the funnies

ALSO BY J. ROBERT LENNON

*The Light of Falling Stars*

riverhead books a member of penguin putnam inc.

new york 1999

# the funnies

## j. robert lennon

RIVERHEAD BOOKS
a member of
Penguin Putnam Inc.
375 Hudson Street
New York, NY 10014

The images of the Bend-A-Family appear courtesy Archie McPhee &
Company, Seattle, www.mcphee.com. The name "Bend-A-Family" is
copyrighted by Accoutrements, of which Archie McPhee &
Company is the retail division.

Library of Congress Cataloging-in-Publication Data

Lennon, J. Robert, date.
The funnies / J. Robert Lennon.
p.   cm.
ISBN 1-57322-126-0 (alk. paper)
I. Title.
PS3562.E489F86   1999              98-42363/ CIP
813'.54—dc21
Printed in the United States of America

1   3   5   7   9   10   8   6   4   2

This book is printed on acid-free paper. ∞

*Book design by Claire Naylon Vaccaro*

*For Mom, Dad, Chris, Mickey, Pop Pop*
*and Skoog, who's got funny*

*The widespread popularity of the strip signifies, I believe, some kind of a subliminal awareness on the part of the readers. . . . The humor, after all, is often quite bland and not particularly effective. Thus it is unlikely that the humor . . . is what interests readers. The probability is, rather, that the representation of pathetic domestic relations cloaked in exaggeration and absurdity really intrigues us.*

ARTHUR ASA BERGER
*The Comic-Stripped American*

*Why should comics be relevant? Should golf balls be printed with ecology slogans? Should circus clowns perform population-explosion skits? Are our martini olives to be wired with abortion information?*

MORT WALKER
*Backstage at the Strips*

# the funnies

**one**

"Dad's dead," said my brother, as if it were my fault. This was Bobby, five years my elder, who once tried to make me drink a bottle of aftershave I had stolen from him. He was fifteen at the time, and I was ten, and he only stopped when he realized I would vomit the aftershave and everything else onto his bedroom carpet. The last word he'd spoken to me, during our last phone conversation a couple of years ago, was *fine*, followed by the climactic silence of an abrupt hang-up. Now, with the telephone receiver in one hand and a backgammon dice cup in the other, I might have welcomed a nice, clean disconnection. Instead the silence was filled with Bobby's measured breaths, rustling mintily in my ear.

I said, "What?"

"Heart attack. In his studio. There's a funeral tomorrow."

I said, "Jesus, when?"

"I just said, tomorrow."

"No, I mean . . ."

A crisp *tsk* reached me, barely perceptible. "Last night. He passed away last night. Bitty's already here, Rose is coming in the morning."

"How's Pierce? Is he okay?"

Bobby's pause again seemed to carry the suggestion of blame, as if our younger brother were a wayward urchin in my charge. At twenty-eight, however, Pierce was the only one of us who hadn't left home, and thus fell under our father's care, whatever that was worth. Not much, anymore. "Maybe when he comes out of his room we'll find out."

"Bobby," I said, "why didn't anyone call me?"

"I am right this minute calling you."

This time I was the one to pause. After several bloated seconds, he said, "Well, Tim, there's been a lot to take care of. We tried last night . . ."

"What time tomorrow?" I said, savoring the interruption.

"Noon. Come early, to the house. And please do not be late."

"Lay off, Bobby." And this was enough to trip, finally, his circuit breaker. My brother Bobby did not blow fuses. He hung up. I gently set down the receiver.

"Roll," said Amanda. She was sitting cross-legged in her nightgown on the floor, inspecting the backgammon board with rapacious pleasure. She was winning. I lowered myself to the carpet, put my hand over the cup, rattled the dice and let them fly.

"Yes!" she said.

"That was my brother Bobby," I told her. "Our dad had a heart attack. He's dead."

She looked up, the afterimage of her predatory grin bobbing gracelessly in her eyes, and I felt bad for her, worse, for a change, than I felt for myself: how did you react to the death of your boyfriend's father, when the only things the boyfriend ever had to say about him were rotten? When, in fact, the boyfriend had, at times, *wished* the old man dead? She rearranged her expression, looked for a time down at her hands, then offered one of them to me. I took it. To her credit, she pushed aside the backgammon board, upsetting the pieces, and pulled herself over. She put one arm around me, then the other. We hugged.

"I'm really sorry."

"Thanks," I said.

"I don't know what to say."

"Me neither."

"Are you okay? How are you?" She pulled back and took my face in her thin fingers.

"Uh, I suppose I'm fine. I guess I have to go. Home. The funeral is tomorrow." My sisters and brothers, I thought, all together at once: when was the last time that happened?

"Do you want me to come? I can get off work. Why don't I come." *Say no*, said her eyes.

"Don't. You'll probably never see them again anyway."

"Are you sure?" she said, with an obvious relief she must have thought she was concealing.

"Sure I'm sure."


That night, while Amanda slept, I sat on the sofa, tugging at upholstery threads torn loose by a previous owner's cat and reading randomly from a stack of five-year-old fashion magazines. Already I was feeling guilty for not going home immediately. But for whom? Not Bobby, who would be pleased to have one more reason to scorn me; or Rose, the oldest, with whom I had barely spoken in ten years. Not poor Pierce, either, who would likely see me as just another conspirator against him. Maybe it was Bitty I should have been there for, the baby of the family, newly married at twenty-five to a man I'd never met but who I bet was a lot like our father.

Considering how eager we all were to disown our childhoods, none of us had fallen very far from the cradle. West Philly, where I lived, was a quick paddle up the Delaware to the family compound in Riverbank, New Jersey. Rose lived in upper Manhattan, Bitty in nearby Frenchtown, Bobby somewhere in the landscaped landscape of Bridgewater. And Pierce, of course, lived in his bedroom. I wondered if the rest of them, like me, hated to travel.

I thumbed through the ragged pile of scrap papers that served as our address book until I came to my mother's number, standing alone on the back of a grocery receipt (hardware, alcoholic bev, bakery, bakery, bakery, dairy). "MOM," it read. "IVY HOMES." And then the number. Before I could change my mind, I dialed it.

"Ivy Homes Care Center."

"Dorothy Mix, please."

There was a long pause, a string of clicks and tones like the language dolphins speak, and a woman's voice. "Yes?"

"Is Mrs. Mix there?"

"Who is this?" said the voice, stern and subdued, like a marriage coun-selor's. Lite rock played softly somewhere.

"Her son Tim."

"She's sleeping now. Do you know what time it is?"

"Yes," I said. "I mean no, but I just . . ."

"They shouldn't have put you through," she said with finality. I hung up.

I hadn't visited her for at least a month—or had it been two? I tried to fig-ure out how that was possible, but of course, as I quickly grasped, it was more than possible, it was true. Small comfort to think that I'd be seeing her soon enough.

Amanda's car broke down fifteen miles from Riverbank, an hour and a half be-fore the funeral was supposed to start. It was a Chevy Chevette. I used to have my own car, a red 1982 Datsun station wagon with a cream interior that I bought in high school and paid for in tiny increments with tip money. I drove it for six years before the brakes needed servicing, and another four before the exhaust system and fuel lines gave out. Beyond that, it was just oil changes and spark plugs. All through art school I used it to lug around supplies, and when I graduated, loaded it with my installation pieces for delivery to galleries. I had slept in it for a year's worth of nights. But not long ago Amanda had somehow convinced me to sell it. Let's just keep one car, she said, the Chevette. It's eas-ier to park. We sold the Datsun and split the money.

So why, I wondered, sitting in the Chevette in the hot July sun, on the shoulder of the only stretch of Route 29 that was not shaded by a canopy of trees, with the driver's side window permanently rolled up, did I feel like I was borrowing it from her?

Under the hood I found the automotive cousin of a coronary: a Cher-nobyl of thick black motor oil steaming on every surface, burst hoses splayed across the car's hot viscera. Gelatinous yellow goo was drooling over the crankcase like spilled custard, and onto the pavement below, where it pooled around my only pair of dress shoes. I was wearing my Sunday best: blue slacks, white shirt, blue blazer, already as sweaty as a gym suit.

Furthermore, I had to pee.

There was a burger place up around the bend, so I started walking, my bladder leadenly somersaulting deep in my gut. I'd driven this road dozens of times, the forty-five minutes back and forth from college, and thought I could remember each trip down to the last unremarkable detail, every song I'd listened to on the radio, every speed trap I'd slowed down for. The homecomings themselves—visits to my mother; half-assed, ill-fated family holidays—were lost to me, as were my unheralded returns to West Philly. How I missed the Datsun: plodding through the terrible heat, I thought I might cry. About my father's funeral, on the other hand, I felt only deep fatigue, as if I'd already been attending it, day after day, for many years.

I relieved myself at Burger Bodega, but the pay phone was out of order, and I had to throw Dad's funeral at the clerk to get my hands on the house phone. I thumbed through a grease-stained Yellow Pages, looking for the service station I always passed in Washington Crossing, the nearest town. Spelling's? Spalding's?

"You mean Sperry Auto," the clerk told me, a rawboned, buzzardly man in a paper cap. "Except it ain't Sperry Auto anymore. It's Sunoco Plus." He stood over the grill, flipping patties with robotic speed, and spoke to me through a haze of meat-scented steam. "Lucky for you I knew that, huh?"

A woman answered at Sunoco Plus, yelling yeah over something shrill and pneumatic-sounding. I told her where the car was. "I'd appreciate it if you hurried," I said. "I'm late for a funeral." For a moment, the noise stopped, and I could hear men laughing and the confident clanking of hand tools, the shrill sound of country music emanating from a transistor radio. If I closed my eyes I could see the radio, balanced on a dented oil drum, layered thickly with years of axle grease and cigarette smoke.

"Well, we'll get there when we get there," the woman said.


The tow truck, still bearing the cheerful Sperry's insignia on the door, was driven by a crabby, tight-jawed mechanic with a handlebar mustache. He wore an orange Sunoco jumpsuit without a single stain on it. "Got Triple A?" he said, hopping onto the pavement.

"No." I had, in fact, a perfectly preserved memory of myself dropping the membership renewal form into the trash two months before. I had gone an entire lifetime without requiring roadside assistance, and decided to spend my thirty-five dollars elsewhere.

"It'll costya," he told me, as if that mattered.

"Well, okay," I said. He glared at me for a moment, then put the Chevette into neutral, backed the truck up to it, and winched the front wheels into the air. I watched this operation with what felt like a woeful, obliged expression on my face. We got in the truck and heaved onto the road, setting a pine-tree–shaped air freshener into pendulous motion where it hung from the radio knob. We listened to the news together, much as we might have if the other wasn't there.

One of my greatest anxieties in life is the possibility of being at the mercy of a man less intelligent than me, yet highly skilled in an arena of which I have no knowledge. As anxieties go, this one is arrogant and impractical, and I am forced to deal with it often. I was unable to restrain myself from saying, "Something just popped."

"What?"

"Something under the hood just popped." I looked at my shoes. The yellow goo had dried, leaving light brown stains on my loafers. I reached down and touched them. Perfectly smooth.

The driver took his time answering. "Tell it to Peg," he said finally.

The service station was much as I remembered it, but it had been painted yellow and blue, and the wooden Sperry's sign replaced by a plastic Sunoco sign, the kind that lights up. There wasn't much to Washington Crossing, a few narrow streets and some traffic lights. People lurched heavily by on the sidewalks. Peg was busy, so I asked to use the phone and was directed by Mr. Mustache to a pay phone around back. Beside the phone was a molded plastic chair with paint spattered on it. I ran my hand over the spots, making sure they were dry, before I sat down and called my father's house.

"Yes?" said Bobby.

"It's me. Tim."

A deep and lengthy silence, the kind that conversations unwittingly fall into and die. "Where are you?"

"Wash Crossing."

"The funeral, Tim, is in forty-five minutes."

"I know," I said. "I had a breakdown."

"You mean automotive," he said.

"Yeah."

"And you want me to come get you."

"Well, I guess so."

"You guess so." This had been a habit of my father's: throwing your words back at you so that they sounded stupid. For a second I considered hitching back to West Philly. Then I saw myself doing it, standing on the shoulder of the road, waving down cars in my rumpled clothes.

"Yes, Bobby," I said. "Please do that. It's at the Sunoco."

"There's no Sunoco in Wash Crossing."

"There is now."

I stumped back into the empty office and placed myself in the path of a dust-caked oscillating fan that had been set up on a file cabinet. The dust, over time, had formed loose confederacies that shimmied precariously in the manufactured breeze. For a while I stood there with my eyes closed, cooling. When I opened them, they fell onto something at the counter: cartoon strips preserved under a sheet of scratched plexiglas. I leaned over, trying to stay in the airstream. Sure enough, there it was, the Family Funnies. My father's comic strip. I got that familiar feeling—a kind of existential loginess mixed with an acute disappointment in the world—that I always did encountering the Family Funnies in the wild. In this one, it's just Bobby and Rose in the car, the two oldest, with my mother and father. The hood's up, and a mechanic's peering at the engine, and Rose is leaning out the car window, and she's saying, "Don't worry, mister, my daddy can fix it!"

Rose, I thought, would probably insist she'd never say such a thing. Then I remembered with a start that I would be seeing her—and the rest of them—in about half an hour. It had to have been twenty years since we'd all been together. We were like a high school graduating class, sticking it out only as long as we had to, then fleeing into the world, diplomas in hand. I could see the five of us only as our comic strip selves: forever prepubescent, compassionate and cute, full of harmless misapprehension and mild rivalry, and immaculately compliant in the delivery of Dad's lousy jokes. If he ever drew us as adults, he wouldn't have enough white space on the page to put between us, enough ink to fill in all the petty resentments and knee-jerk equivocations.

I knew exactly how my father would draw himself dead, though: with wings, and a harp, and of course those blank eyeglasses that obscured all expression.

# two

Maybe Dad conceived of it as a way to control us. In the unbreachable box of the comic strip, we could be charming and obedient, and we would stay that way, year after year. Maybe it was his own puerile self-doubt, his lack of self-control—the classic bad-dad syndrome—that made this seem like a good idea. Whatever precipitated it, the Family Funnies made him rich and famous, transformed him from Carl Mix, rotten father, into Carl Mix, middle-class hero, preeminent architect of Good Clean Fun. And it turned us, of course, into objects of public humiliation, imperfect prototypes for our gleaming, dimwitted twins, who were implicitly held up to us as model kids, as everything we were lamentably not.

"You threw a rod," my brother said, peering into the engine as if it were the mouth of a man I had just killed. He gave me an unapologetic look of appraisal. "Is that what you're wearing?"

"It's the best I've got."

"Jesus, Tim." His face was puffy and his eyes red, and I felt more shame at my own lack of evident grief than I did about my mussed blue suit. Bobby's suit was black, and crisp as crackers. I was sure he had more where that came from.

He plucked a hanky from his breast pocket, wiped his hands on it and folded it with one hand back into the pocket. "Where's that mechanic?" I followed him to the office, which Mr. Mustache now presided impassively over.

"He threw a rod," Bobby told him.

Mustache nodded.

"We have to attend a funeral. He'll be back later." He jabbed his thumb at me.

"Closing at five."

Bobby wrote something on the back of a business card. "Here's the number we'll be at. Contact us when you've looked at the car."

Mustache took the card and, without a glance, secreted it in his coveralls.

"All right, then," Bobby said, and pushed open the door.

Outside he inhaled a giant lungful of coppery air. It rose off the asphalt lot in hot waves, creasing the cars and buildings behind it. "You have to be firm with these kind of people," he said.


It was my brother's habit to get a new car every three years. The one we were in was a brand-new luxury sedan with real leather and wood all over everything, and air conditioning. I hadn't been in a car with working air conditioning in a long, long time, and in the absence of things to talk about I took a lot of deep, theatrical breaths, enjoying the cool. Bobby kept his eyes on the road. He looked almost exactly like our father—square-faced, tan, smooth-skinned—though there was something soft about him, something gentle and resigned, that didn't come from Dad. Oddly, though, he lacked any of our mother's wariness, her sharpness of eye. He would be thirty-six in August, a strange month for a birthday.

"How's Mom?" I said.

He spared me a glance. "What do you think, Tim? She's a mess."

"Worse than before?"

"I'd say so," he said.

Big, heavy branches passed low over us. I thought about my mother, on her birthday months before: alone in her room watching television, a big cache of cheap, cheerful presents crowded onto the bureau. Hair rollers, a hand mirror, dried fruit. Things the staff could afford. I stayed a good hour and never encountered my siblings, although, in their defense, it was a weekday afternoon. I said quietly, "So where's the burial?"

"Burial?"

"Dad's. Where are they burying him?"

"They're cremating him."

Cremating! "Really?"

"It's what he wanted." His expression was forthright and strained, like an expert witness's.

"I didn't know that," I said.

"Now you do."

Bobby owned a medical waste treatment plant, the largest in central Jersey. Hospitals sent him their garbage—everything from latex gloves and syringes to amputated arms and legs—and he decontaminated them using a secret process developed by his partner, a college buddy of his. I guessed that this was no simple marriage of convenience for my brother; he had long been compulsively sanitary. When we were kids, he was always tying his food waste up in plastic bread bags before throwing it out. The sight of garbage dumps and cemeteries tightened him up like a golf ball, an inconvenient affliction if you live in New Jersey. For this reason, his claim about my father's wishes seemed suspect. I couldn't imagine my father considering his own death at all, let alone the disposal of his remains. I changed the subject.

"How's business?" I said.

He turned and scowled at me. "That's sick."

"What!"

"First we're talking about Dad, and then all of a sudden medical waste."

"Okay, okay," I said, unnerved. I tried to come up with something else to talk about, but nothing seemed a safe move, and I clammed up and pretended to enjoy the scenery.

Riverbank is really two towns, which in my mind I've always called Snotty and Inbred. If you were to enter from the South Side, which Bobby and I were about to do, you'd be treated to a quasi-Louisianan tableau: stately old houses with big windows, set back from the road under weeping willows and spreading conifers. There is a country club, two golf courses, some condos you can't see from the road. There is a restaurant called Chez Chien, another called Trattoria Luisini, an antique shop called Jenny's Antique Boutique. This is the Snotty side of town. If you came in from the north, however, you would first have to pass the paper mill, a Russian constructivist nightmare and the subject of countless debates between environmentalists from out of town (college students, mostly) and the Paper Lords, who regularly spouted rhetoric about jobs being more important than fish, etc., etc. Next you'd pass the shotgun row houses built by the mill at the turn of the century for its employees; they still live there, the employees, though the property taxes are apparently getting too high for their mill wages to cover. This is the Inbred part of town. Each group spends much of its time pretending that it doesn't live near the other. My own family, though closer in pedigree to Snotty than Inbred, was and is seen as anomalous. When my grandfather first moved here, he was only Peculiar, and my father retained the title to his death.

We took a left at the Antique Boutique and another at the chestnut stump that marked our house. Bright new cars, looking leased in the shimmering heat, were parked neatly in the grass off the drive, and I pictured Bobby soberly directing traffic in his suit and tie. There was the house I grew up in: squat and brown, like a credit union. Through a break in the hedge, people were visible milling in the backyard. My throat burned. Bobby parked his car in the open garage. "I can't believe your shirt, Tim," he said.

I got out of the car and put my jacket on. It hid most of the stains I'd made. My necktie was still clean; it was the only one I had that had not been given to me as a gag. Artists have predictable senses of humor. "Better?" I said.

He crossed his arms, then nodded.

We turned and headed for the house.


Nobody ever visited us, so the sight of a crowd in the yard was something of a shock. I recognized a few neighbors, a few townies; acquaintances of my parents' I hadn't seen for years. But no names came to me. The backyard is really just the acre of empty space between the house and my father's studio, with a few trees and a birdbath plopped into the middle; the entire thing was as I remembered it, surrounded by juniper bushes and scraggly perennials my mother had planted when she could still do such things. I recognized two women standing near the birdbath. They were my sisters.

Rose was nodding at Bitty, her arms loosely crossed, like a college professor listening to a student plead for a grade change. She looked older, which of course she was. Her face was slack and wary, distrustful of the rote bereavement around her, and she was leaning back slightly, keeping her distance. Bitty, a good six inches shorter, was punctuating her words with frantic hand gestures. She looked good: fresh-faced and blond. Even in her black funeral dress she carried the festive scent of the senior prom.

As far as I knew, Bitty and Rose got on just fine; fifteen years apart in age, they never spent long enough in the house together to grow to hate one another. Much of the stuff that Rose couldn't stand about our family was over and done with before Bitty was born, and even to me, only five years her senior, talking with Bitty was sometimes like talking to the girlfriend who, after one visit, can't understand why you and your folks don't get along. It had been a good year since I'd seen Bitty; Rose I had last seen more than five years before, when I was part of a group show in New York, where she lived. I ate lunch, dutch, with her and her husband, Andrew Piel. In the strip, Rose was called Lindy, as her given name is Rosalinde, the legacy of an otherwise forgotten aunt. But as a teenager she had been quick to distance herself from the name, and by association the comic strip, the family, and her past in general. I couldn't blame her, really.

I steeled myself and walked over. Rose was the first to notice but pretended not to. Bitty's face, following Rose's aborted glance, found me and broke open like a swollen cloud, and emotion poured out of it. "Tim!" She threw her arms around me, and her cheeks, hot with grief, pressed into my neck. She pulled away, taking my shoulders, looked at me with bleary, radiant eyes and burst suddenly into tears. "Oh, Tim, I can't believe it . . ."

"Hello, Tim," Rose said. I said hi over Bitty's shoulder. Andrew was nowhere to be seen, and neither, I noticed now, was my mother. Were they off somewhere together?

I felt terrible for Bitty. I had forgotten how much she adored our father, and he her; it was almost as if we had lost a different parent entirely. She was Daddy's girl. We stood there holding hands for a minute, her dress sticking to her like a wet washcloth. "I'm so sorry," I said, like a sympathetic neighbor lady.

"I was just reminiscing with Rose," she said.

I glanced at Rose, who produced a disapproving smile.

"I was remembering going to Manasquan," Bitty said, wiping her face with a tissue pulled from her purse. "Remember they were dredging the ocean? And there were all those little shells? I made bracelets for Dad and Mom. Rose wasn't there, I don't think."

I did remember, though only vaguely. It had been one of those half-baked save-the-family outings, which unfortunately worked. "Didn't Pierce get bit by something?" I said. "A crab?"

"A jellyfish. His leg swelled up." She frowned. "Where were you, Rose?"

"I don't know. New York, working."

I was trying to remember Bitty's husband's name. Mark? "Bitty," I said, "I'd like to meet your husband."

"Mike?" She swiveled her head. "He's around. Oh, Tim, I missed you." We hugged again. "We have so much to talk about."

As a rule, this was not something people said to me. "Sure," I said.

Rose began to look agitated, and I realized she was making a move to touch me. But how? I started to extend my hand, but she seemed to be leaning toward me, so I quickly opened my arms to receive her. We hugged loosely, like fourth graders slow dancing, and perfunctorily patted each other's backs. She said it was good to see me. I said it was good to see her. She looked at the back of her hand, then reeled it in and cleared her throat. "Andrew's picking up Mom," she said, as if I'd asked. "Oh, God, what a mess this is."

"Where is Pierce?" I said. "Is he around?"

"I don't know," Rose said. "Probably inside, smoking." Among my younger brother's many quirks was a tendency to smoke indoors only.

"I just can't believe he's gone," Bitty said, shaking her head.

"Believe it," said Rose.

"Rose!"

Rose seemed to rally around this new, incisive role in the conversation. "Bitty. He drank and smoked to beat the band."

"He didn't!" Bitty whined. "He indulged a little now and then."

"Hmm," said Rose. We all waited to see what would happen next. Rose inhaled sharply, a near gasp, then let her breath out over several long seconds.

Bitty blinked. I dug deep for a sad smile, plastered it on, and ducked away to look for my little brother.

It would be a lie to say the house hadn't changed at all, though everything was in exactly the place it was when I left home twelve years before. The change was the dirt, a dozen years of it, coating everything like an oil slick. The kitchen and dining room had been kept up okay—I imagined that Bitty or Bobby and his wife had cleaned them from time to time—but the halls were dark and close, and the open closets, their musty contents gloomily bared to passersby, drained the rooms of their light. One of my mother's final acts of remodeling had been to turn my room into a guest bedroom, so the bright red and green stripes had been papered over with a headache-inducing geometric pattern, and my childhood bed replaced with a carbuncular brass affair that had been in her parents' guest bedroom years before. It looked all right, actually, and when I peeked into the now-empty closet to check for the crucifix I'd hung there as a child, I found it was still there.

Pierce's bedroom had once been a sewing room, and was the size of an unusually large closet. The door was shut. I glanced at my watch: quarter to eleven, almost time to walk up the street to the church. I knocked. "Pierce?"

No answer. Rose was right: I could smell cigarette smoke. I knocked again. "It's Tim."

Nothing. After a minute I called out again—"Pierce?"—and pressed my hand to the door. Did I open it or not? It depended: on Pierce's state of mind, on my rights as a former tenant here, on the bonds of brotherhood and the disgrace of estrangement. I could have stood there all day, but it was late and nobody else was going to come get him. I went in. My brother was lying on the bed in a beautiful dark gray suit and the shiniest wing tips I'd ever seen, smoking.

"I knew you'd barge in," he said.

"It wasn't precisely barging."

"How long were you out there?"

"Since I said your name the first time."

"I've been listening to you, Tim," he said, his voice irresolute, teetering in an upper register. "You've been out there for fifteen minutes, at least." He stubbed out his cigarette in an ashtray on the floor and hauled himself off the bed. His suit hadn't a wrinkle on it, though his face bore the red marks of the corduroy pillow he'd been asleep on. Pierce had always had extremely fair skin, and now it seemed nearly transparent.

"I looked in my old room, but I got to yours just now."

"Hey." His hands fluttered around his head, as if swatting the words away. "Shut up, all right?" He twirled his fingers in his ears, then pulled them out and looked at the tips.

When Pierce was ten, he looked like he was nineteen. Now he was twenty-eight and he still looked like he was nineteen. He suffered from chronic undifferentiated schizophrenia, an illness he once described to me as a foul brown paste that had been smeared on him and that he couldn't get off. Now he waggled his hand in the air before me. "You driving?"

"Walking. It's at St. Lucia, right?"

"Nobody *walks* around here."

"Oh."

"And then it's off to the pyre!" He raised his eyebrows.

"Oh, right," I said. I raised my eyebrows back at him. "Bobby said he'd always wanted to be cremated."

"Bobby's full of shit, as usual." He cracked his knuckles. His hands were like mice, skinny, relentlessly in random motion.

"Well, he's driving us, I guess. Amanda's car died on me."

"That'll be fun," he said, slouching past me into the hall. He stopped and looked back. "You're still living with that poor girl?"

"What do you mean, 'poor girl'?"

Pierce shrugged. "Oh, you know. She seems so . . . doomed."

"Doomed," I said.

He gripped his head with both hands and made to throw it at me. "Whatever."

Here is Pierce's story: my father began the Family Funnies when Bobby was born, and for five years the strip was just Bobby, Rose, our parents and a dog, Puddles, who in real life would be dead before I arrived. Then the cartoon version of my mother grew fat with me, and I was introduced as a chunky buffoon lugging a pacifier around. I was two, both in the strip and in real life, when Mom next got pregnant. In real life, the pregnancy ended with Pierce. In the strip, the pregnancy just ended. Nothing. No baby, no explanation—only the cartoon Mom, slim as a cigarette girl again, and us three kids.

There must have been some sort of uproar at the syndicate, but what were they going to do? The Family Funnies, by that time, was a major merchandising cash cow—a new development for comic strips—and thousands of greeting cards and T-shirts and coffee mugs couldn't be wrong. The Public would forget.

Nobody in my family did, though. And I was old enough to notice the desert that sprung up between my father and mother when, three years later, Bitty was born into our house and—without warning—into the strip as the fourth child of the Mix family. My father had skipped Pierce entirely, and bestowed upon the cartoon Dot, my mother, the apparent miracle of spontaneous procreation.

It would be an oversimplification to say that this was the central conflict of our family. In a sense, though, it stood for all the others. So, by association, did Pierce. Whatever problems he was destined to have later, this certainly didn't help.

# three

Pierce and I drove to the funeral with Bobby and his family: Nancy, his wife, who was four or five months pregnant and sat with the front seat reclined nearly as far as it would go, and his six-year-old daughter Samantha, who sat between us in the back. Pierce kept doing things with his hands.

"What are you doing?" Samantha demanded. Already I could see the church; it was only four blocks away.

"Don't bother him, honey," Bobby said.

"Pierce is just nervous, Sam," Nancy said, obviously nervous.

Pierce palmed Samantha's head. "It's true. I may eat you." He growled, and Sam giggled, and then we were there.

We spilled out into the church parking lot. I helped Nancy from the car while Bobby set the alarm. It chirped like a parakeet.

"Thank you," Nancy said, looking at the ground.

"Maybe you'd be more comfortable with the seat up."

"No," she moaned, shaking her head. "I have a little condition." She moved around the car to Bobby and took his arm. Pierce and Sam led our group, holding hands.

The church was the one we had gone to when we were kids. It was also the one in the strip. The Family Funnies was a churchy cartoon, and since their aging was arrested while Bitty was still a baby, the cartoon us persisted in their religious devotion long after our actual family had lapsed spectacularly. Every Sunday strip involved church. There were the ones in which Bobby proudly sung the wrong lyrics to various hymns, the ones where Rose asked probing and misguided questions about ecumenical matters, the ones where we're all in the car on the way to or from the church, being cute. To be fair, a few of these things actually happened. But mostly, like many other FF stand-bys, the church cartoons were a crock.

We found seats. I was just getting comfortable, no small feat in the un-cushioned wooden pews, when I happened to notice the casket, burnished, be-flowered and shut tight on a rickety-looking metal stand at the foot of the altar. Something scaly uncurled in the space below my diaphragm, an almost sexual feeling like the one you get driving fast over rolling hills, and I gripped the pew in front of me. Where were my parents? Of course I had never been here without them. I looked down the pew. Nancy was weeping silently into a hanky. Bobby was stoically not. Pierce and Sam were poking each other and snickering. What was I supposed to be doing? Crying? I was seized by a weird, infantile terror, the sort you feel when you dream yourself naked, among strangers. I scanned the church for Rose's dark, frizzy hair. When I didn't see her, I checked my watch. A little after eleven. Out of the corner of my eye I could see that Bobby was doing the same thing.

It was all happening too fast: the heart attack, the funeral, the cremation. While everybody else was nursing their grief, getting used to the idea, I had been doing stupid things: sleeping, playing backgammon, walking along the side of the highway in soiled clothes. I was the only one who hadn't studied for the big exam, and I alone would fail.

And then Rose appeared, my mother at her side. Mom did not look ter-ribly frail, as I had anticipated, despite her walker and pronounced stoop. She looked angry. Rose tried to take her elbow, but she jerked her arm away. Be-hind them plodded Andrew Piel, his gray ponytail tucked conspicuously be-hind the collar of his jacket. There was a murmur in the church as Mom sat down, as if she were not a widow at all, but a bride.

Her presence was not the comfort I had anticipated, so to calm myself I gave the church another quick once-over. There were more people here than there had been in the yard; it looked like half the town had turned out. I no-ticed two people I didn't recognize at all sitting fairly near my mother. One, a plump, curly-haired woman about my age, daubed at her eyes in the third row; the other, a thin, gristly little man in his forties, sat at the far end of the first row. He was leaning forward, his elbows on his knees, like he was watching a ball game. I wondered how these people knew my dad.

Father Loomis strode up the center aisle, stepped deftly around my father, and fixed himself behind the altar, still looking exactly as he did in the Family Funnies: wispy hair, aviator-style glasses. He nodded to each side of the congregated—about a hundred and fifty of us, total—then launched into a little speech. "We are here to witness the passing of a great man. Carl Mix was an artist, a humanitarian, a pillar of both the business and social community . . ." Blah blah blah. People began to whimper immediately.

Instinctively, I turned to my mother. For some minutes she sat perfectly still, her little puffball head steady as a boulder on her thin shoulders. And then, like a child, she turned and scanned the crowd, her eyes narrowed in search of someone or something. I managed to catch her gaze, and when she noticed me she smiled and brought her hand up next to her face, then wiggled her fingers in a little wave. I waved back.

If she had seen what she was looking for, it wasn't evident to me. She eventually faced front again, and as we all stood and sat and knelt and prayed, she seemed to grow weary and finally leaned heavily against my sister, apparently asleep. Rose did not turn to her. But Andrew Piel did, and put his arm around my mother like he might a pretty girl on a second date. This improved my opinion of him considerably.

After the funeral the cars revved up for the trip to the crematorium. Pierce and Sam had grown closer during the service and now, in the back of Bobby's car, whispered conspiratorially to one another in a strangely humorless way. Nancy hissed at them, through her profuse and earnest tears, that they were having too much fun, and for once I agreed with her. To accommodate the reclined seat, I had my knees spread as far apart as they would go. I entertained briefly the notion of reaching over the headrest and stroking Nancy's coarse blond hair. "Relax," I would have told her, but I kept my hands to myself.

The crematorium turned out to be a new building right next to the Dairy Queen on Route 29. It was stubby and industrial-looking, but made to appear taller with vertical grooves that had been carved into the concrete walls; its nicely groomed grounds were dotted with sapling sugar maples held upright by stretched ropes. The parking lot was beautifully black and flat, the yellow lines bright as neon lamps. Next door, a dozen screaming boys were clambering out of a pickup truck, the winners of a little league game come to celebrate with a hot dog and ice cream. I wanted to join them. Instead, I followed Pierce and Sam through the heavy glass doors, which Pierce held open for me, and into a dark, plush, air-conditioned lobby.

I felt a hand on my shoulder. "This way, sir," said a gelid, androgynous voice, but I was blinded by the sudden dimness and could see nothing but my brother's egg-white neck, bobbing and glowing before me like swamp gas. I followed down a hallway paneled with thick knotty boards, and turned where a man in a black suit and gleaming wristwatch was gesturing through a door.

My eyes adjusted. The room we had entered was much like a small collegiate lecture hall, with seats—bleachers, really, padded with red upholstery—arranged in concentric semicircles around a curtained proscenium. Canned organ music trickled out over the crowd. I looked around quickly to make sure I had actually come to the right place, and saw Bitty holding hands with a stout man I'd never seen before. Mike, I figured. She noticed me and managed a brave smile through the sheen of tears and sweat that had control of her face, and I smiled back. The froggish Mike smiled at me, a frog's smile, wide and anthropomorphic. I nodded at Mike. Mike nodded back. Finally, fed up, I looked away.

Here came my mother, apparently out of Rose's hands, cruising through the milling mourners with her walker like an arctic icebreaker. My heart pitched, and I went to her.

"Mom?" I held out my arms. "It's me, Tim."

Her eyes widened and she veered off to the left, knocking her walker into the leg of the gristly man I hadn't recognized earlier. "Out of the way!" she barked. He turned to me and, with a look that indicated a long and complex acquaintance, raised his eyebrows, as if to say: What are you gonna do with 'em?

I caught up with my mother and took her arm. It was thin and muscled, like a distance runner's. "Mom!"

She turned on me. "Where's my son!" she said. Her eyes were clear and blue as marbles. She had turned sixty-eight this year and looked, with her brilliant white head of curly hair, about a dozen years older. For a moment I saw Rose in her and recoiled in surprise.

"It's Tim," I said. "It's your son Tim."

She stared at me and her gaze softened. "Oh, Timmy," she said, and let me hold her a moment. She had never called me that in her life. That had been my father's name, invented for the convenience of the strip: Lindy, Bobby, Timmy, Bitty.

"Let me get you settled, Mom."

"Well, all right," she said. I led her to the front bleacher and moved her walker into the aisle, close enough so that she could reach it. In a second Rose strode in, her rabid eyes darting.

"Oh, Jesus Christ, Mom," she said, a little too loudly for the small room.

"This man was helping me sit down." She said this smugly, as if Rose had been found wanting in her duties. Rose pouted.

Andrew walked in and, smiling tactfully, put his arm on Rose's back. "Hello, Tim."

"Andrew," I said, shaking his hand. I wanted him to like me, and so tried to return the smile. It was a strain. Why all these smiles, more than I'd ever been given, at such a grim occasion? I had returned so many today, I didn't know if I could take another.

"You all sit," my mother said. "Take a load off those dogs."

"You bet," Andrew said, and plopped down next to her. Rose took her seat with a sigh. The rest of the front row, I noticed, was filled with townspeople. The room had the unlikely air of a puppet show or company picnic, the lame static electricity that preceded any third-rate entertainment. It occurred to me that this was probably how Riverbank felt about my father in general: not the local attraction they wished they had, but all they had nonetheless.

I climbed up the carpeted aisle and found an empty place right under an air conditioning vent. The muted gurgle of voices surrounded me, and I closed my eyes and considered that I felt the same way as Riverbank. He wasn't the father I wished I had, but all I had nonetheless. At least that's what

I pretended, when during college I asserted my independence from the Family Funnies and its author both: what could have been easier than opposing something so wholesome and unironic as the strip, someone so wrapped up in his invented innocence as my father? What could have come more naturally than a thankless and inconvenient career as an installation artist, to the spurned middle child of a well-heeled alcoholic cartoonist?

So why, then, having done these things, did I feel like such a shit? My siblings had taken on the responsibilities of marriage and independence, risen above their petty resentments to become real people. Even Pierce, stuck as he was in the quagmire of his own head, was the true rebel of the family, torturing our father with his presence right up to the bitter end. Only I had proved myself weak and shallow, just like Dad.

Things grew quieter as more people found their seats, and when I opened my eyes I found myself seated next to the plump woman who had wept at the church. She had a round, pretty face and thick-framed glasses too conservative to be hip and too ugly to come off as dignified. They were the glasses of a woman twice her age. I got nervous.

"You're Tim," she informed me, sticking out a doughy hand.

I took it. "Yes."

"I'm Susan Caletti. I was your dad's editor."

"Really?" I said. "I thought what's-his-name was his editor, Burn. The syndicate guy."

"Dead," she said flatly, then turned red. "Sorry. His brother took over the syndicate and didn't want to deal with any actual cartoonists. He farmed them out to his underlings. I got your dad. Like, a year and a half ago."

"Ah."

"He was an interesting man."

"Thank you for not saying he was great."

She reddened again. "Oh. Well." She coughed. "Well, hey, I'll just leave you to your thoughts, okay? But we'll have to talk later." I couldn't for the life of me think of anything we would need to say to one another later, but I bit the bullet and composed another polite smile.

By this time, everyone who was coming seemed already to be in, and the dolled-up greaser who had been standing outside the door quietly closed it.

There were no windows in the room; the only light emanated from recessed bulbs in rows on the ceiling. As if on cue, these lights dimmed, and simultaneously the curtains hummed open on mechanized runners, revealing my father's casket, alone on stage like a brooding soliloquist. It was resting on some sort of conveyor, and beyond it, two little doors were visible, outlined by a red glow. It took several seconds for everyone to process all this, and as they did a stunned hush fell over the room. We were going to watch him tumble into the fire?

Apparently we were. Beside me, my father's editor gasped. Fresh sobs broke out in the crowd.

And then, with appalling suddenness, the doors clanged open and the conveyor kicked into action, emitting a ghastly throb that drowned out the organ music. I felt a breath of hot air gust past me. Somebody screamed. The conveyor was slow, but the casket had little distance to cover, and in seconds was sliding under gravity's pull down a little incline toward the inferno. The back end tipped up, like the prow of a sinking ship, and like that, it was gone.

*Wait!* I wanted to yell, but it was too late. The room was in the grip of an appalling silence. It dawned on me that I never got a chance to look at the old man. The doors swung shut.

Nothing happened for a moment, then the curtains drew themselves closed. For a moment the music swelled to an ear-splitting level, then was quickly corrected. I saw my brother Bobby sitting with his family, his hands on his knees, his eyes implacably aglow, the way the Vikings must have looked when they pushed their dead out to sea. Down in front, the gristly man stood up to leave, and throughout the room other people started to do the same.

Back in the lobby I picked up a pamphlet from a discreet oaken stand and read through it out in the sun. There were several lurid photos, a lot of gibberish about Final Journeys and Eternal Peace, and at the end, a short paragraph devoted, I supposed, to the inevitable macabre tech-heads. It described the "Assumption System," its "state-of-the-art Interactive Theater of Rest," the team of compassionate mortuary and clerical experts who had striven for maximum numinous effect while retaining simplicity and grace. I thought there was little about what I had seen that could be described as simple or graceful. At the bottom of the last page, just above the address and phone, I noticed an italicized message: *Come in for a free demonstration.*

They actually fired up the incinerator for any yokel who strolled in? I pictured Bobby sitting alone in the bleachers, his face slack and calculating, watching the curtains part and the iron doors yawn open into the flames.

Later, at the house, while everyone was enjoying wake food, I went into my father's bedroom, shut the door behind me and called Amanda. She answered on the first ring.

"Yeah?"

"Hey," I said.

"How are you?"

"So-so." I told her about the crematorium, leaving out the part about my self-censuring revelations. She cooed her amazement and sympathy. "I have some unfortunate news," I said.

"Okay."

"The car croaked. Bobby thinks it threw a rod. There's a mechanic in Washington Crossing looking it over."

"My brother's Porsche threw a rod once."

"No kidding."

"Well, whatever," she said. "How are the sibs?"

"Fine." It was a very easy conversation, like all of ours were. One of us said something and the other said something. It was comforting; we could have done it all day.

"Is there any way you can get home tonight?" she said finally.

"It doesn't look that way."

"I wish you would. Can you get a ride or something?"

"I should be with my family," I said. I felt the guilty titillation of the lie in the back of my throat. "For a day or two, anyway."

"Yeah, okay," she said. Everything was okay with Amanda, or so she said. It wasn't really, though: a lie for a lie.

"So I guess I should go."

"Sure."

"Goodnight," I said, though it was not yet two in the afternoon. "I love you."

Afterward, I sat on the bed, smelling the cigar-soaked air. Before me was my father's bureau. His wallet was still sitting there, a handful of change, his wristwatch. I pulled the top drawer open. Briefs. He was the only man in the family who wore them. Pair after pair of black socks. I took a pair out, took my own shoes and socks off, put his socks on. I dug in the back of the drawer for the shoe polish I knew was there. I polished my shoes until the antifreeze marks were gone. Then I put the shoes back on, put away the polish, put on his watch and took the money—about fifty bucks—out of his wallet. I looked at myself in the tiny hand mirror he had stashed in his undershirt drawer, then pocketed that, too. I felt like I was ten years old.

**four**

The crowd outside was thick and noisy and filled with people I didn't want to see, let alone receive condolences from. Buffet tables had been set up and covered with paper, and Nancy flitted clumsily from table to table like a bumblebee, unwrapping plates and bowls and straightening up after those who had helped themselves messily. It was a losing battle. I looked at my wrist and realized I was wearing both watches, mine and my father's, so I took mine off and dropped it into my jacket pocket. It was mid-afternoon. I hadn't eaten since nine.

I wasn't three feet past the door when Salvatore Francobolli, the mayor of Riverbank, grabbed my arm in the sweet spot just above the elbow. He was a high-strung, red-faced fireplug of a man with wild tufts of gray hair above his ears, and none on top. "Timmy," he said. He had always called us by our Family Funnies names, even once we had grown up. "Can't tell you how sorry I am. Riverbank has lost a great man."

I winced. "Good of you to say so."

"So, we're going to go ahead with FunnyFest. Early this morning I called an emergency meeting with the town council. We decided that this, of all years, was the year to go all out. Sort of a public coping, if you will. With our grief." He was still holding tight to my arm. With his free hand, he clutched a half-eaten blob of fried dough.

I flexed my fingers, trying to recover my circulation. "Sounds good," I said.

"You'll be here, I trust? We'd like to get the whole Mix clan involved."

"That'd be quite a feat."

"So you're coming!"

"I don't think so. When is it?"

"Couple weeks."

I shook my head. "I'll be back in Philadelphia."

Mayor Francobolli grinned in a conspiratorial way. "Ah, I think you'll reconsider, Timmy, I do. Think about your responsibility to Riverbank." He released my arm and the blood needled slowly back into it. "People are counting on you."

"I doubt that," I said.

He laughed, high and long. Heads turned. "You kill me, Timmy," he said.

FunnyFest started about ten years ago, once news of my father's fame reached our town. It began as a little marketing diversion dreamt up by somebody at the syndicate: convince the town to have a summer fair, complete with food stands, dunking booths, etc., and have Carl Mix show up and draw pictures for a buck a pop. The syndicate would throw in some cash, and would take a cut, as usual, of the FF product pushed over the course of the day.

But Francobolli, whose only real official function as mayor was cannonballing into the Delaware during the then-already-defunct RiverFest, sunk his hooks into FunnyFest as if to save his life. He advertised all over the state, in newspapers and on telephone poles, on television and the sides of buses. And when the day finally came, it was a blowout: thousands of people, many times the population of Riverbank, filled every parking space from Lambertville to Titusville, bought every ice cream sandwich, drank every drop of iced tea, whisked away every piece of FF merchandise within ten miles of my father's studio. Francobolli was reelected by an unusually wide margin. The festival had been an annual tradition ever since: the fourth weekend in July, every July.

Oddly, FunnyFest seemed to be my father's great joy in life, despite the fact that, as he grew older, he grew to hate more and more people with greater and greater intensity. Generally he spoke to nobody in town except during FunnyFest, when he became glib and effusive, shaking hands and patting shoulders like a politico. This annual appearance ensured, I suppose, that he would continue to be regarded as a charming eccentric in Riverbank, rather than the arrogant bastard people probably suspected he was.

But now, of course, he was dead. I'd always connected FunnyFest exclusively with his enthusiasm for it; as a result it seemed absurdly gratuitous to hold it ever again. Now it appeared to have been a sort of heritage festival all along, a small community's flailing attempt to invent a history to supplant the actual one, the one in which the reeking pulp mill attracts the working class at slave wages, and they gentrify in spite of themselves.

By all means, I thought, throw yourselves a party. But I'm not going to "appear" at it.

I loaded a paper plate with food: greasy Italian sausages simmered to the color of shoe leather; steaming spinach pies in a crumbling, buttery crust; tepefied Waldorf salad. I pulled a canned beer from a cooler of half-melted ice. A table away, Bobby touched Nancy's shoulder, then whispered something in her ear. Her face crumpled like a Dixie cup, and she glided, holding back tears, through the back door of the house. Bobby crossed his arms and resumed her vigil over the food in a more dignified manner.

"What's up?" I said to him.

"What, what's up?"

"Nancy. Is something wrong?"

He shot me that judging look again. "You saw her. She's making . . . it isn't good for her, behaving like that."

I knew what he meant. She's making a fool of herself, he was going to say. Once, he walked out of a play I was in at my high school, very loudly, while I was onstage delivering my handful of lines. My mother told me he got sick, but later he told me the truth: he couldn't stand to watch me make a fool of myself.

I swallowed a bite of sausage and watched my brother as he scanned the yard, looking for foolishness. Fresh hatred blossomed in me like a bulb after a long, dull winter. I felt curiously vital.

.   .   .

"Tim," said my sister, "this is Mike Maas. I guess you sort of met at the . . . you know, earlier."

Mike took his arm from around Bitty and dangled his hand in front of me. I shook it, but already Mike's attention was elsewhere, on the beer I had carelessly stashed under my dinner arm, and which was now splashing copiously onto my remaining spinach pie.

"Hey, yeah," he said, still clenching my hand. "Where'd you get that?"

I gestured with my head. He released me, patted Bitty gamely on the arm and angled for the cooler.

"Nice fella," I couldn't help saying.

"He's a private kind of person," Bitty said, crossing her arms.

"So! Married!"

"Married."

"And now that makes you . . ."

She nodded. "Bitty Maas. It's not bad. I wasn't too attached to Bitty Mix. If I had any monograms, I could still use them." She picked at her lip, then mouéd the lipstick back over it. "So you are dating . . ."

"Amanda. Living with, actually. Same old place."

"Wedding bells?"

"Uh, not anytime soon, I'm afraid." I noticed, over her shoulder, the gristly man from earlier peeking in the windows of my father's drawing studio. The windows were made of frosted glass. My father once told me, while drinking, that he dreamt only in diffused light, that nothing in a perfect world would cast sharp shadows. I remember misunderstanding this and thinking that all the objects were fuzzy in his dreams. I tried without success to draw this dream world many times as a child.

"Do you know that guy?" I said.

She turned. "The squirt from the front row? I was wondering about him."

Here, from across the yard, came Mike Maas. I took a swig of beer. "I think I'll go check him out," I said.

I carried my teetering plate over to the studio door, which the man was pushing against with both hands.

"Hi," I said.

He didn't turn around. "Mm-hmm." His hair was the sickly color of newsprint, and I could see stringy muscles jerking at the back of his neck.

"I don't think I know you. I'm Tim Mix."

The man straightened himself—he was maybe five-six, a couple inches below me—and turned slowly, like a horror flick victim. He had a tiny head and clunky tinted glasses with invisible frames, from behind which beady green eyes were cannily bulging. He stuck a hand out, amiably enough, and said something that sounded like "Tandoori."

"Pardon?"

"Ken Dorn," he said. He smiled. "I am a big fan of your dad's work. I came down from New York for the funeral."

"How'd you know about it?" I said. I tried not to sound wary, but was genuinely curious.

He half-smiled and raised his eyebrows. "I have connections with the syndicate."

"Oh," I said. "You're a cartoonist."

"Yeah."

"Are you here with Susan?" I pointed to my father's editor, who was standing in the center of the yard, squinting into the birdbath.

He shook his head no. "I know her," he said. He advanced another half-smile. I felt like I was supposed to be in on something.

"So what strip do you draw?"

He shrugged. "I ink in some of the biggies. 'Whiskers,' 'Nuts and Bolts,' 'The Deep.' "

I was impressed. "The Deep" had long been one of my favorites on the comics page. It took place on the ocean floor, where a variety of aquatic characters exchanged trenchant and witty observations on life in the sea, which naturally were really about the foibles of everyday human life. For a mainstream strip, it was pretty funny.

I'd never met any comic strip inkers. These were people who apprenticed themselves to the popular cartoonists, and did the finishing work on daily strips. How much effort this entailed depended on the cartoonist. Some did much of the inking themselves, and the inkers simply filled in large dark patches, like the night sky repeated from panel to panel. Other cartoonists barely outlined the strips in pencil, and left the detail work to their inkers. Some even let the inkers in on their "jam sessions" with other cartoonists, where gags were conceived. Most inkers did a lot of the grunt work, like doing drawings for merchandise and answering fan letters with approximations of the cartoonist's signature. My father was a bit of a maverick, though: he had never hired them. He did all his work himself. For this reason, he was a prime target for dissatisfied inkers; they were more likely to land their own strips someday if they attached themselves to somebody famous. I wondered if Ken Dorn had ever pestered my father for a job. I imagined that he had, and for a moment felt bad for him.

"Look," I said, setting my food down in the grass. "Did you want to see the studio?"

His shoulders fairly pitched forward, toward the door, before he caught himself and translated the gesture into an expansive fake shrug. "Why not?"

I reached up into the eaves, expecting to find the key my father had hidden there for the past twenty-five years. The hook was still there, but the key was gone. I looked down at the door, hoping it might have been left unlocked, but instead I found a typed message on slick cream-colored letterhead. It read:

> This property has been temporarily sealed by the executor of the owner's estate, until such time the owner's will has been read and the new owner established. Said will shall be read at 9:00 am EST, July 10, at the offices of Silvieri, Earheart and Caldwell, 1430 Market Street, Trenton, New Jersey.

I said, "Well, that's interesting."

Ken Dorn rubbed his elbow. "That's business," he said.

Of course I had known about the will. Malcolm Earheart was my father's lawyer, executor and college buddy, his partner in the old days for golf and tennis. As a child I called him Uncle Mal. He was a tall, willowy, buttoned-down man with a mildly pompous affect that I didn't recognize as such until I went to college myself. Was he here now? I hadn't seen him in years, so I mentally added white hair to the picture I already had and browsed the begrieved: a gently churning sea of penguinesques in their mourning dress, their dinner plates bobbing before them. But none of them was Mal. Ken Dorn, meanwhile, had vanished.

Hard as it may seem to believe, I hadn't given the will a lot of thought. For one thing, I wasn't sure how much money Dad actually had; for all I knew he had been giving it all away as quickly as it came in. He was not a spendthrift, anyway, as the squalid house had confirmed.

More significantly, I had, since leaving home, mounted the bandwagon of a subculture in which money was supposed to be meaningless—the world of art. Money was said to corrupt, of course, and all anecdotal evidence pointed to the ultimate truth of this maxim; the work of artists who had "sold out" lost favor instantly among their peers, even as it garnered increasing public attention. Relative poverty was a matter of pride to my friends, and much of our talk about art revolved around the emptiness of work made to sell.

Lately, however, I'd begun to have a problem with this. Most of my unease came from a creeping conviction that my work was irrelevant and insular at best, simply awful at worst. I used found objects from the streets of West Philadelphia as my materials, and assembled them in our apartment's extra room to evoke scenes easily accessible in their original form not thirty feet from where I worked. I was, in other words, making little outsides indoors. I had never sold a single piece.

And so I was, as etiquette demanded, perpetually poor. I made money from odd jobs; Amanda put food on the table with a coffee shop shift and the faux-primitive jewelry-making business she'd begun to supplement her painting. I worried about things like excessive long-distance phone calls and sudden rent increases. I panicked regularly about the car (justifiably, it turned out). These little stresses kept uneasy company with the minor scrapes and contusions of my relationship with Amanda. Consequently our lives were not romantic. We were mildly unhappy. We had very little sex.

Of course it was easy to blame money, easy to slaver over the thought of a giant inheritance that would free us from humiliating employment and let us concentrate on what really mattered: our work, our relationship. But, as you can see, I was beginning to wonder what kind of life might come from total immersion in those two things, neither of which I appeared to be very good at.

All the same, it is a rare man who is immune to the American Dream, and I was not that man. Thus, I banished, with a deftness only possible after long experience, all thoughts of fabulous wealth from my mind. If there was one thing all my siblings agreed on when we were children, it was that low expectations were always appropriate, in any situation.

That night I found an extra key to the studio in the junk drawer at the corner of our kitchen, and went out for a look around. I turned on the lights and found a scene utterly familiar, yet peculiarly changed: the objects that had been so mysteriously charged for the young me were now dispiritingly inert and literal. The flat files, after art school, were no more exceptional than a chest of drawers; the pencils and pens seemed so mundane that for a moment I could not picture my father using them. The room was long and thin like a chicken coop; you could have parallel parked three cars comfortably inside. At the very back was a makeshift kitchen: a mini-fridge and a coffee maker, several half-drunk bottles of liquor and a glittering stonehenge of glasses balanced on a card table. A bookshelf was filled from top to bottom with spiral notebooks. I knew that these were filled with rough pencil drawings for the Family Funnies. My father eschewed the hardbound sketchbooks favored by some artists; he found them pretentious.

Elsewhere was a small iron safe, nearly buried under a stack of magazines (*National Geographic, American Cartoonist, Playboy*). I tugged on the handle. It was locked. I made a mental note to try cracking it. There was a filing cabinet filled with accounting papers, correspondence, and newspaper and magazine articles, and a huge bulletin board covered exclusively with FF drawings sent to my father by admiring children. I spent long minutes staring at the board, and remembered feeling intense jealousy at it as a child, even recalled vandalizing an earlier version of it with a felt-tipped marker. I wasn't punished. Dad just put up new ones.

And there was the drawing board, the one he was said to have died at. It was an adjustable architect's drafting table, tilted at a twenty-degree angle. Someone had taken the papers away and wiped it perfectly clean, save for the years-old scratches and faded ink stains.

I pulled open a flat file drawer at random and found an unfinished cartoon. It was, like almost all my father's cartoons, a single large frame. It took place in the kitchen. My mother was standing, cooking something in a skillet, and a child was behind her, pointing at the stove. My mother's face, though distorted as all our faces were (my father drew our heads as elongated ovals, for some reason tilted on their sides, so that it looked like we were all carrying watermelons on our shoulders), bore a sleepy impatience as familiar to me as my own reflection.

But the child was unfinished, only an outline without a head or clothes, and the cartoon had no caption. What, I wondered, could it have been about? And why did he abandon it? The background—a cleaner, less quirky version of our kitchen—was fully drawn. Perhaps he couldn't decide on a child. Or maybe that weirdly accurate expression on my mother's face was too much for him to set loose in the papers. Where did he draw the line with Mom? What was too true to print?

I was closing the studio door behind me when I got a funny feeling, like I had left something inside. I opened the door and switched the lights back on. What was it? I rubbed my eyes over every flat surface. Keys? A wallet?

I found myself back at the bulletin board. The drawings were mostly awful: awkward and disproportionate in ways even cartoon characters shouldn't be. There was our family with Superman flying overhead, a picture of Lindy/Rose wearing, for some reason, an Indian headdress.

But one was almost exactly right, so right that I thought at first that my father had drawn it himself. It was a picture of the whole family, pre-me, pre-Bitty, playing tug-of-war, Mom and Lindy on one side, Dad and Bobby on the other. The girls were winning. It was done very professionally in ink, and the background of trees and grass was very much in my father's minimal style.

Even the mud puddle in the middle of the two groups had something of his line to it—that slapdash, abbreviated naturalism so effortless it melts from the page—and the situation—the tug-of-war—was peculiarly appropriate, though my father never drew anything like it, to my knowledge.

When I looked at the signature, I knew it was what I had been looking for. It read, in a surprisingly mature slanted script, "Kenny Dorn, age 15."

# five

Neither Pierce nor I was in any mood for wrestling our father's Caddy to Trenton for the reading of the will, so I called Bobby for a ride. Samantha answered and said he and Nancy had already gone, leaving her behind with a neighbor. "I wanted to *go*," she complained. "Uncle Pierce said I could sit with him." Next I tried Bitty at her place in Frenchtown. I got Mike Maas.

"Hi," I said. "Mike. This is Bitty's brother Tim."

Mike Maas cleared his throat. "Yeah, hey."

"Listen, is she around?"

"She's in the bathroom," he said. He had a phlegmy voice that sounded much older than it was. For a moment I entertained the notion that I had dialed the wrong number, and the middle-aged stranger on the other end was playing along, deadpan.

"Well, I don't really need to talk to her. I'm just wondering if you guys could swing by for Pierce and me on your way to the reading. Of the will."

"It's not exactly on the way," said Mike Maas.

I said nothing. This was something Amanda had taught me. When you asked somebody for a favor, and that person said something that strongly resembled no but was not quite no, you just waited silently until that person broke down and said yes.

"But, you know," he said, "no problem."

"Oh, great. See you around eight-thirty, then." I hung up. Already I didn't like Mike Maas very much. I wondered briefly why my sister had married him, then decided that I didn't know my sister well enough to reckon such a thing. This realization saddened me and I thought that maybe it could somehow be set right, somehow we could get to be friends. With a heavy heart I went down the hall to find Pierce.

The previous night, I had turned in as soon as I returned from the studio. I remembered tiptoeing through the house, so as not to wake the many guests I assumed were staying there too. But it had become clear, in the groggy minutes after my travel alarm went off in the morning, that there was nobody around but Pierce and me. Rose and Andrew must have gone back to New York, and dropped my mother off at the home; no cousins or uncles or aunts appeared to have come at all. The house felt weirdly desolate, and in my childhood bed, cluttered with the ghosts of every nightmare I'd ever had, I did too.

It was ten after eight. I knocked on Pierce's door. I could hear him in there, breathing, and decided to just go in.

"Howdy," he said with factitious cheer.

"Bitty and Maas are picking us up in twenty minutes," I said. "Are you getting dressed?"

He was wearing a pair of white boxer shorts, smoking a cigarette and running his hand over his chest. "My skin feels fake. Everything feels fake," he said. He looked up at me with real despair. "I can't go. I feel like a fraud."

I sat down on the edge of the bed and lit a cigarette of my own. Amanda didn't smoke, so I didn't either, usually, but here it felt right. With Pierce, trust was a precarious thing. "How's it been lately?"

He shrugged. "Not so bad. I'm on these pills." He gestured in an indefinite direction, away, with his hand. "They get rid of the extra people, but I never feel like myself anymore. My skin is like, numb."

Pierce did not hear voices, per se, as many people with his illness apparently do, but he had always talked about getting out of the crowd or getting away from all the hubbub when there was almost nobody around. Once, I took the subway back from the Italian Market just as a Phillies game was letting out, and the crowd in my car was enormous and loud, and I immediately thought of Pierce. I figured that feeling was what he was talking about.

"We really have to get moving," I told him.

He shook his head. "He isn't going to leave me anything," he said. "He's going to yank it all out from under me, I can just feel it. The house is going to get sold and I'm going to be on the street." He sucked on his cigarette with eerie calm, and the smoke seemed to invigorate him. "I'm not going to fucking Trenton for that."

"Why would he do that?"

"He ignores me, man. We haven't spoken in something like a year. I don't even exist."

I took a moment to digest this. "You've been living together all this time, and you haven't talked to him? In a year?"

"Nope. Isn't that nuts?"

I agreed that it was very strange. Pierce said, "Oh, Jesus, this is just worthless. I don't know why we're even talking. You should get out of here, really. I don't know what I'm going to do."

After a minute, I took the cigarette out of his mouth and stubbed it in the ashtray. Then I did the same with mine. I went to his closet and pulled out the cleanest jeans and T-shirt I could find. I tossed the shirt onto his chest. He just let it lie there. I bent over his feet and started pulling the jeans onto him. Finally, he said, "Oh, fer Chrissake," swung his legs off the bed like they were a couple of prosthetics, and pulled the jeans on himself. When it looked like he'd gotten things more or less under way, I went to the bathroom to brush my teeth. The mirror was so thickly stratified with dust that I could barely see myself. I cleared a hole in the grime, the way I would in a clean mirror steamed, and my hand came away greasy and gray.

Pierce walked in yawning while I was washing my hands. He shut his mouth fast when he noticed the hole. He leaned forward until his nose was nearly touching the mirror, and stared at himself for a full minute. Then, having done nothing else, he turned and left the bathroom.


"You're wearing that?" Bitty said from the passenger seat, apparently to both of us. I noticed that the clothes I had picked out for Pierce were almost identical to the ones I had earlier pulled from my own bag.

"I wish people would stop asking me that," I said, too quickly. Bitty was wearing a businesslike dress in sort of an unbleached flour color, and pearls.

Mike Maas had a suit on, but no tie. He was about two inches shorter than Bitty.

"Okay, whatever," she said.

Mike was the kind of bad driver who believes with all his heart that he is the only good driver on the road. This particular type of driver drives fast because he thinks he can do so safely, and does not use turn signals because they are irrelevant and inefficient. Those driving slowly are doing so because they don't trust their own abilities, which are scant. I'd once had a roommate who explained all this to me. He too was this kind of driver.

A gravel truck was traveling the speed limit in front of Mike and Bitty's Toyota 4-Runner. Every couple of minutes a piece of gravel clicked off the windshield. After a while Mike had had enough. "This is bullshit," he said, and moved to pass, accelerating violently, keeping his eyes focused straight ahead. Bitty glanced out the passenger window, presumably for a look at the man who had caused the delay. The man wasn't looking back. Mike jerked the car over to the right lane, then leaned heavily into his seat like a monarch who has just ordered somebody beheaded.

Trenton hummed dully beneath a hazy hot sun and some half-assed thunderheads that looked like invading UFOs from a cheap sci-fi movie. Mike seemed to know where the parking spaces were; he careened down a maze of one-way streets to a parking meter that might as well have had his name printed on it.

"Got quarters?" he said to Bitty, and she dug into her purse. To my surprise, Pierce produced several quarters from his pocket and passed them to Mike, who stared at them briefly before lunging from the car and plugging them into the meter.

We walked. "You know where we're going?" I asked.

"Yeah," said Mike Maas. "It's near my building."

"So you work in Trenton."

"Uh huh."

We walked several blocks in the heat. Pierce didn't seem bothered by it; he was the only one of us whose forehead wasn't brilliant with sweat. At an Art Deco building that looked uncannily like an enormous jukebox, Mike pulled open a heavy glass door and plunged inside. Bitty jumped forward and caught the door as it closed behind him, and she held it open for me and Pierce. I thanked her and she raised her eyebrows.

We took an elevator to the sixth floor. The doors opened into a wide carpeted hallway. Before us was an empty reception desk and a padded bench, each covered in the same carpet that was on the floor, a dusty sort of gray. I imagined that it hid dirt nicely. My mother was sitting alone on the bench.

"Mommy!" said Bitty. She sprung from the elevator toward her and planted a noisy kiss on her cheek. My mother's eyes flapped open and she shied away from Bitty, startled.

"For the love of Christ!" she said.

"Mommy, it's me, Bitty."

Mother squinted. "Ah, Bitty," she said, though it wasn't clear if this was, finally, recognition, or simply a conversational habit she had adopted to avoid embarrassment.

I went to her while Pierce and Mike loitered before us, their hands in their pockets. "Hey, Mom," I said. "It's Tim. Do you remember me?"

"Yep," she said.

"Okay. Are you doing all right?" I sat down on the bench opposite Bitty, who clutched Mother's right hand as if it were a baby sparrow.

"They came and got me out of bed," she said.

"Are you tired?"

"I was, but now I'm pretty much awake."

"That's good."

"So what brings you here?" Her voice was bright, the way it might be for a pleasant but unexpected guest.

"I'm here to hear Dad's will."

She frowned. "He was going to leave me that old breakfront. But you know he never did? That really burns me, even to this day. Julia got it, the little hussy."

Bitty leaned over her and gave me a look. "Why don't we go in, Mommy?"

"Well, all right," she said, dragging herself to her feet. She shook us both off. "I'm not infirm, you know."

But of course she was. She teetered for a moment, like Wile E. Coyote suspended, by the power of his own ignorance, above a yawning chasm, then buckled. Bitty and I caught her by the arms. Her bones pulled against my fingers through her thin skin, and she said, "Ouch."

We pulled her gently up. "You're okay?"

"Had a little spell there," she said. This is what she used to say when she got drunk and fell down from that. She was lighter now, it seemed by half. I looked up at Pierce, who was staring at her like she had just been dropped into the law office hallway from outer space. Mike Maas kept flinching toward us, as if to help.

"Why don't you go in, Mike," said Bitty.

"Oh, yeah." He turned and headed for the smoked-glass doors at the end of the hallway. We followed, with Pierce bringing up the rear. Mike held the doors open for us this time.

Rose and Bobby and Nancy were already there, along with Susan Caletti the editor, and a tall, pot-bellied man with jet-black hair. They all sat behind the burnished mahogany table that filled the room, my brother's family and Rose around the tall man, Susan a few seats away.

Rose blanched. "Jesus! Where's her walker?"

"I didn't see it," I said. My mother was scanning the room, scowling.

"I put it behind the desk," Rose said, exhaling loudly. She clomped past us into the hall and came back wielding the walker like a lion tamer with a wooden stool. She swept around us and placed it before Mom. "Here you go, Mom," she said.

"Oh, yes."

"So," Rose said. She put her hands on her hips. "Is this everybody?"

"I don't know," I said. "Aren't cousins supposed to crawl out of the woodwork to claim their slice of the pie?"

"What cousins?" Rose sounded angry, like the cousins were waiting in the lobby with six-shooters and burlap sacks with dollar signs printed on them. I looked past her to the tall man. Bobby was seated across from him, asking quiet questions.

"Who's that guy?" I asked quietly.

"Ha, ha," said Rose.

"No, really," I said. "Do I know him?"

Bitty released Mom, who had taken hold of the walker. "You don't remember Uncle Mal?" she said.

At this, Uncle Mal met me with a grim smile. "Hello, Tim, Pierce," he said. "Hello, Bee."

Bee was Uncle Mal's name for Bitty. She loved it. When he came to the house, he used to bring her bee things: little plastic bees, stickers with bees on them, and once, a spiral notebook with a giant cartoon bee on the cover, pollinating a wide pink flower. For months she spent her weekend afternoons sitting at the kitchen table, writing stories in it about her and Uncle Mal. She let me read one once. It was about a killer robot that threatened them with violence; Uncle Mal talked the robot out of it, and the three of them went and had a picnic. It was a strange story, full of peculiar details. A crush of Bitty's from the TV at the time had a fluffy, feathered haircut, and in the story Uncle Mal did too. It was an expressive head of hair, tossing and tousling in the air as the story ebbed and flowed.

But now it was exceedingly thin, and dyed a deep, implausible black. He wore it clumped and spiky, like a wet Marine. And though he still had the same sunken chest, into which his necktie dipped like an old clothesline, Mal had developed a shocking paunch. It stuck out over his belt as if tied there with rope. He looked like a former basketball star who now managed apartment buildings for a living. I must have gaped.

"I look a little different," he said.

"Well, it's been a while."

Bitty left Mom's side and tiptoed around the table to him, planting a kiss in the oily fuzz over his ear. "It's good to see you," she said.

"Always good to see you, Bee. I'm so sorry about your dad." He looked up at me. "You too, Tim."

"None of this seems real," I said, and meant it.

He nodded solemnly. "How are you doing, Pierce?"

Pierce shrugged. "You know."

"Mmm-hmm. Why don't you all have a seat?"

Mal watched me as I helped Mom into a chair and walked around behind her to my own. I nodded to Susan as I sat down, and she nodded back. What was she doing here? Did she expect some inheritance from my father? Had they been close? Her face was such a rictus of discomfort that I could read nothing else into it, and her hands squirmed against each other in full view, leaving a damp shadow on the shiny tabletop.

Mal had a thick manila envelope in front of him, his giant hands spread flat on either side. "Well," he said. "We might as well get this under way." He turned the envelope ninety degrees on the table, reached into it and pulled out three things: a few pieces of textured, watermarked white paper, a thin white business-size envelope, and another envelope, identical save for a slight bulge in the middle. Both of these envelopes were signed across the flap—I recognized the crabbed version of my father's careful hand—and stamped and signed on the front.

"It's a very simple will," Mal said. Bobby's eyes widened. "The six of you, Rosalinde, Robert, Timothy, Pierce, Beatrice and Dorothy, are the only heirs."

I glanced over at Susan to see what her reaction was to this, but she was sitting perfectly still, her hands folded, watching Mal. He began to read the preliminaries: sound mind and body, and so on. The only other sound in the room was the air conditioner's arctic hiss, and muffled traffic noise from outside.

"To Dorothy, my wife, and my children Rosalinde, Robert and Beatrice, I leave my extant liquid assets. These are to be divided equally into funds which I have already established in their names. In addition, I have established for my wife, Dorothy, in her name, a fund for the maintenance of her care until her death, such fund as will be attended to by the executor of this will." He looked up, smiling sadly at my mother, whose eyes were elsewhere.

"To Pierce Mix, I leave the contents of the bank account already established jointly in our names, the house at 12 Old Dock Road, Riverbank, New Jersey, the attached garage, the 1984 Cadillac El Dorado, and the land surrounding the house and garage, save that land on which my cartoon studio stands. To Pierce I also leave this envelope, its contents, and all rights and claims attached to its contents."

Mal held up the bulging envelope and set it down again.

"Save those items already mentioned, I leave my worldly possessions to my wife and all my children, to be divided as they see fit."

He paused a moment here. Had I not heard right, or had my name not been mentioned along with the liquid assets? Could it be that I would get no money at all? The thought crowded my head like a mouthful of stale bread. Nothing! I was getting nothing!

"To my son Timothy," Mal read, perhaps more slowly now. "I leave the Family Funnies comic strip, all merchandising, reprint, animation, book publishing, advertising and other rights as set forth in my name by Burn Features Syndicate, Incorporated, and the cartoon studio behind 12 Old Dock Road, Riverbank, New Jersey, the land it stands on and its full contents (and all rights to all drawings therein) under the following conditions: that he is able, three months from this date, to produce a week's worth of daily Family Funnies strips of his own devising and execution, to the satisfaction of a board of Burn Features editors and directors set forth below." Mal proceeded to read from a list of names, none of which I heard. A silence gathered in the room with guerrilla stealth. People were looking at me.

"I don't get it," I said, my voice dying in the chill air.

"He left you the comic strip," Mal said. "To draw."

"That's all?"

"This too," he said, and pushed the second envelope toward me. It had the approximate heft of three or four pieces of paper.

I turned the envelope over in my hands. TIM, it read, in faint ballpoint ink. When I looked up I met Susan's eyes. She was gazing at me expectantly, like a lover naked under a thin sheet.

"Excuse me," I said, and walked out.

# six

I found a men's room in the hallway, pushed the door open, and locked myself into a stall, where I sat down on the toilet and ripped open the envelope. Inside was a handwritten letter. It read:

Tim—

Well, I imagine you're pretty pissed off right now, being as you didn't get any money from me. Of course if you can pull this off you'll get all the money you'll ever need and then some. Not that money's important to you. Or is it?

We both know that what you're doing is a lot of bullshit. I tried the genius painter thing when I was in college, and I wasn't any better at it than you were. Actually, I was probably a little better. But that's not the point. The point is that it isn't right for you and never was, and you only did it to get away from your mom and me and that house. Can't say I blame you for that. I was a real asshole sometimes, that's for sure, and your mother was too. But now you're thirty years old (maybe more, depending on how quickly I knock off) and it's time to get your act together, like it or not. God knows what a pain in the ass that is, so here's your chance to do it the easy way.

Why me? you're thinking. Of course you are. Look at your brothers and sisters, Tim. Bobby's already got his little chunk of the pie, Lindy's told us all to go to hell, Bitty is married (we'll see how long that lasts), and Pierce, of course, is hopeless. It's the same old song, Timmy, you're not living up to your potential. You're the only one who can still make yourself a decent life. You're down in West Philly with that little girl of yours, but she's not any good either, and besides, you don't like her. Face facts! Say what you will about me, but I did whatever in hell I wanted, when I wanted, and I'm happy I did. Mostly, anyway.

I've included a list of the supplies I use. If you're going to do it, do it right. Finished cartoons go on 2-ply Strathmore plate; you stick a week's worth in an envelope with cardboard and ship them to New York. Do your prelims in pencil on 16-lb layout bond. Sketch with a Wolff "B." Finals with a Globe Bowl point and letter with a Speedball B-6 round. Brushes are MORALLY WRONG, got that? This isn't art school, it's the strips. The other stuff you need's on the list, along with the product numbers for all the important things. Also, I've got you set up with Brad Wurster, out in New Brunswick. He's a real genius, he gives lessons to all the young punks who can afford it. He's the best there is. You'll go to him five hours a day, five days a week. When you make your decision, call him at 224–8935. He's always home. You think FF is a joke, but it sent you to art school, so you'll keep it the way it is.

I said I was mostly happy I did what I did. The only problem was your mother. We tore into each other like nobody's business. Don't do that, all right? That's what'll happen between that girl and you if you don't watch it. Your lives will go on being boring until one day you'll wake up and blame her for it, because you won't want to admit it's your own damn fault. And she'll do the same thing. And there'll be fights and drinking and all the stuff that ruined your mom and me. Now I'm sounding like a sap. But that woman was my one great failing. I bet she'd say the same about me. We screwed up and probably screwed all of you up too.

You won't want to do this at first, but you'll come around. There's more to it than meets the eye.

Dad

The accompanying list was long as my arm: sandpaper, palette, rubber cement, kneaded eraser, etc., etc. I shouldered out of the stall, crumpled the papers and hurled them into the trash can, screamed, spun around, kicked the door so that it gonged on its hinges. Then I stood perfectly still, breathing heavily, for several minutes.

Gathered, I went to the trash can and pulled the papers out. Did he think he could get away with this pop-psychological semi-apology for all the heartlessness and gloomy self-indulgence he'd inflicted on us over the years? But of course he had, and he was doing it right now. I smoothed the letter out against my leg, fresh sweat breaking out under my arms and on my back. I'd keep it as testament to my enduring patience. Someday, when I'd made my own fortune without him, I'd read it and laugh at what a supercilious twit he was.

I smoothed back my hair in the mirror—for once, I noticed, I didn't look like a penitent awaiting the lash—and flung open the men's room door. I almost knocked over Susan Caletti. She brought her arms up before her face, as if I were about to sock her.

"Jesus!" I said. "Sorry."

She backed up a step. "That's okay."

"Where is everybody?" The hallway and conference room were empty.

"They left. You were in there awhile." She smiled, pushing a wavy clot of hair away from her face. She looked terribly uncomfortable—her dress was navy blue and heavy-looking, with her ankles popsicle-sticking out of it, sunburned to a lurid pink.

"So I guess you're giving me a ride home?"

"I guess I am."


Susan Caletti drove a tan Subaru station wagon that looked to be from the early 1980s. It was in great shape. I told her this as we wended our way out of Trenton, the air conditioner gusting clammy warm air into our faces.

"Yeah, I had a boyfriend who waxed it every weekend, so I sort of caught on. It feels a little funny doing it out in the street, but whatever."

"Where do you live?"

"TriBeCa," she said, and added—with a practiced, muted jubilance—"rent-controlled."

"There's no rent control in West Philly."

She took her eyes from the road to offer me a surprised glance. "No?"

"Our rent's gone up something like four times in the past two years."

"Too bad."

Her driving was quietly competent, a rare thing. She seemed even to be enjoying herself. As if reading my mind, she said, "I like driving in cities, especially non–New York ones." We were getting on Route 29 via a narrow entrance ramp. She paused to jockey for position against a pickup with wooden fence rails. The pickup backed off and let her merge. "It's funny, I don't really think of it as a part of real life. It's like a video game or something."

"That could get you into trouble," I said.

"Hmm. I suppose it could."

We rode in silence for some minutes, watching trees and houses creep by. Susan didn't turn on the radio. We were coming into Washington Crossing when she said, "So have you given it some thought?"

For a second I didn't know what she meant. I had been thinking about Amanda's car, and began to look for the service station where I'd left it. Then I remembered. "Oh, sure," I said.

There was the station, up ahead. The Chevette was parked outside in the sun, all the windows clamped firmly shut. "So?" Susan asked.

I turned to her. "Are you kidding me? Of course not!"

"Are you sure?"

"Yes, I'm sure! That strip has been the bane of my existence my entire life! It's stupid!"

"Okay, okay," she said.

"Sorry."

"All I'm saying is don't be hasty. Your dad . . ."

"Don't tell me about my dad, please."

"Right, okay." She opened her mouth, closed it again, then sighed. "Just let me say this. From the standpoint of publicity, it's preferable for us to keep it in the family. It's a family thing, you know?" We were on a straightaway past a meadow, and she took a moment to look at me. I kept my eyes out the windshield. "And the other thing is that it's easy. There's really not much you have to do. Your dad didn't really do much except draw his daily strips. We just send you your checks."

"Susan, with all due respect, I've already made my decision."

She poised herself to speak, her shoulders pitched like a linebacker's. But finally she relaxed into her seat, nodding. The willows and ranch houses of South Side Riverbank came into view.

At the foot of our driveway, she stopped the car. The air conditioner had finally cooled it off, and I envied her the drive back to New York. She opened the ashtray and pulled out, from a pile of nuts, bolts, rubber bands and coins, a creased business card. She handed it to me.

"In case you have second thoughts. Your dad said . . ." She stopped short, her eyes on the river glittering in the distance.

"Oh, go ahead and finish."

"Your dad said it would be good for you. Maybe that's true."

"My dad has never known what's good for me."

She met my gaze and held it, for the briefest moment, then put the car back into gear. "That may be true too," she said.


There was a message on the answering machine for me. It was from the Sunoco station in Washington Crossing. They had an estimate on the Chevette.

I called back and got the woman I'd talked to when I broke down. "You threw a rod," she said.

"I kind of figured that."

"Yeah, well, it's gonna cost you six hundred bucks. We gotta get a new engine, okay? And there's one up in Ringoes we can get you used for about four hundred, and believe me that's a real good deal, and then labor's two hundred, and I know that sounds like a lot, but it's the best we can do in these particular circumstances."

"Oh."

"So we need a decision from you on whether to go ahead or not on it."

"I'm wondering if the car's even worth fixing."

"Well, that's a possibility."

"I'll have to get back to you," I said. "It's technically my girlfriend's car."

I hung up and stood a moment by the phone, waiting for inspiration. Six hundred dollars! On the day I was supposed to have become rich! I grabbed a pencil from the grease-spattered mug next to the stove and snapped it in two against the edge of the counter. This felt good, so I did it to all the other pencils too. Then the pitiful theatricality of the gesture struck me and I put the pieces back into the mug and wiped off the counter with a damp rag.

I called Amanda. She picked up on the first ring. "It's me," I said.

"Hello, me."

"More bad news." I waited a few seconds. "It's the car. It needs a new engine."

"How much?" she said.

"Six hundred bucks."

"Hmm." In the background, at our apartment, I heard somebody say "What?" "Nothing," replied Amanda.

"Who's that?" I said.

"Nobody."

"Oh, come on."

"It's Ian," she said. "I know how you hate him."

"I don't hate him," I said. "Why would you say that with him around?" Ian was our upstairs neighbor. He borrowed things and played "whimsical" little "jokes" on me when I wasn't home, like adding dead birds or dandelion chains to my installations, or filling my sneakers with bread crumbs. I hated him.

"Don't worry, Tim," came Ian's voice, shrill even far from the phone. "I can take it!"

"Don't let him into the studio, please."

"I don't know about this repair," she said. "Are you sure they're not just ripping you off? You can look like a sucker sometimes, no offense." This refreshing frankness suggested that they had just been talking about me.

"I'm sure, Jesus Christ."

She was silent, briefly. "Tim?"

"Amanda."

"Did they read the will?"

"Yes," I said.

"What'd you get?" Her voice was small and quiet, as if it were coming out of a dictaphone.

"Nothing," I said.

"You didn't get *nothing.*"

"I got the comic strip," I said. "If I can get it together in three months, I get to draw the Family Funnies, and I'll live in my father's studio and be him. That's my inheritance. An endless, meaningless task."

This time the pause was longer, a nice slack length of rope to hang the conversation with. "Are you going to do it?" she said.

"Of course not," I said.

She sighed. "No, of course not."

"What?" Ian was saying, "What?"

"Ian, shut up!"

I said, "Look, we're not going to have any money anytime soon. We have to decide about the car."

"I guess we let it go, then. I guess we don't have a car."

"I suppose that's best," I said.

"Unless you sell a piece or something," Amanda said, her voice brassy and false as an audition. "Maybe that'll happen, do you think?"

"Oh, fuck you."

"Yeah, I thought so." But whatever emboldened her before had drained away, and it was just her speaking now, woeful and hushed. "So are you coming home?"

As much as I didn't want to be in this house, with its sticky patina of dust and big empty rooms, I wanted even less to be back in the cramped apartment with Ian listening to us from above, and my clumsy and unappealing work, my feelings for which were maturing from constructive doubt to outright disdain. I thought of Susan Caletti, puttering up the New Jersey Turnpike in a gentle cloud of cool air. For a second, I thought about what a year of the Family Funnies would earn me, and how long I could live on it afterward. I swallowed hard.

"Tim?"

"I need a little time to think here," I blurted. "I have to think things over."

Amanda cleared her throat. " 'Things'?"

"Yeah, things. Everything. All these new developments."

"I see."

"I don't think you do," I said, a parting swat. "Your dad didn't just die, okay?"

"Oh," she said, "I'm sorry," as if awakening from a long sleep. "I'm sorry, I didn't mean . . ."

"Look, just don't worry about it, okay? Just give me a few days and I'll work out a plan."

"Right," she said. "Regroup."

"Exactly. Okay?"

"Okay," Amanda said.


Something was wrong in the house. I walked from room to room, struggling to figure it out, but only when I noticed through my parents' bedroom window that the Caddy was missing did it come to me: the place was empty. I was alone. In a family of seven, with a mother who didn't work, a father who worked at home, and a brother who rarely left his bedroom, this was a rare circumstance, and standing in the dusty quiet I thought I could remember every other instance of it in thirty years. They were all pretty much the same. My father, racked by a sudden recognition that he was a bad parent, would declare a family outing, and one of us (whoever was quickest) would declare themselves violently ill. Bobby was most convincing: never reluctant to purge himself, he could vomit on demand. Rose was second best, milking her nascent menstruation with enormous skill; she would double over with sudden cramps and fold herself onto the floor like an old blanket. I was third. I got headaches. My mother would lead me to my room, pull down the shades and lay a damp washcloth over my forehead. I was actually brought to the doctor once; my mother was certain I was having migraines ("Your great aunt Sarah had 'em, goddam her"). But I was pronounced healthy, much to my relief. Pierce, even when he was far too young to be left alone, had only to announce he was staying home, and nobody would question him: my father, true to form, didn't actually want him along. Occasionally he would be locked in his bedroom for safe keeping. And Bitty, equally true to form, always wanted to go.

After everyone was gone, I generally got out of bed and went straight for the kitchen, where I consumed great handfuls of anything rationed, forbidden or nutritionally counterproductive that I could find. Afterward I rooted through my parents' underwear drawers, read Bobby's hidden skin mags, abused myself and watched television until I heard the car in the driveway. By this time my headache would be real, and I could climb legitimately back into bed.

In response to the memory, or maybe to the morning's disheartening conversations, my head began a tentative thrumming. I rooted in the kitchen drawers and turned up a bottle of fossil aspirin, the crusty old tablets half-buried in a dune of analgesic dust. A threadbare washcloth found encrusted over the tub-edge wilted under cold water. I lay back on my bed, the washcloth folded across my brow, and fell into a shallow nap, where I had a nasty dream. In it, I was driving Amanda's Chevette, and Amanda was directing me from the passenger seat. The car was filthy inside and out, slathered with some kind of tacky black goop. It kept getting on my hands and clothes.

"Left!" Amanda screamed. "Right!"

She was steering me toward obstacles, and when I hit them, parts of the car broke or fell off. And though I was doing what I was told, she was outraged, and pummeled me with her bony fists. "You dumbfuck!" she said. Meanwhile the landscape threatened, grew darker and more treacherous with every passing second.

There were a lot of people watching me drive, healthy, happy people waving banners and flags, as if we were part of a parade. They groaned with disappointment every time we smacked against an object. What were they doing out here, in this awful place? What was *I* doing out here? The dream ended abruptly when Amanda steered me into the base of a huge black volcano.

I woke unrefreshed, spooked by the silence, and found myself missing the usually unnerving presence of my brother. Where did Pierce go? Who did he see? I had no idea. But I supposed the same questions could be asked about me, and the answers would be no less disappointing. The sun hung shockingly low in the sky—it was already evening. I had missed most of the day.

I went to the kitchen and drank a glass of ice water. Then I pulled Susan's card from my pocket. BURN FEATURES SYNDICATE, INC., it read. SUSAN CALETTI, EDITOR. A telephone number.

And on the back, another number, handwritten beside a capital H. I dialed this one. After five rings, a machine answered, and I almost hung up. Then the familiar clatter of a manhandled phone.

"Hello? Hello? Hold on." The taped message droned on a second or two, then stopped. Susan came back on, her voice syrupy with sleep. "Hello?"

"Susan?"

"Yeah, oh, hi."

"This is Tim Mix."

"I know," she said. "I'm good with voices. Excuse me, I just woke up."

"Me too. Sorry about that."

She coughed, and I heard the whisper of fabric being adjusted. "So what's up?"

From where I stood, I could see through the grubby sliding glass doors the entrance to my father's studio.

I switched the phone to the other ear, the way a person does a hundred times during a long, wrenching conversation. "I'll do it," I said.

**seven**

Friday night in Riverbank meant ice cream and miniature golf, two things that, despite my best efforts to hate them during my college-era anti-hometown period, I still loved with unnatural passion. There is no miniature golf in West Philadelphia, and never was. There was no soft serve either, not in the time I'd lived there. I set off on foot for downtown.

I had spent the afternoon avoiding my responsibilities as author of the Family Funnies. There was the studio to clean out and begin work in; there was Brad Wurster to call, to set up my lessons. I needed supplies, I supposed. It was July 10th, and I had until October 7th (three months after my father's death) to become a cartoonist. I felt no urgency. October seemed so far away, like a description of autumn from a long, boring novel, and I couldn't think of any reason why my task should not be absurdly easy.

As a rule, people in Riverbank rarely walked places in summer; they either sat on their porches, watching people drive by, or drove somewhere themselves. This rule of thumb applied equally to the North and South sides of town, though the cars were different. People stared as I strolled along the sidewalk, at first from deep behind stands of trees, then increasingly, the farther north I got, from crumbling cement porches with wrought-iron railings. As I walked, I could hear the river meekly yammering two blocks to my left, and ahead the dim lights of downtown glowed wanly against parked cars.

For the first time in many months, I felt good. I felt better than good, in fact—I felt terrific. I replayed my conversation with Susan in my mind. She had told me that we would meet—"Come to New York if you want," she said, "or I'll come there, whatever"—to discuss my progress, and the syndicate's plans for me. We talked about interviews I would eventually have to give, and a conference I would attend in the coming months. I hadn't done anything at all, and people were taking care of me; people had my comfort and work in mind.

No matter that it wasn't meaningful work. It was work, one way or another, and I would find a way to like it.

Custard's Last Stand stood at the intersection of Main and Cherry, catty-corner from the Episcopalian church. It was illuminated by massive parking-lot streetlamps, swaddled in halos of light-drunk moths, that towered over the eighteen golf holes like skyscrapers. The course was packed. I pulled open the saloon-style half-doors, ducked past the vestibule bug-zapper, then got myself into line behind a hefty family of five. Bon Jovi was on the radio. I hummed along. When it was my turn, I ordered a vanilla cone dipped in quick-drying butterscotchlike goo, then carried it, along with a wad of napkins thick as a Penguin Classic, to the chain-link fence that separated the paying miniature golfers from the spectators.

The Custard's Last Stand course was famous throughout the county for its thirty-foot plaster statues. Custer himself was central, his arm thrust into the air clutching his saber, his mouth a great black gob rendered wide, to indicate a battle cry. There was an Indian named Rain-in-the-Face, who, I learned as part of a school project, claimed to have personally cut out Custer's heart on the battlefield at Little Bighorn. Also present was Tom Custer, Custer's brother, who (I reported in the same project) was so badly mutilated by the Sioux that he could only be identified by the tattoo on his arm. There were other figures, but none as large as these three, so that the course seemed warped by a strange foreshortening. Custer's legs straddled a tricky pond, over which golf balls were supposed to roll via a thin metal bridge. Tom Custer had a loop-the-loop wrapped around his legs. If you hit the loop just right, the ball rocketed straight into the cup. And Rain-in-the-Face, in a bizarre assimilation of divergent cultural icons, had a windmill sprouting from his abdomen. His skin was painted bright red, even his ankles.

I ate my ice cream on the only free bench. It was free, apparently, because the view from it was blocked almost entirely by a large cardboard broadside, lashed to the fence with twisted bits of clothesline. I peered around it for a while, watching the teenagers flirt in their shorts and basketball team T-shirts. Boys mugged, knocking against each other and stealing each other's hats. Girls rolled their eyes and fixed their hair. Then my focus shifted abruptly and I saw what the poster said.

**FunnyFest '98**

**fun*prizes*games*autographs**

**Don't miss this year's celebration! Meet Carl Mix IN PERSON!**

**Also, kids!!! Meet your cartoon favorites Lindy, Bobby, Timmy and Bitty LIVE IN PERSON!**

**Ride tickets on sale within—don't forget to VOTE!**

**Saturday, July 25, Delaware Fairgrounds**

There we were—Bobby, Rose, Bitty and I—living it up on a Ferris wheel, eating cotton candy and Italian ice, so flat-out riled that our parents could only shrug their shoulders in exasperation. Oh well! Kids!

But live? In person? Could Francobolli have actually scheduled us into the 'Fest, or would we be portrayed by actors? For a moment I considered actually going, to see what form the impending debacle would take.

I finished my cone and went back into the restaurant. The line was gone now, and a few families and cooing couples leaned across tables toward one another, talking loudly. I asked about ride tickets at the counter.

"Fifty cents a pop," a kid told me.

"That's cheap," I said.

"Yeah, well it takes like ten to ride the friggin' bumper cars."

"Oh," I said. "What's this about voting?"

"Jussec." The kid bent over and rummaged beneath the counter. When he surfaced, he was holding a printed postcard.

I took it. "Thanks," I said.

When I got outside I looked at the postcard under the golf-course lights. It showed a cartoon of Timmy—of *me*—sitting on my father's shoulders, holding a magic marker the size of my arm. We were facing a tall printed sign attached to a pole, and the sign said RIVERBANK. There was a big black X markered over the word.

With growing horror, I flipped the card over. It read:

VOTE!! for your favorite NEW NAME for Riverbank, New Jersey!
I WANT Riverbank changed to . . .

   ( ) Funnyville

   ( ) Mixville

   ( ) Familytown

   ( ) Funnytown

Pick one, affix stamp, and drop in a mailbox! It's that easy!

The mailing address was "Name Change Headquarters," with a P.O. box in City Hall. I couldn't help noticing that there was no box you could check if you didn't want the name changed at all.

The ice cream, which had felt so good going down, was beginning to churn stickily around in my stomach, and I felt a mild and time-honored nausea. My hands were gummed with drippings. I shoved the postcard into my pocket and started walking home.

Pierce had not come back, so I made my way into a dark house. There were no messages on the answering machine. I would, at some point, have to call Amanda with my new plans, but after considering the telephone for a few minutes decided that I wouldn't do it now.

If I was going to be a cartoonist, I thought, I would have to start acting like one.

In my bedroom, I took the key that Mal had given me from its envelope and slipped it onto my key chain. There wasn't much on there: my copy of the mailbox key in Philadelphia, the two keys to the apartment and a thick aluminum bottle opener from a state-run liquor store on Market Street. I dropped the keys into my pocket and headed for the studio.

There was a smell to the place I hadn't noticed before, a sort of dry, cigary bite in the air. I walked to the back and picked a bottle from the forest of booze on the table, then poured a few fingers of rotgut into a drinking glass. It was a "Whiskers" glass from a fast food tie-in of many years before; the cartoon cat glared with famous apathy from behind half-lidded eyes. The liquor lapped at the fringes of Whiskers's smug smile. I pried open the mini-fridge, which had lain untouched for days. There was a tiny freezer in it, with a tray of rimy ice cubes the size of dice; I plunked a handful of these into the glass and went to the drafting table, where I sat down on my father's orthopedic office chair for the first time. I switched on the overhead lamp, and its light flooded the drawing surface, making explicit the hints of scratches and stains that covered it. Immediately I wondered where to put my drink, then almost as quickly found the answer—a wooden stool at shoulder level, the seat discolored with water stains.

Poor Dad, I thought.

Everything I needed was within reach. Paper was in a low flat file to my right, inkwells on a card table to my left, pens in a plastic Philadelphia Eagles cup stuck into a crude hole on the drawing board. I helped myself to the paper: it was thick and had a shiny finish. Final draft stuff, I thought, so I rooted for something else, and found it, a thinner, rougher sketch paper. I pulled a pencil from the cup and stuck it into a nearby sharpener. It ground itself pointy with a cheerless wheeze. A few preliminary strokes produced a dark, clear line; some gentle brushings left a nice shading.

It had been years since I'd actually handled art supplies—my work had taken on such workmanlike redundance that I had little use for the finer tools of my trade. Now I felt nostalgic, as the lines unrolled themselves under my hand. I was doing something small and precise. I was a lefty, like my father, and as I sketched—nothing in particular, the crook of the desk lamp, the edge of a table—I automatically tilted the paper clockwise forty-five degrees, to avoid smearing. I wondered if my father did this too. I tried, without success, to remember what he looked like while working.

After a few idle minutes I rolled the chair back to the large flat file in search of a cartoon to copy. I opened a drawer at random.

What I came up with was a fairly recent one, which I remembered from the *Inquirer* funny pages; it was a daily strip with a handwritten caption, apparently an early draft, as the figures were a little less refined than they usually were in the paper. Like all my father's originals, it was about three times the size of a printed strip.

In it, Lindy and I were standing with our mother. It looked like Lindy was being reprimanded, possibly for something she had said to me, and she had her arms crossed and a defiant pout on her eight-year-old face. My mother's finger was extended in the classic scolding-mother manner, and she had her mouth open. The caption, between quotes, read: "It's not what's on the outside of a person that counts, but what's on the inside." And the visual punchline of the panel was what hung in a thought bubble above my head, which I contemplated with a precocious stroke on an incipient goatee: the outline of Lindy's bare body, filled not with her external features but with her skeleton.

Ha-ha, I got it. But looking at it now, from my father's point of view, it seemed a weird kind of auto-voyeurism, an unsavory peek into the reeking roil of his subconscious. In effect it was less an opportunity for a joke (misunderstandings of the spoken word were a common topic in the Family Funnies) than an elaborate contrivance designed to allow my father to draw my sister's innards.

Not that her innards had anything to do with documented human anatomy. For one thing, she only had about six ribs. Her femurs were no longer than her humeri. And her skull, elongated as it had to be to fit the established FF head shape, looked less like a human bone than it did the fossilized remains of a Cenozoic-era forerunner of the horse.

There were a few conclusions that could be reached from this cartoon. One, of course, was that my father had drawn it without thinking at all, that he had simply trotted out a cartoon to fit the crappy yuk he had dreamed up. Knowing my father, I didn't buy this for a second. Another possibility was that he suffered odd morbid obsessions that occasionally made it onto paper. This seemed likely in fact, given the strip's often bizarre traffic with the deceased. We were always waxing maudlin about dead relatives in the strip, particularly grandparents, and these would materialize in the air above us in billowing empyrean robes through which big fluffy wings invariably poked. There was also a running joke about an endomorphic spook who haunted the house, leaving chaos in his wake and leaving us kids to take the blame. Ghosts filled entire pews at church. Cemeteries were as busy as train stations. Seeing my sister's deformed childhood skeleton threw me for a loop, and I groaned inwardly at the sudden thought of muscles and blood vessels tangled among my own bones, dark and wet inside me like centuries-old plumbing.

The third possibility was that my father was aware of the inchoate weirdness of cartoon biology, and just wanted to get it out in the open. Of course the skeleton looked strange; it had to, and he had simply pointed this out in a witty sort of flourish.

I decided that the second and third possibilities were compatible. Why not? I felt like I was making progress, understanding the strip through my father's eyes. I flipped over my sketch paper and moved the ink drawing to the right side of the table, then cracked my knuckles, ready to go on to the copying.

First I outlined my mother's head: one quick loop, and I'd start filling in. But as soon as the pencil left the paper, I knew it was all wrong. Something about the chin area. I should have fleshed it out a little. I corrected it without erasing: still not enough. The next line was too much. I scribbled the entire thing out and drew another line.

This one was better. I added hair without too much trouble, then tried eyes.

Terrible.

I erased them and redrew them, this time more slowly. Just little oval dots underneath quick, straight dashes, like notes between lines in a musical staff. And above them, eyebrows like fermatas, wide and expressive.

Awful, completely awful.

I drew another head, then another and another. I couldn't get any as close as the second one had come. I filled the page with aborted heads, then flipped it back over and wedged some more in among my earlier drawings. Finally I took out a fresh sheet and got the head and hair on my third try, then drew and erased the eyes a dozen times, until I had worn the paper through. I tried eyes only, never got them. I did twenty noses, each one perfectly fine, perfectly believable, but not one of them my cartoon mother's.

I gave up on Mom and worked on Lindy. Mom was in three-quarters profile, but Lindy faced front. I did her head easily, then attacked the mouth. It looked bad. I did a few more, then redrew the head, but now that was off. I did this for about three hours, and refilled my glass as many times, until soon I was drunk and could barely keep myself from sprawling facedown on the drawing board.

Which in fact I did, with a sickening slump, my nose mashing into the gashed, galosh-scented surface. My mouth marshaled its drool, which had begun to trickle between my cracking lips, when a creepy déjà vu struck me, and I bolted upright, sending the thread of spittle sizzling onto the lamp.

What was that all about? I wasn't so crocked that I couldn't imagine how I must have looked, laid out agape over my scribblings: like Carl Mix, helplessly infarcting in the humid summer dark. It was time to quit for the night.

## eight

On Saturday morning I swallowed another handful of aspirin and called Brad
Wurster. Outside, it was a beautiful sunny day, but despite the open sliding
doors off the kitchen, none of this brilliant light seemed to be getting into the
house. It filled me with renewed despair. The phone rang over and over, and
just as I was about to hang up, a groggy voice came on the line.

"Yeah."

"Is this Brad Wurster?"

"Yeah."

"This is Tim Mix. Carl's son? I'm taking over the Family Funnies and I'm
supposed to take lessons from you."

This time there was a short delay before he said "Yeah." Both of us waited
after that.

"Well," I said, "I wanted to set up some kind of schedule. When do we
start? Do you have a studio I should come meet you at?"

"We start Monday," said Brad Wurster. His voice was gravelly, and to say
that this was an understatement was itself a considerable understatement. He
sounded like his throat was so coated with scabs and lesions that it might seize
up at any second and eject itself through his mouth, like a transmission
abruptly shifted from fourth to reverse.

"What time?" I said, pen poised above a pad that had the name of a psy-
choactive drug printed on it.

"Seven," he said.

"Seven?"

"Seven to noon, Monday through Friday. Then you'll go home, eat lunch and practice until six. Weekends are yours, but only a fool would skip drawing, especially someone who has so little time as you."

"Better practice weekends . . ." I said, scribbling. "Okay, where are you?"

"Three-thirty-one Church, apartment A, New Brunswick. It's the door in the back. Not the one with the devil painted on it, the one with the cut glass window. Knock and enter. Do not, under any circumstances, let the cats get out."

"Oh, no, I won't."

"Good. I want you to prepare drawings. Give me about twenty sketch pages, that Wolff paper your dad uses. Cover them with Family Funnies characters." "Family Funnies" sounded, on his tongue, like a fraternal order of concentration camp doctors.

"Twenty pages."

"At least. Have a good weekend, Tim Mix."

"Oh, hey, sure," I said. But he had hung up.

I couldn't go out to the studio, not so soon after my dramatic failure and collapse of the night before, so I decided I would try to clean the house. Our house was laid out along fairly simple lines; the living room and dining room were at one end, the bedrooms and bathroom at the other. There were only five bedrooms, so for the first five years of her life, until Rose moved out, Bitty didn't have her own. Instead, she was shuttled from room to room depending on the prevailing mood of the family: who was pissed off, who was happy, who should be rewarded (by not having Bitty in his or her room), who should be punished. She was never with our parents, though, unless she was unusually calm and happy, which is perhaps why she still liked them today.

Once, there was a Family Funnies television special. My father drew all the backgrounds and storyboarded the animation, but the inking and character drawing was done by other people—the only time he ever loosened his grip on the reins. Besides the obvious oddness of hearing someone else's voice come out of my own cartoon mouth, there was something weird about this special. It took several viewings for me to piece it together: the house.

While some rooms, the kitchen and dining room, for instance, were the same in the daily strip as in real life, almost every other setting was purely opportunistic. If a gag required that Bobby and I had to watch television across a huge, empty room, then that room appeared in the strip without regard to the real house. If Lindy had to sit under a spreading chestnut tree, then a grove of them sprung up in the yard. If Bitty wanted to swim in the pool, a pool yawned instantaneously open. The TV special, it turned out, was so packed with recycled gags from the dailies that a huge amalgamation of appropriate settings had to be created for it, all of which existed in the same imaginary space, in the same half hour of television time. The resulting house was massive and impossible, riddled with paradoxes the way a pine board is riddled with knots.

When I was eighteen and a college freshman, I mapped it. I stayed up all night getting high, rewinding and replaying the videocassette and rendering a rough architectural drawing on newsprint. There were at least thirty separate rooms, many of them occupying the same physical space; some seemed to have no connection at all to the house, emptying into hallways that didn't exist. This ridiculous house was ten thousand square feet, easy, not including the free-floating rooms. My drawing looked like Frank Lloyd Wright through a kaleidoscope, a sort of prismatic Prairie School. I sent it to my father, with a giant hazy question mark superimposed over the whole thing, and never heard about it again.

Plotting my cleanup, I couldn't help but see the imaginary house superimposed upon the real one, with all the attendant dirt of two dozen extra imaginary rooms. The task seemed all but insurmountable. My only recourse was to doggedly slog through each room armed with cleaning supplies, and apply them liberally to every visible object.

Of course I had trouble turning anything up that could be used to clean. There was no vacuum, only a frayed whisk broom and an elf-sized push sweeper with rotating stiff brushes. I picked the latter and pushed it around on the living room carpet, to no apparent effect. Though it was the middle of the day, I turned on some lamps. Their shades were covered with cobwebs and dead bugs. I employed my ratty washcloth to wipe down every surface. I moved the chairs and sofa and gathered the dust into my hands. The sliding doors were stained horribly with dirt and rainwater and cigarette smoke; I found a bottle of Windex sans spray nozzle and flicked it onto the glass with my fingers, then wiped it clean with toilet paper. The light in the kitchen and dining room doubled in intensity.

I was wiping down the walls when I heard the Cadillac pull in and the door slam shut. Pierce walked in through the front door, came directly to the living room and sat down on the couch. Dust clouds blossomed around him. He was dressed in the clothes I had picked out for him a couple days before.

"Hi there," he said, for, as far as I knew, the first time in his life.

"You're awfully chipper."

He frowned. "What's that supposed to mean?"

"Nothing," I said. "You seem happy."

His eyes smiled sleepily. "I was with my lover."

"Your lover?"

"Yes," he said. "My lover. She's this woman, and I . . . have sex with her." He ran his hand over the couch cushions, which in the renewed light were gray as granite. I couldn't recall their original color. "I haven't sat on this couch in about two years."

"You don't watch TV?" I said.

He stared at the TV for a moment. "I think I forgot about TV. Isn't that funny?" He laughed. I knew better than to call attention to it this time.

"Yeah."

"Do you feel different?" He was grinning crookedly at me.

"In fact, I do. I feel a lot different. I decided to draw the Family Funnies. For a while. Also I am now a guest in your house."

Pierce nodded, with a little impatience, I thought. "Yeah, yeah. Except I'm thinking of a specific thing. You know. Dad is dead. When I found him I didn't know what to think about that. But now, I've had a little time to mull it over, and I've decided that, you know, I'm kind of glad to be alone."

I swallowed hard. "When you found him?"

"In the studio." He pointed his thumb out toward the yard.

"I didn't know you found him."

He blinked. "Somebody had to, right?"

"I guess," I said. I groped for the right words. "How did you . . . feel about it? Not to sound like a shrink."

He slumped back on the couch, renewing the ambient airborne dust. "Healthy."

"Healthy?"

He nodded. "I'm really alone. I mean, sometimes now I can even believe nobody's watching me."

"Well, there's me," I said. "You're not really alone."

Pierce shook his head. "No, no, you don't fill up the house like he did. It was his house, you know what I mean? I couldn't have sat here when he was alive. I'd start thinking he was going to kill me in my sleep for it." He seemed to consider this and laughed. "That's really something. Do you mind if I sit here some more?"

"Go right ahead. If you don't mind the dust."

"No, I don't mind." He nodded. We watched each other for a few seconds, appraising ourselves and each other as brothers, as a family. Then I picked up my rag and set upon the walls again.

I took the Caddy to Ivy Homes. The road it was on was unfortunately called Old Horse Pike, but since this simply wouldn't do, the nursing home was given its own tiny street, on which it was the only building. This street was called Ivy Place.

Ivy Homes sat on its man-made hill like an expensive and calamitous hairdo. It lurked behind a barrier of uncannily round shrubs and perfect green grass, tended obsessively to by outsourced landscape professionals in embroidered uniforms. As usual, they were there when I parked the Caddy and got out.

At the desk I tried to ignore the fat man bellowing incessantly in the vestibule. I remembered him from past visits; the staff seemed powerless to stop him and had apparently stopped trying. I walked down the long reeking hallway to my mother's door, which as always was open. She unsteadily half-stood, gripping her walker, to greet me. I kissed her cheek and she kissed mine.

"Tim," she said.

"Hi, Mom." I tried not to betray my extreme surprise at her lucidity; it caught me off guard. I sat on the edge of her bed and she lowered herself back into her chair. Above us, gripped by a hanging metal stand, a small black-and-white television droned quietly. I thought, can these people see such a tiny picture?

I once worked as a short order cook at an all-night restaurant and bar in West Philly, called Tory's. Though it had survived in the same place for years, it had a fly-by-night, thrown-together look about it, with no matching tables or chairs and a couple of grimy pinball machines, one of which didn't work. At two each morning, sheets of plywood would be leaned against the bar as a makeshift wall, and I would stand behind them cooking breakfast. There was one waitress. Her name was Janet, and she was astonishingly crisp and beautiful, with a starched white apron she bought herself, meticulously shined shoes and smooth black hair gathered in a yellow clip at the back of her skull. Working in the middle of the night, behind that plywood wall, I would finish orders and call them out, and Janet would appear to whisk them away, as stupefyingly incongruous in that place as the Queen of England. This is how my mother looked to me here: Ivy Homes was no place for someone who knew where she was. I could feel my heart gumming up.

"Are you here from Philadelphia?" she said, trying to get her brain around the situation. "Or are you staying at home?"

"I'm at home," I said. "With Pierce."

She nodded. "Your father's dead."

"Yes."

"I forget, over and over." She shook her head. "Today I'm remembering a lot. I remember the funeral, I think. Was it in some sort of movie theater?"

"You're thinking of the crematorium."

"Oh, hell, yes. Now why on earth did your father go and ask to have that done? He'd not mentioned it a single time."

"I suspect it might have been Bobby's doing."

She blushed. "Tim, tell me what your brother does for a living. It's slipped my mind."

I told her. "Oh, sure," she said.

"Mom," I said. "I came to tell you something. I'm going to take over the comic strip. Do you remember the will?"

She nodded. "Mal looks like a washed-up blackjack dealer with that dye job."

"So you do remember."

"A little."

"Dad left me the strip," I said. "At first I didn't want to do it, but I thought hard about it and decided I would. I need the money, for one thing."

"For one thing."

I looked at her eyes. They were clear and blue. "The only thing, I guess."

For some time, we sat quietly, saying nothing. My mother's eyes closed slowly, and I thought she had fallen asleep. I was getting up to go when she said, "No, wait." Her eyes opened. "Do me a favor, Tim."

"Yes?"

"When you draw, don't make me out to be the simpleton your father did. He used to tell me it was all made up, that it was a made-up family, but I knew that was what he thought of me. He thought I was stupid. Don't make me like that anymore."

"No, of course not."

"You say that," said my mother. "But I know you. You're your father's son, more than Pierce, more than . . . more than . . ."

"Bobby."

"Than him, even." She was crying. Her whole face was wet. When had this started? I hadn't even noticed. But I just sat there, listening. "There's more of him in you than any of your brothers and sisters. You can be cruel, to your girlfriends, to yourself especially."

"Mom—"

"Don't interrupt me. This shithole is my home and you won't interrupt me in my home. Don't you dare make the mockery of us your father did. Don't you dare." Her entire body was trembling now. I got up and went to her. I moved the walker aside and I knelt on the ground and held her, but she didn't react at all. She only wept, and her body was so thin, so hard that it seemed inconceivable that she'd borne children. It seemed like the only thing that could come out of her was bits of herself, chipped away from the whole like splinters off a dead tree.

After this, we could only watch television, side by side so that we would feel close but wouldn't have to look at one another. I sat on the floor. It wasn't long before she really fell asleep, and I got up and left.

Driving home, I wondered how often my father had visited her. I hadn't seen him there since he moved her in, but that wasn't saying anything. I wondered how it felt being him, sitting in his studio, drinking, knowing that the mother of his children lay baffled and pissed in an adjustable bed, miles away from home.

He could have cared for her himself, I thought. I could. I could turn the car around, sign the papers to have her sprung, and bring her back to the house. I could hire a nurse to help. But I didn't turn around.

It isn't my house anyway, I thought.

## nine

I cleaned all evening and Pierce continued to sit and watch, a revelatory gleam swirling in his eyes. It was as if it hadn't occurred to him that it could be done. The more light that came into the house, the more life seemed to flow back into him. When I asked him to get up from the couch so that I could spank the dust from the cushions, he gathered a few of them in his thin arms and followed me outside. He coughed in the clouds of dust that rose, and when we were finished I sat down, exhausted, on the back porch to watch the sun set. Pierce disappeared inside for a few minutes and came out with two glasses of ice water.

"I didn't know what you drank," he said. He set the glasses down on the little cast iron plant stand my mother had once used as a drink table.

I tried to remember a time that Pierce had offered me anything. As a kid, he stole—nothing big, nothing that you'd notice right away, little things, like a comb or a pencil sharpener or rubber bands from my extensive and gratuitous collection. These thefts were calculated to have as little effect as possible on their victim so that they could continue unpunished. I let them go; Rose never did. She throttled her things back out of him with uncompromising ruthlessness.

I accepted my ice water with thanks, and Pierce sat down across the plant stand from me, in an identical rusted folding lawn chair.

"I went to see Mom," I said.

He sipped his water carefully, so as not to spill. "What did she say about me?"

"Nothing," I said. "She knew who I was and everything."

"Really?"

"She made perfect sense."

"Wow," he said, frowning.

"Maybe she ought to move back in here," I said without thinking. "I mean, I could stay awhile. And help."

He sniffed. "And then what?"

"I don't know," I admitted.

"I think she probably would kill me if she could," Pierce said, after some consideration. "If it was an easy thing to do. I think, if she tried, I would probably let her."

There was a noise from the bushes on the far side of the yard, and I was left to chew on this statement by myself. We both looked up to find the noise taking the shape of Anna Praegel, a plump, mildly sexy fiftyish neighbor who occupied, with her frequently absent husband Marty, the riverside house behind my father's. Pierce's, I reminded myself. Anna was holding a glass pitcher full of something and two glasses.

"Uh-oh," Pierce said.

"What-oh?" I asked him.

"Yoo-hoo!" said Anna Praegel. I remembered little about her, save for an ironic affect so deep that it was barely recognizable as irony. She was educated "overseas" (she had said more than once, mysteriously) and claimed to resent the American Housewife, showing such resentment by imitating that housewife in a mocking way. Thus her greeting, which, unless I missed my guess, she thought to be "archetypically housewifey."

"Hi, Anna," I said. Even as a kid I was instructed to address her by her first name.

"Tim-o! I haven't seen you in ages!"

"You too."

"Are you back for just a little while or have you come home to roost?"

"I don't exactly know," I said. The substance in the pitcher appeared to be iced tea. Lemon slices bobbed in it. I guessed that, for whatever reason, she had skipped the funeral.

"So what brings you here?" she asked.

Pierce leapt into the silence that followed this question with, "Have you been away, Anna?"

She narrowed her eyes, suspecting, I thought, contempt. "Marty and I were in Cannes."

"And you just got back."

"This morning. Marty's away at a conference already."

"And you haven't talked to anyone in town, have you."

She narrowed her eyes further, until she looked asleep in an anxious dream. "No," she said. I suddenly realized what Pierce was getting at.

Neither of us said anything. Pierce picked up his water and the ice clinked in the glass. Anna said, "Is your father home, boys?"

I looked at Pierce. His face was flat and impassive as an empty saucepan. How does he do that? I thought.

"Boys, I asked you a question."

It was me who finally spoke up. "I'm afraid he passed away on Tuesday," I said. "Of a heart attack."

Her eyelids flapped open for only a second before they squeezed half-shut again. The Ironic Housewife was gone. "Bullshit," she said. She licked her lips. I understood suddenly that my father and she had been lovers.

"No, he's dead." And I was not unaware of the pleasure I got out of saying this so bluntly, and disliked myself for it. My skin actually crawled.

She stood very still, her eyes closed, a long time, and the pitcher tilted, spattering iced tea on the cement. I felt it, splashing my legs like rain.


Sunday morning I got up at seven, tramped out to the studio and made a gigantic pot of very muscular coffee. I watched it as it brewed, the Mr. Coffee gurgling before me like a good baby. At the drawing board, I moved Friday night's glass to the floor, gulped half a cup black, and pulled out a thick sheaf of Wolff B sketch paper. Immediately I started drawing from memory the cast of the Family Funnies, beginning with my father, his foggy eyeglasses blotting out his eyes, and following with my mother, Lindy, Bobby, and so on, down to the dog, Father Loomis and a variety of neighbors (pointedly none of whom, I noticed, was Anna Praegel).

It was a liberating way of going about things. The drawings were terrible, but there were a lot of them, and I figured this, far more than any lame attempt at "quality," was what Brad Wurster was after. I had finished ten pages by ten A.M., not a bad pace. I stretched in the chair, got up, poured more coffee. It was too stale to drink. I turned off the burner and went into the house. Pierce's bedroom door was shut, and I could smell cigarette smoke. The answering machine was blinking: one, two calls.

"Tim, this is Susan. I just wanted to check on your progress, see if you've called Wurster, et cetera. We should meet this week. Maybe you could come to New York. You have my card."

Beep. "It's Amanda." Her voice had a morbid resonance to it, like she was calling from a mausoleum. She sighed. "I miss you, sort of. Call?"

I fished Susan's card from my wallet and dialed her home number. When she answered I heard a lot of talking going on and some quiet jazz music playing. "Yes?"

"It's Tim Mix."

"Oh, hey," she said. "Let me pick up in the other room." I heard her ask someone to hang up for her, and then a few moments of labored breathing before Susan came back on the line. "Okay!" she said to the hanger-up, then to me: "How's the cartooning?"

"Oh, coming along," I said. There was a breezy informality to her manner—whatever fun she was having was leaking through the line. "What's going on there? Party running late?"

"No, right on time," she said. "Brunch."

"Ah."

"So do you want to come up to New York this week? Expense account. Lunch is on Burn Features."

"You bet."

"Obviously it's the weekend, so I don't have any messages for you from corporate. But I'll know later in the week. Maybe Thursday? Are you free then?"

"Us cartoonists have nothing but time on our hands," I said.

"Ah, yes. Why don't you meet me at eleven for dim sum? Have you been to Delicious Duck House?"

"Never." She gave me an address in the Village and I wrote it down. "I can't do dim sum, though." I told her about Wurster. "Late lunch?"

"Oh, okay."

"You seem to have a thing for brunches."

"Two large meals early in the day. That's how my family always did it. Are you saying I'm fat!" She said this in a mock-hysterical voice. Was she happy to talk to me? I got the feeling she was. I tried to conjure up a picture of her in my mind, but all I could remember was zaftig and fair, like a pastry.

"Uh, no."

"Yeah, well. See you Thursday."

When I hung up, I immediately dialed Amanda, to avoid giving myself time to think about it. She dropped the receiver answering, and for several seconds I heard her fussing with it. "Hello? Hello?"

"It's me."

"Hey, stranger. Are you coming home tonight?"

"I have an appointment at seven tomorrow, in New Brunswick."

Silence. "So you're going to do it." It was hard to read her tone: a kind of wry mock-impartiality, like an NPR newscaster.

"I guess I am."

"And you're not coming home?"

"I didn't say that," I said. But I had meant it, hadn't I? Now, however, it seemed that I had changed my mind.

"So you *are* coming."

"Sure."

"Will you make it home for dinner? I'll cook for a change, har har." Amanda was the house cook, usually. It was a bone of contention between us that while I was perfectly willing to cook, she was not willing to eat what I made. She thought I should learn to cook more elaborate and—she said— "subtle" food. You can take the man out of Tory's, but you can't take Tory's out of the man.

"Seven okay?" I said.

"Yep."

"Well, I'll see you then."

"Kiss kiss."

I was well into my next ten pages of drawings when I realized that I hadn't asked Pierce if I could use the Caddy. I took a break sometime around one and knocked on his door. He didn't answer.

"I know you're in there," I said. "I'm just wondering if I can take the car tonight and tomorrow, until around five."

The creak of bedsprings. "Where are you taking it?"

"West Philly. Then New Brunswick and New York."

"Somebody's going to rip it off."

"I'll be careful," I said. "I'll lock all the doors." No answer. "I'm really in a bind here, Pierce."

"Whatever," he said finally. I stood by the door for another minute until I realized this was just what he was always accusing me of doing. Then I went back out to the studio.

When I was finished I had twenty-two pages, smeared with sketches. They looked nothing like Family Funnies characters. The sight of them filled me with despair. In a few frenzied hours I had managed to demote the FF cast, if such a thing were possible, from paper-thin buffoons to abject cretins. My mother's stylish shapeliness came off as frumpy and slutty, and all of us kids looked like malnourished ragamuffins begging in the street.

I found my father's leather portfolio jammed between the file cabinet and flat file, and stuffed it with my sickly sketches. On my way back to the house, I tossed it into the trunk of the car.

Traffic was bad on 95 South. A truck had jackknifed at the Coleman Avenue exit. I sat wedged in the bottleneck for over an hour, and when I finally squeezed through, found the open highway transformed into a Formula One fantasyland, where everyone seemed to have forgotten that the roads were policed and drove well over eighty in all lanes. I held close to the limit, two-fisting the wheel all the way to Vine Street. For some reason, a thin layer of sand coated the floor of the car, and as I drove it worked its insidious way into my shoes.

By the time I got home I was an hour and a half late and noxious sweat had broken out in my armpits. Amanda was waiting for me. "I called and called!" she said. "Pierce had me half-convinced you'd made off for good."

"Traffic," I said. "Accident. Not me."

This seemed to quench the fire in her eyes. They were good eyes, green and expressive, the shape of flying saucers. One pupil had a notch in it, like the pork roll my mother made us for breakfast when I was a child, and so she had a special contact lens. We kissed. It was so easy, so good that I forgot I had been dreading it.

We ate cold Pad Thai. I took a hot bath, and Amanda led me still warm from it into the bed. For the first time in days, I felt like I was somewhere I belonged. We made rare and surprising love. We slept.

But in the morning I went to the extra room and looked at what I had been working on. It was untitled, like all my work. There was a latex cast of the sidewalk; an old couch, left for the trash, that I'd found; a garbage can with an apartment number spray-painted on it, filled with "clean" garbage I'd gathered and painted to look rancid. It was dreadful. Worse, it was an exercise in pretension, saturated with the embarrassing conviction that I could create new contextual meaning for a scene simply by moving it into my apartment. Yet here it was, the only thing I'd thought about for the week leading up to my father's death.

I remembered his letter, still in the pocket of my sport coat, which was now balled up in my duffel bag in the vestibule. *It isn't right for you and never was,* it said.

"So," Amanda said, behind me. I jumped.

"Jesus!"

"The Genius, Regarding his Masterpiece."

"I want to set it on fire."

She punched my shoulder. "You set me on fire last night, baby. Heh heh."

"Oh, hey, yeah." I didn't know what to say.

"So you've got an appointment. Your new employer?" She was smiling, but the question was pointed and a little defensive, which tone I was supposed to notice.

"My tutor. Brad."

"Sounds hunky."

"We'll see," I said.

She took my hands. In her loose nightgown—a St. Vincent DePaul find from the week we moved in together—and her bowl cut, she looked like a child, someone the ten-year-old me would date. "We haven't talked about this, you know, Tim."

"I guess we ought to."

"You're pretty much moving out, I gather."

"It won't be so bad," I said. "We're not so far away."

"I suppose not. There's still the car, by the way."

"Oh, God . . ."

"I know," she said, sighing dramatically. She tapped an imaginary wristwatch. "You have to go."

"Sorry." We stood inches apart, her arms crossed, mine hanging limp at my sides. Finally I reached up and rubbed her shoulders. It was a lame gesture, but she let herself be placated. I managed a smile, then went to the bedroom to pack up some more of my clothes.

There was a smell the two of us made living in the same place, and it was here now, where we'd slept. I could remember what her life smelled like without me: coffee, paint and houseplants, with a whiff of bleach from somewhere. We'd met at a party in art school, got drunk, fooled around, and didn't see each other again for five years, when we did exactly the same thing. The second time it stuck. Everything from then on in was opportunistic: around the time I was kicked out of my building, her absentee roommate, who'd gone to France to pick grapes and never returned, made it official. My temporary stay stretched into years. Our two cars turned into one. Our smells commingled.

And I noticed this because the night before, the place smelled like her again, just her. I might have been gone a year, for all my nose knew.

Packed, I lingered in the bedroom, watching a dog eat garbage in the alley through the narrow rear window. It was time to go, but I was having trouble: she would be out there, waiting with my parting kiss, and though I had practically become one, I didn't want to feel like a guest.

**ten**

In the American West, if you want to go someplace, there's only one way to get there. That's what I brought away from the irritating, rain-soaked road trip I took with Amanda one summer through Montana and Idaho. All our shortcuts, inferred from the road atlas, turned out to be long, muddy mistakes.

But there's something to be said for that kind of simplicity: if you want to go, you just do it. You don't worry about the route. This is not the case in New Jersey, where all roads lead everywhere, and route mapping is not simply a skill necessary for efficient travel, but a kind of aesthetic category, ripe for pseudo-intellectual cogitation and debate.

To get to Brad Wurster's studio, I could take Route 95 North from Philly past Trenton, then take 1 North to New Brunswick. Or get off 95 around Bordentown and take 130 to New Brunswick. There was, of course, the New Jersey Turnpike, or scenic 27 through Princeton and Kingston. I could even, given enough time to waste, go back through Riverbank, get on county 518 in Lambertville, and tool at about thirty-five miles an hour all the way to Kendall Park, just a short hop to my destination. Each route had, of course, its elegant little perks, which I knew well from my many bored high-speed drives in high school: the Mister Icee outside Franklin Park, the driving range at Cranbury, the water slide by Penns Neck, on a road otherwise choked with car dealerships and strip malls. But it was all a game, really; it was five-thirty in the morning, I was already late, and I would have to take the turnpike.

I listened to talk radio on the way. A guy named Manny was unleashing an ill-informed and redundant invective against the current gubernatorial administration, and the show's host tried vainly to uh-huh him back to planet Earth. I couldn't remember the governor's party affiliation; she was one of those Democrats who love the rich, or a Republican with a short haircut, crouched in some ideological foxhole in the no-man's-land of waffledom. Manny was insisting that she had had numerous extramarital affairs while a member of the state senate. The host, a smooth-voiced baritone named Bill, said, "Well, Manny, I haven't heard those allegations myself."

"Every last word's true! I got a source at the *Star-Ledger* . . ."

"You see, I'm wondering, Manny, if that issue is even relevant to our discussion. I mean, we are talking about the Clean Water Bill here. And besides, let the innocent among us cast the first stone, or whatever."

"Hah?"

"I mean, are you willing to say you've never fooled around yourself?"

"I ain't governor of New Jersey, Bill!"

New Brunswick was not yet fully awake at seven, which was when I pulled into town. I followed the directions Brad Wurster had given me, but they depended heavily on specific landmarks, one of which—a McDonald's with an elaborate glassed-in playground—I happened to have missed. I found myself in the parking lot of a shopping center that was home to a supermarket, a stereo store and a cellular phone shop, rifling through the phone book for a city map. I located myself on Chemical Road, near the edge of town, and found that Wurster's house was clear on the other side, in a skein of whorled suburban streets marked Parkside Village. I tore the map out, feeling terrible for it but promising myself to put it back later, and picked my halting way through town.

Parkside Village was not what I expected. It appeared to have been named after a predictably sterile planned community, but encompassed a much larger area that included Wurster's neighborhood, a low, dark collection of run-down ranch-style houses with fenced yards. Most of the grass here was dead, done in by broad shade trees. The ambient temperature dropped by ten degrees, and in the excessive comfort of the Caddy, I felt like I was still in bed, floating under cool white sheets.

I pulled into Wurster's driveway at quarter to eight, popped the trunk, grabbed my drawings and jogged to the house. Giant pines stood in the yard, trimmed down to the trunk to a height of six feet. The door Wurster had described on the phone—the one with the devil painted on it—could hardly be called a front door, though it stood on the front wall; it was situated far off to the right and had what appeared, through its frosted window, to be a sagging metal bookcase pushed up against it on the inside. The devil himself was badly faded and crudely done, I assumed by a previous owner. His smile, an attempt at the customary maleficence, made him look like a dipsomaniacal birthday party clown. Warped, cracked clapboards showed through the house's begrimed red paint. I found the back entrance, as instructed, and knocked on a screen door fitted uncomfortably into its frame, as if it had come from a different house entirely. "Hello?"

Brad Wurster appeared instantly out of the darkness, like a television screen just switched on, and glared at me. "Late. Not a good sign, Tim," he said. His in-person voice was a vaguely authoritative muck and matched his appearance: hard, grim features set in a wide, flat face; dumpy clothes too heavy for the weather; slim, tall, muscular body. He looked like a Marine gone to seed on a deserted tropical island. The door swung open and rattled against the house, and even without the bug-stained screen between it and me, the interior looked impossibly black and bone-chillingly cold. I stepped inside.

"Air conditioning?" I asked.

"Nope." My eyes had not yet adjusted to the dark, though I could see light glowing faintly through dirty windows around the room. They all had bars on them.

"This way."

I followed him down a narrow hallway, goose pimples exploding along my arms and legs. Several cats of various colors dashed past in the opposite direction. Wurster led me into a windowless room illuminated by a long fluorescent daylight-spectrum lamp. The quality of light gave the room a crisply surreal presence, and lent Wurster himself the mien of a bowler-hatted Magritte businessman, practiced and peculiar. Beneath the lamp was a long drawing board, scrubbed white and uncluttered by any papers.

"Have a seat," he said, gesturing toward a small wooden stool, the kind you spun to raise and lower. I gave it a spin and sat down. Already I was uncomfortable. I was wearing shorts, so my ankles had grown cold in the chilly air, and the seat's several long cracks pinched the skin on my thighs. I wriggled around like a schoolboy.

"Let's see 'em," said Wurster, holding out his hand. I unzipped the portfolio and handed him the sheaf of drawings.

He spread them on the drafting table and examined each in total silence for over a minute. I sat there for nearly half an hour, watching what few charming touches I thought I'd managed wither under his gaze. Finally he handed them back, the tendons of his head straining against the skin.

"These are terrible. You don't understand cartooning."

My embarrassment blossomed into offense. Understand cartooning? "What do you mean by that?" I said.

"You don't know the first thing about it. You're trying to make these people look like people. Cartoon characters don't look like people. The Yellow Kid did not look like a person. Dick Tracy does not look like a person. Cartoon characters are deformed freaks we are convinced are like us. You try drawing like this"—he waved his hand at my sketches, lying askew in my lap—"and people aren't going to believe it for a minute." He shook his head.

"So where does that leave us?" I made sure the anger was clear in my voice. I wondered what my father had paid him to do this. I wondered, in fact, how my father knew him at all.

"Square one," said Wurster. He handed me a sheaf of sketch paper—the same I had done my own drawings on—and a pencil. "Today we're going to draw telephones."

"Telephones?"

"That is, we're not going to try to accurately represent a telephone on paper. We are going to distill the comic essence of a telephone into a drawing. We are going to do a caricature of a telephone. Is this getting through to you?"

"Sort of."

Wurster lunged up off his stool and stalked out of the room. I thought for a moment that he had already given up on me. What did he expect? I had never done any of this before. I was about to go find him when he returned clutching a telephone—two, actually—their cords dangling behind them along the floorboards. He sat down again and slammed the phones onto the drawing board. "Which one is better?" he said.

"Better?"

"Yeah. Which of these phones is the better one."

One was a black rotary, the kind with a heavy cradle and a thick bludgeon of a receiver. The other was a pink princess phone, with pushbuttons. I pointed to the black one.

"I like that one better."

"Why?"

Why? "I don't know. It's just . . . I don't know."

"When was the last time you saw a princess phone in the comics?"

"Never, I guess."

"You guess. I'll tell you the last time I saw one. A couple of months ago in 'Sybil.' That comic strip is a piece of shit." He laid one hand on each phone. "This one," he said, lifting the black phone, "is funny. And this one is pathetic." And he flung the princess phone out the door, where it dinged against the hall wall. I heard the frenzied toenail clicks of a fleeing cat. "Now. I want you to tell me why this is funny."

I stared at the phone a long time. I knew, intuitively, that it was funny, or at least more funny than the princess phone, but how could I qualify such a feeling? I decided that I must answer this question correctly, or I might fail at everything, my lessons, the strip, my inheritance. Something stirred in my chest—anxiety, I thought—but when it rose through my throat and escaped, it did so as a slightly maniacal chortle. Wurster's eyebrows arched, much like a cartoon character's.

"Well?" he said.

"It looks like a little guy. A little blocky mouse guy or something." I pointed. "The receiver looks like a couple of ears." I fired off an involuntary giggle.

"So what are you saying about it, generally speaking?"

"It's got a personality. The other one's just a plastic blob."

"So . . ."

I wasn't catching on. "So what?"

"If it's got a personality," Wurster said, "we can make fun of it." He pushed the phone aside and produced a piece of paper and pencil. In seconds, a fully rendered, undeniably hilarious, living phone had appeared on the page. I laughed out loud. It was suspended inches above a shining coffee table, tilted slightly, and cast an amorphous smear of a shadow; the receiver hung above it, rotated slightly toward the frame. The cord between them jittered in the air like an earthworm.

"That's great!" I said.

"What's it doing?"

"What's it doing? It's ringing."

"How do you know? There's no boldface 'ringggg' hanging over it. There are no hites, no agitrons, no briffits."

"Excuse me?"

"Hites and agitrons indicate movement." He made marks on the page: some quick parallel lines, trailing a flying baseball; some little eyelash curves, around a goofy-looking guy's head. "Hites mean something's going in a certain direction, opposite the lines. Agitrons indicate shaking, or a back-and-forth motion. This is a briffit." He drew a little cloud, behind the hites. "Sometimes objects, particularly those moving quickly in a linear way, leave briffits. But none of these are necessary. Humor lies primarily in implication. Everything about the phone I just drew is implied—its movement, its noise. If I added agitrons to it"—he drew in a couple of them—"it isn't as funny anymore."

He was right. To my amazement, the drawing was mostly ruined.

"I want you to understand that most cartoonists are stupid and lazy." He said this with a half-yawn, as if he were sick and tired of its being true. "Take 'Whiskers,' for instance. I inked that one for years. It's the worst kind of shit. All the jokes are having-a-bad-day garbage about dating and dieting, and the main character's a fucking cat." He drew, with amazing speed, the chubby and insipid Whiskers, his eyes as big as oranges. "And the visual stuff is cheap and unimaginative. Big goofy eyes, huge toothy shit-eating grins, pies in the face. I hate it."

"What about the Family Funnies?" I said. "I never thought of it as being any better than 'Whiskers.' "

"The jokes suck," Brad Wurster said, looking into my eyes. "But the drawings are masterpieces of efficiency. Your father was terribly misunderstood."

"I see."

He shot me a doleful frown. I suddenly felt bad.

"Tim," he said. "I don't think you do."


We drew telephones from eight-thirty until noon, nonstop. For two hours, every single drawing—at least seventy-five of them—was horrible. I either filled in too much detail or not enough, over-personified or didn't at all. Wurster was patient with me, more than I would have expected, and by eleven o'clock he was taking my hand in his and drawing with it, drawing perfect, outrageous telephones, so that I could feel, he said, what it was like. By the end I was exhausted. My hand felt like I had been whapping it against a wall all morning. Wurster walked me to the door and into the sunlight, where my skin gulped the warm air, and told me never to show up late again. "This is not supposed to be fun," he said. "It's work. Your father knew that."

"I don't think you knew my father very well," I told him, zipping up my portfolio and heaving it into the Caddy. "Not as well as you think you do."

"That's probably true," he said. He was standing on his porch, arms crossed, looking every inch a prison warden. "But neither did you." He turned and opened the door, then paused a moment and turned back to me. "Dress more warmly next time. It's hard to draw when your muscles are stiff."

"Okay."

He nodded. "Okay, then." And went inside.

That afternoon I ate lunch in the studio and drew phones. It wasn't fun at all. I took a little break and cleaned the place out a bit—let some air in through the door and cracked open the windows, which hadn't been open, apparently, in some time.

At quarter to six, I drew something I liked. It was a phone that had been knocked off a table. The cradle was tipped up onto its back, and the receiver was flung far away, the cord stretched out taut at an oblique angle to it. Somehow—and I wasn't pretending to myself that it was anything more than an accident—the drawing was both funny and sad. I chuckled and set it aside.

But after that, the remaining fifteen minutes stretched out ahead of me like hours. I rubbed my eyes and switched off the lamp. I would quit early, just this once.

## eleven

Each day, Wurster and I worked on a different inanimate object. This made me uneasy. If a week went by in which I didn't draw a single Family Funnies character, it was, I couldn't help but think, a week wasted. I made the mistake of telling Wurster this. "First I have to make you into a cartoonist," he said, in the kind of voice an obsessive-compulsive might use to potty-train a child. "In general. You must acquire competence, don't you see that?"

Tuesday we drew tables, Wednesday, chairs and sofas. Sofas in particular gave me trouble. There was a certain lunatic puffiness to them that, properly done, could make them look both buoyant and massive at once; my sofas only looked flabby and lopsided, like jelly donuts. In my drawings I stacked telephones on chairs and chairs on sofas, occasionally happening upon a kind of weak whimsy, but mostly producing labored junk. Still, most of them were passable to the untrained eye. I could do an interior background for most strips without too much difficulty, if I had to.

The Sunoco station left messages on the answering machine both Monday and Tuesday. Pierce never answered the phone, and this was working to my advantage regarding the car, which I had yet to make a decision on.

But when they called on Wednesday afternoon, I had just returned from my session with Wurster and was next to the phone when it rang. It was a princess phone, and when I picked it up, I felt a mild distaste for its clammy arch against my palm.

"Bobby Mix?"

"That's my brother. He's not here."

"Look, we've had this car for practically a week now, okay?" It was her, the Sunoco woman. There was a whiff of threat to her voice, as if I might soon find myself hog-tied in the trunk as the car glacially rusted at the bottom of the river. "So is somebody gonna pick it up, or are we gonna fix it, or what?"

"Oh, that's my car," I said. "I'm sorry I haven't called you back. I've been really busy . . ."

"Yeah, well it's not like the mall here, we don't have the kind of room where we can have extra cars just lying around. So what are you gonna do about it?"

I knotted the phone cord, then pulled it apart. The connection crackled. "Don't fix it," I said. "I'll just junk it."

"Well, get it outta here, then."

"Okay, okay. Look, do you know where I can take it? A junkyard or something? Can I pay you to tow it?" The fifty dollars I'd taken from my dad was down to ten now, and I'd had fourteen with me from before.

She told me they knew where to take it, and that I should come and clean it out, if that's what I was going to do. I looked at my watch. My practice session was going to have to start late. I hung up, ran my aching hand under cold water for a few minutes, wiped off my face and started for the door. Then the phone rang again.

"This is Eugene, from the garage," a man said. "You're junking this thing?"

"Yeah."

"I'll give you two hundred bucks for it."

"Really?"

"Yeah. I'll strip it, then tow the rest to the junkyard for you. How's that?"

"Great," I said.

By two o'clock I had the two hundred in my pocket and a cardboard box of Amanda's things rattling in the trunk of the Cadillac. It felt good to be free of the car, finally, but now that I had gone ahead with selling it I wasn't sure what I should do with the money. In the end, I put a hundred in an envelope and sent it to West Philly. I'd explain over the phone.

That evening I drew sofas, sofas, sofas. Once, when I got bored, I tried to draw Bitty sitting on one and ruined the entire thing.


Thursday afternoon I drove to New York and parked on the street about ten blocks from Delicious Duck House. It was hot out, but I kept cool walking in the shade of the tall buildings. The neighborhood was kind of a Microchinatown, just two blocks long, and great smells swirled around me as I passed the restaurants' doorways.

Delicious Duck was the skinniest restaurant I had ever seen. It was wide enough to accommodate only one long row of tables jammed up against the south wall; the maximum seating for any of them was three people. This row stretched all the way to the back of the place, which, once my eyes adjusted to the dim, proved to be another entrance, an entire city block away. The kitchen was in a room off this long hallway. I loved it. I found Susan munching a fortune cookie at a table near the kitchen doors.

"I hope you don't mind," she said. "I like watching them come in and out."

"That's okay." I took the seat across from her, so close our knees nearly touched, and gestured at the cookie. "Where'd you get that already?"

"The people before me left it." She held out the fortune to me. It read, *You may soon be dealing from a full deck.*

"Is it working yet?" I said.

"As soon as we've eaten."

Susan ordered a few things for both of us without asking me what I wanted. This came as a relief. I didn't want to make any decisions. When the waiter was gone, we looked frankly at each other for a minute. I noticed the thickness of her glasses—a quarter inch, at least. The idea of glasses always scared me. What if you lost them, and then had to drive somewhere? What if they fell off at a huge rock concert, and then you had to find the car? Like the rest of the Mix organization (save for Dad, who wrecked his sight with close work), I had 20/20 vision. I said, "How bad is your eyesight?"

"Oh, four hundred something," she said, blushing. The blush was comprehensive, wrapping around her head like a wet pink washcloth. It vanished quickly and left a barely perceptible glow.

"Sorry," I said.

"Don't be silly." She took off her glasses and rubbed them clean on her blouse, a businesslike navy silk thing that clung to her shoulders and upper arms and breasts. Her face, without the glasses, invited touch, the way a tennis ball invites picking up. If she had been crying, I would have wiped away her tears. But of course she was doing no such thing.

"So," she said, replacing the glasses. "How are things with Wurster?"

"Weird," I said. I told her about the frigid house, the pages of telephones and furniture. She nodded, knowingly.

"Uh-huh. Heard about it before. He knows what he's doing."

"So how does he know my father?"

"You don't know that?" she asked. Her eyes widened, as if to take in the fullness of my ignorance.

"No."

"He inked the TV special. The main characters and all that, the animated parts. Your father wouldn't accept the usual team of animators, so Wurster said he'd do it alone. It came in way late but under budget. You've never heard this?"

"Never."

She nodded. "He took your dad, uh, seriously." Another blush. "Sorry. Not that he shouldn't be . . ."

"No, no," I said. "I know it's fluff."

"But he thinks your dad was some kind of genius. The drawings, I suppose." She watched a waiter hurry from the kitchen balancing huge platters of steaming food. It made me hungry. With a demure throat-clearing that portended a white lie, she said, "I can see that, I think. Maybe."

"Yeah." I nodded. "So."

"So."

"So tell me about Wurster," I said. "What's his story? Why doesn't he have his own strip?"

She shrugged. "He can't get one together. God knows he's tried. My boss has a file full of his, uh, efforts. Panel after panel of these wonderful drawings, but there's no story at all. He has a narrative dysfunction."

"I see."

She gave me a look. "Okay," she said. "Here's an example. The last strip he sent us was called 'Elliot Dunfee.' It's just about this guy hanging around in his apartment. There's no setup, no punchline. Elliot fries some eggs, he gets the phone, something new in each panel. The drawings are usually in chronological order, or maybe there'll be some extended task Elliot has to do, like wash his car. And maybe the last panel will be Elliot dropping the hose and getting himself all wet."

"But is it funny?" I asked.

"Oh, yeah. Yeah, it's really funny. But in a wry way. There isn't that laugh you get when you're surprised by a joke. You just slowly break into a grin." She demonstrated, mugging puzzlement, then spreading a wide smile across her face, like honey across a piece of Wonder bread. I laughed. "I think he's published in the indie comics," she said. "Comic books, I mean, where you can do the postmodern kind of thing. His stuff doesn't really fit there either, though. I suppose he could do a one-panel gag strip or something, but I think he thinks it's below him."

Our food came, and we ate it. Neither of us spoke, recognizing as we did the superfluity of conversation. In my family, to talk during dinner was an oddness my father would not tolerate; we had to eat together, but we did it silently. Amanda could never deal with this habit. Several times per meal, she opened her mouth, then snapped it shut in frustration. Eventually we bought a small television at a junk store and set it up on the dish drainer during meals, so that there was something to distract us from each other.

Every once in a while I stole a glance at Susan. She was neither loud nor piggish, but she ate efficiently and with great speed, her chopsticks scissoring in the air before her like conductor's batons. My food was nearly gone before I realized how much I was enjoying myself: meals at home had been marathons of discomfort, and with Amanda they were tinged with a long-standing guilt that she did nothing to discourage. I was actually eating, in relative repose, with another person.

Susan finished first and waited with her hands folded while I put away the last pieces of rice. I set the chopsticks down in an "X" on the plate before me and raised my head.

"Wow," I said. "This place is great."

"Oh, good. We should conduct all our business meetings here." It hadn't occurred to me that there would be more, but I supposed that if I was going to be a cartoonist there must be. I began to get excited.

"So," I said. "You said something about news from corporate."

"Oh. Actually, not really. I mean, I thought I might." She reddened. "All I know is that they're eager to meet you and see your drawings, and all that."

"No news is good news," I said.

"I should tell you, though." She lifted her eyes from her empty plate and pursed her lips. "They'll probably have another guy lined up."

"What? For the strip?"

She nodded. "Just in case you, you know, don't work out. But they want to go with you, being as you're in the family, and it was what your father wanted."

"Oh."

"Do you think it's going all right?" she said. "Your drawing?"

"I don't know," I admitted. "I may not be good enough. It's harder than I thought."

Now she frowned openly. "Well, you have the home court advantage. If you'll pardon that metaphor. My dad is a rabid Knicks fan."

"Sure."

"I know you can do it, Tim. Really. Just keep drawing, that's all." She smiled a little, a quick thing that vanished immediately. "You didn't bring anything, did you?"

"Drawings? God, no."

She picked up the check and gave it a surreptitious look. "Well, bring some next week. If you want, that is."

"We'll see," I said.


When I got home, Pierce was crying. I could hear him from down the hall. I wasn't ready to hit the studio yet, though, so I found myself staying in the house, the kitchen specifically, kneading methodically at the floor with a dishrag. The dirt came up in strata, like latex paint from an apartment cabinet. I rubbed along with the jerking rhythm of Pierce's sobbing until I could no longer take it. Then I got up and went to him.

I didn't knock, just walked right in. He was lying in a ball on the floor by his dresser, shaking like a junkie. If he was embarrassed by my entrance, he didn't show it. I knelt on the ground next to him and said, "Pierce, what's the matter?"

He gulped air, coughed, finally blurted, "You know."

I thought for a moment that he was dipping into one of his paranoid troughs again, that he meant he thought I could read his thoughts. Then it struck me that I should know, I was his brother.

"Is it Dad?" I said.

"It's like g-getting out of *jail*," he gasped, and he wheeled off into sobs again, one after the other, like squalls of rain.

I let myself sink to the floor and sat there, my legs crossed. The last time I'd sat on his bedroom floor, Pierce and I were kids, and we were playing with our Lego space station, and he was crashing his spaceships into everything. He assembled all the buildings loosely, so they would shatter spectacularly when he wanted them to. And then, like that, I was crying too, as if some forgotten part of me, a part that had chugged along invisibly without any problems for my entire thirty years, had suddenly wrenched itself horribly out of whack, had cracked in half and let out this stupid, impossible flood. And it was not the kind of cry I'd had, with great catharsis and eventual relief, a thousand times before; it was more like a torrential bloodletting in which some vital humor was gushing forth and could not be recovered. With dawning horror I understood that this was my confidence draining away: not only the kind that let me do my pathetic art, or believe, however faintly, that I could become a cartoonist, but the kind that let me stumble daily out into the world. I held my head in my hands and let snot dribble through them. Was this what it was like to be Pierce, all the time?

We didn't touch. My gut ached from the ceaseless heaving of this absurd grief, and when it decided to finish it did so as quickly and unexpectedly as it began. Pierce was already done. He took a box of kleenex from a pile of several lying on the floor next to his bed and offered it to me. I grabbed a handful and honked into them, then he did the same. The sound was like a rusty safe being opened after years untouched.

"Well," I said. "Let's finish the job I started."

"What's that?"

"Cleaning the place out. The clothes, the junk. Let's get rid of it all." I looked at my watch. It was five in the afternoon. "Before nightfall."

Pierce's eyes blinked as if against a bright light. "Okay, sure." He seemed scrubbed out from his crying jag. I was not, from mine, and was jealous.

We hauled everything we could out of closets. There was nothing of it that I wanted. This was a new feeling to me, wanting nothing, and as we worked I probed it and turned it in my hands, marveling at its novelty. It didn't make me feel free, only that there was nothing worth having—a sensation, I perceived, of ambiguous worth. The trunk of the Caddy quickly filled, and then the backseat, and then the passenger seat. We uncovered old silk suits, worn once to conferences or dinners; shoes that must have cost hundreds of dollars. We balled up evening gowns and scarves and blouses and jeans, clothes our mother hadn't worn since she'd lived here and had forgotten along with almost everything else. Briefly I wondered if we ought to offer some of these things to Bobby and Rose and Bitty. But I knew that, though they might later profess to have wanted them, they would mostly be relieved they were gone. I thought about how long it took to truly bury the dead. There are cultures and religions in which they still have access to the living, and I thanked my lucky stars we weren't in one, because there would be no sleep for us.

We made five trips to the Salvation Army drop box, filling it nearly to capacity. I wondered if I would soon see people walking around the North Side in my parents' clothing.

That night, I was cleaning my parents' room in almost total darkness. I had begun when there was still some light, and been too consumed by the task to notice its gradual ebb. Now there was only moonlight to clean the room's single window by, enough for the job. Too much, even. I felt like it was shining right through me, chilling me from the inside out, like a microwave oven in reverse. Visible from this vantage point was my father's studio, and I noticed that the lights were on inside it.

Could I have left them on? I remembered turning everything off the night before. "Pierce?" I called out. He was cleaning Rose's room (later Bitty's, then a guest room and lately storage) down the hall.

"What?"

"Were you in the studio today?"

A pause. "No."

I turned back to the window. The lights switched off.

I ran outside and stood in the backyard, listening. A rustle in the bushes? I went to the studio, opened it, and flipped on the lights. Nobody was there. When I turned again to look out into the yard, I noticed the key, hanging where it always had on a nail under the eaves. It was swinging gently there, as if pushed by a wind.

I locked the door before going back inside. In the kitchen, I put the key with the other spare, in the junk drawer. I stood a long time, staring at the keys nested in a tangle of twist-ties. A low-grade hunch was unfolding itself in my head.

Pierce was where I had left him. He was wearing yellow rubber gloves and scrubbing a wall that would need to be painted. I said, "What was in your envelope? The one you got from Dad?"

He shrank from me, clutching his damp rag close. "Why do you want to know?"

"I'm just curious."

"Some kind of key."

"What kind?"

"Not like a door key."

I realized I was speaking loudly, and quieted myself. "Can I see it?"

Pierce seemed very afraid. He led me to his bedroom and fished the envelope from a drawer. Inside was a long, thin, squarish key with a simple notch at the end. I had worked at a bank part-time in high school, so I recognized it right away. "This is to a safety deposit box."

"Really?" he said, but it was a reflex. He was no more interested than he had been.

"You're not even curious about it? About what's in it?"

He looked away at a wall for a second, his arms crossed over his skinny chest. "Probably just the title. To the house, you know."

"Probably," I said.

"I gotta lotta work to do, man," he said, quiet as his shuffling feet against the carpet. We stood there where we had cried, filling the room with our breaths, for another minute before he left.

I remained, holding the key. One key to each son, I thought. Was that what had made me think of it? I wasn't sure. Suddenly, though, it seemed like less of an accident that Pierce and I were living under the same roof again.

**twelve**

Friday I got in trouble with Wurster. I hadn't drawn a thing the night before, and so had nothing to show him, and he called me every foul name I'd ever heard and made me draw house interiors without pause for more than an hour overtime. By then, the gray light and the scent of perspiration had turned the studio into a locker room, and as I walked out into the sun, I could feel its rays greedily drinking the moisture off me like a swarm of sweat bees.

At home, I turned the car over to Pierce, who said he would be away all weekend. We stood in the driveway while he twirled the keys on the end of his finger and darted his eyes from side to side.

"Where are you off to?" I asked innocently.

"Nowhere."

"Same place you went last week?"

He frowned. "What do you know about that?"

"You said you were with your lover."

"Did I say that?"

"Yes," I said. "You did."

"Hmm." He frowned. He was still frowning when he got into the car, started it up, and shut the windows tight. As he pulled away I could hear the circus music he liked to play blaring from the stereo.

Pierce had always had a thing for the circus, though to my knowledge he had never been to one. When he was a child, he had a flea circus. He collected

the fleas from our dog, who frequently brought them inside during the summer; many times I saw him patiently combing the dog's fur and corralling
each flea into a mason jar. He ordered the circus items from a catalog of eccentrica that he had turned up somewhere: little hoops and brightly painted
thimble-sized wooden platforms; a crow's nest on a long thin dowel. He kept
it all locked in a trunk in his bedroom and wouldn't let anyone see it. Letters
came in the mail for him, addressed in shaky, faint handwriting. He would read
the letters, rapt, then barricade himself in the bedroom, and I would hear the
banging and scraping of the flea circus being unpacked, and then only hours
and hours of silence.

One day, a man showed up when nobody was home but me, Pierce and
Bitty. He was perhaps six feet ten inches tall, and had to stoop to get from room
to room. He had huge ears the size of his palms and thin gray hair. Pierce
brought him to his bedroom and shut the door, and through it Bitty and I
heard the shadow of a mumbled conversation: first the man's deep, monotonous voice, then Pierce's sibilant eight-year-old mutter. They were in there a
long time. Then the tall man came out, nodded to Bitty and me where we sat
on the hallway floor, and left the house.

Pierce didn't come out for another half hour. He carried his trunk past us
and into the backyard. He went to the garage, came back out with a can of
lawnmower fuel and a box of matches, and before I could stop him set everything on fire. We watched it burn. Every few seconds a piece of glass would
go with a loud crack. Our parents returned just as the flames began to die
down. I was held fully responsible and grounded for a month.

I remember being terribly sad about the entire thing, not my punishment
(which I even relished, as it freed me from the obligation to play with the
other neighborhood kids, who didn't like us) but the entire miserable event.
The strange man in particular had been a loathsome revelation to me: his face,
cadaverous and lousy with melancholy, was among the ugliest I had seen. But
Bitty had enjoyed it all. Her eyes glistened with peculiar delight to the inscrutable mutterings coming from behind Pierce's door, and she laughed out
loud at the fire in the yard.

This, historically, had been Bitty's reaction to events that didn't fall into an established category. She found weird things funny, even when they were macabre weird or disgusting weird. I read her diary once while home on vacation from college, and learned that she had laughed at some poor boy's penis, and it withered like a forgotten houseplant.

When Pierce's car was out of sight, I went inside and called her. I didn't know what she did with her days. She hadn't held a job since she married Mike; whether this was a matter of his insistence or her convenience was not clear. I hadn't seen their house, though it was reportedly very nice. I didn't know what she liked or what sort of people were her friends. When she answered, she spoke very quietly, as if a baby were sleeping nearby.

"It's Tim," I said. "Did I wake you?"

"Oh, no," she said.

"I was thinking we could get together. Maybe have some lunch tomorrow."

"Oh!" she said. "Oh, that's a terrific idea. I have just the place. Do you want to see a movie too?"

"A movie?"

"There's this movie I want to see, but I can never seem to get myself out of the house." She was still very quiet. I asked her if I was calling at a bad time.

"No, no," she said, but offered no other explanation.

After we had hung up, I remembered that Pierce had the car all weekend and called her back. This time she took forever to answer. After perhaps ten rings, she said, "Yes?"

"It's me again," I said. I asked her if I could have a ride. That was no problem with her.

"Mike's doing yard work all day. He isn't going to go anywhere. He got these new tools."

We agreed she would pick me up at noon, which would get us to the two-thirty movie with time to spare. "Oh, I'm really excited, Tim. It's like a date."

"Well, not quite," I said.

My assignment for Monday was to draw the heads and bodies of the Family Funnies characters: not their faces or clothes, just outlines, in various odd positions. Wurster had made me a list. It was difficult to read, scratched as it was in pencil on a piece of legal paper, but I could make out:

bitty hands behind head
carl shaking hands w/self
dot shooting pistol
bitty kicking football
bobby taking pants off
bobby sucking toes
timmy drawing self
timmy eating sandwich

There were fifty items, each equally daunting. I was embarrassed to admit to myself that I hadn't considered drawing the characters actually doing things; I had only envisioned them head-on, their arms at their sides. Hard as this is to believe, it was a hallmark of my way of thinking. I narrowed tasks to a manageable level, then concentrated solely on the streamlined, and solvable, versions, forgetting the original problems entirely. I turned on my light and set upon the list, drawing each in quick succession, as badly as necessary, then scrutinized the results to see if I'd done anything right. I tried to apply what I'd learned about inanimate objects to the characters: what typified an arm? What was leggiest about a leg? With the children, there seemed to be one set of rules, as we all had the same infantile chubbiness, despite our real-life age differences. But my father had another set, and my mother another still.

What is funny about a child's arm or leg is not necessarily funny about an adult's, unless that adult is supposed to look sort of childlike. And what is funny on a man is not necessarily on a woman, and vice versa. I drew desperately. It seemed like each inch of progress toward a visible plateau brought ten new and previously hidden plateaus into view. The sun crossed the sky outside. I drank the rest of the scotch. At around seven, I went inside to make some dinner.

There were six messages on the answering machine. Every one of them was a hang-up, and the last had been an hour ago, according to the creepy computerized voice that announced each one. I listened to them again, trying to make out some telltale sound in the hissing blankness leaking from the speaker, but there was only the desolate click of disconnection. I found a can of beans and heated them up with a little garlic and onion, then ate them out on the patio. I wondered what was up with Anna Praegel, if she was taking my father's death badly. I tried to peek through the bushes, but there was nothing to be seen, only the faint glimmer of an empty yard.

I worked in the studio. After a while, certain things about the characters' bodies became clearer: the little Y that folded skin made on the children's arms and legs but not the adults', the trick to the black shock of hair at the back of my mother's head, my father's slump. I had a copy of the Family Funnies Grand Treasury, fifth edition, open on the table beside me, and I referred to it often.

I was slowly coming to terms with my father's considerable, if largely squandered, talent. There was something he held back in these drawings, something deep and strange, that through years of refinement he had managed to designate solely by vague implication. That slouch he gave himself, I think, expressed backhandedly a despair he was loath to express explicitly. It was a great and subtle slouch, just the faintest forward collapse of the shoulders, the merest fold of gut jutting out over his belt. He looked like he was in constant danger of toppling over, onto his face.

And equally remarkable was my mother's enduring sameness. She always possessed, underneath the Sunday dresses and food-stained, child-grimy aprons, the slim and sexily muscled chassis of a roller derby star. Her hair was always drawn as the same dreary black pith helmet, and her clothes existed outside time, lacking just enough detail so that the willing reader could fill in whatever he liked, could make her into whichever foxy housewife or doting mom figure he wished. It was pretty gross, but also impossible to reproduce. With practice, I could draw a person who looked like her, but I could no more render the delicate balance necessary to recreate her cartoon essence than I could dig my father out of the ground, prop him up at his table and make him do it for me.

And there were things about her I could barely bring myself to draw: her breasts, the curve of her thighs as they disappeared into her crotch. Other cartoonists filled in such things with studied sketchiness, as if they were of no more consequence than a ball cap or raincoat. It seemed I had a prudish streak, though, at least when it came to Mom.

So for most of the evening I drew around my father's facility, looking for a compromise that could fool people. It wouldn't fool Wurster, but maybe it didn't need to. The sun sank. I drank and drew.

When I turned off the desk lamp, I heard something outside, a crackling in the weeds. I froze. Whoever it was was behind me, at the back of the studio, and was moving toward the far end, which abutted the Praegels' yard. I stood quietly and turned off the overhead lights. The sound stopped. For a moment, a head was framed dimly in the frosted glass, and then it was gone.

I lunged across the darkness and flung open the door. Somebody screamed, very near me. It was Amanda.

"Jesus Christ!"

"What are you doing out here?"

"Looking for the goddam door. God!" She stamped the ground. Her face was hard in the ambient moonglow and looked to be near tears. "You're out here at"—she looked down at her watch, tilted it into the moonlight to read it—"one in the morning?!"

"It's that late?"

"Yes!"

We glared at each other across the couple of feet that separated us. Amanda was panting. She wore the kind of clothes—sweat pants, an old flannel shirt a few threads away from ragdom—that you threw on in haste, rushing to the hospital or escaping a house fire. Her narrow shoulders rose and fell in an uneven rhythm. I waited until about a second before it was too late, then went to her. She held me loosely, like she might have held a stranger, and I pulled her closer in response, and she let herself tighten against me, and I tightened more still, until we had begun something that neither one of us thought it prudent to stop. "How did you get here?" I said over her shoulder.

"I borrowed a car from Ian."

She sighed, and I did too, and I loosened my grip on her a little, as an offer to her, to let her do whatever she had come to do. Her arms slid off my back. She stepped back and dug into her pocket. "What's this all about, please?" She was holding the envelope I had sent, with the hundred-dollar bill inside.

"Oh," I said.

" 'Oh'?"

"I sold the car for two hundred bucks." I told her what had happened. "I'm sorry. I guess I should have called. I meant to."

"At least to let me know what you were doing, Tim."

"I know."

She sighed again and turned toward the house. "Is there anyone in there?"

"No. Pierce is away."

"I'm not going back to Philly tonight."

"Of course not."

"So," she said.

"So let's." I took her arm and pulled it, gently, and we walked together to my brother's house.


We made love in front of the television. An infomercial for a line of skin care products was on, and its spokesperson was Davy Jones, the former singer and tambourine player for the Monkees. His skin was no good, despite his endorsement. Amanda lay naked at the couch's end, and for the better part of an hour I touched her, kissed her in an effort to make myself desire her, and though she went through the motions of pleasure, even probably felt it in a base and detached way, she knew that this was what I was doing. When desire came to me, it was in the form of a removed fascination, as if I were seeing her for the first time, were seeing a woman's body for the first time, past curfew under a picnic table at the pavilion out behind the public pool, and this desire was ravenous and impossible to exhaust, even after we had done all we could for one another and were too sleepy to continue. We lay listening to Jones's shtick, our hearts fluttering against each other's skin. It had been like this once before, our first time, long before we fell in love. And we understood, but were too weary to say, that it was the same now: we were not in love. Sleep reached for me and I shivered, fumbled for the remote to switch off the set, pulled the rough blanket Pierce had draped over the back of the couch onto our bodies. Amanda curled against herself, like an insect desiccating on a windowsill. I tried to mold myself to her body but couldn't match its shape.

In the morning I found her munching cereal in my boxer shorts and T-shirt, watching me from the easy chair at the end of the sofa. I remembered the night before, and realized I would think of it often, for a long time, even when I had mostly forgotten the dynamic of our meager life together. I had to pee, and so stood and walked naked to the bathroom. I came back and wrapped myself in the blanket. It was early, not yet hot out. Amanda had finished the cereal and the bowl sat empty on the arm of the chair, the spoon sticking out of it like a tail.

"Good?" I asked.

She nodded. "Want some?"

"Sure."

She got it for me and returned. I took it, spilling a little milk on myself, and ate. Amanda watched until I was done. I set the bowl on the floor.

"Am I right about this being it?" she asked.

"I think probably."

"Can I ask why?"

I looked around me at the house, still grimy but now lived-in, almost alive itself. "I don't know if I can tell you."

"Figures."

"I'm assuming it's not just me," I said.

"No." She had been touching her fingers to her toes, like a child, but now stopped and looked at me. "I'm not seeing anybody else, or anything," she said. "But there's no more reason for going on than there is for stopping, is there? That isn't good enough for me."

"It shouldn't be."

She laughed bitterly at this. "Thanks, Doc."

"I'm sorry about the car."

"No, I am. If we'd kept yours we might still have a car." She smiled. "We might still be together."

"Are we apart already?"

"We are. Maybe I should go."

"You don't have to—"

"Don't be stupid," she said. "What would I do here all day? Not be your girlfriend." She stood, picked up both bowls and brought them to the kitchen, where she washed them. She came and knelt before the couch, picked up her clothes, changed into them, then leaned over to kiss me. "Goodbye."

"I'll come and move out as soon as I have the car."

She stood by the door, biting her lip. "I'll leave at eight Monday night and won't come back until morning. Come then."

"Okay."

She opened the door. I called out, too loud, "That's it?"

"That's it. Don't say you're sorry." I held the words back. "I hope this works out for you," she said, passing her eyes over the room. "I mean that sincerely, Tim. I won't say no hard feelings, because I have some, but I do mean that."

"Thank you."

Her chin creased, but instead of crying there, in the house, she pushed open the door with her foot and said goodbye. I said it too, but she was already gone.

## thirteen

All morning I sat under the blanket watching Saturday morning cartoons and letting regret choke me like a plastic trash bag over the head. First I regretted letting Amanda leave, then agreeing to draw the strip, then moving in with Amanda in the first place, until I had regretted my way back to my childhood and all its petty humiliations, like stealing a bong from the hippie neighbors' garage and kissing an unpopular girl on a dare. On the TV, animated characters became entangled in perilous adventures, then extricated themselves. Children ate sweets and enjoyed toys. I forgot about the time.

"What are you doing?" said Bitty from across the room. I jumped, and the blanket slid most of the way off me before I had the presence of mind to grab hold and pull it back.

"Ohmigod," I said. "What time is it?"

"I'm a little early." She looked at her watch. "Mike's cutting the grass. I couldn't hear myself think."

"Right, okay. I was just . . . I lost myself."

She dropped into the chair Amanda had watched me from. My sister was dressed as if for a summer date: a blue denim skirt, thin white cotton short-sleeved sweater, pumps. She sighed and hoisted her purse onto her lap, as if she was going to take something out of it. But she didn't.

"You're looking very New Jersey," I said.

She looked down at herself, then at me. "Hmm. You look like you're on a bender."

"I'm not. Not yet."

She squinted. "What are we watching?"

"I have no idea."

We stared at the set for a few minutes more. Bitty sighed again, so I got up and went to the bedroom to throw on some clothes. I was at the end of my T-shirt cycle and would have to launder soon. When I came out, she was gone. Through the windows I saw the door to the studio standing open.

I found her in front of the flat file, looking at drawings with her purse hanging weightlessly from her shoulder. Her frown was as miserable as a kicked dog's. "Are you actually working in here?"

"Yeah. I'm taking lessons."

"Are these yours?"

"Those are Dad's."

She looked up at me. "Really? Dad did these?" The drawings seemed to be ink sketches, the kind I knew he occasionally sent to fans who wrote him letters. Bitty herself was in one, holding an apple as big around as her head.

"Yep."

For several seconds, she seemed in awe of the pictures, and I opened my mouth to tell her to take them. Then she dropped them back onto the others, as if to preempt me, and pushed shut the drawer. She composed herself and walked out of the studio. "Well, I'm famished," she said over her shoulder. I followed.


Mike and Bitty's Toyota was the kind of rugged car that is often pictured atop mountains in television commercials, surrounded by dumbstruck goats. I didn't understand why. Our part of the state had no mountains in it, and Mike and Bitty were not the type, apparently, to leave it. They didn't ski, and had never vacationed together, as far as I knew. Bitty's driving was competent and slow, and at four-way stops she waited until all other cars were out of sight before she pulled away.

Close up, she looked charmingly seedy. Her hair was roughly cut, as if by hedge clippers, and her makeup, at one time a seamless and carefully applied mask, had been dashed on. The hem of her skirt was frayed, and as she drove she picked at the loose strands, pulling them farther away from the whole. Her sweater was loosely woven, and the bra underneath allowed her nipples to show clearly through. I anchored my gaze out the window and found us out on Route 518, heading toward Hopewell.

"Where are we going?" I said.

"AJ's."

"In Princeton?"

"Mm-hmm."

AJ's was a pancake and coffeehouse on Nassau Street, known for its enormous variety and high prices. Still, it was always packed. When I was in college in Philly, I had a group of friends I went to Princeton with to see rock-and-roll shows: the campus eating clubs frequently hosted huge parties at which many of our favorite bands—loosely musical rat-faced outfits with gratuitously improbable names—exerted themselves. Afterward, since there were no bars in town, we would go to AJ's to sober up. There was always a two o'clock rush there. I'd never been during the daytime.

As we passed through Hopewell, conversation inexorably turned to the Hopewell Head. Hopewell was notorious for a murder case that was cracked there in the 1980s. Apparently, a pimp from Atlantic City had killed one of his prostitutes; to cover up the crime, he cut her into pieces and scattered them around the state. The Head was discovered in a creek next to a Hopewell golf course, not far off the road.

"Remember the guy who found it?" Bitty said.

"He was a caddy or something."

"I was on the debate team with him."

I turned to her. She had produced a candy bar from somewhere and was eating it. "You were on the debate team?" I said.

"Uh-huh."

"What else did you do in high school that I don't know about?"

She chuckled. "Lots." She folded the wrapper over the end of the candy and stowed it under the seat. "Remember when the Badenochs' old shed burned down?"

"Not really."

"Pierce and I did that."

"What!"

"We got drunk together and we went out trying to set things on fire. But it didn't work. We didn't have any kerosene or anything, and the matches kept going out. But that shed was like, it went up like a tinderbox." She wiggled her fingers in the air, indicating flames.

I paused a moment to digest this. "Do you remember when Pierce set his flea circus on fire?"

Her jaw dropped, and she banged the steering wheel with both hands. "That *happened?!* Were you there?"

"So were you," I said.

"All these years I thought I imagined that whole thing, it was so weird. Do you remember the tall guy with the hoop earrings?"

"Not the earrings."

She shook her head. "Fuckin'-A," she said, and from her tone I knew that it was a high school phrase she hadn't used in years.


AJ's was packed with bespectacled Asians, no doubt foreign students who couldn't afford to go home for the summer. Their food battled for table space with rambling mounds of books and papers. The menu had two panels; on the left was the pancake list. Apple, Banana, Buckwheat, Buckwheat Apple, Buckwheat Banana, Buckwheat Blueberry, Buckwheat Pear, fifty pancakes long. The coffee list, on the other half of the menu, was similar. I ordered a cup of cherry-flavored coffee and buckwheat pear pancakes. Bitty got decaf and buttermilk cakes. The waiter looked familiar. He had a gaunt face and a strange beard: muttonchops reaching for a meticulous black checker of hair on his chin.

"Do you know that guy?" I asked Bitty.

"Nope. He's cute, though." I watched her eyes follow him across the room.

"So," I said.

She smiled. "So."

"How's married life?"

She shrugged. "Dull. I guess."

"Tell me a little about Mike," I said. "How'd you meet?"

"How'd we meet," she repeated, as if it were a peculiar and probing question. "Okay, I guess it was at a picnic. My friend Sheila got married to a guy named Steve, and Steve works with Mike, and they had a picnic and introduced us. We fooled around in the pool."

"Neat," I said.

"I suppose. He's an odd one, that Mike." I couldn't read between the lines of this comment, which sounded like it was said about a mutual acquaintance of ours whom neither of us had seen in some time. Her face went mildly dreamy, and her eyes took to a shaft of sunlight, following dust motes through the air.

"How so?"

She shrugged. "Mysterious. Occasionally explosive. Sexually devious. Not that you want to know that."

"Not exactly."

"Do I love him?" she asked the hanging lamp over our table, as if this question had been posed. "I suppose I do. He asked me to marry him. It was a surprise. I said yes."

Our coffee came. Bitty began to sip hers without preamble. I set to adjusting mine, sprinkling in a carefully measured spoonful of sugar, dripping in the cream. It was real cream, too, not milk. The smell of cherries rose as I stirred. I took a sip. Combined with the lingering flavor of toothpaste, which had not long ago been in my mouth, the coffee tasted exactly like cough syrup. I could not conceal my disappointment.

"Why would you order that?" Bitty said. I looked at her unadulterated decaf with envy.

"I don't know."

"I've got it," she said suddenly.

"Why I ordered?"

"Who our waiter is."

"Who?"

She waggled her finger at me. "Paul Crumb. That guy is Paul Crumb."

I turned. Indeed, it was Paul Crumb. Paul was the valedictorian of my high school class, and had been roundly hated by almost everyone. He was generally considered a genius, and went to study particle physics at Caltech. Now, a dozen years later, he was pouring flavored coffee at AJ's. We had all hung out with Paul at one time or another; he had a nice car and his older brother bought people beer, something Bobby would not have done for me if I had paid him double. I remembered my betrayal of Paul with agonizing clarity. I was one of a small group who set him up with an imaginary date, then spied on him as he waited on the street for half an hour, by himself. We had all been the victims of similar jokes, and since he was the only guy we knew more gullible than we were, we jumped at the chance. It was curiously unsatisfying. I never spoke to him again.

Paul Crumb brought us our pancakes. I smiled perfunctorily, Bitty generously. Paul didn't smile back. I smothered the pancakes with syrup and took a bite. They were not entirely unappealing, tasting one moment like a breath of spring air, the next like a sofa cushion.

We couldn't speak while eating, so I listened to the other people around us. To my right, two women were having what sounded like a business lunch. After a few minutes, it became clear that one was giving the other a color analysis, the kind that helped you get dressed in the morning. Are you a Winter? A Summer? I stole a few glances at the women. They were regular, thirtyish people, sort of attractive. Both were utterly rapt. The customer turned out to be an Autumn. "No offense," said the analyst—whose clothes, I thought, were ill-fitting and strangely colored—"but that outfit is all wrong for you." The customer nodded, looking down at her clothes as if she had just spilled something gluey and slightly toxic on herself.

For a minute I wanted to get up and stop them. I wanted to tell the customer woman that she looked fine and that there was no reason to pay for the other woman's advice. *Shame on you,* I wanted to tell the analyst. But it became clear that they were both perfectly happy and having a good time, and it was none of my business. My mouth clogged up with pancake and I swallowed hard, suddenly lonely. I thought about my frequent breakfasts out with Amanda, and the great time we invariably had at them. I wondered what she was having for lunch: probably nothing. She didn't eat when she was under stress.

Bitty paid our bill. It felt strange, accepting this from her; I used to buy her ice cream with the money I made raking yards, in exchange for her doing the household chores I was responsible for. But I had no money of my own, not until the strip was officially mine. I felt like the ne'er-do-well prince of a deposed royal family.

We went to the multiplex outside town to see *Benny II*, the movie Bitty had been looking forward to. It was a strange movie, apparently the sequel to a popular film about a dolphin, which I hadn't seen. The main character, a marine biologist named James, had been a boy in the first movie, and had been saved by the dolphin, Benny, in some kind of sea disaster; now he was involved in a righteous plot to sabotage a Japanese tuna boat known for its inhumane treatment of dolphins. Benny was recruited for the cause, and led other dolphins in a salvo of head-butting against the ship, saving James and his new girlfriend, who had been captured by the greedy fishermen. Benny was a friendly and clever animal. His motives seemed far purer than humans'. As the credits rolled, Bitty's body shook with sobs. At first I thought she had broken down, and would soon reveal to me some awful personal problem, or talk to me about our father, but as we got up to leave I realized she had been moved by *Benny II*.

Out in the parking lot, we couldn't find the car. People were everywhere. For the life of me I couldn't recall any landmark we'd parked near, and neither could Bitty. We decided to go into the mall the theater was part of, in the hope that the crowd would thin out. We found a slatted bench next to a huge fake ficus tree and sat down.

"Nice ficus," Bitty said. "Are you bored?"

"Oh, no," I lied.

"I am."

I watched a child drag his mother into a video game arcade. "You can't play the beat-ups," the mother said.

"What was your wedding like?" I asked Bitty.

She shrugged. "We went down to Atlantic City. Mike wanted to be married by a sea captain."

"In Atlantic City?"

"Well, we didn't find one. We got married by a justice of the peace. He took us out onto a pier." She sighed. "I love the shore."

"I haven't been for ages," I said.

"Well, it was a little cold, the water. But we went in." She dug into her purse and pulled out a cigarette. I didn't know she smoked. Then she said, "Do you think Rose hates me?"

"I doubt it. I mean, I don't know. How would I know that?"

"She treated me funny at the funeral."

"Maybe she hates us all."

"Maybe," Bitty said. "We go up to Newark Sundays to eat dinner with Mike's family. They laugh and joke and have a good time." She looked at me, holding the cigarette in the air like a question. "We never did that. Even when we weren't eating. I mean, I'm not stupid, I know that other families are different, but you know, I just sit there getting more and more pissed off at them. I want to tell them, 'Shut up! All of you shut up!' They're smug, is what they are."

"And Rose?"

She smoked. "We invited them over for dinner. Andrew, specifically. And this look came over him, like, Oh, Jesus, I want to say yes but Rose is going to be pissed. And sure enough: he comes back to us later saying, I don't think we'll be able to make it."

"Poor guy," I said.

She shook her head. "No, he loves her. They have each other, I mean. He's a nice person and all, Tim, but he doesn't care if they get chummy with us or not."

"It's that important to you?"

"Actually, yes, it is. Mike has his brothers and uncles. I want a sister. It's not a hell of a lot to ask."

"It's a lot to ask of Rose."

"No kidding." She seemed disappointed by the cigarette and, finding no ashtrays, put it out in the giant ficus pot. "The last of my college friends has left Jersey. There's nobody to hang around with."

"What about Mike?"

"Mike's Mike. He's a smart guy, but he acts dumb around his dumb friends and their dumb wives. I get lonelier around them than I do alone."

"Have more lunches with me," I said.

She smiled. "Yeah, okay. How lonely are you?"

"Lonely."

"We all are, aren't we? Pierce, duh, no kidding. But Rose and all that hate, hate, forget, forget, and Bobby, with his rules. I bet fucking Bobby's like taking a driving lesson."

"I wouldn't know."

She stood up and kicked my shin. "Like I would," she said.

We found the car about forty feet from the front door of the theater. While the AC cooled down we split the rest of Bitty's candy bar. It was extremely soft and got on our hands, and we sat licking them off and listening to the radio. I felt like we had made a breakthrough: or, more precisely, we discovered that there had been nothing to break through besides our own apathy and/or laziness. When she dropped me off we kissed each other's cheeks.

I wanted to call someone, to tell them what I'd done, though I understood that to most people, having lunch with a sibling was a negligible accomplishment. Even so, my appetite for conversation had been whet. I picked up the phone and listened to the dial tone, hoping someone might occur to me. No one did, though.

# fourteen

My cleaning jag had left me feeling jittery and unfulfilled, so I spent the rest of the afternoon purging the studio: though I'd had the windows cracked open for days, it still had the same musty ripeness my father had left in it. I took the car-washing supplies from the garage—rags, sponges, a stiff brush misshapen by years spent jammed into the corner of a box—and filled a bucket with warm soapy water.

The first few items were hard to throw away, but after that it was easy. I filled a garbage bag and a half with old newspapers, food containers and xeroxed pages from books. I crawled around on the floor and pulled the dusty corpses of pencils and pens from under the baseboard heaters. I threw the empty bottles into a box for the recycling center.

In the end, the source of the smell turned up under the drafting table, pushed all the way to the wall: a china dinner plate covered with cigar ends and ash. I emptied this into a trash bag and washed the plate. Then I crawled back under to see what else was there.

To my surprise, it was this: 35-15-24, the combination to my father's safe. I found it written on a piece of masking tape, curled upon itself in a gray snarl of dust and hair; I only noticed it because it stuck to my finger as I tried to throw it out. Maybe it had been fixed to the underside of the desk.

I tried the combination in vain several times without success. To fiddle with the dial I had to crouch, and my Achilles tendons stretched themselves out to an unnatural length, giving me the feeling that my feet might snap off at any moment. Was this an ailment common to theives, safecracker's ankle? Finally the tumblers clicked in an expectant way, and when I tugged at the handle the door swung silently open, as if by magic. I lowered my butt to the floor and peered inside. There wasn't much: an old book, a manila envelope. I peeked into the envelope first and saw only cartoons. No money. I set it aside and opened the book. It had been published in 1922, by the Trenton Star Press, and its title page read:

Where Dat Kitty?
*a Cartoon Treasury by Galway Mix*

Galway Mix was my grandfather, whom I knew only as a wheezing old man in an armchair, a crotchety Irishman, barely comprehensible through his thick brogue, who was obsessed with inclement weather. I also knew he had drawn a cartoon for the newspaper once, but I never knew what it was about or for how long it had been published. I turned the page and saw a thin cartoon black man, dressed in frayed overalls with shafts of wheat sticking out of his pockets. The man's lips were white and thick as croissants, puckered around a dark stupefied O, and his eyes bulged out of his head like a toad's. His hands were snarled in his hair, and he was hovering several inches above the ground.

Of course it was the most racist cartoon I'd ever seen. Underneath it were the words "To Carl, who wants to be a Cartoonist," and below that was my grandfather's signature. He had drawn another, rougher picture of the black man's face and added "Love, Pap."

I turned to the first page. There were four three-paneled cartoons. The first one went like this: in the first panel, the black man was in a chair, rubbing his stomach. His voice bubble read, "Ooo-ee, I'm hongry for some corn pone!" A small cat was rubbing itself against his legs. In the second, he was pouring some batter into a pan, and saying, "Hmm . . . Where dat kitty?" In the third, the corn pone was finished, steaming in its iron skillet, and the cat's head was sticking up out of it, charred and frazzled. The black man was doing what he had been doing on the dedication page: jumping in astonishment, gripping his head.

As it turned out, every single strip was like this. The black man chose a task, lost the cat, then found the cat somehow entangled in the task. "I loves the banjo," the man said in one strip, as he strummed. "Where dat kitty?" he wondered in the second, and in the third, the cat's head had punched its way through the sounding head of the banjo and wedged itself between the strings.

I read the whole thing. The cat turned up in an automobile engine, a horse's mouth, a chicken coop, a well ("I's thirsty!"). It was awful and great simultaneously: a formal puzzle to be "solved" over and over, a clever series of means to the same worthless end. I was reminded of Wurster's grueling exercises, and how they were supposed to make a good cartoonist out of me. In a way, this had happened to my grandfather. The strip was, its over- and undertones aside, endlessly ingenious. It was also, much like the Family Funnies, utterly shallow.

For the first time in a solid week of actual work, I was reminded of what a pitiful contribution I was making to the world of creative enterprise. Who needed the Family Funnies? What kind of people enjoyed it, week after week? I could see them now, with their perfect teeth and golf-inspired clothes, gathered around the kitchen table, complacently tittering at the Sunday comics. If my grandfather was anywhere near as smart as my father, then he must have faced the same problem: do I make the comic strip something worth doing, or do I just do it? And it appeared they made the same decision.

I put the book down and pulled out the manila folder, then slid the drawings from it. For a second, I wasn't sure what I was looking at: my cartoon mother, standing, a look of consternation on her face, my father's head looming goofily over her shoulder. Then I noticed they were naked. I turned the drawing on its side. Her legs were parted slightly, his hands clamped over her breasts. Visible between her legs was the base of his penis, shaded in with a couple of quick lines. Folds of boobflesh squeezed out between his fingers, and his eyes were half-closed over a look of intense and slightly sinister desire. And her face: that irritated expression barely masked something else, an intense and embarrassed pleasure.

I turned to the next page. More of the same, this time her on top of him, and then after that a rogues' gallery of sexual poses and acts I had not ever previously imagined my parents privy to. My mother dominated each drawing, her breasts and crotch, and her pained features.

Why had he done this? Somehow his boozing and ranting and womanizing just didn't measure up to the sheer indignity of these drawings: not only was my mother forced to act out his fantasies, she was made to dislike it, and then to enjoy disliking it. It was the secret expression of my father's desires, and it was his apology for them, and it was his justification for doing it in spite of the apology.

But in the end it was him I felt truly sorry for. If drawing those pictures was a lonely act, keeping them in the safe was an act of profound desolation. It was as if he'd kept a chunk of the heart that would kill him suspended in a jar, so that he could moon over it whenever he wanted, up to the day he died.

I put the drawings back in the envelope. Then I stuffed it, along with the book, into the garbage bag.


Later, after my trips to the recycling center and the dump, I curled up on the couch and watched, for the first time in years, the Family Funnies television special. It was a Thanksgiving affair, washed in the appropriate earth tones and bright fall colors. The special first aired on a Thanksgiving Day sometime in the late seventies, and I remembered gathering in the living room with my family to watch it. Dad was drunk in protest. He had gotten louder and louder, and made increasingly less sense, as our meal progressed, and by the end the rest of us had stopped trying to carry on our own conversations around him and began to pack, like squirrels sensing the imminence of winter, as much food into our bellies as we could fit. During the special, I struggled with the sleep-inducing properties of turkey, knowing that if I fell unconscious my body would eject most of what I'd eaten. From the panicked expressions of nausea on my siblings' faces, I could tell they were doing the same thing.

It was with considerable relief that we received the good news: Dad liked the special. The plot was silly, really—the Thanksgiving turkey is stolen, an angel appears to Bobby in church, our dead dog Puddles saves the day—but Dad snorted and cackled at his own jokes, repeating them at top volume in a slurred voice and spilling liquor in wide wet arcs all over the living room floor.

There could have been no clearer evidence of our real family's divergence from the one we were watching on TV. While the FF Mom bustled about in her apron and heels, making preparations for the big feast, the actual Mom was slumped glowering in an armchair, rhythmically clenching and unclenching the fingers of one hand and rubbing her temple with the other. The more frenetic and demented things became on the screen, the gloomier they got in the living room, until my father's laughs turned to sobs, and we were all sent to bed. I stayed awake a long time, plugging my ears with my fingers and trying to remember each and every scene of the Peanuts special, which came on next and which I was missing for the first time ever.

Tonight, however, I attempted to focus on the bizarre animation of Brad Wurster. In one sense, the special was much like others of its time: cheesy animation, with fewer drawings per second, and backgrounds that, for simplicity's sake, didn't move at all. But in another sense it was strangely accomplished. Wurster had taken the limitations imposed on him by the special's budget and created a subtly disorienting, visually arresting semi-masterpiece. I turned the sound down to blot out the context and watched the images move in slow motion.

Wurster seemed to break an obvious rule of animation, which was that all parts of a character's body, if moving, should be doing so at once. Instead, he moved about half of a character's body in one frame and the other half in the next, so that it possessed, at full speed, a strange unbalancedness that complemented perfectly the situation on the screen. Bobby, when he gazed up at the altar and saw the friendly angel, seemed to sway, barely perceptibly, in the pew; his eyes closed one at a time and opened the same way. My mother, nonplussed at the turkey's disappearance, looked like her head was about to bobble right off her shoulders. It was as if the actors portaying my family had been replaced by passionate but unpracticed Eastern European understudies. I stared transfixed until I got too hungry to go on, then I turned off the set and walked downtown, still dazed, in the day's last light.

Custard's Last Stand was curiously lethargic, as if the throng had just received some mildly bad news. People engaged in measured conversations.

Teenagers hatched plots in subdued groups. I got into line and quickly grew bored waiting, and so scanned the customers in front of me to see who was slowing things up. That's when I noticed somebody familiar. A short man with a guarded posture, like he feared sudden arrest by rogue cops. I waited until he was given his food, then watched him turn around.

It was Ken Dorn. I tried to remember where he said he was from. Hadn't he come some distance to attend the funeral? What, then, was he doing standing, as he was now, at the big window in Custard's Last Stand, watching kids play golf? I studied him as I waited for my hot dog. Rain-in-the-Face, in a neat trick of perspective, seemed ready to plunge his giant wooden axe into Ken's head.

Dorn stiffened, as if he knew he was being watched. Maybe he did. I averted my eyes before he had a chance to turn, and when I accepted my food from the cashier I made sure not to look directly at him. If his presence had something to do with me, I didn't want him to know I knew he was here. But I could see him at the corner of my eye, watching.

That night, I fell into a strange and intense sort of concentration. I sat in the studio for hours, drawing, oblivious of the time, of the room around me, of the place where the pencil met the paper: it was more like a single entity, part me, part comic strip, part pencil and paper, that created images by subtly changing itself. And as the night wore on, I began to feel *myself* changing, as if at first I'd failed to absorb Wurster's training, which had only now found my muscles, where it guided them from character to character, from prop to prop, each more refined than the last, each more convincing.

But that's as far as it went. My heart still wasn't in it, even if my body was. Still, I felt as happy as I'd been all day—no great feat, admittedly—because, for a change, I was getting somewhere.

## fifteen

Wurster liked my new drawings, or at least didn't find them particularly offensive, and we spent the week immersing ourselves in the work, poring over the FF Treasury and making lists of images, situations and combinations of characters that were likely to pop up in Family Funnies cartoons. I worked on a few minor characters, like Father Loomis, the neighbors and Puddles the dog. We discovered that Puddles was always drawn in profile, always sitting (even when the strip was about him, as when the family was leaving for a trip and he was sad, or the family was returning from one, and he was happy)— an unexpected shortcut, and one less thing we would have to worry about. I let myself be consumed by the strip, despite my considerable misgivings, feeling the kind of fullness a condemned man does after his sumptuous last meal.

I mentioned to Wurster that I had watched the Thanksgiving special. His face darkened.

"I think it's great," I said. "Your animation is unreal. Have you done any since then?"

He waited a long time before saying, "They stifled me at every turn," and beyond that he wouldn't talk about it.

Wednesday night I called Susan, thinking I would return to New York for lunch. I had found that, while working, I got excited thinking about it; the trip, the connection to Burn Features and the free meal were the only things I had to look forward to all week long. She wasn't home, so I left her a message and went back to work, with instructions for Pierce to come fetch me if she called.

Pierce, true to form, had slipped into a funk. He had returned from his weekend trip looking haggard and paranoid, and when he walked into the house he seemed surprised to find me there, as if all that had gone on were a delusional nightmare he thought he'd rid himself of. He spent most of the week indoors, in his bedroom, and I didn't dare ask how his visit had been, let alone who this mystery lover was or what she did with her time.

Meanwhile I had decided to do something with my mother over the weekend—possibly even get her out of the home, if she was feeling well enough, and bring her someplace nice, perhaps Washington Crossing Park, for a picnic lunch. I tried talking to her on the phone, but without my face there to remind her, she repeatedly forgot who I was and segued spontaneously into conversations with other people. I found myself playing the part of her late sister, my grandfather and (apparently) a maladroit plumber who must once have given her a bum deal: "No, ma'am," I assured her in a mushmouthed plumber's voice, "of course we'll pay for the water damage."

Susan called back around sundown, which was coming noticeably earlier in the day. I heard the phone ringing through the open doors of the house and studio, and when Pierce didn't come to fetch me, I went in, curious. Pierce was nowhere in sight but the receiver was lying on its side on the countertop. I picked it up and listened.

"Hello? Hello?"

"Susan!"

"Oh, hi," she said. "You called."

"Yep. Lunch tomorrow?"

"Actually, I was thinking," she said. "Since I'm going to see you Saturday, why don't we bag it this week?"

"Like, a bag lunch."

"No, like let's cancel."

"Where are we going to see each other Saturday?"

There was a brief silence. "Uh, FunnyFest?"

"Oh," I said. "That's right."

"You forgot?"

"Just for a minute."

She cleared her throat. "I don't want to butt in, you know. But I think you ought to go. People are probably very sad about your father. They're kind of expecting you."

I thought about the mayor's gleeful wheedling at the wake. "I don't like this, Susan."

"You won't have to do anything, you know. Just sort of be around."

"Nobody even knows who I am."

"Sure they do. Look," she said, "let me chaperone you. I'll buy the food."

"Well, if you put it that way, sure," I said.

Susan parked at the house Saturday morning. She was wearing sunglasses, a pair of cutoffs and a white T-shirt. "You look different in your civvies," I said. She did. She looked festive, vaguely sporting, if not athletic. She stepped through the front door.

"Nice digs," she told me. We stood before each other, unsure of what to do, of what our tenuous business relationship demanded. In the end I stuck out my hand and we shook. Susan snorted. "Well," she said.

"Well."

"I've never seen the studio."

"Really?" I had pictured her and my father enjoying gin and tonics in the doorway, with a fan trained on them.

"Really," she said. She looked around. "Where's your brother?"

"I guess in his room."

"Ah."

We went out to the studio and I showed her around. She paused before the drafting table and ran her hand over it, and peered into the open, empty safe. "It's so small."

"Well, you know. It was just him."

She nodded, then took off her sunglasses. We looked at each other. "So are you having fun?" she said.

"Fun? No, not exactly." I told her about the week's work.

"You think you'll be ready?"

I shrugged. "I don't know anything."

We walked to town. It was ten o'clock, time for the mayor's opening speech, though I was nearly certain he would start late. When we arrived at the dusty town park alongside the fairgrounds, the bandstand was empty and a few people were milling around, eating fried dough out of paper napkins. Around us, in a huge ring, the food vendors were lighting up the charcoal for the first wave of meals. Children stood patiently with their parents, waiting to be titillated. Family Funnies shirts were being staple-gunned to plywood planks, and coffee mugs hung on brass hooks. I spied several rent-a-cops loitering near the food, and beyond the park, at the river's edge, the fairgrounds were knotted with mechanical rides: a Ferris wheel, something that looked like a tilt-a-whirl.

Susan and I walked to the fried dough stand, the only one that seemed to be doing business this early. We ordered two pieces each. Susan, as promised, paid.

"Hey, he oughta be paying, right?" demanded the dough fryer. He turned to me. "You oughta be paying for this pretty lady."

I tried to chuckle, a rasping, malformed sound that had to be metamorphosed into a cough. "Could I get a receipt?" Susan asked.

"What, are you kidding?"

Next to the booth, I listened to a young family talking to a rent-a-cop. "What do you mean, he's dead?" the mother was saying. "We came all the way from goddam Greenwich, Connecticut for this!"

The vendor scribbled something on a piece of waxed paper with a magic marker and gave it to Susan. "Thanks," she said, but he didn't say anything back. We wandered to the center of the circle, where no one else was standing, and waited.

"I have a bad feeling about all this," I said.

"Don't be a sourpuss." Her mouth was white with powdered sugar, and I reached across the space between us to wipe it off. Her face felt cool. Suddenly this seemed wildly inappropriate, but she only thanked me. "Though it'll just get all dusty again."

"This is true."

"Why have we come out here, by the way?" she said. "Shouldn't we be under some trees?"

I shrugged. "I guess so." But I lingered. I didn't want to sit near the rent-a-cops. Once, briefly, when I was about four, I had a thing about rules. I became convinced they were all false. It wasn't a rebellion, just an obsession. I don't know what led me to believe it—probably something I'd seen on television—but for at least a week, I went around breaking every rule I could remember having been given: I scribbled on the walls in crayon, I stuck a butter knife into an electrical socket (it didn't go in all the way), I ran through the house and built forts out of the furniture. Bobby and Rose spent the week giving me disapproving glances, but I kept thinking: you guys haven't figured it out yet! You're missing your real life!

It all ended when I shucked off my mother's hand at a crosswalk and charged into traffic, nearly causing a pileup. A beat cop (the only one I have ever seen in Riverbank) saw what I had done and, to my amazement, arrested me, handcuffs and everything. The handcuffs didn't quite fit, so all the way to the station—and we walked, right down Main Street—I held tight to them, so that nobody would think I was trying to escape. The cop led my mother and me to a holding cell and made me step inside. I asked for a tissue for my freely running nose, but the cop told me, "You don't get tissues in prison. You have to trade your cigarettes for them."

I cried, "I don't have any cigarettes!" then fell to the ground sobbing.

At that point my mother had had enough and rescued me. She told the cop off right there in the station, and he must certainly have realized he'd gone too far, because he stood with his head hung and took it, then let us leave. For a long time, I believed my mother was commanding and invincible—a long shot from Dad, with his droopy grin and arbitrary regulations. Mom was my hero. What struck me most about this memory was that, until now, I had completely forgotten not only the incident, but my years of awed respect for my mother. It seemed like a lot to forget, and I wondered what else I had forgotten.

Susan must have noticed my reverie, because we didn't move to the shade, only stood there in the gathering heat while people massed for Mayor Francobolli's dedication. I could see him now at the foot of the bandstand in his suit, leaning slightly back to compensate for his paunch. He was talking to some official-looking men I didn't know. Why a suit? I wondered. He'd only have to shed it to jump into the river for the big kickoff, a tradition that had made the crossover from the old festival.

As he scaled the bandstand steps, the mayor noticed me in the crowd—the center of the field was still largely empty—and waved to me. I waved back. He made his way to the lectern and thumped his fingers against the microphone; a screech of feedback swept over the park. People groaned.

"Christ," I said.

"Reminds me of the rock clubs I used to hang out at," Susan said.

"You were a teenybopper?"

"I was a bass player."

"Hello!" bellowed the mayor. He waited, like an elementary school principal addressing his student body, for the crowd to greet him back. A weak mumble went up.

"I'm glad to see you all here for the opening of FunnyFest 'ninety-eight!" he said. "This year is a special one. Our attractions, our prizes, are some of the most spectacular ever, and we have more food and gift vendors than ever before, thanks to the really stellar efforts of my Director of Publicity, Vasily Rowe!"

One of the men he had been speaking to waved from a patch of worn grass next to the bandstand. A few ragged claps died in the air. The mayor went on. "But most of you have probably heard the great tragedy that has befallen FunnyFest, Riverbank, and the world: Carl Mix, the creator of FunnyFest, I mean the Family Funnies, died of a heart attack not two and a half weeks ago." Somewhere, people booed. It wasn't clear if they were booing my father, the mayor's mention of my father, or death in general. "But we have decided to continue FunnyFest, this year and forever, much as our favorite comic strip will continue, at the hand of Timothy Mix, Carl's son, who is with us today ladies and gentlemen right over there give him a hand!"

Francobolli gestured vaguely in our direction. I slumped, mortified, as people swiveled their heads to see who, precisely, I was. More clapping, though not as much as there might have been had I waved. The mayor prattled on about community spirit in the face of tragedy, and heads reluctantly turned back to him. I whispered to Susan, "I can't believe he did that."

"Jumped the gun just a little," she said.

"You can pick up a schedule at any one of the ticket stands here at the 'Fest, or at any restaurant or shop in town, all of whom would appreciate your business." He paused for a brief giggle, an effervescent sound like soda pop gurgling into a glass. A breeze picked up and blew several of his note cards away. People scrambled to retrieve them, but the mayor had already resumed, now a little less confidently. "And there are . . . uh . . . rides, thank you Vasily, and plenty to eat, and events here and in the fairgrounds all day long, and to-morrow. And be sure to cast your ballot at any ticket booth for Riverbank's new name!" More cheers and boos. "And now, without further ado . . ." Fran-cobolli stepped to the edge of the stage and tore at his clothes, baring his sunken chest with a manly, button-popping yank, and pushed down his pants to reveal a pair of bright Hawaiian swimming trunks. He was laughing as if tickled, and a few game members of the crowd laughed along with him. He had some trouble with the shoes and socks, and I wondered why he had worn socks at all, had he known he was going to do this.

"This is tremendous," Susan said.

"That's one way of putting it."

Once he had gotten the pants fully off, Francobolli held them high in the air, letting his belly laughs carry over us on the wind. He moved back to the mike. "To the river!" he called out, and this time a few people did respond with a weak "To the river!" "To the river!" he said again, and this time a resound-ing reply: the crowd had filled in behind us like Indy cars revving at the start-ing line. When Francobolli jumped—remarkably nimbly, I had to admit—to the ground, the crowd flowed around us like blown sand through a dune fence, and I began to feel the anxiety that comes from watching other people em-barrass themselves.

"So what are we doing here?" Susan said. She had pushed her sunglasses up onto her forehead, and her eyes gleamed with such delight that I thought she might begin tearing off her own clothes. For a second I figured she wanted to leave FunnyFest entirely. Then I realized that she was planning to follow the mayor to the bridge.

"Avoiding that?" I offered lamely.

"Don't be a poop."

The bridge was several hundred feet from the bandstand, to the south of the fairgrounds. The crowd surged: across the open field, between the food vendors, who proffered their stuff weakly in our direction as we passed, between the giant maples to Bridge Street. We were not allowed to join the mayor on the bridge, for fear of its collapse. The rent-a-cops created a theoretical barricade by blocking us with their bodies. The crowd feinted, retreated, then finally gave in.

"I sort of wanted to see it go down," Susan said.

A rescue team had been assembled: there was an ambulance, its lights flashing ominously, parked in the grass, and down by the water, two medics with a stretcher and a couple of guys wearing swim fins, flapping the fins at each other and laughing. Meanwhile, the stripped-down mayor had reached the center of the bridge, where he peered over the edge at the rushing water, still high from spring rain, and at the concrete abutments that held the bridge up. He shuffled over a few feet. The men in suits were with him, and briefly I amused myself with the image of them joining in the leap, but they both stood far from the railing, where they stared at their shoes. One was holding a stepladder.

The mayor raised his hand in the air, casting a hush over us. "Ladies and gentlemen!" There was no microphone, and he was forced to scream. He motioned to the stepladder man, who unfolded the stepladder and positioned it against the railing. The mayor climbed it, and stood, tall for once in his life, on the steel railing of the bridge. I could see, at the far end in Pennsylvania, a few people hanging around, marginally interested in the peculiar spectacle of our town. "Ladies and gentlemen," he repeated. "Let the Funnies begin!" And with that, buoyed by the infectious cheer of the massed burghers, he leapt, his baggy swim shorts billowing around his pus-white thighs, and plunged into the Delaware.

And this time, even I cheered. Why not? Already a few wiry, nervous types, mostly adolescents, were scrambling down the bank on the south side of the bridge to watch him surface. I felt the mob edging that way, even as their screams died away. We followed. Susan's hand found my arm in the crowd.

Her skin was warm, and it was difficult to tell where she left off and I began; I felt larger, as if now, attached as I was to my editor, I had new and joyful access to a strange and exciting world.

Then I noticed that the cheers had died away. I was standing on a riverbank with several hundred people, all silent. What was the problem?

The problem was that the mayor had not surfaced. The rescue guys calmed their flippers. The ambulance lights, which for some reason had never turned off, lent the scene a weird, done-deal air, as if the mayor's body had already been dragged, bloated and ashen, from the muddy water.

We watched and waited. Someone somewhere began to cry. And then, at last, Mayor Francobolli burst from the water laughing. He laughed and laughed, sweeping downstream like a sodden log, and the cheers erupted again, mine along with them, and the divers dove in and ferried him to the shore. And still he laughed, staggering up the bank, his chest dark with wet hair and his flabby arms triumphantly cleaving the air.

It was easy to forget that this entire hullabaloo was about my father. Most people already had, I guess. For a moment I wished I could be a Fan of the Strip, so that I could have as good a time as everybody else.

## sixteen

We were beginning to feel the logy halfheartedness that comes over weary people on hot days, so we found a tree near the entrance to the fairgrounds to take a breather. The next big event in the field wasn't scheduled to take place until two, and the crowd made its way toward the rides. More people were arriving now, staggering past us through the gates, sweaty after the trek from their cars. A clot quickly formed at the ticket booths.

"I suppose we'll need tickets," I said.

Susan unzipped the butt pack cinched around her waist and produced a thick fistful of ride and game tickets.

"Where'd you get them?" I said, impressed.

"Custard's Last Stand," she said. "You know the place I'm talking about?"

"Know it? It's the site of my unsupervised self-upbringing."

"Cool," she said. "I also voted for the new town name."

"No kidding! You don't even live here."

She shrugged. "No one asked. I voted for Mixville."

"I'm flattered."

"Hmmph. Maybe it was a vote for your father."

"He's probably snorting in his grave."

While Susan leaned, sighing and shut-eyed, against the tree, I took a moment to give her a long look. Her ankles were very close to me, not ten inches. They were heavy and dotted with razor stubble. She had funny knees, with an anatomically mysterious swirl to them, like the surface of a cinnamon bun. Her thighs were thick, her cutoffs cool- and comfortable-looking on her, and her arms, poking out of her T-shirt, were freckled and hazy with fine brown hairs. She was the kind of person somebody's mother might call solid, who wore her glasses so close to her face that they seemed to have grown on it. I felt compelled to put my head in her lap, but didn't.

"You're looking at me."

"What? No I'm not."

She took off her sunglasses and squinted at me. "That's okay. There's nothing else under here to look at."

"I wasn't," I protested, weakly.

She crossed her arms over her chest. "I thought you lived with a girlfriend."

"Used to. I'm about to move out." How did she know this? I decided Bobby or Bitty must have gotten to her first.

"Ah." She cleaned off the sunglasses with a corner of the shirt and shot me an appraising look. "I'll tell you my story if you tell me yours."

I shrugged. "Fair enough." I found myself strangely excited at the prospect, and remembered my college days, and the girls who dumped me, and the other girls I spilled my guts to, who someday later would also dump me. It seems in description like a vicious circle, but I kind of liked it: a steady rhythm of disappointment and elation I could rely on. In retrospect it was pathetic, and there was something in Susan's question that made me think she knew all about it, that she could see right through me to the essential shallowness of my heart. I proceeded with caution.

I gave her the short form, the one without the sex on the couch and the sad, empty cartoons. It felt strange, composing the story from the actual events of life. I'd never attempted to talk about Amanda; I hadn't the need nor the audience. I pushed gently at the sore spot in me, and it hurt enough for me to turn away as I talked. My eyes fell onto the Ferris wheel. It jerked forward as the seats filled. In the gondolas, people waved their arms in the air, pretending fearlessness.

When I stopped, Susan fell silent for a time, and I imagined that she too was looking at the Ferris wheel, which now gained momentum and began to turn with what, after the gradual admission of passengers, seemed a harrowing speed. But when I looked at her, she had her sunglasses folded in her shirt pocket and was gazing off toward the river, down where the mayor had been fished out. She said, "It was about six months ago for me. My fiancé, actually. Getting married was all his idea. I wasn't at all sure if he was the right guy, even *a* right guy, but I figured, hey, I was over thirty, a little, and I'd passed a pretty doable three years with him, two shacked up, and maybe falling in love was not at all like you hear it is, and was mostly just what had happened to us, which wasn't much." Her eyes refocused and fell on me. "You still want to hear this?"

"Yeah, sure."

She started at the beginning, filling in far more detail than I had. She was once an editor at a cookbook publisher, and the fiancé had been, and still was, a food photographer, who couldn't cook to save his life but knew a good-looking meal when he saw one. They met at the publication party for a cookbook written by a famous talk show host's chef. A lot of the talk show host's friends were there—movie people, some sports figures, a U.S. senator. Susan found herself pushed into a corner with the photographer, who complained to her about the buffet tables, that the white tablecloths showed stains, that the food wasn't being replenished fast enough. Susan complained about the chef himself, his proud arrogance and mustache yeasty with recent meals.

"I should have known," Susan said. "Complaining in the first five minutes. We complained all night."

They became lovers, attended parties together, slept over a lot. Their relationship consisted mostly of talking about the collective output of mankind, or at least Manhattan, ferreting out the poseurs, seeking honesty with a dogged, almost desperate persistence, yet remaining more or less aloof about one another's hopes, fears, etc. "The standard stuff," she said. "Too boring for Lyle. We were normal people, and he was not interested in normal people, and for the time being neither was I."

Lyle suggested he move in with her, as she had the larger apartment in the better neighborhood, and so he did.

"Now at this point," she said, "I figured the lid would come cracking off this arch little critic thing we had going, and we'd start spooning out the goo. But it didn't happen." If anything, they became, thanks to the sheer volume of their critical output, even more detached. Their everyday discourse had the tenor of a book review: mild enthusiasm thinly obscuring deep disdain. "For me, the dissatisfaction was about the dissatisfaction. I mean, I liked everything but the constant nitpicking. That sounds foolish, I know, but I suppose I had invented a rich inner life for Lyle that in retrospect it seems he didn't have. Or if he did, it wasn't the one I'd imagined."

She began to prod him a little about his feelings, question his criticisms. It became a game, an extension of the old detachment, but this time focused on him. Then he began to do it back. For the last six months, both were on edge most of the time, though they never thought to stop and make a truce. Apparently the game itself still felt normal—it was, after all, a version of what had held true for two and a half years—and Susan didn't connect it to the anxiety she was feeling. "I had just switched jobs, to Burn Features. I figured I was stressed over that."

Then, one night, they were playing the game, criticizing a movie they'd seen in which a woman leaves a man. Susan argued she had every right to leave; Lyle thought she had a responsibility to him.

"But she didn't see it that way," Susan said.

"But that's the way it was," Lyle said.

"Not for her," Susan said.

"Everybody doesn't get their own personal view of things that they can act on," Lyle said. "There have to be rules. Or I could go committing heinous acts whenever I wanted."

"But you wouldn't. Most people don't want to."

"Because the rules have told them they shouldn't."

"What if there were no rules? What would you do if there weren't rules?"

Lyle considered a moment. "Leave you."

That hung in the air for a moment. Then Susan said, "What rule is keeping you?"

"I owe it to you to stay."

"You owe me nothing," she said. So he left.

"I thought we were still playing the game," Susan told me. She licked her lips. There was something terrifying about her face in its pure and open expressiveness; the whole of her could be seen there by anyone who wanted to look. It was as if she'd left her car unlocked in a bad part of town. "There was no change in tone," she said, "no escalation of emotion, nothing. He just walked out, then came back for his camera equipment in a few days."

I had been plucking grass from the ground between my legs as she talked, and now when I looked down I noticed a small bare circle, which I had cleared. "I'm sorry," I said.

"Don't be." She shook her head. "I hated him. I'm not just saying that, either. I hated him all that time and didn't even notice. That's how clueless I am. I let myself be in love with a guy I totally hated, and when he left me I cried like a little friggin' girl."

"And now?"

"Now I don't even much like me."

We went on some rides. Susan headed straight for the tilt-a-whirl and insisted on riding it over and over, with the unhinged scowl of a mad Civil War lieutenant driving again and again, with tragic hopelessness, into enemy lines. Afterward we tried the Ferris wheel. It turned out to be pretty slow after all. Several times it stopped turning entirely, due to some ominous mechanical trouble, and as we swung in silence at the top of the world, I looked down at the crowd and picked out the Family Funnies characters in their plush, outsized costumes, frolicking maniacally in the dust below. "Is that you?" Susan asked, pointing.

"I think that's my brother."

We watched in silence as the surrogate Bobby made his way through the throng of revelers, throwing his arms in the air, doing little dances. It was disconcerting, like watching Mickey Mouse get drunk. Then I noticed Mal. He was sitting on a bench, holding an ice cream cone and gazing into the sky, perhaps at the Ferris wheel, perhaps at me. His glasses, reflecting sun, were twin glinting blobs that made my eyes pucker. I held up my hand against them.

What was he doing here alone? I couldn't recall ever seeing him at FunnyFest before. Once, he even told me that he didn't like what my father turned into during the 'Fest, when Riverbank took him into its greedy arms.

Or was I making that up? Come to think of it, I couldn't remember it actually happening. With the afterimage of Mal's glasses still burning in my eyes, everything seemed to have an equal chance at truth or falsehood. Even my childhood memories were open to interpretation. When my sight came back, Mal was gone, and the Ferris wheel jerked into action.

After the ride, I wanted to find the characters, to see how the costumes looked close up, but they had all disappeared, as if evading me. I forgot about them for a while, but when Susan and I were waiting in line for foot-long hot dogs I saw my mother ducking behind some shrubs that ran along the fence about forty feet away.

"Can I leave you here a second?" I said. "I want to check something out."

"Sure."

I walked along the bushes, trying to find the gap the false Dot had passed through. For some time, I could see nothing. Then, feet: giant orange cartoon feet, milling around barely visible behind the hedgerow. I ducked down as far as I could, closed my eyes, and plunged through the branches, emerging in a peculiar cul-de-sac, a gumdrop-shaped space between the shrubs and the weathered wooden fence that demarcated the fairgrounds' border. It seemed to have once been the site of a ticket booth or power station, now removed. In it stood six teenagers, smoking marijuana, each dressed up as a member of my family. I identified the Tim costume immediately by the striped T-shirt I was always made to wear in the strip. Its inhabitant, a thin-faced girl with a squint, held my head under her right arm.

"Hey, man," she said. "I know you."

But I didn't know her. I didn't know any of them. There was something familiar about each, though: a bend of the nose or an expanse of forehead that might have been hallmarks of Riverbank's stagnant genetic pool. But the girl I didn't recognize at all.

"You're me," I said.

"Yeah, yeah." She had a slightly ironic well-I'll-be tone that I didn't much like.

The others giggled. They were all boys. Somebody said, "Small fucking world."

I realized I was terribly out of place here, that the costumes had not been worth looking for, and that in finding them I had stumbled upon a hostile and unfathomable miniculture. I didn't understand teenagers at all anymore. Where my generation had embraced irony with a taste for its novelty and its shock value with adults, these kids breathed it like pure oxygen, taking more power from it than I had ever thought possible, and crushed earnestness like it was so many soft drink cans. When they seemed sincere, they were really taking irony a step further, mocking the very concept of speaking one's mind. What adults thought of them one way or another was of no significance. I feared them terribly. "Uh, sorry," I said. "Wrong turn." I ducked back under the bushes, leaving my ass exposed to any number of punting feet. Somebody snorted, and then they all did.

"Where did you go?" Susan asked when I got back to the doggie stand. When I told her, she frowned. "If this was Disneyland, they'd get fired just for taking the heads off. Did you know that? At Disneyland, that's just cause for instant expulsion."

"I had no idea."

We walked around, eating. Most of the attractions were, in fact, food-related; vendors sold everything from falafel to pork rinds to chicken lo mein. One enterprising man had named his menu items—standard American stuff, burgers and fries—after characters in the strip. So far, nobody had stopped him. I thought of ordering a Coca-Cola à la Carl.

"Oh, look!" Susan said. "There's a Timburger!"

Sure enough, there was. My burger had gouda cheese and bacon on it and cost six dollars and fifty cents.

I was beginning to feel a bit creeped out. Besides the prevailing depersonalization of myself and everyone I was related to, the place was swarming with children. Children made me uncomfortable. They had a smell, a confectionary pissiness to them, and all the self-possession of an escaped pack of zoo animals. For a moment, I had a gruesome epiphany, much like the stoned realization that a muscle, your tongue, was filling your mouth: that all around the fairgrounds, purchased food was being transformed into *Kinderfleisch*. It was happening now, right now, as I thought about it! I felt woozy and reached out automatically to Susan to steady myself. Her shoulder was hot and round and fit in my palm like a peach.

That's when I saw Ken Dorn. He was standing alone just outside the fairground gate, eating what looked to be a Timburger. When he saw us he grinned with devilish self-satisfaction, as if he had engineered our nascent acquaintance for some as-yet-concealed personal gain. In retrospect it seems like he must have walked toward us, but if memory serves, we were *drawn* toward him, as if toward the darkened entrance to a funhouse.

"Hello, Ken," I said, trying to preempt him. He was still grinning.

"Timmy," he said, "Susan."

"What are you doing here?" Susan asked him flatly.

"Oh, just surrounding myself with the trappings, you know."

She looked at me. "You two know each other?"

"We met at the wake."

"Oh, right." She bit her lip.

"How's the drawing going, Tim?" Dorn asked me. In his tone was something of the teens I had earlier encountered.

"Better, better. Harder than I thought."

"Yes, it's actual work, isn't it."

We stared at one another, me attempting to figure him out, to exhume his motives, whatever they might be; him seeming to know everything about me there was to know. I finally looked away, back at the fairgrounds.

"You're getting along with your new artist, I trust?" I heard him ask Susan.

"Swimmingly, thanks."

Suddenly I was tired. Maybe it was the heat, but part of it must have been Dorn. I didn't have it in me for a conversation with him; he begged a profusion of second guesses I didn't feel like making. He droned at Susan and Susan droned back, and I stood with my hands in my pockets and my eyes half-shut until they stopped.

Susan pulled her car into our driveway. "Well," she said.

"Well."

"Nice day, huh?"

"Very. Do you have a place to stay?"

She shrugged. "I can find a motel."

"No, no, no," I said. "Stay at our place." I quickly added, "I can sleep on the couch. You take my bed."

"Oh, I couldn't."

"Or my father's."

She grimaced, and it was decided.

Inside, I knocked on Pierce's door, while Susan shut herself in my bedroom. "Pierce," I said. "Are you up?"

"I am lying down," came the measured reply.

"My editor's staying over. I'm taking the couch."

"Your who?"

"Susan, from the syndicate?"

A long pause. "Oh, okay." He sounded better, in possession of some rudimentary grip. I hadn't seen him all week, and from my own observations and evidence from the bathroom, deduced that he hadn't bathed or showered during that time.

"We were at FunnyFest all day," I said. Silence. "It wasn't too bad, you know. In fact it was silly. The mayor almost drowned."

Pierce said nothing, and I regretted saying anything. Then he said, "I don't think any of that is silly."

"Whatever you say," I said automatically.

"That's what I say," said my brother.

## seventeen

In the morning I woke determined to spend some time with my mother. I lay on the couch, still groggy, working out the logistics. Susan could go off to FunnyFest alone, I supposed, and I could take the Caddy to the nursing home; maybe I'd bring Mom down to Washington Crossing, if they'd let me. This seemed like a plausible scheme, and afforded me the momentum to get up and rummage through the fridge for picnic elements. What I found was less food than archived material, so I pulled on the dishwashing gloves and began deaccessioning, lobbing each fungal mass into the trash bag until there were only unopened condiments left, inertly maturing in their glass cloisters. I sponged down the shelves, put on some pants and headed for the South Side Market, five or so blocks up the street. Their prices were insane, geared toward shoppers who would rather pay four dollars a pound for butter than wait in a checkout line with poor people, but I was driven, and charged it all to a crusty old credit card. I came back to the sound of the shower—Susan, I supposed, was up—and bustled around the kitchen making sandwiches and fresh iced tea.

The bathroom door opened, and footsteps came toward me down the hall. "Sleep well?" I called out.

It was Pierce standing there, his cheeks scrubbed raw and sunken like ruined vegetables. His voice came out quiet and cracked. "Fine, I guess." He eyed the sandwiches.

"Do you want one?" I said.

He nodded. I took a sandwich out of its plastic bag and handed it to him. He took a little bite off the corner, then began tearing off huge chunks with his front teeth, as if he had just chased and killed it on the savanna. I watched him while I made another sandwich.

"Another?" I said. He swallowed the last bite, then shook his head no, so I bagged the fresh sandwich too. I gathered together my makeshift lunch and put it in a paper grocery sack, then slid it into the austere recesses of the fridge.

"Have you been eating?" I asked him.

"Mostly raisins."

"Just raisins?"

He shrugged. "Other dried fruits, too." He put one gently shaking hand on his stomach. Already his cheeks looked a little fuller, though that might have been my imagination. "Other things seemed poisoned, somehow. I'm a little worried about the sandwich."

"How'd it taste?"

He nodded. "Good. Going on a picnic?"

"I thought I'd go visit Mom, maybe take her out to Wash Crossing."

"Can I come?"

"Yeah, sure. Should I make you another sandwich? For lunch?"

He looked at the pile of ingredients, eating them with his eyes. "Would you?"

"Absolutely."

He stuck out his hand, to steady himself against the counter. "I think I might lie down for a bit."

"Maybe you ought to."

He walked halfway across the living room before he stopped, his hands out at his sides like a dancer's. "Tim?"

"Yeah?" His voice had the quality of a wax-cylinder recording, tremulous and faint.

"There's somebody else in the house, man."

"It's my friend, Susan. My editor. Do you remember?"

"No."

"She's in town for the weekend. I told her to stay in my room. Is that okay?"

He made it the rest of the way to the couch, supporting himself with delicate gropings of the chair, the end table. "That's cool, sure," he said.

I sat down with him. We turned on the TV, but since it was Sunday there were only religious shows on. Pierce noticed the Family Funnies videotape lying out by the VCR. "Were you watching that?" he said.

"Yeah. Brad Wurster did the animation, you know. He's the guy teaching me cartooning."

He was silent for some time, touching his face lightly, like one might a lover's. "I don't think you ought to be doing this whole thing. You can stay here forever for all I care, in fact that would be really cool, but you should get some kind of job instead."

I took a minute to let that sink in. "Do you have any reason for telling me that?" I said. "Because it's really hard to pass up. It's a lot of money."

He snorted. "Money corrupts, bro," he said, half-ironically. "And besides that, you won't ever stop. And you're too nice a guy to do it."

Nice. The innocent chime of it filled me with gratitude. I reached out and touched his shoulder, and he nearly jumped out of his seat.

"Jesus!"

"I'm sorry! I'm sorry!" I backed off a few inches, trying to stifle the urge to touch him again.

"It's okay, but. Man alive." He shuddered. I waited for him to get back on the subject of me and the strip, but he never did, only held himself against an ambient and imaginary chill. I heard movement in the hall.

"Hi," Susan said. "Pierce. Remember me, Susan?"

He managed a smile. "I guess we never officially met."

She extended a hand to be shaken, and I cringed, but Pierce took it gently. "Forgive my, you know, inhospitality. I'm coming off a spell."

"Sorry." She seemed not to be made uncomfortable by this, and I was relieved.

"Well, you know," Pierce said.

There wasn't much to talk about after that. I told Susan to help herself to breakfast—I had bought some cereal—and that Pierce and I were headed for the nursing home. "I can meet you back here at some point," I said.

She nodded. "Well, okay," she said, and headed for the kitchen. I felt like I had let her down, and didn't know what to say. What were the rules for accommodating one's editor-friend? I had no idea. I was baffled enough to want to cry.

In the Cadillac, Pierce said, "She's cute."

"You think so?"

"Yeah. Are you, you know?"

"No!" I paused to swerve around a dead animal. "I like her."

"She's cool."

I half-turned to him. "What's your girlfriend like?"

"She's a witch," he said.

"That's not very kind of you."

He shook his head. "No," he said. "She's a *witch*. Like, a wiccan. Herbs and spells and shit. She lives in the Pines."

I thought about the sand I'd seen on the floor of the Cadillac. It was still there now. "She's a Piney? You're dating a Piney witch?" A lot of people do not know that there is a giant forest in the middle of New Jersey, called the Pine Barrens. It's all trees, sand and cranberry bogs, and is home to the cleanest natural water and most isolated people within five hundred miles.

"I wouldn't call it dating," Pierce said, but I could see he already thought he had said too much. I didn't say anything more about it.

The first thing I noticed at the nursing home was Bobby's car, parked at the far end of the lot, away from the other cars. I pointed it out to Pierce, and he nodded. "I forgot," he said. "They come on Sundays. It's like, their day."

"They don't like it when other people come? Does Rose come weekends?"

"Rose comes Tuesdays, I think. Mornings. Bitty during the week, but I don't think lately." He slumped in the seat. "I'm sure he'll be pissed. Whatever."

We found Bobby, Nancy and Samantha in my mother's room, sitting in a small row of identical aluminum chairs. Nobody was saying anything, and my mother's eyes were closed. Everyone but Mom turned when we entered. "Hi," I said to them and grinned to show that I meant it.

Bobby stood up. "This is unexpected," he said. He looked weary. The ruddy plumpness that usually came off as healthy now seemed like the result of some sort of infection, as though his thick skin was going to slough right off.

My mother's eyes were open now. "Well. Is this a party?"

"Hey, Mom," I said. She squinted at me. As far as I knew, nothing was wrong with her eyesight.

"Boy," she said. "They let you dress like that in church?"

I had dressed, unconsciously, in what Susan had worn the day before: cutoff jeans and a white shirt. "I didn't go to church."

"It's Sunday!"

Pierce spoke up now, almost at a whisper. "Mom, how are you?"

"Seems like I'm everybody's mother."

"Uncle Pierce," said Samantha. "Are you sick?"

"Samantha!" Nancy said. To my utter astonishment, she reached out and slapped Sam full in the face, letting off a sound like a dropped volume of an encyclopedia. Nobody said anything. Samantha did not cry. I hugged the paper bag tighter to my chest, and it crinkled hollowly.

"What in the hell was that?" my mother said.

"I haven't been feeling too well, no," Pierce said. "But I'm a lot better today. Nancy," he said, turning, "don't ever hit a person for my benefit."

"It has nothing to do with you," Bobby said.

Nancy didn't speak, but her expression betrayed a kind of horror at what had transpired. The guilty hand covered her mouth and she took a deep breath around it. Everything about her said *I'm sorry* and everything about Bobby— the deepening folds of his chin, his thick hands spanning his knees—said *don't apologize*. Samantha's face bore the handprint in deep, livid red.

I broke the silence by holding up my paper bag. "Mom," I said. "I brought you some food. I was thinking maybe we could take you out to Wash Crossing for a little picnic. Do you think they'd let us do that?"

She smiled politely. "You're so nice to invite me on a picnic," she said.

Bobby said, "This isn't your day to visit, Tim."

Nancy, with a sound that nearly made me hit the ceiling, cracked her knuckles.

Samantha excused herself and got up to leave the room. Nobody stopped her. After a moment Nancy followed, offering Pierce and me a varnished smile on her way past.

"I'll check on springing her," Pierce said, and left.

My mother, alone with her oldest sons, looked blithely at us as if we were handsome strangers. "I'm interested in this picnic," she said. "Are both of you fellows coming along?"

"Mom," I said, sitting down. "It's Tim." I took her hand. Bobby looked down at the entwined hands, curious and slightly disgusted, as if they were a pair of trysting housepets. "I was here a couple weeks ago. We've been talking on the phone."

"Of course," she said, obviously lying.

"She isn't going to remember," Bobby said.

I didn't look at him. "That's okay."

Pierce returned with the news that, though they would let us take her out, we had to have her back by lunchtime.

"But we're going to eat lunch," I said.

"Yeah, well. They said the food wasn't the point."

"I'm very excited," said my mother, her eyes gleaming.

"She needs structure," Bobby said. "That's what that's all about. Or else she forgets herself. She gets sad."

"Do you want to come along?" I said to him. He seemed possessed by a deep misery that I was afraid to touch, for fear it might rub off on me.

I think he did want to come. But he didn't look at me as he said no.


The nursing home let us take a wheelchair. Apparently she wasn't standing up on her own at all lately, and Pierce and I had to lift her by the elbows and maneuver her into the seat. She seemed very small there. We rolled her out to the car and helped her in. "Are you comfortable?" I asked her, buckling her up.

"Oh, yes. This is a nice car."

"It was Dad's, do you remember?"

She frowned. "Dad didn't drive, now did he?"

I wondered who she was talking about: her own father? I had not met him, as he had died before I was born, or very soon after, I couldn't recall. "I don't remember," I said. It was strange to me that she could be so incoherent today after the relative sharpness of two weeks before. It was easy enough to extrapolate into the not-so-distant future. What would go next? There were not many parts of her left to fail.

Pierce, sitting in the back of the car with the wheelchair, seemed to be thinking the same thing. The three of us were silent for most of the drive. My mother's head swiveled, her eyes flickering over the landscape like searchlights, seeming less to take it in than to project onto it. What they were projecting I couldn't figure. What did this stretch of road mean to her now? What, for that matter, did it mean before? I realized that a large part of my family past, which had meant nothing to me before, was lost to me.

It seemed like my family had always been a clean slate, its future hazy and irrelevant and its past nonexistent. I remembered arriving at college to find my fellow freshmen embroiled in heated discussions about their various ethnic and geographical backgrounds, as if it were imperative that these details become a part of public record, as if without them it would be impossible to be themselves. I felt out of place and slightly snubbed, though never jealous, precisely. Amazed was more like it, the way I might have been if I had found they were able to see more colors than I could, or breathe underwater. Family history was a novel, if worthless, principle, as far as I was concerned. Until recently, that is.

But now I was feeling more left out than ever. I thought about the paltry breakup story I had told Susan, how it was likely to be the most fleshed-out account of anything worth hearing that I could offer her. I wondered, dimly, why she seemed to like me at all, and if perhaps I had overestimated her opinion of our friendship, when in fact it was simply a diverting function of her job as my editor.

Despite my impression that FunnyFest had drained the recreation from every town for miles around, Washington Crossing Park was quite crowded.

We had to push my mother's wheelchair over several hundred yards of footpath to find a pleasant enough tree to sit under. It struck me that we hadn't brought a blanket: no use worrying now. For her part, my mother settled nicely into the entire situation, as if it were a weekly occurrence, which as far as I knew it could be. She sat placidly in the wheelchair, moving her fingers in her lap much like Pierce had back on the day of the funeral. There was a briskness to her, in her bright dress and clear gaze, that belied her condition, a simple economy that made me feel clunky and gratuitous for being able to walk, to remember, to carry on a conversation. I gave her half a sandwich, and she ate a little bit, spilling a few ingredients onto her dress. I picked them off for her. Pierce, seeing she wouldn't finish, made short work of the other half-sandwich.

My mother was frowning. "What do you call it when you think you remember something?"

Silence. "I don't know," I said.

"You know, I've-seen-this-all-before."

"Oh! Déjà vu!"

"Yes," she said, "of course." Then, for a long time, she didn't say anything at all. Pierce and I waited. She closed her eyes, breathed deeply. The frown lines smoothed. Finally Pierce went back to eating.

"Were you going to say that this was all familiar to you?" I said. "This park?"

She didn't open her eyes. "Oh, yes. You boys, this park, that deer, over there in the trees." She pointed toward the park entrance, where a convenience store and gas station were set back from the road.

I looked harder for the deer, knowing it wasn't there but feeling no less inept for not seeing it. What I could see, with a sudden exactness, was myself, the way she was seeing me: a bare outline, shaped like a man, into which any memory or desire—or, in their absence, nothing—could be poured. "Mom, do you remember us?" I asked her. "You remembered me last time." I felt Pierce's hand on my arm. "Don't you remember us at all, your sons Tim and Pierce? Mom?" I realized I had raised my voice. "Mom?" I said.

"Tim," said Pierce.

But my mother cried. "I'm sorry," she said simply, and of course it should have been me crying, me apologizing, but it wasn't.

The doctor at the nursing home told us that our mother had a problem with the artery in her neck that was preventing blood from reaching her brain in the usual amounts. As a result she forgot things. Maybe they could have operated if it were a few years before, he told us, but she was far too frail now, far too deep in senile dementia caused by "environmental factors," which of course meant, in this doctor's opinion, that she drank herself to it. This, anyway, was the unspoken subtext to our conversation, which occurred by chance in the hallway outside her room. It was clear the doctor, a droopy oaf with a dirty shirt collar, considered my mother's problems her own damn fault, and was sympathetic in only a professional sense.

Pierce and I didn't say much on the way home. The doctor was right, of course, about her drinking, and it was my fault as much as anybody's. I sporadically came home for the holidays, just like everyone else but Rose; I noticed her frequent trips to the kitchen to check on food that had already been served and eaten, the insults flung at my father as the rest of us slipped out the door to see a movie. I noticed the empty liquor bottles, stacked with heartbreaking care in the clear glass recycling bin in the garage (and certainly whatever gene coded for this kind of behavior explained Bobby's as well).

But most of all, I noticed, as Bitty did, as Bobby and his wife and, later, his daughter did, that whatever grit had gotten into the gears of their marriage and necessitated such gross overcompensation involved Pierce. I could remember my father spitting on him over a dessert, my mother throwing back her chair with such force that it gouged a chalk-white divot in the dining room wall. And there was a time, early on in the drinking, when Pierce banged on the bathroom door, behind which she had locked herself, pleading for her to open it, that he felt terribly afraid, that he thought we might all try to kill him, and hearing her reply, "Oh, God, Baby, not you. I can talk to anybody but you right now." And of course we decided that, in her drunkenness, she had mistaken Pierce for Dad, and spent the rest of the night talking Pierce out of his paranoia, not entirely successfully. And there was the matter of Pierce's absence from the strip, which none of us ever questioned, because after all Pierce didn't belong there. He was obviously a little crazy, wasn't he? What place did he have in America's favorite family cartoon?

Of course, we should have just gone and asked Rose what was going on. There had to be a reason she didn't come back. But we decided to see Rose as a quitter, as the primary aggressor in the breakup of the family, and for a long time that made things a little easier.

# eighteen

I ran around FunnyFest in a fever, looking for Susan. It wasn't that I had anything in particular to say to her, but at the moment she was the only person I
knew in town who didn't know things I didn't want to know, or forgotten
things I did want to know. I had developed a sudden and highly specific fear
on the way back from the nursing home: that my brother and I would live in
the house together as eternal bachelors, Pierce growing gradually less crazy
and me crazier until we met in a highly eccentric middle ground, where we
would remain until we had both reached an age too advanced to measure. At
that point nobody would be able to tell us apart, and would have no reason to.
I was one hundred percent sure this would happen.

Susan was not to be found. I saw a lot of familiar-looking people—high
school acquaintances or their parents and siblings, I guessed—and they made
me feel more than a little bit amnesiac, as if I had once had a real family and
a sprawling group of loyal pals and had scorned them all without realizing it.

I had just passed a rickety-looking espresso-and-chai stand in front of
the roller coaster when a young girl jumped up from a bench and called out my
name. I recognized her, after a moment's confusion, as the girl who had been
wearing the Tim costume, the one I'd talked with behind the bushes. She
flounced up to me, her face absurdly serious, like an undercover agent's. She
was wearing a colorful striped tank-top and, beyond all reason, given the heat,
a pair of dark blue jeans with flaring cuffs. A cigarette—clove, by the smell—

dangled with studied perilousness from her right hand, and she switched it to the left to shake my hand. "Hey," she said. "Gillian Millstone."

"Tim Mix."

"Sorry about my buds yesterday. Those guys are all dorks." She shook her head gravely. "I wanted to talk to you, man."

"About what?"

She studied my face a second, then turned suddenly coquettish, twisting her body half-away from me and producing a wry smile. "You look like your brother," she said.

"Which one?"

"Piercey."

"I see. And you're . . ."

"Yeah, his girlfriend, sort of, I guess." She straightened, flicking the cigarette aside and dropping the coy flirtation like a dusty rug snapped in the wind. "That's what I wanted to talk to you about."

I shook my head. "I don't think I want to know about that," I said. "I'm looking for somebody, really." And I started edging away.

"The chubbette? Is she your girlfriend?" She was following me.

"No, my editor."

"Oh, a business relationship."

"You could say that."

We were walking freely now, fast, with her close behind me. "It's not our love I want to discuss with you, Tim. It's just I'm worried about him. He's a little obsessed lately."

I came to a stop before the entrance to the Centrifuge of Death. There was a large wooden cutout of me, the cartoon me, holding its hand out at head level. The voice bubble above me read, "You must be this high to ride!!"

"Lately?" I said. "He's always obsessed. It's chronic."

"It's aggravated by stress," she said seriously. "Hey, my dad was a shrink before he croaked. I know nuts."

"I'm sorry," I said.

"Which part?"

"Your dad being dead."

"Yeah, well. So's my mom." She shrugged. "What are you gonna do?"
She tilted her head toward the ride, a massive black cylinder the approximate
shape of a tin of Christmas cookies, which had spun to a stop and was letting
off nauseated-looking passengers. "Come on, I'll fill in the blanks on the
ride."

I laughed. "That? Forget it."

"Don't be a wimp, Mix."

"I don't have tickets."

She dug into her jeans pocket and pulled out a wad of crumpled tickets big
as a fist. "We stole a bunch from the booth. The goober who runs it hides the
key under a rock."

I sighed. I didn't want to talk to this girl, nor go on this ride, yet the combination seemed so ludicrous as to be, on this day, inevitable. She winked at
me. "Come on. Everybody's doin' it."

This was demonstrably false. The stragglers coming off looked like the
remains of an army battalion decimated by friendly fire, and we were the last
two people in a line of seven. I shook my head no, no, but there I was, climb-
ing up the steel stairs, clomping across a metal platform, approaching the
curved black door. The twin iron doors of the crematorium occurred to me
and I froze at the threshhold, but Gillian Millstone pushed me in.

Unlike, say, a coffin, the Centrifuge of Death was almost completely unadorned on the inside, save for a series of thin steel dividers that marked rider
compartments and the wide safety belts that dangled between them. Gillian
grabbed my hand and dragged me clunking across the floor, pushed me into
a compartment and wrapped the seat belt around my waist. I half-expected to
be injected with some sort of truth serum, but instead she gently punched my
gut. "You two have the same bod, except you've got a little more meat
on you."

"That's not saying much."

"Guess not."

She strapped herself in next to me, then reached over and grabbed my
hand. Her face poked around the divider, and of her I could see only that
face, the tips of her breasts, her shoes and the flare of her jeans. A metallic
groan issued from beneath us, and we slowly began to turn. In half a minute,

we were spinning at breathtaking speed, and the entire apparatus began to tilt. Gillian screamed. I screamed. I pictured all the blood in my body pooling at my back, my spine swimming in it. I pictured the Centrifuge breaking free, rolling toward the river, crushing revelers in its path, sinking slowly in the water while I struggled to extricate myself from the belt. The sky and treetops wheeled madly, and I shut my eyes.

For the rest of the ride, Gillian Millstone told me, at a near-shriek, her story: that her parents, both doctors, were killed two years before in a plane crash in Montana, where they had gone to attend a conference on expert witnessing; that she had fought to be declared an adult a year early to prevent falling into the custody of her aunt and uncle, whom she detested; that she lived alone in an old house in the Pines once owned by her grandfather, and lived off the money from the sale of the family home and grew cranberries in a bog; that she met Pierce when he drove into the Pines and tried to drown himself by plunging the Cadillac into a nearby pond. The pond had been insufficiently deep. She had the car towed at her own expense.

She said she loved Pierce, that he talked incessantly about our father and acted like he wasn't really dead, and that the Pines was the only place where he never felt him watching. That his greatest fear now was the key he had been willed, that it represented dangerous knowledge, that he didn't deserve to have it, that he could not rid himself of it lest he suffer dire consequences, that because of it his father could still control his thoughts, his death notwithstanding. And throughout this gush she held my hand tightly, her fingers linked with mine, and sweat from her palm mingled with mine and disappeared in the wake of the Centrifuge's crosswinds.

We leveled out, slowed down. The last revolution was the worst, when the spinning had slowed too much to seem incredible, thus potentially imaginary, but was fast enough to toss my meager lunch around in my stomach like a whirlwind of autumn leaves. I wrenched the belt free, staggered off the ride and out into the world, listing slightly to the left. I found a bench and collapsed into it. Soon enough I felt Gillian collapse there next to me. I flinched. The ride seemed a betrayal, though nothing untoward had occurred. I thought about the cool sensation of another person's sweat evaporating from my hand.

"So will you help me?"

"Help you?" I gasped.

"By helping Pierce."

"By doing what? He doesn't need my help."

"You could open the safety deposit box for him, find what's inside. He trusts you. If there's something in there that would scare him, something that could convince him your father still holds power over him, you could lie."

I opened my eyes and looked into hers. They had taken on a startling and persuasive intelligence. I considered this, in light of what I now knew about her. I could see it, her and Pierce.

"I bet you're good for him," I said.

"He needs me."

"I can't lie to my brother. Whatever's in there, I'll have to tell him."

"That's selfish," she said. "That's you holding onto a habit because it's easier to do that than to take responsibility for him. He wants you to be responsible for him, you know. He trusts you."

"You said that."

"It's true."

"Before I came back here, I hadn't been close to him in years. Why would he trust me?"

She shrugged. "Beats me."


I finally found Susan standing in the middle of the food vendors' circle, blankly glancing around through her glasses, as she had at my father's wake. I noticed for the first time that the circle looked much like a ring of covered wagons, cowering in the dust on a prairie of the American West, shielding itself from an attack by marauding Indians. Susan seemed unaware of any such attack. She took a bite out of something in her hand, and as I came closer I noticed it was a corn dog. She saw me, made a move to hide the corn dog, then gave up and brought it back into view.

"I'm so embarrassed," she said. "The ultimate popular culture nostalgia cliché food. Would you believe I've never had one before?"

"Hmm," I said.

"Really, this is my first."

"I'm sorry," I said suddenly, surprising myself with my vehemence.

She started. "About what?"

"Leaving you to your own devices this morning. Not letting you know I'd be going out to see our mom."

"Good Lord, Tim, I don't care about that. I'm a big girl."

"I'm just not used to dealing with all these new people," I said. "And old people too. Not that you personally are hard to deal with."

"No offense taken."

"I don't feel like myself," I said. "Do you know what I'm saying?"

She nodded. "I never feel like myself. Or rather I never feel like the person I think of myself as actually being, the sort of Platonic ideal of myself I always picture doing the things I'm about to do. And then when I do them this other person takes over and screws them up."

We stood silently in all the commotion, nodding. Susan offered me a bite of her corn dog. I refused, still queasy from the Centrifuge of Death, but I didn't tell her this, and I feared that this rebuff without explanation would give offense. Then I came to my senses and simply let it go. It was a wonderful feeling, like dropping a box off at the Goodwill.

"Is this on?" came a shrill voice, then a squeal of feedback. I turned to see the mayor, perched on the bandstand with a brass band setting up behind him, peering at the microphone as if it were a mutant strain of lab rat.

"Speaking of clichés," Susan said.

"Hello? Hello?" The mayor was wearing a Family Funnies T-shirt, the one with a picture of Bobby saying, "Why's it called a tea shirt? There's no tea on it!" He also wore a deep, rich tan he hadn't had the day before.

"It's five o'clock," Susan said. She pulled a folded schedule from her shorts pocket. "Time for the election results."

"I forgot about that."

Francobolli was fumbling with his notes now. A few people had gathered in the field, not many. I wondered how many townspeople had actually voted.

And then, something very strange happened: I became suddenly, inexplicably happy. It came to me like a faint, delicious scent swept from a distant place, and tumbled over and over itself, snowballing inside me, taking on weight. I shifted my feet to support it. Then the mayor coughed, bent to receive a sealed envelope, and just like that it left me. But its faint impression remained, lending me lightness, the way an extra bat gives the slugger in the on-deck circle his effortless swing at the plate. I hopped once, then again, testing it.

"What?" Susan said with a puzzled smile.

"Nothing, nothing."

The mayor gave a brief speech. He talked about the things that made Riverbank great, its natural beauty, its notable figures of the past, then segued into my father, then into the town council's decision to change the name in his honor. He clawed at the envelope.

*Not Familytown,* I begged him silently.

"Ladies and gentlemen," the mayor announced. Behind him, the trombone player raised the trombone to his lips and adjusted the slide. "I'm pleased to report that our town is now called . . ."

A beat, in which only the distant sounds of the rides and riders could be heard.

"Mixville! Mixville, New Jersey!" And as the band ripped into the air with a ragged vaudevillian vamp, the mayor yelled, drowned out by the sound, "Welcome, one and all, to Mixville, New Jersey!"

I looked around, at my new town, the one named after my family. People were clapping, infected by Francobolli's manic exuberance. I was unsurprised to spy Ken Dorn hunkered among them, looking vaguely Teutonic in a gratuitous leather vest and khaki hiking shorts, and he eyed me from twenty yards away with a knowing smirk, as if he could read my mind. But I was just as sure that he couldn't. *Try your damnedest, Ken,* I told him silently. *You will never know me.* And I turned to my editor and accepted my great, ironic handshake that for the moment I thought I deserved.

# nineteen

Monday morning was relentless in the wake of my undone cartooning work, with the curve of the pen itching away at my bones, Wurster hanging over my shoulder, barking instructions, the house's oily cold clinging to my skin and clothes. By the time I got out, the early clouds that had been massing on the horizon had arrived and gushed forth their rain, and the heat wave had finally broken. I blinked in the bright gray light, listening to water dripping off trees.

When I got home I asked Pierce for money. I hadn't wanted to do this, but I had been letting him pay for groceries and gas for weeks now, and he hadn't appeared put off by it.

"Oh, yeah, okay," he said. We were in his bedroom, where he had been playing solitaire and smoking cigarettes. He got up and went to the closet. I heard some clunking around from there. When he came out, he had a neat handful of twenty-dollar bills, which he handed to me.

"You've got cash in there?"

He shrugged. "Yeah."

"Where from?"

"The account Dad left me. I got a lot out at once." He sat down on the bed, reluctant to meet my eyes. "Banks make me nervous."

I glanced at the money. It was a thick little pile, and I had to restrain myself from counting it. "Jesus, Pierce, thanks."

He shrugged. "It's nothing."

"It's a lot."

"I don't want to talk about it."

His tone was dismissive. But I lingered, letting my eyes navigate the room, wondering if he had other things stashed here: drugs, old photos, letters. "Speaking of banks," I said, and felt the temperature in the room drop half a degree. "That key."

He bent farther over his game, emphatically flipping cards into piles.

"Are you going to look and see what's in it? Aren't you curious?"

"Nope," he said.

"Not even a little bit?"

He placed a club onto the pile slowly, his hand shaking. He straightened but didn't look at me. "It's just the title. Or something."

"Or something?"

He didn't answer. He didn't go back to his game, either. He just sat there, staring at the closet doors as if into a deep darkness, where the ominous outlines of things were barely visible. After a while I looked down at the money in my hand and felt like a thief. Not long after, I left.


I was running out of certain supplies, so I decided to go to the art store. Nobody was around now that FunnyFest was over with, and the streets were empty of cars. Shopkeepers propped their doors open, letting in the cool summer air. A woman sat cross-legged on the floor of a clothing boutique, painting her fingernails.

The art store was in a small converted town house just off Main Street that was also home to a music studio. I'd often gone there with Dad, and while I poked through the dusty rows of art supplies I could hear the muffled sound of scales artlessly played on a variety of instruments. Occasionally an instructor would grow bored with one of her students and begin playing something beautiful, and I would stand transfixed, listening.

When I got there I found that little had changed. The proprietor, a barrel-shaped man in his sixties, was standing on a ladder, repainting the hanging sign that had read "Riverbank Art Supply." He had finished the first few letters of "Mixville." When I approached he looked down and called to me. "Timmy Mix!"

"Hi," I said.

"You remember me? I used to sell your daddy his pens and paper."

"Sure do," I said. "I'm here for the same stuff."

"Yeah, yeah!" he said. "Hear you're taking over!"

"Looks that way." I pointed to the sign. "How's it going?"

He shook his head. "No offense," he said. "But I'm not voting for that Francobolli next time around. This here's a pain in my ass. I gotta send out change of address cards, for Chrissake. All of a sudden I'm living in a different town."

Inside, I noticed one other customer. He looked familiar to me—a fifty-ish man, thin hair, wearing khaki shorts and a blue chambray shirt—but I couldn't place him. We passed in an aisle and he smiled at me in a comradely way. I gathered a few items—pens and pencils, fresh paper, all from the list my father had included with his letter, which I kept in my wallet. Overhead, something that sounded like a cello grunted through something that sounded like Bach. I went to the counter, where the familiar-looking man was already waiting for the proprietor. "Hello, Tim," he said.

We shook hands. "Hey, uh . . ."

"It's Father Loomis," he said. "You didn't recognize me."

"Oh! No, you know, your clothes . . ."

"Not very priestly."

"Uh-uh, no." I smiled at him. There was the ecumenical collar, tucked discreetly under the work shirt. He looked weirdly like his Family Funnies counterpart, who almost invariably was depicted at a great distance: behind his pulpit, in the background of one or another whispered misunderstanding over matters ecclesiastic. I'd been having a lot of trouble drawing him. He had spread out his purchases on the counter: red sable brushes, cadmium red and cerulean blue oil paint, turpentine. I said, "You paint?"

He blushed. "Oh, yes, a little bit here and there . . ."

"What sort of thing?"

"Landscapes, mostly. You know, glory of God and all that." He said this with more than a little irony. I liked him. "So," he said, "I hear you're in the driver's seat now."

"That's the rumor."

"How's it going?"

I told him briefly about my lessons, how easy it all seemed at first, and how hard it turned out to be. "I have new respect for my father," I managed to say, "as an artist."

He nodded expansively. "Your dad was a strange man, Tim." His face froze a little at this; he thought he had gone too far. "I mean, he was complex, very complex. A troubled man. There was more to him than people know."

"I've guessed that."

"Pardon me, I've said too much."

"Oh, no," I said. "I'm very interested. He seemed so . . . covert, I guess."

Father Loomis wagged his finger in the air, and nodded faster now. This had obviously been on his mind. "Yes, yes! At our last confession . . ." But then he stopped himself. "Well, he had a lot of guilt, Tim, a lot of pain. He made his mistakes, you know, but . . ." He reached out and touched my shoulder. "He was a good man. I truly believe that. He was a friend. I think there will be a place for him in God's Kingdom."

"Great!" I said moronically.

The proprietor appeared, red-faced and paint-spattered, and rung us both up. When I went outside with my purchases, Father Loomis was standing on the sidewalk, gazing up into the sky. "Yes," he said. "A lovely day indeed," as if this had been the subject of our conversation.

"It was good to see you," I said.

"Oh! You too! It would be nice to see you a little more often. Sunday mornings, perhaps."

"Oh," I said. "Well . . ."

He waved his hand in the space between us. "No, no guilt please. I have to make my pitch, though. There was nothing wrong with your father a little extra prayer wouldn't have fixed." He raised his eyebrows. "And maybe a little therapy."

"Maybe a lot."

We had a quick laugh together. Something of the previous day's rush of happiness had stuck with me, and the new, cool air tasted like lemonade. Father Loomis and I said our goodbyes. And then—I guess it was something in the way he had spoken that made me think of it—I said, "By the way, when was the last time you saw him? For confession, I mean."

We were standing half-turned from one another, gazing up at separate patches of sky. Father Loomis shrugged. "A few weeks, I guess."

"A few *weeks?*"

"Well, yes."

"He was coming to you up until he died?"

I realized I was making him uncomfortable. "Yes, Tim, he was."

"Wow," I said. "Sorry. I just didn't know."

"Well. You never know everything, I suppose."

"I guess not." Father Loomis was shifting from foot to foot, and I decided to let him off the hook. I raised my hand, bid him a good day, and left.


That night I drove to Philly and got my stuff. There wasn't much. A few records, some clothes. I left all the furniture and dragged the remains of my art studio out onto the sidewalk. Most of it went into the wet, reeking dumpster out back, where it landed with a deadened clang on the bottom. It didn't look out of place there at all. The trash can that had been part of my work-in-progress I left on the curb, next to the one it was modeled on, and the two stood there, identically scratched and dented, like a frowzy set of twins waiting for the school bus.

Before I left, I opened and closed each of Amanda's drawers, looking at the clothes there. I set the box of things from her car on the bedroom floor. Maybe I cried a little. Mostly I felt the bulky and annoying weight of things, which massed to ruin the otherwise modest pleasure of clearing out of the place forever. I shut the door on the apartment's dim double in my mind, which though closed would always be there, taking up space. Then I dropped my key on the coffee table and closed the door on the real apartment. I went home and slept badly.

One morning that week, when I got to Wurster's house, I found him sitting in a lawn chair in the middle of the cool, shade-ruined yard. He was drinking a glass of iced tea and squinting. "Good morning," he said. It wasn't something I'd ever heard him say before.

"What's up?"

"We'll be doing something different today. You mind driving? I don't drive."

"Oh, no, that's all right." In fact, I had been, for perhaps the first time, actually looking forward to our session. I'd been working on a portfolio of the characters, one drawing of each of them doing ten different things, and I thought it was going extremely well. I was beginning, in fact, to believe I could start doing full strips.

"Good," he said. "Put your work away. We won't be talking about drawing today." He stood up, stroked his chin. "Actually, that's not true. It's always about drawing, one way or another. We'll be implying about drawing." He walked to the Caddy and got into the passenger seat. I stowed my work in the trunk with some consternation, climbed in beside him and started the car.

"So what is this mystery topic?"

He fastened the seat belt, and when he was through gave it a sharp tug. "Gags. What kind of driver are you?"

"Careful."

He leveled me a skeptic's glare. "Are you, now?"

"Yes! I'm very careful. What about gags?"

"We're going to make up gags. We're going to see how good you are at Family Funnies humor."

"Oh, great," I said, pulling out.

"Drive the speed limit, please," said Brad Wurster.


We went to the Brunswick Plaza, one of the early malls: a single-story quarry-tiled complex with no skylights and a central fountain, dark with thrown pennies, that juggled filthy warm jets of water. Wurster and I walked slowly around the fountain, our hands in our pockets. He nodded every now and then.

"Well?" he said.

"Well what?"

"What do you think?"

I looked down at the fountain. A soaking child was kneeling at the water's edge, raking the cement bottom with a grubby hand. He came up with a fistful of pennies and ran off, trailing damp footprints. "I think it stinks."

Wurster shook his head. He took two small spiral notebooks and a couple of pencils from his shirt pocket and handed me one of each. "You're going to have to be more specific than that," he said. "The Mix family is at the mall. I want you to sit on this bench and make up five gags about this fountain."

"Five!"

"For starters, yes." He took a seat on the bench. "We'll compare notes in a little while."

I sat beside him and stared hard at the fountain, concentrating this time. It wasn't very funny. He began to push his pencil almost immediately, a maddening sound, like mice scrabbling in a cell wall. It took me twenty minutes to come up with any jokes, and by the time half an hour had passed my little notebook read:

> ~~bitty wants to go swimming~~
> lindy holding bittys hand, says 'bitty wants to know
> how come we cant go swimming'
>
> stranger kid floating in fountain
> timmy says I'd sure like to go swimming
>
> bobby ~~saying how come they~~ telling timmy if you
> throw your pennies in there god gets 'em
>
> lindy

This was as far as I got. The fountain was so perfectly vapid, so meaningless and foul, that I might have believed it was specifically constructed to befog my comic sensibilities. Furthermore, I didn't know how to draw water. Resigned, I turned to Wurster and admitted I was finished.

"Let me see," he said. I gave him my notebook. He read it carefully, then pointed to what I'd written. "This one about God is pretty good. You got one of the common FF themes in there. I like that. The other stuff, though . . . you get a twenty-five percent. That's an F."

"Gee, thanks, teach," I said. "What have you got, then?"

He handed me his notebook. The gags covered several pages in his neat, heavily slanted handwriting.

    1. Lindy tells Bitty, "It's called a fountain 'cause
       there's lots of money *found in* it."

    2. Timmy says to Carl, "How come we don't get one
       of those in the bathtub at home?"

    3. Bobby says to Carl, "How come we can't throw
       dollar bills in there?"

    4. Drawing shows lots of kids playing in the fountain;
       Lindy tells Bitty, "It's the fountain of youth,
       because it's got kids in it."

    5. Bobby says to Bitty, "It's not a sprinkler. You can't
       run through it."

"Hmm," I said. "Not too bad."

"One and five are terrible," Wurster said. "But four will do." He cracked his knuckles. "Okay, we've got two we like. You draw mine and I'll draw yours."

"Really? I've never tried a whole cartoon."

"It's time. Go to it."

I made several test sketches of the fountain of youth gag: in one, Lindy and Bitty were sitting at the edge of the pool with their feet in the water; in another they were on a bench, off to the side. In the end I decided to put them left of center, standing in the foreground; the fountain was visible in the background, small enough to obscure my poor draftsmanship. Kids frolicked in it. Lindy was bending over, her finger held up like a teacher's, while Bitty, in a typical pose, had her hand in her mouth. It looked all right to me—something that an expert inker, which I was not, might be able to make whole. When I was done I found that Wurster had already finished his. He handed it to me.

I was amazed. My father might well have done it himself. In the background of the strip, a woman—endowed with that flawlessly bland matron sensuality that all women had in the Family Funnies—leaned over her child, who was tossing pennies into the fountain. And in the foreground, Bobby was telling me the punchline, the one about God getting the pennies, and I was listening. Bobby's expression was perfect in its groundless confidence, while mine was one of effusive awe, both of what he was saying and that he knew it at all. It was marvelously stupid, exactly the kind of thing the guy who cleaned the fountain would cut out and tape to his fridge.

"Wow," I said.

"Let's see yours." I gave it to him. He nodded. "Okay, sure. You could ink this up into something half-decent, couldn't you?" He handed it back and stood up. It was time to move to a new site.

I was frustrated enough with Wurster's effortless aping of the strip that I stayed an extra couple of seconds on the bench. Wurster was already walking. "Why is it," I called after him, "that everybody can draw this goddam strip but me?"

He turned around. "What's that supposed to mean?"

"Just what I said. I don't even know why I'm up for this job. You ought to get it yourself. Or Ken Dorn."

His eyes bugged out, and he took a step forward. It was a funny step, the kind you might take toward a caged lion in a poorly maintained zoo. "What did you say?"

"You ought to get the job."

"Did you say 'Ken Dorn'?"

"Yeah, Ken Dorn. You know him?"

Wurster sat down again, his eyes never leaving my face. "How do you know him?"

"He was at the funeral," I said. "And at FunnyFest. He's been hanging around town."

"Riverbank?"

"Mixville."

"What!"

I explained the name change to him. He shook his head. "For Christ's sake. How stupid."

"Well, whatever. But Ken Dorn."

He brought his finger to my face. "Ken Dorn is a leech, Tim. He'll grab you and suck all the blood out before you know what hit you, and by that time you'll be dead in the water."

I unmixed his metaphors and offered a respectful nod. "How do you know him?" I asked.

Wurster shook his head and stared off into the depths of a shoe store. "That's not important," he whispered.


That Friday, at lunch in New York, I got an idea of what Wurster was talking about. Susan had been gloomy and evasive the entire meal, and while we were eating—the time I would least expect her to speak—she put down her chopsticks and sat up straight in her chair. "Tim."

"Mmph?"

"I have a confession to make."

I finished chewing and raised my head. Already the rhythm of the meal was draining away from me. "What?"

"Remember I said the syndicate would have somebody else . . . on deck? Just in case?"

"Yeah?"

She turned her head to watch a waiter glide by. "It's, uh, Ken Dorn."

My innards tingled, as if girding themselves against an impending nausea. Still, I was not surprised. Before I could respond, she said, "I only found out a week ago. And then, bumping into him at FunnyFest . . . it just looked strange. I should have told you then."

"But they still want me, don't they?"

She nodded. "Well, yeah, sure. I mean, I hope."

"You hope?"

"I found out about this through a memo from Ray Burn to the syndicate's law firm. They were working out the legalities of turning it over to Dorn. Who gets the merchandising rights and all that."

I said, "I guess Dorn would."

"Well."

"Well?"

"This memo was asking the lawyers to look into Dorn not getting the merchandising rights. That is, the syndicate getting all that."

"I don't understand."

"I think . . . I think maybe if you get the strip, you get merchandising money. But if Dorn gets the strip, the syndicate would keep it all. I think."

I gave this a little thought. "So you're saying it's not in their best interests to go with me."

She opened her mouth. It took a few seconds for anything to come out of it. "Uhh . . . no, not exactly. We're talking about your father's dying wishes, here. I mean, they still want you. At least I think. I mean, no, they definitely do. Why would they be pumping money into this thing otherwise? Free lunches, et cetera." She didn't look like she was convincing herself. She let the et cetera hang in the air a moment, then plunged, embarrassed, back into her food. Now I set down my chopsticks.

"Susan," I said. "I don't want to do this if I'm just going to get screwed."

She chewed and swallowed, and stared at her plate. "Well, there are things you can do to impress them. Go to this conference, for one thing."

"Conference?"

"The cartoonists' conference I was telling you about? Next weekend?"

"Oh, right."

"And then meet with Ray Burn. Tell him you mean business. Dorn would be a hard guy to sell, to work with. He's a notorious weasel. Everybody hates him."

"And you can set this up?"

She nodded quickly. "After the conference, sure."

"So now what?" My food looked sticky and unappetizing on the plate, like it had just been dragged from the bottom of a lake.

"I, uh, got the day off," she said. "Maybe we could go somewhere? The Met? A bookstore? A drink?"

"A drink sounds good."

"On me," she said. "Not the syndicate."

## twenty

In fact, we had several drinks, at an ill-lit NYU student hangout with framed portraits of art-film stars on the walls and peanut shells all over the floor. We got sort of drunk. This is not something I had done with someone else for a long time, and it reminded me of college, and long, dazed walks back to my dorm in the dark. In retrospect these walks seemed like the best moments of my life: unhurried, mildly challenging, directly preceding sound sleep. I was so lost in the memory of them that when we spilled out onto the sidewalk afterward I was shocked by the bright diffuse light of an overcast summer day in New York. I smelled pretzels. We traced the smell to Washington Square Park, and sat eating in a little island of grass bordered by orange snow fences, where some kind of water-line maintenance was going on.

"I can't go home," I said. "I'm drunk."

"The Museum's still open," Susan mumbled, studying her watch. "Let's go there."

But we never made it. Our cabdriver didn't yet know how to get there. He feigned professional indignation, as if the Museum were in the South Bronx, surrounded by crack-happy street gangs, before letting us off, for free and apparently at random, outside a movie theater, which we found ourselves staggering into like twin Mr. Magoos through an open manhole. The movie playing was a revival: *It's a Mad, Mad, Mad, Mad World*. It was three hours long.

It took us most of that time to find one another in the dark. The star-studded cast was scampering blithely around the base of the big "W" where the money was buried when I finally turned my head blearily toward hers and found her looking blearily up at me, and our lips blearily met. And then our arms were around each other and we were kissing, kissing, and it felt very, very strange. The air conditioning was too cool and I touched the nubbly bumps on the skin of her arms. On the screen Jonathan Winters's childlike voice was rising out of the din, and he said something that, in my alcohol-and-hormone-induced delirium, sounded like "You're making out!"

Making out! I hadn't heard anyone say that since about 1980, and I turned my head to the screen. But all that was going on there was digging, and back in our seats Susan was kissing my neck. And so I turned back to her, and the credits rolled.

But in the street, nothing. We had gone to the rest rooms to unrumple, but something must have happened there—perhaps the sight of ourselves, just beginning our fourth decades, wan and haggard in the unflattering fluorescent light—to pluck us out of our respective spells. We simpered, embarrassed, at one another. The sun had finally come out, just in time to start setting. I had homework to do.

Still, we walked all the way downtown, saying little, not touching. It was a good walk, a necessary walk, as the last remnants of alcohol rose to my skin and evaporated into the city air. When we got to the Caddy we stood facing each other, smiling politely and not looking each other directly in the eyes. The day had lost almost all its light.

"So," I said.

"So," she said.

I began to lean forward, just a little, and she did too. Then someone down the street yelled and we turned our heads to see, but there was nothing. And then my hand was on the door handle and Susan was a step farther away, and so that would be all.

"So call me," she said, then corrected herself: "I'll call you. Whenever I know something. About the conference."

"And Ray Burn."

"Yeah, sure." She smiled, I smiled.

"Thanks," I said. "I had a great day." Though I wasn't sure if that was true. Great? Different. Unexpected.

"Yeah?"

"Sure," I said.

Her face darkened, just a little. Had I not sounded convincing enough? I was embarrassed and looked away.

"Well, until then," she said.

"Okay, great." I opened the car door and got in. She walked off. And I was suddenly saying, "Susan?"

"Yes?"

She half-turned, her face full of something: hope, fear, humiliation? It was red, anyway. No matter what I said, it would be wrong. I said, "Thanks again."

A moment of silence. Then, "No problem," and she was gone.

All the way home, I half-listened to talk radio, and thought incessantly of her breast's gentle pressure against the crook of my arm.

Pierce was asleep, but the kitchen counter had been cleared entirely of dishes and food residue and wiped clean. And sitting in the middle of it, like a surprise birthday gift or suicide note, was the safe-deposit box key. No explanation, though none was needed. Tomorrow he would go, I supposed, to the Pines, and I would be going to the bank.

There were three banks in Riverbank—that is, Mixville—and only two of them were open Saturday mornings. Of the open ones, I remembered having a childhood passbook savings account at Riverbank First National, and knew that Riverbank National Bank and Trust was closer, right out on Main Street. I went to RNBT first. Downtown was uncrowded, save for a small, just-awakened crowd milling around the bakery. I stopped there myself and bought a scone, perfectly serviceable and still warm.

RNBT was in the process of becoming MNBT. They had had a vinyl sign printed up with the new town name on it, and this hung from ropes over the illuminated sign; the lettering on the door had already been changed. I was impressed and abashed.

When I showed the safety deposit teller the key, she assured me that it was indeed one of theirs, and passed me a stack of forms. I had to sign in, as usual, but there were some other hoops, relating to my father's death, that had to be jumped through.

"I'm not actually in charge of his money," I said. "I don't have power of attorney or anything."

"Where did you get this key?" she said.

"It was left to my brother Pierce."

She winced, as if she had some dire connection to Pierce I didn't, and couldn't, understand. "And why isn't he here himself?"

"He doesn't want to be the one to look."

"Can't you bring him in here with you? Then he could stand outside."

I looked down at the half-eaten scone in my hand. "He doesn't . . . like banks," I said.

"Hmm." She asked me for my driver's license and social security card. She asked me what my father's mother's maiden name was and made me verify his address. Then I signed the forms and she opened the gate. "But keep that out of here," she said, pointing at the scone. I set it in front of a closed teller station and followed her in.

She made me wait outside the vault while she pulled the box from it, then led me to a cramped booth containing a small desk, a pen on a chain and a reading lamp with a green glass shade. She set the box on the desk. "Let me know when you're through," she said, and clickety-clacked back to her window.

It was a long, narrow box, gray with sharp corners. The lid came up with a feeble creak. Inside was a small sheaf of papers and an envelope. I looked at the papers first: titles to the property and car, dental X-rays, birth certificates of Dad, Bitty and Pierce. Some low-denomination savings bonds, never cashed in and possibly forgotten.

I put these things aside and gingerly tore open the envelope. The paper was bright white, not aged in the slightest. Inside there was only another key, this one to a door lock or padlock. There was nothing else. I pulled the key out. It had the number 134 etched into one side, and on the other was a yellow sticker, half of which was rubbed mostly away by a succession of rough fingers. Only a few words were visible:

orage

lphia, PA

I looked again into the envelope: surely something else was in there. But there was no explanation, no note. I rifled through the papers, nothing. I pocketed the key, crumpled the envelope up and dropped it into the wastebasket. Then I closed the box and left the room.

"I'm done," I told the teller. She gave me a look indicating that she was pleased to hear it. She disappeared into the vault with the box and returned with the key. Meanwhile I discovered that my scone had been disposed of. There were still a couple of crumbs there, standing out pale against the black marble counter where it had been sitting.


My assignment for the weekend was to come up with twenty-five stripworthy gags. These would form the basis of my work for the next month and a half. During the last two weeks of my tutelage we would prepare the six dailies and one Sunday that would constitute my submission to Burn Features Syndicate, would decide my fate as a rich and goofy pop artist or pretentious loser living with his brother. I wasn't sure, considering the two, which suited me better. By that evening I was forced to confront the fact that neither was particularly suitable, and that despite my doubts I had no other conceivable options. I wanted to sit around and discuss this with somebody, but I couldn't see calling Susan so late at night, and incidentally making a fool of myself. So I sat quietly, fighting off sleep, and worked on the gags.

I had decided on a system while returning from the bank, and stopped in the mini-mart for a stack of 3x5 note cards, the kind without lines. I had this idea that lines would make the jokes seem less funny, a task they would likely need no help accomplishing. At home, I dug from the hall closet an old typewriter, a black war-era Smith-Corona in a battered black case that my father had used briefly in his stint as a newspaperman, and hauled it onto the kitchen counter. I sat on a wooden bar stool and rolled in card after card, tapping out every stupid gag I could think up. I didn't worry too much about their quality, only the redundant mechanics of their production: off the stack, into the machine, think up the joke, type it out, out of the machine, onto the stack. By the time I gave up I had about forty, most of them worthless. Under the gray fluorescent kitchen light, the only one burning in the house, I thumbed through the pile. *Calendar says Jan 1, Lindy says to Bitty Time to make your New Year's revolution. Dog curled on Dot's lap, Timmy saying It's Mommy's laptop! Mailman coming up walk, Bobby looking out window says If he was a girl would he be a femailman?*

And those were the best of the lot. I set the finished stack next to the empty stack, pushed the typewriter back and lay my head on my arms.

For a short time around my sixth Christmas, my father went on "vacation" and "I" "took over" the strip for him. That is, my father went nowhere, and the cartoon Timmy became the in-name-only author of the strip. At first I was horrified. The drawings were artificially childlike, with arms and legs rendered as sticks, and trees and shrubs as thick brambles of scribble. But they were clearly the work of an adult: all the subtler rules of motion, of bodily line were fully articulated, and the images were laid out on the page with clarity and grace.

The gags themselves were all about my parents—child's-eye views of the sober complexities of adult life. There was an arrogance about this I was already old enough to resent. I was not stupid, as people generally believe children to be, and already deeply suspicious of anything either of my parents did. I would never have made the kind of "cute" assumptions this series of strips—about a week's worth—attributed to me. For example: of my father, laboring over some papers, I was to have said: *Daddy has to pay his bills to Santa.* As if my family would ever have bothered with the Santa Claus deception. Elsewhere, "I" drew Dad shoveling the car out of a snowbank. The caption read: *Daddy loves playing in the snow.*

All the same, I ended up welcoming the week's worth of attention these strips brought me. People stopped on the street to tell me what a good little cartoonist I was, how I'd be sure to have my own strip someday. Father Loomis gave me a gift: a pen, which eventually found its way out of my room and into my father's studio, where it was forever lost. I felt a little like a superstar, and people wrote letters to me from all over the country. Rose hated me; so did Bobby. I played exclusively with Pierce the first two weeks of January, building things out of Christmas Tinkertoys and watching television.

Until now, I hadn't thought of that week of strips as prescient. But the connection felt all too clear: an attention-grubbing fake taking credit for something that wasn't his own, something that itself was not worth the paper it was printed on. There was no doubt anymore; my father was a failure, and so was I. However accomplished his cartoons, his gags remained second-, even third-rate. His story, like mine, was one of squandered potential.

I slid off the stool, dragged myself to the light switch and turned it off. I was as lonely as I'd been in months.

During the night, I woke to a noise from somewhere in the house. It manifested itself in the sex dream I was having as my murky lover's rough moans; what it really was, I understood once I had fully awoke, was the kitchen stool being pulled out from under the counter. Pierce? I thought. There was some shuffling, a click, then giggling: a pause, a giggle, a pause, a giggle. I listened to this for a minute or more, the still air screaming in my ears, until one of the giggles became a full laugh, and then I knew it wasn't Pierce. I looked around the bedroom for something to crack him over the head with, and found only my bedside lamp, a ceramic travesty in the shape of a woman's head bearing a fruit-filled basket. I yanked the plug from the wall and crept out into the hallway.

No light issued from the kitchen. The giggler was in the dark. I padded as quietly as possible, the lamp heavy in my hand, raised as high above my head as I could reach. Its plug dangled down behind me and knocked against my heels.

I peeked into the kitchen to find a tiny flashlight beam illuminating a small hand and my gag cards. The hand was picking through the cards, its owner chuckling at each one before embedding it back in the pile with a delicate turn of the wrist. I knew who it was before I switched on the light.

"Ken Dorn," I said.

"Oh, these are priceless, Timmy. Really wonderful stuff." He flipped off the penlight and dropped it into the pocket of a leather jacket. On his head, slumped like a baked eggplant, was the kind of cap worn exclusively by robbers in cartoons. " 'If one of them's a panty hose, why aren't the two of them panty hoses?' That is rich, rich!"

"What are you doing in my house?"

"Your brother's house, Timmy." He turned, grinning at me with pinprick eyes. "You got the strip, remember? You live in the Family Funnies now."

"Ha, ha." I calculated distances. The telephone was closer to him than me.

He followed my eyes to the phone, then picked it up and handed it to me. "How are you going to dial with that lamp in your hand?"

I was shaking, unnerved by my residual fear and infuriated by Dorn's presence. He showed no sign of leaving. I put the lamp on the floor and picked up the receiver.

"All right, Timmy, all right," he said, sliding off the stool, and I didn't dial, a failure that I regret to this day, much as I regret not punching the high school English teacher who dragged me up in front of the classroom and gave me a humiliating and painful wedgie. "Don't get all bent out of shape. You left your door unlocked, if you want to know."

"That doesn't mean you can just walk through it," I said.

"The truth is," he said, tapping the pile of note cards straight, "you don't like me around because I represent your greatest fear, right?"

"Which is what?"

"That you can't even do this strip right, even when it's been dropped in your lap. Even though you didn't have to work for it at all."

I had no response. I suppose this was a fear of mine, but it was a cornflake next to the grain silo of fears I was shadowed by.

"So," Dorn went on. "I suppose that chippie of yours has told you I'm in line for the job?"

"She found out by chance," I said.

Dorn laughed again, the same nefarious snigger that had chilled me in the dark. "Come on, Timmy. She just didn't want to hurt your feelings. She knew."

He zipped up his jacket and ran his hand over his head. I said, "Get out, Dorn."

"You got it, Timmy." He backed up to the sliding doors and pushed one silently open. His eyes wheeled, taking in the house once more. "It turns me on just being in this place."

And then he was gone.

I sat in bed, the fruit lady lamp plugged in and burning, and read over my cards again and again. Tomorrow I would try to do just as many. Maybe even illustrate a few in pencil, to give me something to discuss with Wurster.

Much later, as I lay still, letting my anxiety amplify every faint sound from outdoors, I let my real fears take on their full sagging shape: that, in fact, I *would* be good enough to do the strip, but would let myself think it was the best I could do. That Dorn had been right about Susan, that she'd lied to me to save my feelings, that our embrace in the movies was an open expression of desperation and I had been making a fool of myself on all fronts and still was. And would be, over and over, knowing all along it was what I had chosen and what I would continue to choose, despite all the available alternatives, because it was the easiest thing to do.

## twenty-one

When Pierce came home Sunday night, I was still at the counter, sorting the gag cards into bad, awful and workable piles. I was on my third pass through, having only come up with nineteen workables, in the hope of finding a few bads I could improve. Thinking up more was out of the question: I was burned out.

I could tell Pierce was highly agitated even before he came into the circle of light cast by the kitchen lamp. He tossed his bag onto the couch in the dark of the living room and stood there, panting.

"Pierce?"

"Hey," came his voice, weakly.

"How was your weekend?"

There was only his breathing for a moment. Then he said, "I talked to Gilly about your talk with her. I didn't even know about it before I left the key."

I didn't know what I was expected to say. "Yeah. We went on the Centrifuge of Death."

"She said she told you not to tell me anything."

"She did," I said. I wondered what kind of good this girl was doing my brother, an established paranoid, by hatching plots behind his back, then gushing to him about them a week later. I wondered if he knew she had been dressed up as me at the 'Fest.

"So are you keeping it from me?"

"Of course not," I said. "I told her I wouldn't keep things from you."

He stepped slowly into eyeshot. He looked tired. "She told me that too," he said. I could see the mess this was making in his head and put down my stack of cards.

"Look, I went and examined everything very carefully. There wasn't much. The deed, the title to the car, legal junk, pretty much like you said. There was only one odd thing." I waited a second. "Do you want to hear it?"

"I don't know."

"It's not so bad."

He groaned, it seemed to me with a little irony. Okay, then, I thought, he's doing all right. He slumped down on the stool across the counter from mine, began picking at something on the back of the typewriter and said, "Hit me."

I felt in my pocket for the key, then set it on the counter.

"Oh, crap," he said. He picked it up and brought it to his face, closer than perhaps was necessary. He read aloud the fragments of words once, then twice.

"What do you think?" I said.

He put down the key, rubbed his eyes with the balls of his hands. "Oh, shit, Tim, who knows." He looked up grinning sadly. "I hate mysteries. Really I do. I hate the whole fucking past, and all the garbage everybody in our family did to each other, and everybody in other people's families did to each other and to our family. Every time a little mystery pops up it's like a tumor in my head, and it grows and grows until all I can think about is all the things I don't know and all the things people are keeping from me, and the reasons they might be doing that." He reached out and pushed the key across the counter at me. "I mean, if people are doing anything behind my back, why can't they be doing everything?"

I picked up the key and dropped it in my shirt pocket. "That's a heavy load."

"No kidding." He gestured with his head at the disappeared key. "What do *you* think?"

"Storage company in Philly?"

He nodded. "The family skeletons?"

"Could be." Though our skeletons had always shunned the closet, clattering around right out in the open, like bathrobed houseguests.

Pierce picked up the note cards and read through them. He kept doing this for several minutes after I thought he would certainly stop. Finally he said, "Man, every time a new strip came out, I felt like he had stolen a little piece of my soul."

"Like those isolated people who were afraid of cameras."

"I hate cameras too," Pierce said.

I gathered the cards up and put them aside. I was exhausted, too much so to talk to Pierce any longer. I got up and made sure the sliding doors were locked, though I understood there was no point in telling Pierce about Dorn's break-in. "You know," I said, sounding more irritated than I really was, "you're not even in those strips. You've got that going for you."

Pierce slid off his stool and headed down the hall. "You're not looking hard enough," he said. "I'm in every one of them."


I did a lot that week, though the main thing I did was not call Susan. She didn't call me, either. But it seemed that the burden of calling had fallen to me, and though, reviewing the weekend's events, I could find no concrete reason I should bear it, I took it upon myself anyway. Perhaps it was just my natural predilection for guilt, and if so, then I deserved it. Unfortunately this same tendency was also at work in my relationship with Amanda: though our breakup was a long time coming, I still felt compelled to prolong it, so that I would keep on feeling bad. This is why, after spending a lonely and grueling Thursday evening drafting cartoons for Wurster, I called her instead of Susan.

I half-expected, half-hoped to find the apartment embroiled in a raucous, libidinous party, which in the reeking bog of my imagination would leak out the telephone earpiece like corn syrup and relieve me of my obligation to be unhappy. Instead, she answered on the first ring, and the room behind her yawned into an aural emptiness that made the dank house seem crowded by comparison. Before I'd even said hello I was struggling to contain the guilt.

"It's me," I said, as sprightly as I could muster.

"Yes, hi."

I could hear the vigorous dabs of a paintbrush against canvas. Nonetheless I asked what she was doing.

"Working."

"Is it going okay?"

"Yeah, better than usual."

There was a long pause after this, a challenge to me to say something worthwhile. I was not up to it, and said, "So, what's up?"

"Um, Tim, did you just call to chitchat? Because you might remember that you dumped me, and now I'm trying to use all the free time to do something useful."

"Jeez," I said, already sounding like a seventh grader. "Sorry to be wasting your time."

"Used to be it wasn't a waste of time, because I could pretend it was an investment in my emotional future." Dab dab dab. "But now . . ."

"I get the idea."

"So have you anything important to discuss?"

I marveled at this arch construction: have you anything? Something new, tossed at me to show what I was missing. And in this state, I missed it. "I guess not. I only wanted to talk."

"Let me guess. You have a new girlfriend, and she doesn't fit quite perfectly into the little abscess in your heart where I used to sit."

"Fuck you, no!"

"What then?"

I sighed, stammered, already admitting defeat deep down, already chastising myself for this foolish phone call, which in the long run would only make things worse. "Okay, nothing," I said finally. "I guess I was thinking we could be friends."

"Ah," she said, "Just Friends."

"Never mind, then," I said.

"I shan't." And that was that.

*Shan't?*

.  .  .

I finally called Susan at her office after my Friday session. My fingers were so cramped from inking and re-inking the same strip over and over that I could barely hit the tiny buttons, and I dialed the wrong number once before I reached her.

"Susan!" I said.

"Hello?" A long pause. So much for never-forgetting-a-voice.

"It's Tim Mix."

"Oh, hi."

"I'm calling about the conference, and to see how you're . . ."

"It's at the Bridgewater Holiday Inn," she said, "do you know where that is?"

"Well, I know how to get to Bridgewater."

"Okay. Well, you go . . ." And she gave me unnecessarily detailed instructions, which I dutifully jotted down on the crusty block of Post-It notes that had been left by the phone. I decided to flow with the cold currents, and so earnestly parroted the traffic lights and street names and rights and lefts, tossing in an uh-huh here and there in the hope that cordiality could be jump-started.

"So . . ." I said, when she was through, "are you thinking you're going to be there, maybe?"

"Oh, no," she said. "No, I have obligations with other clients this weekend."

"Oh."

"Look," she said breezily, "I want to apologize about last weekend. That was terribly inappropriate. I hope we can put it behind us, you know, and work together civilly."

"You make it sound like we were in a fist fight," I said.

"You could say that." A long pause while that sunk in. "Look, Tim, I think that with us both coming off bad relationships and all, the last thing we need is a . . . a thing, clogging up the gears." Her voice was sick with the confrontation, however minor. "Don't you think?"

"I guess."

"So you're on a panel Sunday. 'Taking Over the Old Strips.' It's at eleven in the morning, and they said you'd find the room on the general schedule . . ."

"A panel? What do I do on a panel?"

"I dunno. You sit and talk with other cartoonists in front of a bunch of people, I suppose."

"Ah."

"Well . . ."

I felt the call slipping away from me—had I had a grip on it to begin with?—and said quickly, "So, do you have time for lunch? In New York?"

A sigh. "I really can't today, Tim, I'm sorry."

I imagined myself as a kind of Promethean figure, doomed to sit on a high peak, enduring brusque phone calls from women I have offended, every day for eternity. My crime? Bringing bathos to the mortals. "Okay," I said, taking my medicine with a whimper.


Working in the evening, I heard a car pull up into the driveway, and its door open and close. I peeked out and saw the back half of a big, brown, unfamiliar sedan. Then I heard Pierce's voice, the sound of the screen door, and silence.

Dorn had made me paranoid. I was dying to know who had come. On the other hand I didn't want Pierce thinking I was spying. I decided to wait it out and spy later, when the visitor was leaving.

I was drafting a word-mispronunciation gag. Lindy was sitting on the floor among some messily stacked books, and Timmy was standing nearby, talking to someone outside the panel (another common weirdness of FF Wurster and I had isolated during the week). Timmy was pointing to Lindy and saying, "Bobby likes strawberries and Bitty likes blueberries, but Lindy likes liberries!"

The crisp, inarguable stupidity of this delighted me. Certainly it could pass as an original FF strip, and I figured that, if I got it right, it would be included in the final packet I submitted to the syndicate. I might even bring it to Ray Burn, if Susan still felt like setting up a meeting between us. I did several pencil roughs of the cartoon, which differed mostly in terms of placement:

should Lindy be sitting on a couch or chair, or should I stick with the floor? Should Timmy be in the foreground, thus larger than Lindy, or at the same depth? I tried all the combinations, and found that Lindy on the floor, Timmy in the foreground worked best. I sketched this out three or four times, doing my best to make Timmy simply look closer, instead of unusually large. One of them looked okay, though it took me a while to figure out why: a stray line coming off Lindy's hair seemed to form a vague corner in the room, implying spatial depth. I filled in the rest of this line and added converging floor lines, and suddenly the perspective all made sense. Excited, I got out the thick paper and Wolff B. Then there was a knock on the door.

I jumped, bashing both knees against the underside of the desk. "Come in."

The door opened and in walked Uncle Mal. He was dressed, incongruously, in a pair of cutoff jeans and a loose, short-sleeved button-down shirt, and his sham black hair was mussed on the left, possibly from driving with the window open. His goofball smile was the most honest thing I'd seen all week. "I thought I'd come out and check on you," he said. "I've visited half your family today."

"No kidding," I said, rubbing my knees. They were throbbing so powerfully I thought I could hear them making a sound, a low electric hum.

"Your mom today, your brother just now. Your father's grave."

"You picked the toughies, didn't you?"

"You're no exception, it seems." His hands clasped each other behind his back, and he looked around the studio, nodding.

"How's Mom?"

He didn't look at me when he said, "Absent, mostly. Barely your mother anymore."

"I know," I said. "We took her on a picnic . . ."

"She remembered. It was all she talked about. She couldn't recall who took her, though. I thought it might be you two." He gave his head a quick shake, the way a dog does brushing off flies, then met my eyes. "So!" he said. "How's the inheritance?"

"Not so bad." I handed him the preliminary sketch. "This is the first official attempt at a cartoon."

He glanced at it a second, then laughed out loud. "Funny."

"You think?"

"Oh, yes. A good likeness, too, of your father's work. Your little pants are quite skillful." He handed the drawing back.

"I appreciate that," I said.

He spent a few seconds idly nodding. He had something to say, it appeared, but couldn't get it out. I decided to throw him a bone. "Hey," I said, "can I ask you about a legal matter?"

His face relaxed. "Sure."

I told him about Ken Dorn, about the merchandising situation with Burn Features. He nodded slowly, seriously as I talked, appearing to relish the gradual unveiling of the problem. For once I could see the appeal of attorneyhood. Problems, all problems, could be applied to an established set of rules for judgment, and solved. The answer to any dispute was there, in the books, waiting to be discovered and applied. He took a deep breath.

"Well, if money was the only consideration here, they'd go with the other guy."

"Oh," I said, crushed at having my own thoughts so succinctly voiced.

"On the other hand, you'd be surprised at how often money isn't the point." He raised a single eyebrow. "Are you going to talk to this Burn guy?"

"Apparently."

"Well, there you go," he said. "Sell yourself." He smiled a little. "If that's not too, uh, distasteful to you, of course."

I shrugged. "I'm accustomed to the distasteful."

He chuckled, then leveled, out of nowhere, a serious gaze at me. A little of the nervousness had returned, and he wiped his face with a pale hand. "So are you learning anything about your father?" He nodded toward the drawings.

"A little of this, a little of that."

"Ah! Good, good. He wasn't all bad, you know."

"I never said he was."

At this his face flushed, and I regretted saying it. "Ah, no, of course not," he muttered, backing toward the door.

"Say, Mal, I didn't mean to—"

"No, no, I'm prying in your work." He opened the door. "I just want to see how you're doing, is all. I . . . I miss you kids. Sometimes I wish . . ."

"What?" I said at last, when he had long trailed off into silence.

He jerked out of it, looked at me as if he'd forgotten I was there. "I wish you'd all been little at once, like in the strip. That would have been . . . a lot of fun."

Poor Mal, I thought: never married, a lover of children, left with such a rotten family to play surrogate parent to. Maybe he was right; maybe it would have been fun. Somewhere in the studio there was a promotional drawing my father occasionally sent to fans, of all six of us crammed into the station wagon beneath the weight of our dozen teetering suitcases lashed to the roof rack, waving toward the frame, as if the viewer were our best friend in the world. It was easy to contrast this with our actual vacations. I recalled a final one, a last gasp effort to a secluded lake in the Adirondacks: Rose was absent, having long since moved out, and Bobby, who had just learned to drive, insisted on taking his own car. It rained, our food was absconded with by forest animals, and Pierce, unable to sleep, flung rocks into the water all night long, keeping us up with the splashing. We left in waves: Bitty got sick the third day, and Bobby drove her and Mom back home. None of them returned. Pierce and Dad and I remained, locked in a proud silence, for the rest of the week, subsisting on mouse-gnawed junk food from a nearby convenience store housed in a tarpaper shack.

But now I could see that we were all Mal had. "Yeah," I told him lamely. "Yeah, that would have been something," but my face must have told a different story, because Mal only flashed a flaccid grin and walked out, making this the third—and I hoped final—conversation of the day that had ended badly.

## twenty-two

Late that night I remembered Pierce had the car on weekends. I tried to talk
him out of it, so that I could attend the conference. "Gillian could always
come out here," I told him. "I won't be around until Sunday night."

He was lying on his bed, reading a paperback novel, but put it down now
and gave this some thought. "She's never been here before."

"Well then, I'm sure she's dying to visit."

He looked at me as if I were insane. "No way," he said finally.

Instead, he agreed to drop me off at the hotel. It was far from being on
the way to Chatsworth, the Pine Barrens town Gillian lived on the outskirts
of, and I couldn't complain. The next morning, I packed a bag with the usual
items, plus a few others I thought might be useful—a sketchbook, a few things
to read—and met Pierce by the car, where he was standing with shower-slick
hair, staring into the distance. He brought nothing, it seemed, but the clothes
on his back.

We listened to the radio, an AM station that exclusively played country
classics: Patsy Cline, Johnny Cash, Hank Williams. The DJ wisely remained
near-invisible, as when he did speak it was with a quavering, spooked voice as
grave as a crow's. The station fuzzed out halfway to Bridgewater. Pierce
reached out and clicked the radio off, leaving us together in the soporific muffled hum of the Caddy's interior.

"So," I said to my brother.

"So," he said.

"What did you and Mal talk about?"

He shifted his hands on the wheel, weighing his answer. "He came out and talked to you, huh?"

"Not about you."

"Uh-huh. Well, nothing, really. Mom. Life. Et cetera."

I said nothing for a few miles, watching the trees drift by along Route 202. "He told me Mom's even worse," I finally said.

"She didn't know him."

"No."

He turned to me. "Let's bring her home, man. I'm serious. Like, right away."

I knew this was right: visits once a week were not enough. She hadn't even her memories to keep her company anymore, save for the stray, out-of-context recollection that floated every once in a while past her mind's eye. Or at least it so seemed; what did I know? I was beginning to get an inkling, through the clumsy lens of my own meager loneliness, of the vast, clinical emptiness of my mother's. "Yeah," I said, feeling my heart shrink to a tiny, cal-lused knob. "Yeah, we have to do that. Do you know the first thing about it?"

He shrugged. "No. Give her medicine? Clean her up, talk to her? What is there to know, Tim? We just give her what she needs."

"It has to be more complicated than that," I said, but he met this with only a silence that persisted for the rest of the trip.


I had no idea if Susan, in her advanced state of indifference to me, had bothered to book me a room in the hotel. I checked in at the desk to discover that she hadn't, though I decided to chalk this up to unavailability, rather than malice. It was quarter to ten in the morning. I asked the desk clerk which way the conference was, and she pointed me toward a double doorway on the left, which opened into a long hallway.

The first thing I saw entering was an enormous woman, stout and dense like a cannonball, wearing a studded leather bikini and scabbard. The latter contained an ornate medieval sword. The former contained, barely, the woman. She was standing at a chipped folding buffet table where two men sat wearing Star Trek Federation uniforms and Spock ears. The three looked up at me at once, goggling as if I was the one in the weird getup.

"Uh, is this the conference?" I asked.

"Oh, yes," said one of the men. "Are you a visitor or a participant, or what are you?"

"Mostly a visitor. I'm supposed to be on a panel."

The other man, who was smaller, began rifling through a clipboardful of papers. "What's your name?" this one said.

"Tim Mix."

A lot of shuffling and frowning. The big lady sidled off, resting a palm on the hilt of her sword. I looked down the hall in the direction she'd gone and saw a diverse and clumsy menagerie of people, bizzarely costumed: a space suit, some kind of animal with a lot of tentacles, a wizard and a witch ducking hand in hand into a brightly lit doorway. "I don't see you here," said the small Spock. "M—I—X, right?"

"Yes," I said, still watching the crowd. Then something occurred to me. "This is the cartoonists' conference, isn't it?"

"Oh, no!" said the tall Spock, and they both laughed. "This is JerCon! We're a science fiction conference! Your con is down the hall."

"Ah," I said. "Thanks."

Sure enough, there was another table at the other end of the hallway. From a distance it appeared to be staffed by contemporary earthlings in conventional clothes. I made my way past the sci-fi people, peeking into ballrooms and meeting rooms. Racks of paperbacks and comic books, loud laughs from panel discussions, where characters in and out of costume spoke from behind microphones set up on table stands. I had no trouble getting registered for the cartoonists' conference, was given a schedule and a hello-my-name-is pin with TIM MIX laser-printed onto it. Next to my name, seemingly questioning the legitimacy of my attendance, was a winking Dogberry, the wily and irreverent canine hero of "Art's Kids." I looked at my schedule. Art Kearns himself was the grand master of the conference, and would deliver a closing speech at tomorrow night's awards dinner. He would be on hand afterward to give drawings and autographs to his fans.

I scanned the list of participants, and came across some of the most famous names in cartooning: Leslie Parr, Kelsey Hoon, dozens of others I knew from my daily perusal of the funnies.

Which, I suddenly realized, I hadn't read all summer. Pierce didn't subscribe to a newspaper, and apparently neither had my dad. Oddly enough, I hadn't even missed them. I made a mental note to pick up a paper and read it sometime over the weekend, if for no other reason than to see what strips of my father's the syndicate was running, now that he was dead.

Meanwhile, the convention people had apparently gotten the news of his death too late to remove him from the list of participants. There he was, drawing and signing in the Red Room, speaking at a panel in the Blue Room, debating Tyro, author of the minimalist strip "The Emerald Forest," in the Brown Room. I wondered who they had gotten to replace him: hopefully not me. I looked at the schedule for Sunday and found:

> *9am–11am: Continental Breakfast Buffet in Ballroom B*
> *11am: Kelsey Hoon draws and signs in Red Room*
> *Panel Debate: Taking Over the Old Strips, Green Room*
> *Tyro draws and signs in Blue Room*
> *12 noon: Leslie Parr draws and signs in Blue Room*

I guessed I was to be in the Green Room at eleven the next day, and decided to attend a panel debate, to see what was expected of me. I was beginning to get excited—not just about the conference, but about cartooning and being a cartoonist. I was feeling, for the first time, a part of something.

I looked at my watch—my father's watch. Ten o'clock. According to the schedule, no panel discussions were going on. All right, fine. Somebody named Sybil Schimmelpfennig was drawing and signing in the Blue Room, and since an open door nearby bore a felt-tip-markered sign reading "Blue," I went in.

The room was not exactly empty, but it was far from its capacity of about a hundred and fifty people. There were maybe thirty gathered around a table at the front, most of them gnawing on donuts and sipping coffee from paper cups, chatting animatedly to one another. A woman sat at the table, her head of dark shiny hair bent over, twitching with the motion of her drawing arm.

It might have been a sixth sense, or perhaps just dumb logic, that made me realize this must be *the* Sybil, author of the strip "Sybil." "Sybil" didn't run in the Philly *Inquirer,* so I didn't get to read it often, but it had spawned a fairly massive T-shirt and coffee mug industry and was therefore familiar. Its basic premise was this: Sybil was a thirtyish woman who worked in an office, and she complained about things. The main things she complained about were men, clothes and food. Recurrent characters were the coworker who always had good luck with men, the department store clerk who sold Sybil clothes, and the deli clerk who made the sandwiches Sybil ate and which made Sybil fat, or so she thought. Sybil always wore black: a black blouse with a white star on the chest, and either black pants or a black skirt. The oddness of the star— what kind of office worker wore such clothes, let alone all the time?—was lost in its ubiquity. Sybil posters were almost inevitable in any office. In them, Sybil was generally seated behind a desk, the papers in her "in" box towering unsteadily over the pile in her "out," and she wore an expression of resigned exasperation. Or, in an alternate poster, usually hung in office break rooms, Sybil sat behind an enormous slice of pie, grinning coyly and saying something like "I shouldn't . . ."

I walked to the front of the Blue Room, which was not blue, stepping over a crushed glazed donut that had been ground into the carpet by someone's heel. I listened in for a moment to the conversation coming in stifled bursts through mouthsful of food. People were talking about other conferences they'd been to. Sybil herself finished up the drawing she was working on and handed it to a thickset woman with puffy yellow hair, who thanked her politely. Sybil nodded and grinned. "Any time," she said. She was dressed exactly the same as her cartoon self, down to the white star. It wasn't the usual pointy American-flag star, but a bulgy one, like a child's toy.

"Hi there," she said. "How do you want it?"

She was talking to me. I came to the table and rested my hand on the edge. Sybil Schimmelpfennig's face, the thin, translucent kind of face you'd expect would flinch whenever it was looked at, was as twitchless and composed as a hunk of marble, and frozen into a grin so fiercely welcoming that I thought she must be mad. She had an unusually large chin. I said, "Uh, want what?"

"Your drawing. What do you want Sybil to be saying? Something about your girlfriend or boss, maybe? What do you do for a living?"

I considered my answer, as Sybil clearly grew impatient. "I'm a cartoonist, actually."

"No kidding?" she said. "What strip?"

"I'm taking over the Family Funnies."

Her expression at last changed, taking on a manipulative edge that unnerved me. She looked like she knew something about me I didn't. "Ohhh. You're Tim Mix."

"Yeah."

"Sorry to hear about your dad."

"Yeah."

"Right, so . . ." Expectant smirk.

"So what?"

"So what do you want here?" She swirled her pen hand in the air, pretending to draw. It was a felt-tip, which explained the characteristic fuzziness of "Sybil." I was thrown, confused that she still assumed I wanted a drawing now that we had been established as professional equals.

"Uh, I don't know," I said. "Whatever you want."

She raised her eyebrows, making my statement seem, in retrospect, provocative. Then her hand flashed into action, squeaking across the paper like a cornered rat, leaving heads, hands, faces in its wake. She was the fastest draw I'd ever seen. She talked to me as she worked. "I'll make you as many as you want, Tim. I love doing it. I don't feel like a full person when I'm not drawing." I noticed now, clipped into her breast pocket beside the star, a row of fresh black pens. "I draw in the steam on the bathroom mirror. I walk past people's cars and draw in the dust on their doors and windows."

"Wow," I said.

She finished with a bizarre flourish, continuing the tangled loop-the-loops at the end of her signature right out into the air, where she swirled the pen around for several seconds before showing me the drawing. It was rough, but looked right out of the "Sybil" strip: Sybil sitting on a bar stool next to a man, both of them with outsized martini glasses in their hands. Both figures had those bubbles over their heads that indicated drunkenness: squeans.

"Whaddya think?" she said, twirling the pen between her fingers.

"Great," I said. "Nice squeans."

"How about you?"

I looked up, feeling the conversation veer away. "How about me what?"

"You," she said, pointing. I inspected the drawing a second time and recognized that the man on the stool was me, getting drunk with Sybil. She had rendered me with cruel accuracy, exaggerating the thinness of my face and the obstinate rumpledness of my hair, and had given my eyes and mouth the same puzzled anxiety they were likely to betray were the scene to take place in real life. "Let's get together in the hotel bar tonight. A lot of the other cartoonists are going to be there. Besides, we have a lot to talk about."

"Really?"

"Our common work, for one thing."

"Cartooning."

She handed me the drawing, which I didn't want. I folded it as politely as I could and put it in my pocket, while she moved her head from side to side, indicating my failure to pick up my side of the conversation. "Not *just.*" When I didn't respond, she threw up her hands. "Duh," she said. "We both draw *ourselves* for a living."

"Oh! I guess that's true."

"Duh," she said again, and then it was someone else's turn to talk to her.


I figured I should call Bobby, as I needed a place to stay. I found a bank of pay phones in the hallway, right in the middle of the sci-fi conference. It seemed the science fiction people, with their outlandish outfits and elaborate imaginary personae, were having a better time than the cartoonists. They all appeared to know each other from way back, perhaps from chance interactions at far-flung intergalactic spaceports, and greeted one another with everything from solemn high-fives to glottal sputterings in invented languages. Samantha answered my call with the strangely formal "Mix residence, can I help you?"

"Samantha, it's your uncle Tim."

"Hi . . ." She dragged out the word, filling up space.

"How are you doing? No school today, right?"

"It's *summer,*" she said.

"Oh, yeah. Listen, can I talk to your dad? I'm in the area and I thought I might visit."

"Is Uncle Pierce coming?"

"I'm afraid not," I said.

"Oh," said Samantha, and the phone clunked down and I heard her call Bobby.

JerCon participants passed by as I waited, leaving the smell of makeup and sweat in their wake. Close up, they looked like they had just crawled out from under damp tarps. Presently I heard Bobby pick up the phone and clear his throat. "Hello," he said, "this is Robert Mix, can I help you?"

"Bobby, it's Tim." I told him where I was and suggested we meet for dinner. "I'd love to get together with just you guys. You and Nancy and Sam."

He thought about this awhile. "Dinner," he said, as if eating in the evening were a quaint, antiquated custom, like wearing goggles while driving a car. "I don't know."

I was unable to contain myself. "Really?"

"Well. Nancy might be planning something."

"You could ask her."

"Hmm."

"I'll do the dishes."

If he was offended by this, he made no sign. "Just a moment," he said, and I heard a beep, and then some quiet, vapid music. I thought: *Hold?!?* He has *hold* at *home?* I was still sorting this out in my head when he came back on the line.

"Why don't you eat with us?" he said, like it was his idea. "We're having roast."

"Great! Can you come pick me up? Pierce has the car."

"Pick you up," he said. "Yes, okay, sure."

When we hung up, it occurred to me that I had planned to ask him other favors: if I could stay over, if I could perhaps borrow the car during the evening, to go back to the hotel. I was warming up to the drinks-at-the-bar idea. But I thought that Bobby might short-circuit under the strain of such difficult questions, and decided to hold off until we'd eaten. Until around eight, I was set. I consulted my conference schedule and stepped out, into the fray.

# twenty-three

I slipped into the Red Room, where a panel discussion was already in progress. It was called "Drawing Animals." I recognized one of the participants immediately: Kelsey Hoon. Hoon drew "Whiskers," of course. I knew him from an American Express commercial he once did, in which he ate dinner with an animated version of his cartoon cat. The cat ate everything, including the dinners of the restaurant's other patrons, who seemed unfazed by his presence: their expressions of alarm as he tipped their plates into his mouth gave way to the charmed smiles of the newly lobotomized. Kelsey Hoon had to pay for everyone's meal: thank goodness for American Express. Hoon was a round little person with thick round eyeglasses and a childish affect. In another life he might have been a zealous scoutmaster, the kind of man kids love and adults fear. He was the one talking while I found an empty seat.

"Oh, no!" he said, giggling. "Certainly you must use thought bubbles! Never speech bubbles! Animals can't talk, in the strictest sense."

There were three other cartoonists up there, identified by little name placards. Dave Guest drew an all-animal strip called "The Island," about a group of animals stranded on a desert island together. One of the characters was a seagull, who for some reason never flew off to find rescuers. I imagined that Dave Guest caught a lot of crap about this. Another cartoonist was named Jane Wooley. I had never heard of her. The fourth was Tyro.

Tyro was a young turk in the cartooning business. His strip, "The Emerald Forest," was very popular in college newspapers and urban free weeklies.

It had a cast of four: two self-loathing gay woodchucks who lived in a tree and often threatened each other with knives; a cute bunny who never spoke and who endured the unrelenting abuse of the woodchucks; and a sexy human waitress with a ruined face, named Naomi. Naomi worked at the café where the woodchucks and bunny hung out. The bunny was named Eldridge. Both woodchucks were named Laird.

Dave Guest said, "Now, Kelsey, that simply isn't true. My strip is an all-animal strip, you see, and therefore the animals can speak freely to one another using voice bubbles. There is that . . . suspension of disbelief, you see." Dave Guest was thin, his face dominated by a wide, gleaming forehead and a pointed chin. "Now our colleague from the dark side here is a different story . . ."

"Tyro!" said Kelsey Hoon. "Yes, you have both a human and animals in your strips, yet you allow them to speak to one another."

"And the bunny never speaks!" said Guest.

"Indeed!" said Hoon. "Now why is that?"

Tyro was not entirely visible from the audience, and people were craning their necks to get a glimpse. He was pale, about my age, with no hair, a hard, shellshocked face and a leather jacket. He slouched in his seat, one elbow flung up above the back of the chair.

His voice came clearly, though he was nowhere near his microphone. "It just is. That's the stupidest question I've ever heard."

"But it can be so discon*certing*, you see," said Dave Guest. A murmur boiled through the crowd. Dave Guest was grimacing, holding out his empty hands as if Tyro might put the solution to this problem right into them, like a gaily wrapped present.

"That's the entire *point,* " said Tyro, leaning forward now, the mike amplifying his voice to a stadium-style roar. "It's *supposed* to be disconcerting. That's the *point.* "

"But is that what the people want?" asked Hoon.

"I don't give a shit what people want. I'm an artist, not a goddam short order cook."

This silenced Hoon and Guest for a moment, and threw the crowd into a moderate hubbub. The previously silent Jane Wooley produced, seemingly out of nowhere, a gavel, which she banged on the table. The mikes fed back.

The crowd covered their ears. "I like 'The Emerald Forest,' " she said. "I understand Mr. Tyro's gist, if you will. His strip's not for everybody."

"You mean it's not for the hoi polloi," Guest said. "We're just not smart enough?"

"Oh, very good!" said Hoon.

Jane Wooley shook her head. "No, no! I'm just saying it doesn't have to be a popularity contest, is all." It might have been the name, but Jane really did appear wooly to me, with a thick ball-shaped head of curly hair and soft, sagging, unfocused eyes. "There aren't many humans in my strip, and the animals actually talk to each other, and they think to each other only around the humans. I'm just saying there are a hundred ways to handle this problem."

"What's your strip called again, Jane?" said Guest, and the crowd booed him. He shrugged, as if he didn't know why they were so upset.

"Now, now, David," Hoon said.

"Oh, I suppose that may have cut a little too close to the quick."

Tyro finally interrupted this with a shout. "Who cares?" he yelled. "What fucking difference does it make?" At this, Dave Guest made a stunned, offended face, the kind that is supposed to seem private but is in fact for the benefit of everyone. "I don't know what we're debating about. You people are so attached to your cute little furry animals and your goddam stupid diet jokes that you don't have the time to think about art! You don't care about ambition, or . . . or genius!" Flustered, he fell back into his chair.

Kelsey Hoon and Dave Guest leaned over the table, exchanging looks past Tyro. "Goodness, Dave," Hoon asked the microphone. "Do you know any geniuses?"

"Well, let's see, Kelsey, I don't believe I do."


I hung around afterward, listening in on people's conversations. Kelsey Hoon's voice was easy to pick out from the general din. It was nasal and high-pitched, like an electric drill. He was holding forth to a small coterie of admirers, which I situated myself on the edge of to listen.

"Oh yes!" he was saying. "There really is a Whiskers! He's a good little boy, a fat little boy." His face lit up at the mention of his cat, and the faces in the little group lit up with it, in a chain reaction of disturbing good will.

"How old is he?" someone asked.

"We're not so sure, you know, but our vet believes fifteen. Or older!" He launched into a description of the cat's daily activities, which in its advanced age seemed limited to sleeping, eating from a bowl and prowling senselessly around the apartment, bumping into things. Kelsey Hoon was riveted by all this, as were his admirers, but I could only appreciate it on the level of intense ironic detachment, which today I was not up to. I moved on.

I found Tyro lurking in a corner of the room, talking to a teenage girl in a halter top and torn jeans. She was nodding vigorously while he talked, which he did without altering his posture—a precarious slouch against the edge of a table—or expression. When I got closer I saw that his eyes were closed. He didn't open them when the girl pressed a little piece of paper into his hand and slunk away, or when I walked up to him and said hello.

"Hey," said Tyro, in a parched, uninflected voice, the kind you'd expect to hear from a gas station attendant in a backwater New Mexican town. We were standing next to the unfolded accordion "wall" between this makeshift room and the next, and I could see the motion of feet beneath it.

"I'm Tim Mix," I said. I told him I was taking over the Family Funnies. He opened his eyes at this. They were dark and small and set far apart on his face.

"Ah," he said. "The enemy."

"You were the last person I expected to see at this thing."

He hauled himself into a standing position and crossed his arms. "If I'd known you existed, I would have been expecting you, I guess." He reached into the pocket of his jacket—wasn't he overheated in leather?—and pulled out a pack of cigarettes, then lit one. This was probably not allowed, but he didn't seem worried. He didn't offer me one. "So," he said, entering into conversation with visible emotional strain. "What brings you here?"

I told him about Burn Features and the struggle for my future. I don't know why I wanted to do this. Something made me feel we were on the same side, though it was clear that Tyro didn't consider anyone to be on his side. I breathlessly asked him why he had come.

He said that his syndicate—Fake Comix, Inc.—offered to send him. "Free motherfucking weekend in hell, that's why I'm here, Tim." He inhaled deeply on the cigarette, obviously enjoying it. "I won't be back next time around, you can bet on that. I might not even be back tomorrow."

"That was some debate," I said, with more than a little irony. He didn't catch it.

"It's a minimalist strip. None of these assholes understands the aesthetic."

"Oh, I do," I said. "I was in college when you started it. It was my favorite strip."

He frowned. "What about now?"

"Now?"

"Yeah, now. Like, the present day? Or are you too busy fucking with your bread machine to taste human pain?" He threw the cigarette down on the carpet half-smoked and ground it out with his shoe.

I could easily have been offended, but I found myself sunk into a trenchant sympathy for Tyro. The fact was, I related to him personally much better than I did to his work. "The Emerald Forest" was funny, and wasn't like anything else, but was so aggressively and self-consciously bleak that it came off, to anyone over the age of twenty-two, as more than a little quaint. Case in point: a recent strip consisted of sixteen panels. In the first, Laird and Laird were joylessly hunting rabbit, with Eldridge along for the trip, smiling his customary wide-eyed, drugged smile. In the second panel they shot a rabbit who looked exactly like Eldridge. In the third they skinned it, and in the fourth they set it aboil in a pot. The next eleven panels were identical: Eldridge watched the pot, grinning. The final panel was just like the previous eleven except that Eldridge had a fat, glistening tear hanging from his left eye.

That was it. Most of the Emerald Forest strips were just like this, so earnestly, familiarly grim that looking at Tyro's work every week could become a form of comfort, like a manicure, or a pint of ice cream eaten in one sitting. In this way the strip was no different from the Family Funnies, which at least had as many as four or five gags going for it, as opposed to Tyro's one.

The crack about the bread machine took the wind out of him. He slumped back against the table. We were in the same boat: about to make a buck and glad of it. I had heard rumors that there was going to be an Emerald Forest television cartoon; in it, the Lairds were said to be heterosexual and a new character was in the works, a fast-talking chipmunk with a Japanese accent. Tyro had not publicly denied this.

"No, I still like it," I said. "Really." I reached out and touched the arm of his leather jacket. I couldn't feel a real arm under there. "Hey, do you know Sybil Schimmelpfennig?" I surprised myself at how fluidly the name rolled off my tongue, like a much-rehearsed line from a German opera.

" 'Sybil' Sybil?"

"Yeah," I said. I pulled the drawing she had made me out of my pants pocket. "She said people are going to be drinking at the hotel bar. You ought to go."

He took the drawing and gave it a cursory look before handing it back. "I hear she's a man-eater."

"I kind of doubt that," I said.


I spent the rest of the afternoon walking around, looking for Art Kearns. He was supposed to be at a debate about the thematic shift in comics after the second World War, but somebody in the Blue Room told me he had laryngitis and was roaming the Ballroom floor instead. The Ballroom was set up as a huge fair, with booth upon booth of comics dealers, merchandise hucksters and collecting freaks arranged in long rows. A few people from the sci-fi conference had wandered in, and loomed near the outer-space-related comic books, pawing over piles of rarities and obscurities tucked into acetate envelopes. I didn't see Art Kearns anywhere, although I hadn't seen a recent photo and was looking, mostly, for an old man wearing glasses.

Several times I thought that the experience would be a lot more fun with Susan around. She would have stories about people. We could get some food together, and probably she would pay for it. My missing her had manifested itself, thus far, only in terms of doing things—looking for people, eating, taking in the novel or unusual—and was therefore, I thought, safe. At the same time it seemed unwise to dwell on her. What difference did it make, I thought, if I was with her or by myself? I could have a good time alone.

And so I did, sort of. I polished off the final hours of the day sitting on a canvas stool next to one collector's booth, reading. The collector had only "Art's Kids" paraphernalia, and had apparently gone to high school with Kearns in West Lafayette, Indiana. He was a willowy, gray-haired old man with a high, mirthful laugh, and he let me flip through everything.

There was one, a full-color Sunday strip, that I read over and over. In it, Dogberry is lying on the floor, waiting to be fed. He licks his chops, scans the room just like an ordinary dog. Then, exasperated, he walks to the kitchen, opens the cupboard, takes out a can of food, opens it with an electric can opener, and dumps it into his own bowl, where he sets upon it with delighted relish. The thought bubble above him reads: "Persistent problems demand extraordinary measures."

As I walked out to the lobby to meet Bobby, that's what stuck with me: persistent problems demand extraordinary measures. That, and the image of a dog, your common retriever, effortlessly manipulating a human tool with his clumsy paws, steadying the rotating can with a single extended toenail.

## twenty-four

Bobby pulled up alone. He was wearing a pair of pleated khaki slacks, a green golf shirt and elaborate running shoes, and looked like someone he'd hire to spray insecticide on the lawn. The air conditioning in the car was going full blast and it chilled the evaporating sweat off my arms fast enough to make me swoon.

"Bobby!" I said. "It's great to see you."

"Good!" He patted my leg, just above the knee, then used the same hand to scratch his nose. He pulled out onto the road and pointed us toward Bridge-water proper. "So!" he said, frowning. "A conference, eh?"

"My editor thought it would be a good idea."

"Sure, sure. Cartoons and all."

"You bet."

There was a tape playing on the radio of some New Age music accompanied by the sound, alternately, of crashing waves, a rainforest and wind. It was like being whisked from Nantucket to Borneo to the Canadian prairie, over and over. With growing horror, I realized that we had already exhausted our supply of conversation, and I fell into a mild panic. "What's this music?" I asked Bobby, whom I had never known to listen to any music at all.

"This? Oh, my, uh, doctor recommended it. Because I get a little tense. While driving."

"Of course."

"I have another one. Whale song. Pretty serious stuff." He nodded, agreeing with himself. I noticed the cassette box lying nearby and picked it up. It was by a man named Benni Magnussen, who was pictured on the cover: long, permed blond hair and a placid Scandinavian smile. He looked slightly depraved. Bobby and I spoke at once, for perhaps the first time ever.

"You first," I said.

"Oh no, you."

"Well, I was just going to ask about Nancy and Sam. Are they doing well? How is Nancy's pregnancy?"

"They are fine," he said, frowning. "Nancy went to her female doctor last week and everything is checking out okay. Sam is a real dear." I saw his fingers uncoiling, coiling again around the wheel.

"And you?"

"I am also fine."

"No, I mean what were you going to say?"

He started. His hair, always the same length, was very still, cupping his head in thick combed waves. It was beginning to go gray and I was pleased to see that he wasn't coloring it. "I . . . well . . . I talked to Mal yesterday."

"Ah."

"He says Mom isn't doing very well." He looked at me now, his small eyes pleading.

"I suppose she isn't."

"So I guess you see her . . . often," he said.

"Fairly. Not enough, I guess."

He pushed out a theatrical sigh. "Well, enough, not enough. I wonder if she really wants to see us, being so, well . . . You know how she is."

I wasn't sure what he wanted. "What do you mean?"

He sniffed and turned his head to the side window, and I could see the neat wide V his hair made as it tapered down his neck. I bet he got it cut about once a week, and I could see him, rigid in the chair, his eyes squeezed shut, surrounded by the sound of electric clippers and hit radio. "I mean," he began, then started over: "I mean, maybe it upsets her too much, seeing all of us. I wonder if perhaps it might be best not to be bothering her all the time. She has everything she needs."

I opened and closed the empty, pristine ashtray. "Actually," I said, "Pierce and I are talking about bringing her home. So she can spend her last days there, with us."

"Oh, no no no!" said Bobby, keening over the sound of Benni Magnussen's crashing waves. "I'd advise you very strongly against that. You don't know what you're getting into, there."

"Well, I'd at least like to wait until after I get through with my cartooning classes. I'll have more time when——"

"No, I mean not at all." He was all business now, his voice taut with authority. "I think it's a terrible idea. She cannot get adequate medical care at home. She will die in misery, in pain."

"It's not like we're going to just dump her on the sofa and leave her there, Bobby."

"Of course not. For God's sake." He shook his head.

"We have some idea."

He turned to me, angry. "Do you know you'll have to do things like treat bedsores? You'll have to take her to the toilet and, and wipe her?"

"Well, yeah."

"Oh, and I'm sure you're going to do all that."

Suddenly I was on the defensive. "Of course we will, if we bring her home. And you too, maybe. It's our responsibility."

"It's the responsibility of medical professionals!" he said, jabbing his finger at the windshield with each word. "That is what we pay them for! That is their job!" After this, he had to take a moment to catch his breath. The tape switched from Waves to Wind, and he lunged for the player and jabbed at the eject button. The tape Heimliched out onto the floor. Neither of us touched it.


Samantha was standing in the middle of the yard, staring at the ground. She didn't look up when we pulled in. Bobby took a deep breath before he opened the car door, then stood up and yelled "Hi, sweetie!" in a frantic falsetto. It was as if he had been taught to greet children by a shrink who had never met any. Nevertheless Sam raised her head and smiled. "Hello Daddy. Hello Uncle Tim."

"Hey, Sam," I said.

Bobby walked to her and spread his arms. Samantha wrapped hers around his flat, sad ass. The yard, a vast slathering of fresh-cut green, dwarfed them, and they looked like lovers lost in the desert, dying of thirst. They parted. "Whatcha got there, sweetheart?"

"Nothing."

"No, on the ground there, honey."

"I was just looking."

"I mean what were you looking at exactly?" He pulled his pants legs up half an inch and crouched on the ground. He ran his hand through the grass.

"Nothing."

Bobby sighed, then stood up. I followed him to the unadorned cement porch, where he pulled out a set of keys. "She won't tell me," he said under his breath. "She never tells me anything."

I was surprised to find Nancy at home, not twenty feet from the door. Bobby closed it behind him and locked it. "Hi!" he called out to her, too loud.

"Hello," she said. She was chopping something in the kitchen. "Hello, Tim."

"Hey, Nancy," I said, and then to Bobby, "Does Sam have a door key?"

"We all do."

"You keep it locked even when you're home?" Their house was deep in the suburbs, a white ranch-style at the end of a long white gravel drive.

"You never know when the crazies will pop up."

He went to Nancy and kissed her cheek, and then turned his head so that she could kiss his. She did. Bobby and I sat down at the kitchen table, where two bottles of Miller High Life were waiting. Bobby cracked the cap on one of the bottles, then got up from his chair, opened a cabinet, pressed the foot pedal on a pink trash can lined with a plastic bag, and threw the cap in. I opened my own beer and stashed the cap in my pants pocket.

"So," Bobby said. "What're we having?"

"Roast," Nancy told him.

"I mean what veggie."

"Corn."

"I love corn." He took a swig of beer.

"Please remember to cut Sam's off the cob, Robert. I don't want to have to remind you at the table. Sam doesn't like to be talked about like that."

He rolled his eyes at me. "Okay, sure, I won't forget."


Bobby didn't cut Samantha's corn off the cob, and she sat quietly staring at it until Nancy asked him to do it. He did.

"Thank you," said Sam.

They all had a funny way of eating. They didn't speak, of course, being Mixes, but they didn't concentrate on their food the way we used to at home. They stared: not at each other, not into space, but at specific things around the kitchen, such as the clock or the window. I remembered watching television while eating with Amanda. This was a lot like that, except without the television. It was less distracting than it might have been, owing to the quality of the food—it was very tasty—and the air, which was being maintained by air conditioning at what seemed the optimum humidity and temperature for a dining family. I set to work on the roast and corn (and applesauce too, which I hadn't eaten in something like ten years) and was finished long before everyone else.

"Maybe I should make some coffee," I said.

The three of them looked up startled, at me and then at each other. Nancy finally swallowed the bite she was working on and said, "That would be just fine, Tim."

Sam and Bobby stared at her, and I pushed back my chair. "That was great food, Nancy," I said.

"Uncle Tim," whispered Sam. "We don't get up."

"Shush, Samantha," said Nancy.

"But he's getting up."

"He's a guest."

I quickly pulled my chair back in. "Oh, that's okay. I'm sorry."

"Tim, make that coffee," said Bobby. His fork, which had been interrupted in flight, still lingered there at the hollow of his throat, mounded with meat. "You're our guest. Go on," he said. "Go to it."

I did. They finished while I was working, and I turned to find the dishes cleared (how had I failed to hear this happening?) and the table re-set with coffee cups and generous servings of cake. I served the coffee and we ate the cake, which was delicious, and then Samantha silently took all the plates to the dishwasher and disappeared down the hall. Nancy produced a newspaper and set it before Bobby, who was absorbed into it in seconds. Soon after, Nancy was gone too, and the sun was going down outside, and there was only the crackling of newspaper and the distant sound of a television.

Presently Bobby looked up. "Do you want a section?" he said.

"The funnies."

He expertly slid the comics page toward me and lost himself in the Sports. I smoothed the paper on the table and read.

Suddenly, in the midst of the narrow, precarious lives of my brother's family, the entire idea of comics—their exhaustive comedic symbology, their primitive perspective, their unbreachable brevity—seemed beyond my understanding. Sybil was eating pie, then trying on a bathing suit; Dogberry was betting on catfights; Whiskers was playing poker with a small circle of mice wearing visors. I recognized that all these things were richly allusive to certain aspects of the culture, but I couldn't for the life of me figure out how. They appeared only as highly stylized, abbreviated images: a flurry of cubist arms fanned in the air over the pie pan; a dog holding dollar bills; mice sitting like humans at a tiny table. Cryptic icons from a mysterious parallel world. Then I blinked, and it all fell into place and made sense. I must have made a sound, because Bobby looked up at me. I pretended not to notice. He went back to the Sports and I read the strips.

In the Family Funnies, Bobby was watching sports on TV: diving. He was telling our father, "They'd make a bigger splash if they did cannonballs." I stared at this cartoon for several minutes, and then at the real Bobby. There wasn't much resemblance, at least not now; in the strip, we were most easily identified by our clothes. Bobby used to wear buttoned shirts and scuffed Wranglers. Now he reposed in his groundskeeper's costume. I wondered when we diverged, finally, from our comic strip selves. Was it a gradual process, or did my father wake up one day and realize he wasn't writing about his family anymore? Did each of us become imaginary at different times? Or were we real all along, honest versions of selves we had stopped being years before? It was impossible to tell. My father's work had barely evolved over the years, except to welcome Bitty and me. While Dogberry had gone from a truly dog-like dog who never had real thoughts to a pompous intellectual who walked on two legs, Dot Mix stayed exactly the same. While Whiskers had grown shorter and thicker, Lindy was always Lindy: skinny, standoffish, pony-tailed.

How sentimental my father must have been, to keep us all so static for so long. It could not have been accidental, only a laborious, obsessive, endless act of will.

I talked one of the cars—Nancy's, as it happened—out of Bobby. He seemed extremely reluctant to lend it to me, though I swore I wouldn't get drunk and promised to be back before midnight. He sighed heavily before handing over the keys. "You understand I will lose major points for this," he said, and I pictured Nancy sitting up in bed, her face slathered with cosmetic mud, briskly erasing marks from Bobby's column in a tiny spiral notebook. He told me I didn't need the house key, as I was to use the electric garage door opener to stow the car, and he told me that the opener made a lot of noise and would probably wake all of them up.

"I could leave it outside."

"No, no, I'd rather have peace of mind than a good night's sleep."

It was a perfectly normal car, a small white sedan with a neat pile of prenatal care pamphlets stacked on the passenger seat. I made several mistakes finding my way back to the hotel, and by the time I arrived it was ten, two hours from my curfew. The beer I had drunk at Bobby's, combined with the palpable tension of his house, had whet my appetite for a cold drink, and I bellied up to the bar without surveying the crowd. I ordered something dark and bitter. Off to the right was a microphone and an elaborate rack of synthesizers, set up under dim colored lights on a small carpeted stage. The words "Midnight Angel" scrolled ominously across a sequined banner.

When the bartender brought my beer I fished in my wallet for money, only to find a five-dollar bill slipped across the bar before me like a bribe. I turned and saw a fuzzy-eyed Sybil Schimmelpfennig, and behind her a tall, serious-looking guy I'd never seen before, standing with his arms crossed.

"Timmy Mix!" said Sybil. She was still wearing her name tag: *Hello my name is* SYBIL. "You made it!"

"Couldn't miss it," I said. "Thanks for the beer."

She reached across me, took her change and tried to tuck it into her black-pen pocket, but a few of the coins missed and fell on the floor. She didn't seem to notice. "Hey, have you met Lowell?"

"I don't think so." I extended my hand to the man. "Tim Mix."

"Lowell Jackson."

"You draw 'Bottle Caps,' right?"

"Yep." "Bottle Caps" was the comics' page's only black strip: all the major characters were black. So was Lowell. It was a good strip, your basic family-living-an-ordinary-and-sometimes-zany-life kind of strip, though it had not spawned the kind of merchandising mini-empire that, say, "Whiskers" or even FF had. There was an edge to it, a barely concealed anxiety that made the standard suburban, capitalist-advocacy strips like mine look slightly foolish. I told Jackson I admired his work and he nodded slowly, as if we were agreeing on a movie or restaurant we both liked.

"So you're the new man," he said.

It took me a minute. "Oh! Oh, yeah. Another couple of months, actually."

"You didn't do today's, then."

"That's a posthumous one from my dad."

He nodded again. "Spooky."

"Indeed."

Sybil was gone, off talking to a chubby middle-aged man. She laughed hysterically at something he said, bending over and clutching her stomach, and the man smiled, looking unsure of what was so funny.

"So how do you know Sybil?" Lowell asked me.

"Just met her. At the conference."

"You think she's good-looking?"

I looked across the bar at her. "Sure, she's okay," I said.

"She keeps saying she's ugly and fat. That girl is not fat."

"No." I took a sip of beer. It tasted good, thick and sharp like carbonated coffee. I wanted to change the subject. "So what got you into cartooning?"

He pressed me with a long, suspicious look. "What, because a black guy isn't supposed to be a cartoonist?"

"Well, no, not exactly . . ."

"We do read the papers, you know."

"Oh, of course, I just . . ."

He suddenly looked at his watch and then out the door, into the hotel lobby. "I gotta see a man about a horse," he said, and was gone. I watched him as he left, talked into a pay phone for a few minutes and headed for the door.

"Mix! Tim Mix!" I felt a hand clap my shoulder, hard enough to make me stumble. It was attached to a telephone-booth-shaped man in his sixties whom I'd never before seen. He looked like a retired sportscaster, with his large gold watch and a puffy red face that seemed to have had a few dents knocked out of it. "You're the spittin' image of your old man, Godblessisoul."

"Oh! Really? Well . . ."

"You know who I am? Last time you saw me you were a little shaver!"

"Ah, I can't say I do."

" 'Course, I might not've recognized you if it weren't for that name tag." He pointed. In fact, *I* was still wearing *my* conference name tag and apparently had been wearing it all through dinner at Bobby's. It struck me as extremely odd that no one had mentioned it. Then I got a funny feeling that this might be the sort of person to poke me in the face while I was looking at my shirt, and I quickly raised my head.

"I'm sorry, I just . . ."

"Les Parr! 'Nuts and Bolts,' second-longest running strip drawn by the same fella in the history of comics, thanks to that Kearns, goddam him!"

"Wow," I said. "I've read your strip my whole life."

He laughed. "Thanks, thanks," he said, though it wasn't a compliment. "Nuts and Bolts" was set in a garage in some rural backwater. All sorts of colorful country folk stumbled in and out of it each day with their dented pickup trucks and cobbled-together farm machines, and engaged Cappy, the plucky mechanic full of folk wisdom, in slangy conversation. Occasionally they all headed for the hills in search of earthy adventure, like discovering a moonshine still or shooting squirrels for stew. The humor, such as it was, depended heavily on the readers' conviction that the country was quaint and inherently funny. Apparently many people believed this, because the strip had hung on since 1945, when Cappy came back from the war. "Art's Kids" was said to have begun publication a few scant weeks before "Nuts and Bolts," and I had heard this was Leslie Parr's pet subject.

He grabbed my arm just below the elbow and leaned close, reeking of aftershave. I adjusted my estimation of his age to a particularly hale early seventies. "Your pop was a great man. A great man."

I made a little room between us by sipping my drink. "Hey, thanks."

"It's got class, that Family Funnies. Not like a couple strips I could name."

"Well, I'm really enjoying work—"

He let go my arm, leaving a hand-shaped cool spot of sweat in its wake, and formed the hand into the shape of a pistol, which he brandished before me. "You know 'N and B' really got started a year before Kearns? Had a little strip in a small-town paper in Northern California. Called 'The Shoehorn Gang.' Wasn't strictly 'N and B' but it was, whaddyacallit, its spiritual cousin." From Parr's mouth, the words "spiritual cousin" fell like lead weights at our feet. "Just because it doesn't have the same name, those ninnies disqualify it. Of course, Kearns's got 'em wrapped around his little toe. Old man doesn't even draw the damned thing anymore."

"He doesn't?"

"He's a quivering fogy!" Parr produced a drink, something clear that magnified his fingers through the glass, and downed it in a single swig. "Can barely hold a pen!"

"So who does it?"

He leaned back, gesturing in the air with his beefy arm, as if it were the entire world supporting the great fraud that was Art Kearns and "Art's Kids." "Minions! Flunkies! Whatever! Living out there on that bogus ranch of his, nodding his little white head." He reached out to the bar—what seemed an impossible distance—and slammed down the empty glass. "You and me, kid. Nothing to worry about there. We're the real thing."

. . .

It was nearly midnight when the unfolding spectacle of Midnight Angel came into full bloom, like a poisonous species of daisy. "Is this on?" asked the singer without irony. She gave her tambourine a tentative shake. She had the long blotchy nose of a border collie and cheeks sunken enough to eat soup out of. Her partner, camped out behind the synthesizers, had his shaggy head tipped back and was squeezing a bottle of eye drops several inches above his face. He turned to the crowd and blinked dramatically, his mouth hanging wide open.

I was groping for the car keys when Sybil grabbed my hand and dragged me from the bar. "Igotta showya somethin'," she said. She was drunk, but seemed not to have lost her manual dexterity. We hopped into an elevator and she pushed the button for the fifth floor. I couldn't remember the hotel being so tall. As we rode, she stared at me with a detached intensity that made me feel like I was about to be dissected. I watched my reflection in the polished steel doors.

Of course I knew what was going on: a blunt, clumsy seduction. I didn't want to be a party to it, but still I followed, stumbling puppily behind her. We went to her room. She used a little magnetic credit card to open the door, then told me to follow her to the bathroom, where she began running hot water into the tub.

I thought of Lowell's question: did I think she was good-looking? Now, watching her watch me in the bathroom mirror, I thought, Yeah, Lowell, sure she is. But she was the wrong woman. Her pocket was still full of black pens. "I'm sorry," I said, meaning it. "I can't." And I fled.

## twenty-five

It was nearly quarter to one when I pulled into the driveway at Bobby's house. The device he had given me to open the garage door was bulky and crude, considering the general level of immaculate newness in the house. It had three large green buttons on it, each the size and shape of dominoes, and looked like something the Army would use to detonate explosives in the desert. I pressed each of the three buttons and nothing happened. I pressed harder. A light blinked on and a sound issued from the garage like a piece of heavy road machinery; the door rumbled slowly up on metal tracks.

Inside the house, no lights burned. Moonlight guided me to a guest bedroom, where I assumed I would be staying. Nancy (or someone) had put fresh white sheets on the bed and stacked several salmon-colored bath towels at its foot, along with matching hand towels and washcloths. The walls were covered with beige carpeting.

There was a nightstand next to the bed. I flopped myself across the comforter, making a tremendous squeak and upsetting the stack of towels, and pulled open the drawer: nothing. I was mildly surprised, having half-expected a Gideon's Bible and a little pile of hotel stationery. It was the latter that I wanted.

I crept back into the hall. Bedsprings creaked behind a door: Bobby and Nancy? Sam? In the kitchen, I opened and closed drawers, looking for paper and a pen in the light of the digital microwave oven timer. I found both under the telephone, and a small safety envelope. Back in the guest room I undressed and got into the bed. The sheets had been tucked tightly under the mattress, and I left them that way, letting myself be sandwiched between them. It felt like I was lying at the bottom of a shallow sea. I propped my head up on the pillows and examined my implements: the pen was a black ballpoint with UNITED STATES GOVERNMENT stamped on it and the pad, perhaps a bit small for my needs, had the punchline from a lightbulb joke printed at the bottom of each page. I looked for the joke setups but didn't find any.

Dear Susan,

I'm sorry, although I don't really know what I'm apologizing for. That doesn't mean I don't think I've let you down somehow, because I have the feeling I did, I just am not sure how. If I seemed funny after the movie last week, maybe it was because I was a little drunk & tired and wasn't sure exactly what was going on. But I know I don't like this not talking, business-relationship thing, and I'm guessing you don't either, so one way or another we should see a little more of each other.

So far so good. I went to gnaw on the pen when I noticed it had been heavily gnawed on already. It took some serious biting to make those kind of marks in hard plastic, I knew from experience. Were they Bobby's? Nancy's? Sam's? It was hard to tell, in this house, where one of them ended and the next began, so uniform was the overall effect. I imagined they would all be embarrassed to know that I was using their Federal Government pen and gag paper.

I wish I could describe the way I'm feeling lately. Something like going to church when you're Jewish. Or eating dog food. Things don't seem to fit. There are things I feel I ought to be doing instead of this, but I don't know what they are. Maybe I'm a little old to be having this problem. Whatever, I keep doing it, because it's new and different, even though I'm kind of repulsed.

That was all wrong, "repulsed." Might she think I was talking about her? I paused a moment and realized that I might as well have been, though she didn't repulse me, not in the vernacular sense, anyway, the sick-to-one's-stomach sense. It was more like an empirical repulsion, the repulsion of two magnets aligned with like poles facing. Maybe all that was necessary to make the magnets do what they were supposed to was flip one around. Me. But I couldn't. Did I want her in that way? Did I want a new girlfriend? I suppose I did. Those people who said they didn't want a relationship right now because they had just come off a bad one were lying. They wanted one even more than before.

I gnawed on the pen after all: we were family. Here I was thinking about Susan, about us. It all seemed too much to expect, love, success. Happiness. I had none of them right now and would gladly settle for just one. The bottom of the page read: *Two. One to change the lightbulb and the other to change it back.*

"Hi."

It was Samantha, standing in my doorway, wearing pajamas with pieces of watermelon printed on them. "Hi," I said, whispered actually, to avoid waking Bobby and Nancy. "Did I wake you up when I came back?"

"No." She stepped in, carefully, as if into a flower bed, and shut the door behind her. "I never sleep."

"Never?"

"Almost never." She pointed to the end of the bed. "Can I sit there?"

"Sure," I said, curling my legs up under me. She climbed on and sat cross-legged next to the fallen towels. I thought she had some piece to speak, but she didn't speak it, so I said, "What do you do? When you're awake?"

She shrugged. "Think. Make up people. Sometimes I read books. Grandpa gave me a little flashlight. Before he died."

"Do you miss him?"

"Sort of." She looked up suddenly. "He's your daddy."

"Yeah."

"Are you sad?"

"Sure."

She looked away, toward the blank black window, and sighed. "What are you doing?"

"Writing a letter."

She leaned forward. "Can I see?"

"No. It's private."

"To your girlfriend," she told me flatly, obviously bored with the idea already.

"Not exactly." I twirled the pen in my hand for a few seconds. "Samantha, how are things around here? Is your dad okay? Your mom?"

"They're okay. I'm getting a sister."

I hadn't known they knew the sex. "What is her name going to be?"

"I'm going to call her Mariette."

"Ah." As with Bobby, I was running out of conversation topics. What do you say to a six-year-old? I began to get anxious that Bobby would find her here, and read something sinister or perverted into our meeting.

"Can I come visit you and Uncle Pierce?" she said. She unfolded the washcloth and put it on her head, not in a silly way but reverentially, like an old lady in church. "Maybe over school vacation. Maybe for Christmas."

This jolted me. Christmas! With my brother, at home! Not to mention Thanksgiving, Labor Day. Holidays with Pierce and Mom, opening her gifts, holding them up to her inscrutable eyes. "Sure," I said. "Any time."

"How about soon, before school?"

"Well, I have to draw cartoons. And you'd have to ask your mom and dad . . ."

She took off the washcloth and dropped it on the pile. "Yeah, yeah," she said, and slid off the bed. I felt jilted, as if by a lover.

"Goodnight," I said weakly.

She turned, ran back, stretched out to me and gave me a kiss. "Sleepy dreams," she said, and hurried out the door.


In the morning everybody ate cold cereal. The options were dumbfounding: every sugar-rich concoction under the sun, each represented by a jolly mascot. I ate the cereal formerly known as Super Sugar Crisp, which in this enlightened age had become Super Golden Crisp, its public image transformed from cheesy harbinger of tooth decay to precious Incan artifact. My mouth ached, but I scooped out every last drop of cloying milk. Looking around the table, I could see the same expression of awe on everyone's face; it was the only moment of unqualified joy I had witnessed under this roof.

My letter was finished, sealed and stamped, thanks to a booklet of self-adhesive American flags I'd found in the kitchen drawer; I left some change for the postage, feeling I'd taken enough already. Now the letter was in the pocket of my jeans, awaiting a mailbox.

After breakfast, I thanked Nancy. She nodded gravely, her eyes still luminous from the sugar high. I kissed Sam on the cheek and she accepted with grace. "Tell Uncle Pierce hi," she said.

"You bet."

"Tell him I love him!" This was irony, something I'd never before heard from Sam, but which seemed to fit. Nancy and Bobby didn't recognize it as such. Expressions of unease overpowered their faces.

"I will," I said.

Bobby drove me back to the hotel. He was strangely chatty. I wondered if he was always like this mornings, before the day defeated him. "Too bad you can't come to the plant. I ought to show you around sometime."

In fact, there was no reason I couldn't go, except that I hadn't been asked. "That would be great."

"Show you the sterile radiating units, they're something else. Had to order them special from Switzerland. And the shredder, which actually is called the homogenizing refuse deintegrator, but we call it the shredder."

"Yikes."

"Oh, it's all perfectly airtight, perfectly clean. Smells like a doctor's office in there, no kidding."

"I don't doubt it."

"Like a trip to the doctor's," he said, apparently to himself. We were silent for a while.

"Sorry I came in late," I said.

He waved this off. "Barely noticed."

"Good."

"So, Tim. Think about what I said yesterday. About Mom."

"You bet."

"I know you think it's the right thing. But you're only doing it for your-self, to feel good about yourself. That's no reason to take an old lady away from the place where she'll be safe."

I wondered if Bobby had really looked at the nursing home. The degen-eration of people's bodies, the madness, the unrelenting smell of urine. I said, "Well, that's food for thought."

We had come to the hotel. A woman with antennae walked into the re-volving door with a man in a robot suit. Bobby didn't appear to notice.

"So keep in touch," he said.

"I will."

We shook. "That was a great visit."

"Sure was."

He nodded. "Okay, right. See you, bro."

I got out of the car, straining to come up with a response. "Right on," I told him, and shut the door. The sound it made was quiet as a breath.


I was among the first to arrive for my panel. To my surprise, there was a name placard already in place for me, along with three others: Bennett Koch, Lynn Bismarck and Ken Dorn.

I actually did an authentic double-take. Ken Dorn? I didn't think he'd ever had his own strip before. The other people I knew of only vaguely: Koch's strip, "Pangaea," had a lot of cute dinosaurs in it, and Bismarck's was one of those serial soap-opera things, the kind that now invariably looked like Roy Lichtenstein paintings, I forgot the name.

But Ken Dorn! I began to get a creepy feeling, like he'd been planted. I entertained the notion that he had somehow replaced me without my know-ing: had I been betrayed by the Burn Syndicate's corporate honchos? Or by the woman I possibly sort of loved? I took the sealed letter from my pocket and turned it over in my hands. I felt like a fool, and thought about tearing it to pieces.

"Timmy Mix. Fancy meeting you."

He was beginning to grow a tiny mustache and goatee, and had gotten his hair shaved closer to his head. "I'd imagine you're brimming over with insights from your training, mmm?"

"Hello, Ken," I said, stowing the letter. "Oh, I don't know."

"Don't know? You haven't taken any notes?" He reached into the pocket of his pants and pulled out a small stack of 3x5 note cards, fastened with a rubber band. "I've been thinking a lot about this. The issues are compelling indeed."

"Well . . . I've never done anything like it before."

"I would suppose not."

"So what strip have you taken over?" I said, trying to sting him. He looked off into the air, though, and crossed his arms in a pose of mock contemplation.

"Oh, I've taken over the inking for a few. But I'm most interested in taking over full creative control." He raised his eyebrows and turned to me, grinning. "Someday, that is."

"Oh, sure," I said, crossing my own arms. I was almost a full foot taller than Ken Dorn. *Push him over,* I thought.

"I was talking to Ray the other day, and he seemed quite impressed with my drawings. I didn't have anything prepared, of course, but it was no trouble dashing off a few sketches . . ."

"Ray? Ray Burn?"

"Yes, Ray Burn. A good man, wouldn't you say, Timmy? What did you talk about the last time *you* saw him?"

I cleared my throat. Dorn leaned back and plucked from a chair a glazed donut and a cup of orange juice. "Well," I said, "he told me I'm the sentimental favorite."

Dorn took a large bite of donut, laughing from behind his closed lips. "So you are," he said, chewing. "So you are."

"Where did you get those?"

"These?" he said, holding out the donut and juice. "There was a table in the hall. Participants only!"

"Then you'll excuse me," I said.

"Of course! See you behind the mike!"

. . .

Everyone seemed to have donuts and juice but me, and if there had been a table in the hall, it was gone now. I stood helpless among the conventioneers, squinting into various rooms. Finally I gave up and was turning to take my place in the Green Room when I saw him at last: Art Kearns.

Kearns was being escorted by a jowly middle-aged woman wearing an "Art's Kids" T-shirt. He clenched her arm with one hand and a scuffed wooden cane with the other. Both hands, along with the rest of Art Kearns, were shaking. He was a large man, even in this sad, crumpled state, still bearing the profile of the Wyoming cowboy he was said to have been before he became famous. He wore a white shirt and bolo tie, and a pair of dirty black jeans; his head was nearly bare, with a little red knoll of blotchy skin poking up through his hair. He was blinking, blinking, blinking his eyes, as if something tiny and painful was lodged under both lids.

He and the woman moved slowly, and they commanded much of the hallway's attention. A few people even set down their donuts and juice to quietly applaud. As they passed me, Kearns raised his head and his eyes met mine. He winked. I couldn't help grinning.


Ben Koch had two donuts, but didn't offer one to me. Lynn Bismarck had only juice. Dorn was finished eating. He and I sat next to each other at one end of the table, while Koch and Bismarck chatted animatedly like college freshmen, obviously falling for one another.

"Oh, you're from Ohio too! Which town?"

"Sandusky."

"Oh, you're kidding me. I have an aunt in Sandusky."

"Really!"

"Ida Loos."

"Well, I'll just have to ask my mother if she knows her. Do you get back much?"

"Not much."

"Well, we'll have to go together sometime!"

"Why not?"

Dorn was oblivious to them, transfixed upon his notes. I tried to peek at them, but his handwriting was indecipherable: thin lines of what looked like chocolate ice cream sprinkles. Several times he laughed privately or raised his eyebrows. I watched the room fill up and wondered if Tyro would come, until I remembered he was drawing and signing in the Blue Room. It was difficult to imagine him doing such a thing.

Koch had the gavel. He whacked it happily on the table, paused a moment to giggle with Lynn, then announced in a loud voice, "Welcome, everyone, to 'Taking Over the Old Strips.' " People clapped. He introduced Lynn and her strip, then Ken Dorn, "who has helped produce some of our finest work for over fifteen years." Dorn nodded. "And at my left," Koch said, "is, I believe, Tim Mix, who you all know as Timmy in the Family Funnies. Let's give him a hand."

People clapped, harder than they did for Dorn. I raised my hand, scanning the crowd for a familiar face. Thus distracted, I stopped waving a few seconds too late.

"Now," said Koch, "let me introduce our topic." He went on at length about the cartoonist's responsibility to his legacy, that perhaps an inherited strip is at best shared with the deceased. He pointed up the need to be honest about making people laugh. "Or cry," he said. "Emotions are serious business. People depend on their funnies. So. There you have it. Does anyone have a question?"

A man stood up in the audience. "I have a question for Tim Mix," he said.

Koch leaned over the table and shot me a smug smile. "Tim?"

"Uh, sure," I said. "Go on." My meek voice boomed out across the crowd and I pulled back a little from the mike and cleared my throat.

"What's it like, drawing yourself? Is it, you know, weird?"

"Uh, not really. I don't think of it as me, really. Timmy's just, you know, a kid. I'm, uh, an adult."

A ragged laugh went up. I didn't understand why.

"Mr. Mix?" somebody asked. "Did your father train you?"

"No. No, he didn't. I'm . . . I'm still learning, actually."

A brief mumble, like a spattering of rain. Then I watched as a large man hauled himself to his feet in the fifth row, pulling up his overalls as if he were about to go out and slop the hogs. His arm pistoned into the air. Ben Koch pointed the gavel at him.

"Tim," the man said, "now you know there's a cartoonists' union, isn't there? Are you a member of it?"

Silence. *Cartoonists' union?* "Uh, no," I said, "not yet. But I'm not actually going to start the strip until . . ."

"And isn't it true your father was never a union man? If I got it right, a few people weren't exactly disappointed your old man, ah, wasn't able to make it to this weekend's festivities."

My head began a mild, plaintive ache. Voices simmered up across the room, and the man's voice carried over them. "A lot of people here would rather see a union man take over, see, especially since your dad wasn't particularly known for hiring from the union. Or from anywhere at all, for that matter. He was, whadyacallit, an outsider, wouldn't you say?"

"Well, uh . . . I suppose he was kind of . . ."

"Sir, sir," came Dorn's voice from beside me, "ladies and gentlemen, please. Let's not gang up on our young man, yes? I'm sure Tim has considered all these important issues, haven't you, Tim?" He laid his hand on my shoulder and patted, gently.

"Sure. I . . ."

"I think we ought to take this opportunity—a great classic's change of hands—to discuss what must be done, what we must do, to perpetuate the great tradition of the funnies." A dull snap as the rubber band came off his stack of note cards. "Let us consider the Family Funnies' place in the canon of daily strips, namely, its role in establishing and solidifying those values the American family holds dear . . ."

And he was off, dodging and parrying probing questions in my defense, explaining how the Family Funnies was written and why it was written that way, and what he would do—in the unlikely event he would draw it—to keep its feet planted firmly on virtuous ground. It was a crock of shit, but I was dead in my seat, all resolve evaporated. The large man was gone, slipped away in the commotion. Lynn and Ben whispered sweet nothings to each other, their snacks left unfinished. And Ken Dorn held the floor, a self-taught expert on my comic strip.

When it was all over, I bummed a cigarette and found a back door to slither out through. I wondered what I thought I was doing, why I had thrown away a perfectly reasonable, if imperfect, life to act out this elaborate failure. The cigarette tasted awful, as a cigarette does when employed as a side dish to a generous helping of self-pity.

It didn't take me long to spy Dorn lurking next to a dumpster at the other end of the building, handing something to the large man from the Green Room. They finished their transaction and parted. The man got into a pickup truck, and Dorn ducked back into the hotel through a green steel door.

I stubbed out my cigarette underfoot, sick of myself, and slunk back inside.

# twenty-six

The Kearns event was a buffet dinner, keynote speech and drawing/signing, to be held in the Grand Ballroom down the hall. It wasn't to start until four-thirty, and I was hungry beyond description. The morning's cold cereal had rushed through me like an electric pulse, leaving behind a dry, slightly scorched taste in my mouth and a yawning gulf in my stomach, though I realized that part of this was probably from making a fool of myself—of being made a fool of—in the Green Room. I set off in search of food, taking a detour at the men's room in the lobby.

Inside, I realized I wasn't alone. This is always obvious in a public restroom. In gangster movies, people often hide from the hit men by standing on toilet seats in lavatory stalls, but to me, such scenes are highly implausible. Every surface in a restroom reflects and amplifies sound. Air currents shift at a human body's slightest motion. In this case, a specific smell tipped me off: the dank, vegetative odor of pot. I ignored it and picked a stall, sat down and did my business, trying to minimize the noise. I got out and washed my hands.

In the mirror I could see a pair of black boots and the cuffs of black jeans, motionless under a stall door. I took a gamble.

"Tyro?"

"Hello, Mix."

There were no paper towels. I forewent the hot air dryer and wiped my hands on my pants. "How's it going?"

"It's fucked," he said. "Want a joint?"

Why not? "Sure," I said.

There was a rustle, then a fat white cigarette rolled across the floor at me, shedding marijuana like a molting pigeon. A lighter followed it, clattering across the tiles. I picked them both up and sat in the stall adjoining Tyro, where I committed my misdemeanor. It had been years since I'd hung out with anyone who smoked. I felt like a greaser.

"I got humiliated today," I said, passing the lighter under the dividing wall.

"It's got around."

"Already?"

"Sybil told me." I heard a deep breath. "She's pissed at you, buddy."

"We had a little misunderstanding."

"Let me guess. She tried hustling you and you wimped out."

"Sort of," I said. "Maybe it was a mistake." I could feel the unsent letter crackling in my back pocket. I considered flushing it down the toilet.

There was a long pause before he said, surprising me, "I like her, but she's too depressed for me. Women read my strip and they think I'll wanna sit around quoting Nietszche with 'em."

"You don't?"

"Hell, no." After a minute, he added, quietly, "It's an aesthetic, not a *Weltanschauung.*"

I smoked awhile in silence, waiting for the pot to take effect. I concentrated, vigilant for changes in my mood. It wasn't until I was thoroughly fed up that I realized I wasn't fed up at all anymore, and the stall suddenly seemed like a perfectly reasonable place to be, with the walls verdant and mildly reflective and a pool of clear water beneath me. I said, "I think I'm falling for this girl."

"Not Sybil."

"Not Sybil."

"So what are you doing here?"

"Being a dick," I said, stunning myself with my crassness. I scrambled to soften it. "I guess."

He coughed. "Want to get something to eat?"

I dropped the end of the cigarette into the toilet. "You bet," I said.

We got microwaved burritos at the Kwik Stop adjoining the hotel, and ate them out on the curb. I couldn't fill myself fast enough, and ended up going in for another. Tyro watched people walking in and out of the store and made up secret obsessions for them. "Ass freak," he said. "Angora goatfucker." I put my head in my hands and watched spilled gasoline trace prismatic amoebas in a puddle of water.

"So Mix," Tyro said. "Why are you doing this shit?"

"Cartooning?"

"No, animal sacrifice."

I didn't want to talk about it. "Hard to say," I said.

"Is it the money?"

Of course that was part of it, but if money was all I ever wanted, I would probably have it already. The truth was that my life was fine, and could have stayed fine indefinitely, but I didn't want fine, I wanted great. So I had to change something. But I had no guiding ambition, and in my fumbling for one seemed to have traded fine for pathetic. I was feeling like I could spend years just trying to get things back to fine again. I wouldn't have said this to Tyro even if I could, at that moment, have formed the complex sentences necessary to do so. All I said was, "Not really."

"So why? Why are you so interested in the Family Funnies?"

"It's my family," I said.

"You're telling me that strip is more interesting than the genuine article?"

"There is no genuine article." This had the ring of gloomy, fatalistic truth to me.

Tyro shook his head. "Bullshit," he said.

We went to the buffet together. I was still hungry, even after the burritos, and loaded my plate with Italian sausage and pierogies, which anywhere else in the world but New Jersey would have been an unacceptable contradiction. We sat at a table with some Fans, who didn't talk to us. Many of them wore Dogberry T-shirts, with Kearns's looping signature under the drawing.

"I hear he still has horses on the ranch."

"Is that so? Does he ride?"

"Oh, I'd imagine he must. Wouldn't you?"

"Well, naturally."

I watched Tyro eat. His exterior calm was astonishing, though it was clear this was not his natural, primeval state: under the table his feet twitched to an obsessive internal rhythm, and he fussed at his jeans and shirt surreptitiously, not out of vanity, it seemed, but of minor yet irrepressible discomfort. I could guess at his childhood: pure nerd until his junior year in high school, when suddenly he became bony and dangerous, a sexual beacon to girls who months before would have had nothing to do with him—cheerleaders, honor students. It made him wary of people who expected things from him. He ignored the Fans and absorbed himself in his food until Kearns was introduced by, of all people, Leslie Parr.

Parr stood massively on the plywood stage, hunched over the lectern like an Army colonel preparing to outline battle plans with his quirt. What he said about Kearns probably looked respectful enough on paper—some saccharine blather about the strip's immeasurable influence and timeless appeal—but his voice reeked so strongly of contempt that I half-expected riot. Nobody else seemed to notice, though.

"Of course, I could stand up here yammering all day, give y'all time to polish off that chicken tertrazzini or whatever you got there"—polite laughter—"but you wanna see the genuine article, and lucky for you we got 'im right here, the mangy old goat of the funny papers, Art Kearns!"

Thundering applause, from all quarters including mine. My cogitations on the curb, which already in the glum aftermath of artificial stimulants seemed no more or less significant than a low-wattage light being switched on in a musty attic full of junk, had no effect on my slavish devotion to Kearns, whom I still considered tack-sharp and dignified, even in his weakened state. His progress to the lectern was prolonged and excruciating, and the applause flagged and reinvigorated several times before he finally arrived, supported by his assistant. She took a moment to steady him before the mike, then sat down upstage on a folding chair.

"Well thanks," said Kearns, his voice thin and crusty as an old piece of wire, and everyone clapped again. Tyro picked up a sausage with his fingers and chomped off a thumb-sized chunk.

"It's a real honor, speaking to you here. I've been in this business a long time. Longer'n you can imagine. And I've drawn a lot of strips, for sure. But it's all 'cause of you all that 'Art's Kids' is still popular. 'Smuch as it was fifty years ago." His oratory trickled out over the crowd like a leak in a cellar wall. All his sentences were of uniform length. I looked around me and found people eating quietly, cleaning off their eyeglasses or squinting earnestly at Kearns, as if in an effort to see the words better. I waited for the introduction to stop and his speech, per se, to begin. But minutes passed, and pretty soon he stopped talking, and after a pause that lingered a beat or two too long, everyone caught on that this had been his speech, it was over, and it was time to start clapping. So they did. Kearns turned from the lectern and his assistant leapt to her feet to support him, and together they walked off, to further applause.

Les Parr was quick to retake the mike. "All right!" he screamed, as if it had not been Kearns on stage at all, but Elvis Presley. His grin was less celebratory than triumphal, and he pointed at Kearns's receding form with what looked, from where I was sitting, like open mockery. "Y'all finish eating, and Art's gonna move over to this table here"—he pointed to where some people were unfolding a buffet table, stage right—"and draw y'all some pictures, okay? All right, let's give the old boy one more hand!"

More clapping, weaker this time. Kearns, who had nearly made it to his seat, half-turned and accepted it, nodding. And then the noise retreated into scabrous mumbled conversation and giggling. Tyro held up his empty plate and nodded his head at it.

"Seconds?" he said.

Afterward, I wanted to wait and meet Kearns. Tyro would have none of it. "I'm history," he said. "More than thirty-six hours in Jersey gives me the willies."

"I understand," I said.

To my surprise, he stuck out his hand to be shook. It was an ironic gesture, accompanied by a pompous fake smirk, but his grip on my fingers was strong and honest. "It was good meeting you, Mix. I thought I'd have to hate everybody."

"Glad to be of service."

"Let me know how things go," he said.

"You'll see me in the funny papers."

He made a face. "Shit, Mix, I can't read that trash. Drop me a note or something."

"Yeah, sure," I said, but we didn't exchange addresses or telephone numbers. He didn't say goodbye either, only made a little pistol with his hand, cocked his thumb and shot me right between the eyes.


The line to see Kearns was nearly fifty yards long, but I got in it anyway. People seemed to be holding things for Kearns to sign or draw on. Was it possible that there was no paper for the cartoonist?

"They ran out," someone told me. "He keeps making mistakes and starting over."

"So, do you have anything . . . extra? You could give me?"

His name tag read STEVE GOPP, WASHINGTON POST. "Nah, I just got these two." He held up a couple of magazine subscription cards, one with a grease stain on the corner. "One of 'em's for my kid."

I scanned the floor for dropped programs or dinner napkins. My own program had somehow gotten away from me. The line, which had seemed stuck, was moving now, and as I came closer to the table I set to the task of persuading myself that asking for autographs was crass and demeaning, and a handshake and pleased-ta-meetcha would be sufficient. Then I remembered I had some paper with me after all.

"Now, you look familiar," Kearns said to me, smiling. His right eye was milky with growths and it was a wonder to me that he could see at all.

"I'm Tim Mix," I said. "Maybe you knew my father Carl. He drew the Family Funnies."

"Nah, that ain't it. You look like my granddaughter's boyfriend. You ride a motorcycle?"

"No, sir."

He nodded slowly. "Kill yourself on one of them things. So," he said. "Whatcha got for me?"

I pulled the envelope out of my pocket and set it on the table in front of him. He turned it over and read the address. "To your sweetie?"

"Kind of."

"Well, we'll give you a little something for luck here." He brought his felt-tipped marker to the envelope and began to draw. His hand shook, teetering at the very edge of his control. When lines appeared, they did so in a rhythmic fuzz, like pipe cleaners bent into shapes by a child. For some time, I waited for the patterns to become recognizable, then finally gave up. Eventually Kearns handed the envelope back to me.

"There you go," he said. "Little shaky, but it's the real McCoy."

"Hey, thanks," I said.

We shook hands. It was like grabbing a branch. "No problem," he told me. "Whatever you got yourself into with that girl, this oughta straighten it out."


Out in the hall, I studied the marks on my letter, trying to decode them. A continuous line, a blobby, smeared amorphism, a hieroglyph at the bottom that might have been a signature. I wondered who, exactly, was drawing "Art's Kids." Had the inkers taken over? Did Kearns even write the gags? The drawing might have been of Dogberry, or of Greta or Funny Hans or Derrie-Do or any other "Art's Kids" characters. Or it might have been the Empire State Building or Richard Nixon.

I surprised myself with my enormous and inexplicable affection for Art Kearns, which was springing up inside me like a kiddie pool filling with water from a hose. I stood very still and let my mood improve. When I felt like a human again, I unpinned my name tag and threw it in the trash, then brought the letter to the front desk to be mailed.

## twenty-seven

Pierce had something on his mind. The Caddy's windows were closed and the air conditioning on, and no music played on the radio. When I shut the door he said nothing, so I said "Hey," and Pierce said "Hey."

He pulled away from the hotel parking lot. "How's Gillian?" I said.

"Oh, you know."

"Not really."

He didn't seem to hear, only grunted and nodded at the sound of my voice.

To fill the time, I played back every disappointing and humiliating event of the past week in my mind, with special attention to the precarious blown moments on the sidewalk outside the movie theater with Susan, and my ignominious retreat from the conference. I thought about the way Susan wobbled from side to side, waiting for me, possibly, to stop her with an arm curled around her waist or an offered hand; the fat man's bushy eyebrows, their blurry meeting place over his knurly red nose. I got myself pretty worked up. I stared at the door, wondering what it would be like to open it and fling myself out onto the pavement, if I would tumble under the Caddy and be pulverized by its wheels, or if I'd spend the rest of the day at the hospital having road gravel pulled out from under my skin by a knock-kneed intern with a pair of sterilized tweezers. I was beginning to shift myself toward the center of the car when Pierce said, "What if it's some sort of trap?"

"What?" For a second I thought he was talking about the car door.

"What if he's laid a trap for me?"

"Who?"

He was frowning the panicked, spasmodic frown of a child about to cry. "Dad."

"Dad?" I said. "Why would Dad lay a trap for you?"

"The key," he said. "It's in a warehouse, right? In Philadelphia. What if it's some kind of trap? It could be a bomb, or like you know those corporate guys who set up a kind of pulley system so that when they intercom their secretary and tell her to come in, she opens the door and it trips a wire that's attached to a shotgun and boom, suicide. Something like that."

For the briefest of moments, this scenario seemed perfectly plausible, and I lost myself long enough in it to delay speaking. Then I said, "Um, Pierce, that's ridiculous."

"Oh, is it?"

"Why would Dad want you dead?"

"He hates my guts."

"Hated," I said. "And he didn't, really." Though there was precious little evidence for that. Pierce extended his arms against the wheel and pushed his head into the seat, as if buffeted by massive g-forces.

I said, "If he hated you so much, he wouldn't have left you the house, or any money to live on."

He seemed to consider this. I thought he was going to speak, but he didn't, not for a long time. He stared at the road, driving with enormous concentration, his lips pressed together and his chin creased. Finally he said, "You know what I was just thinking?"

"No," I said, with a certitude intended to reassure.

"I was thinking how weird my life is. Compared to other people's."

"How so?"

"Well, you know what people are always after. Like, success, I guess. Jobs and love and getting famous and getting elected. And I was just thinking how much I'd like to have those things as goals. I mean, I don't care so much about actually getting them, you know. I just want them to be *goals.*"

I had missed something. "So why aren't they?" I asked him.

He sighed, and I knew that I'd let him down. "Never fucking mind."

"No! No, I'm sorry, I just don't understand."

He spoke with bitter intensity, straining to mask his emotions. "I don't get to have those kinds of goals. I get to try to get out of bed in the morning, and half the time I don't. I try to have a conversation. If I get up, I think, okay, I'm not going to smoke so many cigarettes today, and I'm going to have a conversation, and it's going to last something like ten minutes. I try to open the door to my bedroom. Mostly I can do that, if I've gotten out of bed, and that's pretty great, a thing I can be successful at almost every time I try it." He wiped off his face, which had begun to shine. "Yesterday I dropped you off and today I picked you up, and in between I went to my girlfriend's. I mean, do you know what that's like, being able to do that?" His hands were shaking now, and he held the wheel more tightly, and then his arms were shaking.

"Maybe I should drive," I said.

Pierce took a minute to think it over. "Yeah, okay."

He pulled over and we switched places. For a long time he kept shaking. It wasn't until we had reached the North Side of Riverbank—MIXVILLE read the new green sign—that he asked me, "So how was the conference?"

"It was really great," I said.


I got to work quickly, forcing myself to draw. It had only been two days, but it felt like weeks, and the lines came out wrong every time, veering off cock-eyed or going on a little too long before stopping. The characters were weirdly foreshortened or stretched in odd directions, and their faces gaped blankly out from the page like stickmen's. It was obvious that whatever zeal I'd built up had dissolved over the weekend, and I was only going inexpertly through the motions. All night I tried to get it back, whatever "it" had been, and by two a.m. I had, if nothing else, burned the neural networks more or less back into place. I could draw the Family Funnies again.

Back in my room, this seemed a dubious achievement. I reasoned with myself for several more hours. Did anyone like their jobs? People got dressed every day, went to the office, earned money, but they didn't like it, did they?

They simply did it, because they had to. At least I didn't have trouble getting out of bed in the morning, or opening the bedroom door.

The next morning Wurster could tell that something had changed. He drilled me mercilessly, making me draw the same strip over and over while he walked around the house, tending to his cats, yelling weirdly perceptive instructions and corrections at me from other rooms. But all I could think about was the fact that my letter was being picked up, brought to the post office and sorted by state, bundled with the other New York mail and loaded onto trucks, driven up the turnpike and into Manhattan. I drew my sisters, my brother, my parents, myself. I drew dogs and cats and trees and houses, popsicles and hamburgers and bicycles. I reinvented the language, the props, for a fake drama, enacted by a false family. And I was still doing it the next day when my letter was sorted into a tray and given to a carrier, tucked into a bag and dumped at the front desk of her building, carried to the Burn Features mail room and pushed into her box, then delivered on a cart to her desk, facedown. She sees the bleeding, smeared drawings first, the unintelligible signature, then turns it over. She reads the return address. She opens it, reads it.

She didn't call me that day, or Wednesday or Thursday. Wurster and I worked on the cartoons I'd bring Ray Burn for our meeting. They were fine, as good as I could do, but it made me sick to look at them.

"What is it?" I asked Wurster. "Tell me what the problem is, here."

He shrugged. "There's no problem."

"Of course there's a problem," I said. "Look at them!"

A cat hopped up onto his lap. He lifted it by the belly with great gentleness and set it down on the floor, where it moved off sniffing like a child's electric toy. Then he regarded my current drawing yet again and emitted a tired sigh. "I guess it depends on your standards, Tim. If you're comparing it to your father's work, it's fine. Considering you couldn't draw a month and a half ago, it'll do just fine."

"And?"

He scowled at me, obviously irritated. "And if you're comparing it to Degas, you mean? Well, what do you think? Then it's crap."

He shrugged, fell back in his chair. That wasn't quite what I meant, but I could see why he was upset. I never wanted to be a cartoonist, and he was turning me into one in a matter of months; meanwhile he'd wanted it all his life and could never make it work. I watched him staring at me for a while, then picked up a fresh piece of paper and started inking a new draft.

That afternoon, a Friday, I came home to find the answering machine light glowing with disheartening steadiness, and in a spasm of loneliness resolved to visit my mother. It was not yet dark, but it would be soon, and sitting out in the studio I felt a strange urgency, as if this impending visit, which had no specific purpose, was as important a mission as I'd ever undertaken. I turned off the lights and locked the door, then went to find my brother, whom I didn't want to come along. He was on the patio, staring at the shrubs that separated our yard from the Praegels'.

"How's it going?" I asked him. Ice cubes melted in a sweaty, empty glass on the ground beside his chair.

"Not bad. I've been out here for something like three hours without panicking."

"Good, good."

"Look there," he said, pointing through the bushes.

I saw a form, moving slow circles around the yard. "Yeah?" I said.

"That's Anna. She's been out there as long as I've been here. I think she might be naked."

"No kidding?" I squinted but couldn't make out any specific organs through the branches.

"I think she's going nuts. Isn't that sad?"

"It is."

"Maybe I should talk to her or something."

"That might be a good idea," I said. "Pierce. I'm going to visit Mom, okay?"

He looked up at me. "Okay."

"You're all right alone for an hour or two?"

"Sure."

He watched me a moment, expectant, but I had nothing to give him. I said goodbye and went in to get the car keys.

. . .

It was nearly dark by the time I got to Ivy Homes. One shift was apparently ending and another beginning. Nurse's aides in white pants and blue blouses filed in and out of the building like factory workers, and people picked them up and dropped them off in shabby old cars. I wondered what they made per hour, how long the average tour of duty was, if any of them lasted longer than a year. They were all young—misanthropic-looking student types, summering with the senile and terminally ill.

The attendant at the desk was eating tortilla chips from a colorful bag and watching a sitcom on a tiny TV. She told me visiting hours were long over and that I should come tomorrow. I went back out.

My mother's window was on the side of the building that faced the parking lot of a strip mall. I walked around, past lit rooms where blue figures passed, fussing over the residents, until I stood in a scrappy patch of juniper, looking in my mother's open window. She was watching TV from a wheelchair, and a book was open on her lap, exactly like there had been at home when I was a child. She used to sip from an iced glass of some vile liquor and read during commercials. Seeing this moved me, and I felt like I was in a dream, the kind in which dead relatives return, alive and healthy, and explain that everything, the hospital, the funeral, was a misunderstanding. I tapped on the glass.

She turned and looked through me. "Mom," I whispered, and tapped again.

She wheeled herself over to the window and tapped back, her face expressionless and infantile. I was beginning to think I had done a disastrously cruel thing when she reached up, scrabbled at the catch, and tried to open the window.

It was a terrible sight. She had little leverage with her knees wedged between herself and the wall, and had to splay her elbows on the sill to pull up on the handle. "Stop," I said through the glass. "Mom, stop." But she didn't stop. I could hear her thin grunts, mixed with the sounds of cars pulling in and out of the strip mall. Behind her, in the room, her door stood half-open, and aides walked past, oblivious.

When she had the window open a crack, I wedged my fingers under and pushed up, and the window leapt as if loaded with springs. My mother's face opened up like a treasure chest, and she let out an elated cry. "Come on," she said. "Nobody will know."

I looked behind me and saw no one, so I hoisted a leg up onto the sill and climbed in. The room looked different at night, not so sterile. A table lamp cast a comfortable light. There were flowers on the dresser and I wondered who sent them.

"Hi Mom," I said. I kissed her cheek. Her skin, usually so dry, was hot and moist, as if I had awakened her from a feverish dream.

"Oh! Don't call me that."

"Okay, I . . ."

"Close the door!" She sounded angry and afraid, even as her eyes were thrilled. "They're all asleep."

I went to the door and closed it quietly. "How are you feeling?" I said.

"I've been thinking about you," she said. "I got your note."

"What note?" I sat down on the bed.

She smiled, waved her hand at me in mock offense. " 'What note.' The note you left in my book. At school?"

"At school."

"We're going to . . . I'm going . . ." She began to turn toward the door, as if guided that way by a sturdy hand. Her eyes were full of hope. I followed her gaze.

If it's possible for a normal person to have moments of perfect empathy, then I had one at that moment. It was not a pleasant experience. I had no idea who or what my mother expected to see there, but when I turned it was with the expectation that I would see it with her: a gathering of congenial ghosts popped in from the past, maybe, or a nurse bearing lavish gifts. And though I couldn't see her face when I found only the gray metal door, shut firm against the hollow bustle of the hall, with its yellowed, scotch-taped fire exit map peeling away at the corners, I knew its expression as well as I knew the dreary contours of my own mind. Her disillusion was my own.

"Mom?" I said, my voice every bit as brittle as hers, like a twig dragged through gravel.

"Oh! Suddenly I'm very tired, just now." She was slumped in the wheelchair, her hands curled inertly in her lap. "Don't call me that. It isn't funny."

"Maybe you should get some sleep," I said.

"I was hoping you'd kiss me goodnight."

I didn't know what to say. We sat like that awhile, me with my knees pressed together on her bed, her with her chin buried in her nightgown. Then I went to her and kissed her again on the cheek. She raised her head and her lips parted, and a small, grievous sound escaped her throat. Her eyes were closed, the lids pulsing with the press of blood. "Goodnight," I said, and this time kissed her lips. They were a young woman's lips, warm and soft, and they barely moved under mine. I pulled back and stood before her, wondering what had happened, and how it had happened so quickly: I couldn't have been here for more than a few minutes. Then the door opened.

"Dotty? Your door must stay open . . . who are you?"

"Her son."

"No, you're not. Her son is older." The aide was a middle-aged woman with a round face and wild hair. She looked about to run for a telephone, or a weapon.

"She has three sons. I'm Tim."

"It's after visiting hours. How did you get in here?"

"Uh, there was no one at the desk . . ."

She bustled in and grabbed the handles of my mother's wheelchair, jerking her around in a rough half-circle. Her white head bobbed, her eyes still closed. "You'll have to leave. It's almost time for her bath and brush."

"She's my mother . . ." I felt like a schoolchild, begging to be released to the lavatory.

"You can come and see her tomorrow, in the daytime. Now you'll have to go." She stood behind my mother, waiting. "I'll call security."

I left. The hall seemed much longer than it had the other times I'd come, and I hurried down it, feeling gawky and stupid, though none of the passing employees paid me the slightest attention.

When I passed the desk attendant, she didn't know who I was. She told me goodnight.

I drove around, trying to get lost. It didn't work. New Jersey is a place of many roads, but no matter which obscure county route I picked, it led me to a familiar place. When at last I emerged into the shimmering Trenton suburbs and decided to make my way back home, I got the disagreeable feeling that I was trapped, that there was no place I could go where I wasn't precisely the person I'd made myself into, where I hadn't made the familiar mistakes of my past. Then I remembered my mother and her untethered scattershot of memories and thought I must be the most selfish person the world had ever known.

I wasn't ready for the house and my brother and my bedroom, so when I pulled into Mixville I passed our driveway and tooled through town. There was not much town to tool through. It was late, and even the teenagers were indoors. A couple of drunks I thought I recognized sat asleep under a public telephone outside Main Street's only bar.

And then I found myself at the paper mill. I'd snooped around here a few times when I was a kid. I parked the car in a weedy gravel turnout on the opposite side of the street, then walked around the chain-link fence that separated the mill from the world. The fence was topped with razor wire now—that was something new—and choked with dry growth the weedeater couldn't reach. The boughs of trees hung low over me. I walked hunched.

Finally I came to the riverbank. There was no development here, just the overgrown backyard to the mill, and a lonely line of phone poles stretching into the distance. The mill was dark and silent, but lights and sounds reached me from the Pennsylvania side: another mill there had been gutted and turned into condos, and I could see the orange glow from a barbecue fire and hear the music and voices of a party.

Both mills used to run all night, when I was a kid. I sat in the grass, remembering. And then I got another memory, of fishing in this exact spot, with my father, who wasn't actually fishing but sitting in a folding beach chair with a bottle and a sketchbook. I didn't know how to fish and didn't like it anyway, but my father had bought me the rod and reel because he wanted to do something nice for me, or maybe with me, and so I went along. I sat in the weeds, the pointed ends of grasses working their way into my shorts, and flung worm after worm into the toxic, pulp-thick water, and my father fell asleep.

It wasn't much fun. I remembered wishing I had brought my baseball card price guide, which I had spent the morning in bed reading. But now it seemed that it must have been the best day of my life, and I was full of regret for not having appreciated it at the time.

## twenty-eight

On Saturday morning, after Pierce had left for the Pines, I sat by the phone waiting for the courage to call Susan. Repeatedly it didn't come. I had slept badly and now, as if under the influence of a hundred cups of coffee, my hands were trembling like belt sanders. I had to keep wiping them on my pants.

I decided to try reverse psychology and made myself some actual coffee. It calmed me some, but in place of my nervousness came strange, shapeless sorrow, which bore down on my head and chest like the onset of a cold. I moved around the house with my mug, trying to soothe the painful spots, but they were difficult to find, and slippery once caught. It struck me that my parents themselves were elusive like that, even when they were alive and whole, as well as now, in memory. If I put my mind to it, it was easy to recall the occasional ugly scene, but mostly, when I thought of them, I thought of archetypes, of cartoons: my mother in her threadbare terry-cloth bathrobe with a drink in her hand, her face bent into a half-lidded, skeptical sneer; my father as a drawing of himself, with the slump, the empty eyeglasses, the cigar. There were no artifacts around the house I could use to prick myself with, nothing either of them had been attached to. There were no family traditions I could feel the loss of. What I did feel was a general and shifting sadness. It was not like a tumor that could be excised or a cut that could heal. It was more like a mildly toxic gas I couldn't stop breathing, and, with every breath, producing more of.

Why, I wondered, did they have any children, let alone five? Were we their inconvenient remedy to the empty space between them? Did they think they could reach each other over a bridge of kids? It gave me pause to consider that my purpose in life might only have been to shore up a doomed marriage, which in any case was now over. A dire and oversimplified notion, but my present pinnacle of self-negation had not been arrived at by the sober contemplation of life's complexity.

I got a bus to New York. Once there I would walk somewhere, and probably I would call or visit Susan and make a fool of myself. I began to regret these acts as if I had already performed them. That's when I remembered Rose and Andrew, and decided that now, with our mother growing increasingly dependent and senile, the time had come to make amends with them. I would call them when I got to the city, and if refused spend the day going to art galleries and drinking iced coffee. Satisfied, I bought a paperback at the station, a murder mystery, to read on the bus, and made a mental pact to enjoy myself no matter the circumstances.

And for the duration of the trip, I did. If I didn't exactly leave my anxieties at home, I at least was able to set them aside. It was like they were bulky bags filled with pack-ratted garbage, which I could leave in the adjacent seat, lumpy and worn and distantly reassuring, until I found a suitable place to dump them.


Rose wasn't listed in the Manhattan phone book, but Andrew was, and it was Andrew I got over the phone from Port Authority. He didn't seem to know who I was for a moment.

"Tim?" he said.

"Your brother-in-law Tim."

"Oh! Tim! Well how's it going?" I liked this about Andrew, his perfect pleasure at hearing from anyone surprising, no matter who it was. It was contagious.

"Oh, it's going!" I said. "Doing lots of drawing!"

We talked about that for a while, as if we were sitting across from one another in a restaurant. He asked questions and I answered them. I had forgotten how nice it was to be on the less burdensome end of a conversation, so long had I been talking mostly to Pierce and Brad Wurster, and it made me feel uncharacteristically glib, a far cry from the dolt I'd been at the cartoonists' conference.

"So Andrew," I said finally. "I'm in New York."

"New York! No kidding!"

"Yeah . . . I was sort of hoping we could get together. You and me and Lindy."

"Rose, you mean."

If I'd made that slip to Rose personally, I would have been listening to a dial tone now. "Jeez, right, Rose," I said.

"Uh, well, she's not in . . ." He was stalling, and was bad at it. I pounced.

"Look, I'll just come over, what do you say? Because my bus just got here, and I've gotta do something in New York all day."

"Oh, sure, all right . . ."

"I'll just come right over, okay?"

"Yeah, come over. Come on over."

I took a cab uptown. Andrew and Rose lived on 110th Street, in what I'd heard her refer to as "a decent building," in a tone that encompassed both condemnation and compliment. It looked like any other to me, large, grim and slightly foreboding. A tired, filthy man wearing a ball cap sat at its base, surrounded by garbage. But the neighborhood in general was clean, and people walked along the street, talking and laughing. I found their number on the mailboxes, took the elevator to the fourteenth floor, and knocked on a freshly painted green door with a sprig of dried eucalyptus hanging over the eyehole. I heard steps, and Andrew appeared.

He looked exuberantly comfortable: baggy wrinkled shorts, a T-shirt and a pair of wool socks in the early stages of falling off. He grinned. "Hey!" he said, as if again surprised, and embraced me. I hugged back, stunned myself. He smelled like old-growth pine forest. Behind him brilliant light filled the room, doubling itself on the polished floor.

He let me go. "She's not home yet. Come on in."

I did. It was a spectacular loft apartment. I was filled with envy. The windows were enormous, consuming most of the back wall, and all the furniture, the decor, was chosen to acknowledge and defer to the light: the bookshelves were wooden planks set in rough iron frames that let the light stream through; a hardwood table standing on thin legs was surrounded by metal-tube chairs with vinyl seats. There was glass everywhere, translucent dishes and food stored in decanters. The whole thing had the look of long planning, of fulfilled desires: they had the place they wanted. I considered this an accomplishment, simply knowing what they wanted.

"Wow," I said. "Did you put all this together?"

"Rose, mostly."

"I didn't know she was such an . . . aesthete."

He narrowed his eyes.

"I mean that respectfully," I said. And I did. Perhaps my greatest failing as an artist had been that I had no confidence in my own aesthetic judgment. My pieces all looked like I expected them to; it was my expectation that always proved inadequate.

"I thought you did. Do you want to sit down? Can I get you something? Juice, maybe?"

"Yes on all counts."

I sat on a lumpy tan sofa and Andrew brought me a tall orange juice, which the light claimed before I could lay a lip on it. It tasted like good air.

"So," he said, taking one of the metal chairs. "You haven't told me what brought you here."

I shrugged. "A sort of inner mumbling."

He nodded solemnly, as if this made sense. "How's your brother?"

"Better," I said. "I think. He doesn't seem . . . taken in by his worries so much lately. Not to say they don't bother him."

"No."

"But our mother . . ."

"She's not good." He was sitting on his chair backwards, his legs manfully spread, his face deeply focused on the conversation. Andrew was a listener, which I supposed was what Rose needed.

"Yeah," I said. Then, delicately, "So Rose has been going down there?"

"Once a week, really early in the morning, when she thinks none of you will be there." He gulped his juice, finishing off the entire half-glass in the process.

I was floored by the sheer physical presence of him, the sense of him in the apartment. He was less a man in his castle than a physicist in his lab. He gave me a look.

"What?" I said.

"You know that whatever you say is going to piss her off."

"I don't exactly know what I have to say," I admitted. "I sort of came by accident."

He raised his eyebrows. "There are no accidents." And as if on cue the door opened.

Rose swept in carrying a paper bag. "They were out of the everythings, so I got a couple onions and some salts . . . oh."

We gaped at one another across the dazzling floor. I smiled, or tried to. Rose didn't. She was much taller than she looked elsewhere, and I marveled at the poise and dignity she managed standing there, perfectly flummoxed at my presence. "Hi," I said.

"Well." She set the bag down on the kitchen table. Andrew reached greedily into it and pulled out a thick bagel. "We were just going to have a little brunch."

"Yes. Sorry."

"Do you want a bagel, Tim?" Andrew asked me, and Rose's contemptuous restraint gave way to resignation and she pulled up a chair.

"We have onion and salt," she said.

"I heard. Can I have a salt?"

She handed me the bagel. They bit right into theirs, without applying cream cheese or anything else, so I did the same. We ate. Halfway through his bagel, Andrew seemed to deflate. He got up. "Okay, well, I'm out for a walk," he said. He snatched the keys from the table and hustled out the door, cracking his knuckles. Rose and I finished eating, then she crossed her legs at the thigh and folded her hands over her knee, as if praying for me to leave.

"So," she said.

"So!"

"You want to talk about Mom?" she said. I nodded, relinquishing all hope of some pleasant conversation before we got down to brass tacks. I had come here to postpone groveling to Susan, but falling to my knees and begging for forgiveness seemed a refreshing diversion from the present situation. Rose came to the sofa and sat at the other end, as far from me as possible. It was the most affection she'd ever shown me.

"We can't have her here," she said. She was facing the windows as if speaking through them out into the city, to Andrew. "We talked about it, but really, we're so high up, and the elevator is unreliable, and this neighborhood . . . I know you're thinking, she's so selfish, they could move downstairs or out to the suburbs, but Tim, and I know you're going to think I'm a shit but so be it, I've come so far. I've made the life for myself I wanted, and it was hard. I don't think you can understand that."

"Rose . . ."

She turned to me finally, a brazen, tearful flash in her eyes, and tugged spastically on her earlobe. "I think she ought to be at home. In Riverbank."

"Mixville," I said.

"What?"

"At FunnyFest. They changed the name."

Her mouth hung open a moment, and then she coughed out a single, near-hysterical laugh, and began to cry. She covered her face. I moved to comfort her but couldn't reach, and I feared that moving farther would make her get up, and then I would leave and we would never have this conversation. So I said, "I think you're right. Pierce wants her at home, actually. I didn't tell him yes right away myself, and he got mad at me, but really he's right."

She produced a kleenex and honked into it, then crushed it in her fist. She looked up. "You're going to do that? Bring her home?"

"I think when I get the strip, this fall. I just can't do it before then."

"Right, of course."

"If you feel bad about it, help us. Come down and take care of her." Rose blinked, peering into this future with what looked like real apprehension. "Andrew said you come down every week anyway," I said. "It'll be like that. Just stay all day or something. I'm sure Bitty will do a day too."

"And Bobby?"

"Bobby's against it. But he'll come around."

"Maybe not."

I shrugged. "Maybe not. And Pierce and I will always be there. At least for now."

She looked down at her hands, passing the kleenex back and forth like a juggler. "It's hard for me to be with Pierce. I have bad memories of . . . that time."

"He's a good person," I said. "He's the best of us."

She snorted. "He's not one of us."

"He is," I said. "He's got different problems is all."

Her eyes met mine. They were as deep and alien as bullet holes. I got the impression she wanted to say something, but she never opened her mouth, just stared at me until I had to turn away.

"Get over it, Rose," I said, suddenly angry.

Out of the corner of my eye I saw her shaking her head. "You never *trusted* him, Tim. And then had your trust betrayed. By the time you came along, he'd already ruined everything."

"Pierce?" I said, stupidly.

"*Daddy,*" she said. "Pierce was a drop in the bucket."

I was beginning to tire of this. "I can't understand why you *dislike* Pierce so much," I said. "It isn't his fault he's the way he is. Frankly, Rose, there's a lot more of Dad in you than in Pierce."

"You can say that again." She laughed, a sound like a dish breaking.

Rose had always prided herself on being cryptic and secretive, claiming obscure insight into the family dramas that we could never possibly understand. As a teenager she kept a journal in code, and was so confident it couldn't be cracked that she left the spiral notebook it was recorded in lying haphazardly around the house. She was right too: the hodgepodge of numbers and letters and mysterious symbols eluded Bobby and me, the only people who cared, and a thorough ransacking of her bedroom turned up no Rosetta stone. But there was a part of me that didn't want the code cracked. I wanted to buy her schtick, to take comfort in the thought that someone, at least, knew what was going on.

Now, of course, it was obvious she'd been every bit as addled as I was. I wondered if there really was a key to those journals, if perhaps they'd been as mysterious to her as to us: maybe writing in the journals was an elaborate kind of playacting, and at night in bed she scrutinized the meaningless signs with a flashlight, as if they held the solution to her misery. In that case, her game was meant to protect us, to take the pain of living in that house onto herself, and I had misjudged her.

I stared at her and she, with her long face turned into the sun, must have felt me staring. How many layers of pretense and subterfuge was she made of? Was there a pure, unadulterated Rose underneath, or had she become the things she pretended to be? She was older than me by more than just the years between us.

As if she had read my thoughts, she said, "You're still just a kid." And that seemed about right, until she turned to me and revealed the face she'd assembled to go along with the statement: a contemptuous smirk, her eyebrows arched in naked moral superiority, and the tiniest ghost of doubt concealed underneath, like a thief silhouetted behind a billowing curtain. She was trying to chase me out.

It was hard to resist. I got up, setting my juice glass on the floor at my feet. "Funny how I'm the one taking the adult responsibilities around here," I said, and started to leave.

"Wait," she said, in a voice almost too quiet to hear. I was nearly to the door by then. The room grew tense, as if polarized by our talk, and in the silence the air seemed to glow with its energy. "I'll help. I'll help take care of her."

I looked back: her body was shut tight, knees and hands together, turned toward the windows. I saw the bagel bag lying neglected on the table and I wanted another.

"You mean it?" I asked.

She nodded. "We can work out the details later."

I considered going to her, but I knew she didn't want me to, and to be honest, I didn't want to either. I said, more quietly than I had intended, "Thank you, Rose," and walked out.

.   .   .

I didn't feel like sorting out the mess the conversation was already becoming in my head, and so I tried to put my plan back on track: I walked with the intention of stopping myself every twenty blocks for one thing or another, an art gallery, a cup of coffee, lunch. The idea was to clear my head to make room for the work I'd have to start doing when I got home. Instead, every step seemed to shake loose another anxiety: the cartoon, Mom, money, my future. The coffee I bought tasted stale, and the art I looked at in the usual galleries seemed too aggressive, too eager to please, or offend, or prove something. I avoided inventing a destination, but all the same I wasn't surprised when I found myself in SoHo, nosing around the galleries near Delicious Duck, hurrying past work that deserved perhaps a second look, to get myself back on the street. I studied passersby, letting them take on her shape for the smallest fraction of a second, letting my blood run thick and sludgy with longing. I made no mistake about the longing: it was for a sympathetic ear, for a sounding board. But of course there was more to it than that, and for that undefined more I kept myself from rushing to her building and ringing her from the desk.

As it turned out I didn't have to. I watched her walk into the restaurant from a block away. Once she was inside, I made a run for it, hoping to make it before she ordered, in the event that we might do it together. I found her huddled in the cavernous dim of the place, her sunglasses absently left on, buried in an ornate, finger-softened cardboard menu. She seemed to have trouble reading it.

I thought I could sneak up on her, reach over the menu and pluck the glasses off. I pictured her astonished, laughing face as she looked up and saw that it was me. Instead, she turned her head and my hand brushed her ear, and she jumped back as if I had zapped her with an electric prod.

"You!"

"Hi."

She sighed, shaking her head at the carpet.

"I'm sorry," I said. "I was trying to surprise you. By taking off your glasses."

"Glasses?" She brought her hand to her face and removed them. "Ah. Yes." She let me have a thin smile, and said, "Dare I ask what brings you here?"

"Scrumptious Chinese takeout."

She nodded. "Fair enough."

We ordered food and it was brought to us. "No napkins, no fork, no chopsticks," she told the clerk. We carried out our bags, and since she hadn't told me to go elsewhere, I walked alongside her. We didn't talk. She squinted, having forgotten to put the sunglasses back on. I followed her into her building, a scabby brownstone with a cat on the stoop, and up the steps. She held the door for me.

Her place was what I'd expected. Largely tidy, the furniture covered with pieces of damp clean laundry. Some movie posters and an old formica dinner table, where we sat and opened our bags.

"You got my letter?" I said.

She held up a hand. "Tim. Lunch first."

We took chopsticks from the china mug at the center of the table. I watched her eat. She watched her plate, occasionally fixing me with a wary, slightly hostile glance. But I could tell she pitied me a little—her face, exerting itself in the act of eating, betrayed a crude, practical sort of mercy—and I let myself hope.

I finished first. When she was done, she reached out, took my hand, and pulled me to the couch, where she placed us at opposite ends (I was reminded of my talk with Rose). She said, "I do not want to be the girl you're hanging around with while you're sorting out your various issues."

This took a moment to sink in. "Which is to say forget it?" It sounded true as I said it, and my heart listed.

"Which is to say forget it, if that's all I am to you, or will be."

"I don't think that's all you are to me."

"You don't think."

I chose my words carefully. "I can't tell you that I'm absolutely certain of anything. I am pretty sure I don't want you just because I'm desperate for somebody to talk to."

I was surprised to hear myself say this. She sighed.

"That came out wrong," I said.

"No, it didn't. It was the truth."

"I guess."

"Move closer," she said. "Just a little." I gave her several feet of space, and she took my hand in both of hers. They were cold. "I was watching *Rear Window*," she said. "Get it rolling, would you?"

With my free hand I picked up the remote from the coffee table and turned on the set. It took a moment to find PLAY in the parking lot of buttons, and then I hit it.

"Thanks."

"No problem."

We watched it straight through without speaking. Jimmy Stewart had just started spying on the glum songwriter. The taste of Hunan beef still simmered on my tongue. At some point Susan's hands began to move over mine, and our fingers entwined and pulled apart, tested each other while we watched.

When it was over, I picked up the remote and turned off the TV. I could hear her breathing. She slid into my arms and I lay back, and then she lay back, half-on, half-off me on the thin cushions. We kissed, and kissed again.

"If you break my heart, Mix," she told me, the ends of our noses flattened against each other, "I swear I'll beat the living shit out of you."

"It's a deal," I said.

More kissing. My hand found her back, the place where her T-shirt had pulled from her shorts and exposed a bare inch of skin. She let out a breath.

"Bedtime," she said.

Delighted, I said, "Right."

## twenty-nine

Afterward we seemed far from finished. We stayed very close, saying nothing, finally sleeping, then waking, then trying it all again, and despite the typical trappings of pleasure, I didn't feel like what we'd done had resolved anything. We had crossed over into something new, and though the border patrols hadn't gotten us there were still miles of rough terrain left to navigate. Lying in Susan's arms, I extended the metaphor, adding rattlesnakes and scorpions, undercover immigration agents and idle rednecks with sawed-off shotguns, until Susan absently began stroking my hair and I let my brain shut mercifully down.

It was too late to take the bus home, so I stayed. We went out to eat, and came back to Susan's apartment exhausted and happy, two things I had not been simultaneously for a long time. It was strange trying to fall asleep on a new bed, with a new and unfamiliar presence, and we stretched and rolled and yanked on the sheets until I felt raw. At some point we simply gave in and stopped moving, almost too tired to speak.

Almost. "Tim," she said. "There's a reason I haven't been calling you. Besides this, I mean."

I made an encouraging sound. In my half-dream, her words took on shapes and bobbed in the haze of sleep.

"It's Ray Burn. Your meeting with Ray Burn."

"Whaboutit?"

"He tried to back out. He said he didn't want to see you, but I talked him back into it. You're meeting next Wednesday."

I pulled myself out of the haze and sat up. Moonlight spilled across the bed. The clock radio quietly buzzed beside me. "Why didn't he want to see me?"

"He said there was no reason to bother you until you were completely ready." She was lying on her back, watching the ceiling, which was cracked and bubbled from years of leaks. "But I think . . . I think he was thinking it would be easier to pull the rug out from under you if he never actually met you. He didn't say that; that's just my impression."

I could feel it all falling apart. "So what are you saying?"

"I'm not saying anything. I mean . . . the thing is, Burn is a very bland guy, not too smart, and he doesn't need to be doing this cartoon thing. He's got old money. He just does this for a hoot. So he is very impressionable when it comes to cartoons. If somebody shows him something or tells him about someone, and the person doing the showing or telling is . . . confident, you know, has a little spark, then he'll start believing everything that person says." She sat up too, and put her hand on my knee. "He's, you know, tabula rasa."

"I saw Ken Dorn at the conference. He told me he'd met with Burn."

"Yeah, well, Ron Burn, the old boss, liked Dorn. He thought Dorn was a wit. So Ray sees Dorn if Dorn wants to be seen."

"And Dorn has a 'little spark'?" I said, incredulous.

"Well, no. But Dorn has gotten to him, and Dorn also is trying to make you look bad. Besides, Dorn is the bargain cartoonist, so . . ."

"So I'm history."

"No. You're meeting with Burn, remember?" She turned to me and took both my hands with hers. "Tim, if you want this, you can go into the meeting and wow him. I know you can."

I shook my head, wondering if it was all even worth it. "Did you hear about what happened at the conference?"

"Your panel discussion? Yeah."

"Dorn set me up, you know." I told her about the overalled hayseed and the transaction out by the dumpster. "If he really wants it, he's going to get it."

"Not if you don't want him to. Remember, you're the one who's supposed to get it. As far as I know, the lawyers haven't been able to get around that."

I pulled my hands away and lay back. "I didn't want any of this to begin with."

She waited a long time before saying, "Including me."

"No, not including you."

It was hard to cheer up again after that. We slept, and in the morning ate breakfast together, but there hung between us some general dissatisfaction, something both of us felt but were powerless to repair, either in ourselves or in the other. Susan offered to drive me home, but I refused. "It's your day off. You should enjoy it however you want."

She said, "Will you call me?"

"And vice versa."

"Sure." We hugged. "Did we do the right thing?" she asked me, from over my shoulder.

I brought her face around to mine, looked her in the eyes, and said "Twice," which was, thank God, exactly what was needed for a change.


I tried to do two days' work in one afternoon. It didn't go so well. I figured if I pushed myself I could be finished by the time I got hungry, but instead my dinner—a Custard's Last Hot Dog and an A&W float—proved to be a dinner break, and I was back in the studio by six-thirty, the hot dog still somersaulting inside me. Despite my best efforts, the FF characters would not yield to the pen. I took half an hour to add to my pool of gags and replaced a few of the old, half-assed ones with the new. I was supposed to have six roughs for Wurster by tomorrow morning, and it was pretty clear I wouldn't accomplish this with any degree of technical mastery.

It was well after dark when Pierce got home. I heard the car pull in, then his footsteps across the driveway gravel and the grass. The studio door was wide open, but he knocked on it as if it were shut. "Tim?"

"Hey," I said, looking up. It took a second for my eyes to adjust to the middle distance, a sign I was too tired to be working.

He stepped in. He was dressed in a T-shirt of mine and a pair of shorts cut off from our father's pants, and he hugged himself against the cool of the night. "I'm back."

"No kidding?"

He smiled. "Huh huh huh."

"How's the lady?"

"Gilly's cool. We picked cranberries. She's a real green thumb."

"I don't doubt it."

"Tim," he said. "I was wondering if, if you thought about what I suggested. About Mom."

I put my pen down. "Actually, yes. Actually I went to New York and talked to Rose about it."

He flinched as if I'd taken a swing at him. "You talked to Rose?"

"I think she thinks it's the way to go. I tried to convince her to come down a day a week. To help."

He snorted. "Yeah. Right. She won't get near me."

"I don't know that I understand that."

"She doesn't like thinking other people's problems are as bad as hers." He looked out the door now, as if the answer to this riddle was hiding in the yard somewhere. It reminded me strongly of Rose, the way she was looking out the window when I left her.

"I think it's a go," I said. "I think we should bring her home."

"You do?" His eyes were pleading, as if he thought I might still change my mind.

"Yeah. We'll manage."

I could see the relief washing over him. He passed a hand over his face. "Oh, man, yeah. Yeah, we'll manage okay." He shook his head. "I really miss her, man."

"You know she'll probably never come back, I mean all the way back."

"It doesn't matter," he said. "She'll know she's home."


But it was not as easy as we thought. We had expected to walk in there and roll her out in a wheelchair. A few phone calls proved this impracticable, if not impossible: the fund my father had established to provide for her was difficult to crack. Pierce called Uncle Mal and told him what we wanted, and he said he would get on it. "He's really glad," Pierce told me. "He thinks we're doing the right thing."

Meanwhile, my mother herself grew blurrier and more confused, though her physical health remained stable. I began visiting her more often, trying to get used to the idea of having her around, but it was hard; like a baby, she had difficulty making her needs known, and the subtleties of expression left in place of her voice were beyond me. Several times during the next week, a nurse scolded me for not noticing when she was thirsty or had to be brought to the bathroom, and I was consumed with shame.

The nurses didn't want us to take her away. They seemed to consider our ineptitude a sign of carelessness, and our plan to bring her home a selfish scheme to alleviate our own guilt. None of this was spoken. Maybe it was all in my frenzied imagination. But it was on my mind, and it gave me a lot of food for thought when I noticed what could have been a glimmer of recognition in her eyes, or a sensible sentence that may or may not have been directed at me. I brought Susan in twice. The first time, my mother cooed and fussed over her as if she were a newborn, much to Susan's embarrassment. The second time she cursed at her like a shock jock. We didn't talk so much, Susan and I, about these visits or about how they played into our relationship. It seemed too soon. Susan did get along well with Pierce, though, and one Saturday morning in Mixville the two of them woke before me and made a stack of pancakes together. I was astonished. Pierce didn't even like conversations with other people, let alone complex activities like cooking.

For what it was worth, I felt increasingly like Susan was someone I could be with, even as my doubts about myself were escalating. I held myself back from her, and sensing this, she did the same. What were my motives, with my mother, with Susan, with the Family Funnies? Why was I doing what I was doing? These were the things I overworked myself in order not to think about, in order not to talk to Susan about. I realized this was a stopgap measure, and that something would have to give, but I didn't know which something, and when it would give. So I drew, and waited.

The Monday night before I was to meet with Ray Burn, Pierce and I

drove down to Trenton to meet with Mal about Mom's move. I was not thinking about our mother, only about reworking several cartoons after the meeting, and I found myself uncharacteristically silent for the entire trip. We
bought sandwiches at a deli downtown and brought one to Mal, and we ate at
the same boardroom table where our father's will was read. Mal looked sloppy
and haggard, and I wondered about his private life, if he had lady friends or
friends of any kind. He had never married.

Pierce was picking up the slack for me, throwing himself into these meetings like his life depended on it, and before his sandwich was even gone he convinced Mal to get out his papers and begin going over our options. The two
of them bent over the documents, nodding, speaking in low tones as if I were
asleep and they didn't want to wake me.

It was then that I noticed, from across the table, the similar way their ears
stuck out, pointed at the back and strangely facile, like a cat's. I remembered
watching Pierce wiggle his ears when we were kids, and being frustrated with
myself because I couldn't do it. And their thin heads of hair: Mal's yellow-
white at the roots, more brittle-looking, but both whorled off at the right,
around a little bald spot. For almost a full minute I looked at this curious sym-
metry without judgment, contemplating it as I might a yin-yang or a
Rorschach blot, and then I remembered Rose's cryptic pronouncements and
the pieces fell into place. I must have made a sound because both of them
looked up.

"Tim?" Mal said. "What is it?"

I swallowed the bite of sandwich that had been sitting, half-chewed, in my
mouth the whole time. "Nothing," I said.


We were halfway home in the car when I said, "He's your father, isn't he."

Pierce didn't turn to me. After a while he said, "I've always wondered if
you knew and just never said anything."

"I just figured it out."

"Just now?"

I nodded. "You have the same ears. And something Rose said. I didn't
know what she was talking about at the time."

"Well, now you know." He sounded angry.

"Have you always known?"

"No. Mom told me when I was something like ten. She was drunk." He leaned against the passenger window, and it fogged up where his breath met it. "I don't know why she told me. Mad at Dad, I guess."

I considered this, and his plan for bringing her home, and marveled for a moment at the power of his forgiveness, the way it sustained him. I said, "Does Mal know you know?"

"Yeah."

Trying to reassemble our childhood from this new perspective would be futile, like unlearning a language. I gave up before I even started. "I suppose I'm the last one to find out."

"Rose says she knew when I was born, and suspected it even before. I told Bitty. I don't think Bobby knows. He wouldn't want to, anyway." I signaled and turned onto Route 29. "I don't suppose you'll be hating me too, now, will you?" He said this with studied nonchalance, as if he'd been practicing it for years, but I could tell he was truly scared.

I said, "Of course not."

"Rose hates me, you know that. And Bitty . . ."

"Bitty doesn't hate you," I said.

"She doesn't think she does," he said. "But she does. She hasn't said boo to me since I told her. I remember we were sitting in my bedroom and I told her, and she walked out. I thought she'd tell Dad I knew, but she didn't. She just stopped . . . sistering."

"I don't think Bitty or Rose hates you. Especially Bitty."

"With all due respect, Tim, I don't think you actually know."

"I'm sorry," I said after a while.

"Me too."

Getting home was like coming to an entirely new house. I saw my father, in an inkstained oxford shirt, cracking his knuckles at dinner, offering Uncle Mal another helping. I saw Pierce opening the gifts Mal gave him, always better than the ones he gave the rest of us. I saw my mother hugging Mal at the door. All of it brand new.

"I should go to the studio," I said.

Pierce's lips pressed themselves together. "I should go in the house."

I opened my arms and he stepped into them, and we held each other there in the driveway. He pulled away, crying. "It would have been better if it was Mal," he said. "With us."

"Maybe," I said.

Pierce shook his head. "Definitely." And he went inside.

# thirty

I couldn't decide what to wear to my meeting with Ray Burn. It was Wednesday morning, and I had canceled my cartooning class with Wurster, in exchange for a promise to draw all day when I got back from New York. I didn't tell him that Susan had gotten the afternoon off, faking a chronic illness and its attendant doctor's visit, and that we planned to spend the day together.

Considering my previous wrangles with discipline, I went out to the studio every afternoon with surprising ease. I'd had to drag myself to work in the old days. It wasn't that I was having more fun (though I'll admit there is greater satisfaction in drawing competently than in drawing badly); it was simply that the more work I did, the more I wanted to do. I was turning into a junkie.

Part of my high, of course, was a boost in self-regard: I was beginning, at last, to feel like a cartoonist. Cartooning was making me into a visual thinker, my drawing into a sort of emotive shorthand. I was developing a taste for the self-contained. Oddly, this change didn't seem to come entirely from my lessons with Wurster or the cartoons I studied: it was more like these things helped to uncover what was already true, but hidden, about my artistic sensibilities. I was establishing an aesthetic, something I'd never had before, even when I was trying to be an artist.

All the same, I bristled at the boundaries of my one square Family Funnies panel, and even more at the raw materials available to me inside it: not my family, not even anything remotely close to me, but a coterie of cutout shills employed to deliver flimsy one-liners. I'd been trying to think of the strip as a kind of self-limitation, like a fugue or a sonnet, but even Beethoven or Keats could not have made art out of the Family Funnies.

The irony was all too obvious: not until I had given up art for a career in schlock did I begin to feel like an artist.

My one white oxford shirt had an ink stain on the right arm, but I decided I could wear my blue blazer on top, and avoid taking it off during the interview. I put on a pair of khaki pants and polished some old wing tips I'd salvaged from my father's closet before the big clean-out.

"Looking good," Pierce told me when I came out to the kitchen. He was leaning over the coffee maker, watching fresh coffee drip into the pot. Over the past week he'd been much less gloomy than usual, and often was up and out of his room before I left the house. He had a jittery, anticipatory air about him, as if there was something up his sleeve. I let his statement take a few turns around my head, ran it through the sarcasm detector.

"Really?" I said.

He stood up. "Well, for you."

"Hmm. What are you up to today?"

He shrugged. "Not much," he said, but went on to explain that Mal was picking him up over his lunch hour, and the two of them were going to go see Mom. I was having some trouble getting used to the new genetic circumstances. Knowing now what had been hidden in plain sight for so long, I could see how Rose might stretch her already-strong biases against Pierce into a tacit exclusion of him from the family. But still I looked at Pierce and saw, at first impression, not a piece of Mal or a piece of my mother but a piece of myself. "We're going to try and get her used to the idea of coming here. You know, talk about the neighborhood and the house and all."

"Do you think it's going to get through?"

He shrugged. "I dunno," he said, and I could see that the question offended him more than a little.

I gassed up the Caddy and stopped at the Jersey Devil, a coffee shop and bakery in Titusville. It was a little out of the way, but I had a theory: I figured if I drank coffee in the car and had a pastry to soak some of it up, I wouldn't have to pee until I was well into the Burn Syndicate's building on West 57th. And I needed some kind of distraction on the way to the city, a drive of geometrically increasing intensity that began with shaded country roads and derelict barns and ended with traffic jams and squeegee men.

The shop was mostly empty. A grizzled maniac type hunkered over a steaming cup at the only occupied table, and a pretty girl in denim overalls was talking to the clerk. The clerk looked familiar. He had small round glasses, a fluffy head of curly hair and a large, assertive goatee. He was also dusted with flour. It took a moment, but it came to me: without the flour, he looked just like Leon Trotsky. The girl was saying, in a seductive, sugary voice, "I'm really looking forward to reading your manifesto."

"Helpya?" he asked me brightly. The girl turned and offered a vacant, half-lidded smile, and I felt like I'd just interrupted a sexual act.

I ordered and he gave me my food in a paper sack before turning back to the girl. I had to pull myself out the door, so desperately did I want to stay and hang out with these kids. I was halfway to New York before I sorted out this feeling: it was jealousy, the kind I sometimes got when I caught a glimpse of people doing exactly what they wanted.

The Burn Syndicate occupied the nineteenth floor of a building that, beyond all probability, I had been in before. There was an art gallery on the fourth floor I had once had a piece in. This was probably the high point of my career as an installation artist. The show was called "Garbage, Garbage, Garbage," and the piece I'd shown was, by necessity, only a small chunk of a larger work. It consisted of a metal trash can lid with rotten things hanging off the bottom of it, and was called "Detritus, Risen." The show went on for three days before the gallery was shut down due to fire code violations.

I was early for the meeting, so I stopped in for old times' sake. On display was a series of "drawings" by a woman I'd not heard of. I had some trouble finding them. All I could see were the walls, each painted a metallic dark gray. Nothing hung on them. Then I realized that the walls *were* the drawings: she had apparently taken a pencil—lots of pencils, I supposed—and covered every inch of wall space with graphite and fixative. I took a postcard on the way out and put it in my jacket pocket. It was a white index card "drawn" on in the same way.

On the nineteenth floor, I peed, then waited on a long leather couch in a lushly carpeted room that could have comfortably housed a chamber orchestra and several parked cars. Some distance away, a receptionist sat behind a wide mahogany desk. She kept glancing at her watch, then looking up at me. At about ten minutes past ten, she picked up her phone and spoke to somebody, but I was too far away to hear. She hung up, came to the couch and said, "Mr. Burn will be with you shortly. Would you like a Perrier?" I told her I would and she vanished through a smoked glass door, and returned with a bottle of Perrier, a bottle opener, a cocktail napkin and a small wooden table. She opened the bottle for me, set it on the table and returned to her desk.

I didn't particularly like Perrier, but I stuck to protocol and drank some anyway. It was a testament to both the decadence and puissance of the beverage industry that water could be altered so that it made you belch. After a time, someone came out for me. "Mr. Mix?" he said.

"Yes." It was a young man, some kind of intern or temp, with a round face and thin brown hair. He was wearing a golf shirt, untucked from a pair of jeans, and white tennis shoes.

"Follow me," he said. I got up, grabbed my portfolio and raised the Perrier bottle to the receptionist as I passed, grinning. She wasn't watching.

The temp led me through a labyrinth of cubicles, past offices with their doors slightly ajar. I looked carefully for Susan, who I thought would surely find me before the meeting, but she failed to materialize.

Eventually the temp and I arrived at a corner office, a cavernous chamber with oaken paneling and purple carpet and windows twice as tall as I was. "Wow," I said.

"Yep," the temp said proudly, sitting down behind a huge desk.

I blinked at him. Suddenly it occurred to me that he wasn't young at all, was in his forties and just looked young owing to his childish face, his sneakers. I stood there like a fool, clutching my portfolio across my chest.

"You're . . ."

"Raymond Burn. Niceta meetcha. Have a seat!"

I lowered myself into a leather armchair, looking around for a place to put the Perrier. I opted for the floor. "Uh, well! Thanks! For seeing me!" I said, wondering if the windows opened and, if so, whether I should fling myself out one. Why hadn't he introduced himself already? Why didn't he shake my hand? Why didn't I shake his? I sprung back to my feet and leaned across the desk, my hand extended. The postcard I'd gotten downstairs slipped from my pocket and fell onto the desk, so I retracted my hand, grabbed it, stuck it back into my pocket, held the pocket shut with my portfolio and re-extended the hand to where Burn's was waiting impatiently. We shook.

"Love your dad's work," he said. "Love it! You could say I'm a Fan." He gave the shook hand a surreptitious glance, then wiped it with a handkerchief.

"Well," I said. I sat down again. "Me too."

"You better be, heh-heh. Tim, I was just talking to Ken Dorn the other day. You know Ken?"

"A little."

"Ken was saying he didn't think you had the stuff to draw the Family Funnies. Now, don't get me wrong," he said, holding up his empty palms. "We're committed to you, Tim. You've got the legacy, you see. But I just wanted to know if maybe you had any interest in responding to that statement of Ken's, whaddya think, Tim?"

I set down my portfolio and noticed two enormous dark handprints on my knees. Where had they come from? I looked down at my hands: black, as if I'd been delivering newspapers all morning.

"Sure," I said. "Sure, I have a response to that. Uh, I just want to say that I can do it, sir. I mean, I want to do it, and I'm the right man, uh, for the job . . . and . . ." I picked up the portfolio again. "And I think my portfolio will speak for itself, sir." I lifted the heavy thing over the edge of the desk and set it down, open end first, before Ray Burn. "I think perhaps you should take them out yourself, sir, owing to the fact that my hands . . . I don't know what happened . . . seem to be very dirty suddenly . . ."

He peered over the portfolio at my hands, which I was holding out to him. "Yeah, you got yourself a little mess there, heh-heh."

It wasn't just my hands and pants, of course; it was my white shirt, too, the inside of my jacket. The postcard had fallen out of my pocket again and onto my lap, and I understood now that it was the culprit. I picked it up. The penciled side was half rubbed off: it hadn't been fixed on there after all. I could see the artist's name, scrawled in thick black magic marker, hazy beneath the worn parts. "Maybe . . ." I said. "Maybe you should go ahead and give those a look, sir. While I go clean myself up a little."

He was already sliding the cartoons from the portfolio. "Sure, sure," he said, distracted. I jumped to my feet and headed out of the office at a brisk jog. The maze confounded me. Which way around the desks? It took me several minutes to get back to the lobby. Once in the restroom, I dropped the postcard into the trash and looked at myself in the mirror. A disaster. Not just my clothes and hands but my face, my neck . . . how had I touched myself in so many places so quickly?

I washed my hands with liquid soap from the dispenser, then wet a crumpled ball of paper towels and used them to dab at the huge stains on my shirt and pants. The towels grew dark, but the stains didn't seem to diminish; on the contrary, they spread, losing definition, and my chest and thighs became soaked with dirty water. I took off my jacket before attempting to clean it, then decided to just leave it off, despite the inkstain on the arm. I checked myself in the mirror. I looked like I'd been splashed by a dozen cabs.

Back in the office, though, Ray Burn was laughing. The sound was so shocking, so unselfconscious, that I considered backing out into the hallway until he was finished. Laughing! This was something, I realized, that had been missing: an audience. I stood paralyzed in the doorway, listening to him.

"Mix!" he said. He pounded his desk. It made a sound like a bank vault door crashing open. "This is a gas!"

"It is?"

" 'Liberries!' That's it exactly! What a killer!" He moved another drawing to the top of the pile. "And how 'bout this—'If Puddles doesn't use a fork, how come we have to?' Tim, this is brilliant!"

"Thanks!" I said.

"It's like you're the reinfuckingcarnation of your old man, pardon the

French. You got that same sense of humor. That's what a good strip really needs! A sense of humor!"

I sat down slowly, setting my jacket on the floor. I picked up the Perrier and took a sip. "I think you're right, sir."

"Ray," he said, "call me Ray."

"You got it, Ray."

He set the drawings down, and tilted his head up, toward a corner of the ceiling. I resisted the impulse to look there too. "What was it like?" he said, then looked down at me. "Living with the Maestro?"

"You mean Dad?"

"Yeah, yeah! Did the fans flock to the old home place? Was it a barrel of monkeys? I'll bet it was a barrel of monkeys."

"Oh, sure," I told him. "We had some prime yuks."

And this is what we discussed for the rest of the meeting: a highly selective, often imaginary version of my childhood, complete with adoring throngs, madcap domestic adventures, familial harmony and mountains of fan mail. To my amazement, Burn was utterly riveted. We laughed like old friends. It was fun, in a peculiar way, inventing this zany childhood for myself, and I began to realize that this was what the Family Funnies was all about: fulfilling the wishes of the American family with a delicate, photo-album detachment, letting the reader fill in the blanks with more goofy good will instead of the usual tedium and heartbreak most people's blanks were filled with. I realized that Ray Burn was a completely fabricated person, that he had made, at some point in his life, a conscious decision to let the world fill him up according to his wishes, which he had been letting it do for so long that he no longer had an ounce of objectivity to his name, nor wanted to. Susan was right: tabula rasa. I was impressed with her judge of character.

My departure consisted of a lot of handshaking and back-slapping. My clothes were dry now, and I looked like a third grader's math test, blurry with inept emendations. We thanked each other profusely. I half-hoped Ken Dorn would make one of his mysterious appearances, so that I could gloat.

"Say, Ray," I said at the threshold of his office. "Do you know where Susan is?"

"Susan who?"

"Susan Caletti? Who works here?"

"Oh, sure!" he said. "Little Susie! Yeah, she's down in that last office." He pointed down a long, narrow hallway, where light shined from an open door. "You two know each other?"

"Uh . . . She's my editor here, I think."

He slapped his forehead. "Right, duh! I dunno where my head gets to."

I headed down the hallway, leaving Burn with a little wave. I wondered how long he would remember our meeting.

"What happened to you?" Susan asked me, her eyes wide.

I gave her the short version. "But the main thing is that Burn liked me! We got on like old pals. He thought the cartoons were hilarious."

"He's a disturbing little person, isn't he?"

"Most assuredly."

She gathered her things and we left via a back hallway that emptied out near the receptionist's desk. Susan was wearing some shimmery blue dress thing and a pair of running shoes. I wanted to grope her, and did, in the elevator. She kissed me.

"Tim," she said.

"Oh God. What now?"

"Am I that transparent? I intercepted another memo."

"Where do you find these things?" I asked her. "Do they just cc you every time they print out a secret communiqué?"

"Recycling bin," she said. "The intern leaves copies of everything in there. I think she secretly has it in for everybody." She detached herself from me. "Tim, the lawyers figured out a way around your contract. It's just a matter of choice now: you or Dorn."

"Well, I wowed the chief," I said, feeling my heart sink.

"That does count for a lot. For everything, in fact."

"Except money."

She shrugged. "Except money. But Ray's an old softie. His heart and his head. It's a toss-up, as far as I can see."

"Well, no use worrying."

"No."

I pulled her back toward me. "So the plan?"

"Ah! The plan! You're a Friday visitor, so you've never known the pleasures of the Delicious Duck Wednesday specials."

"And I will now?" I said.

"You certainly shall," she answered, and that did make things a lot better.

# thirty-one

That Saturday I woke to find Pierce sitting on the couch, playing solitaire with a deck of naked-girl playing cards. He had a look of controlled boredom on his face, as if forcing himself to act like a normal person while he weathered a particularly trying inner squall. I got myself some cereal and sat on the easy chair, facing him.

"You're home," I said.

He carefully did not look up from his card game. "Gilly's coming."

"Here? Really?"

"She's picking me up. We're going to go to Philly."

"Philly!"

He nodded, then pulled from his pocket the worn-out warehouse key. I hadn't seen it since I found it in the safety deposit box. "We're going to find what it's to."

I tried to conceal my excitement. I hadn't forgotten the key, but I'd filed away semipermanently the curiosity connected with it, sure that Pierce would never get around to finding the warehouse. I asked him how they were going to look for it.

"Gilly has a plan," he said. It seemed that the two of them had spent much of the previous weekend poring square-eyed over the Yellow Pages and a street map of Philadelphia, marking with colored sticky dots the locations of every self-storage warehouse in the city. They were going to go and look for the right place in her car.

"But there have to be dozens of warehouses," I said.

"Two hundred fourteen."

"You're going to go to two hundred fourteen warehouses in one day?"

He shook his head. "That's where Gilly's plan comes in," he said, his eyes gleaming. Apparently Pierce had some sort of aura that Gillian could detect surrounding his person, as did everyone. People related to a person were said to share elements of that person's aura, and it was possible to sense a person's presence from his possessions or from items that were once his. It seemed that Gillian planned to go to each warehouse, ascertain if any Pierce-related aura was hovering about, and decide to inquire about the key based on that determination. As Pierce described the plan to me, in the same pained, earnest voice he might have used to tell me about a ball game or a television program, I began to feel like the world had vanished around me while I slept and been replaced with another one which, though similar, differed in certain subtle, disturbing ways.

"Aura?" I said. "Really?"

"Oh, yeah. You've got one, Mom, Mal, everybody." He said that two hundred fourteen was too many warehouses even to drive by, but that Gillian would be able to sense the correct general area by a method of "emotional triangulation" she had devised herself. It involved a hand mirror and a candle, among other less palpable elements. "It's some sort of witchy thing," Pierce said. "I don't totally understand it."

My cereal had gone a bit soggy listening to this, so I took a few contemplative bites and considered the plan.

"Not to take the wind out of your sails," I said. "But it sounds a little wonky to me."

He shrugged. "Yeah, well . . ."

"Do you believe in that stuff?"

He pursed his lips, thinking. "I believe in her," he said finally.

"Well, okay, good."

"She thinks I need to go find the place. She says it's like there's a little part of Dad that isn't fully dead, but wants to be, and I have to go put it to rest."

"Can she talk to the dead?" I asked.

He looked shocked. "Of course not!" he said, turning back to his game. "Don't be ridiculous."

I was standing in the yard watering the bushes when a little red Ford Fiesta with an ankh painted on the hood pulled in behind the Caddy. Gillian Millstone tore herself from the car and ran across the yard to me like a four-year-old. She was wearing short shorts and knee boots and a University of Massachusetts sweat shirt. "Hi!" she yelled, and threw her arms around me with such force that I dropped the hose. I thought at first she had mistaken me for my brother, but then she said my name and that she was happy to see me, and I decided she was just an extremely friendly kind of person.

"You look happy today," she said.

"I sort of am." It was true. Fall was a week from beginning, and, for better or worse, my stint as a cartoon journeyman was coming to a close. In a few weeks everything would be different. Even considering the vast gulf between the best-case and worst-case scenarios, this prospect gladdened me, and when Gillian untangled her skinny body from mine I felt a little twinge of regret.

"It's good to see the old place again."

"I thought you'd never been here," I said.

"I've driven by," she said. "I get good vibes from it, anyhow."

I nodded, thinking about the warehouse plan. "I wish I could say the same. So, Gillian."

"Yeah."

"This plan of yours. Do you think it's going to work? I mean, you can actually detect . . . auras?"

She smiled at me, and I saw in her face a surprising intelligence—calculating, though not in a bad way. What was the chance of picking out the place at random? What was the chance of your parents getting killed in a plane crash? I got the idea Gillian had the numbers. "A little," she said. "I'm better at detecting your brother."

"How so?" I asked her.

She shrugged. "He wants to believe we'll find it. But not too much. Know what I mean?"

I picked up the hose, which had soaked my shoes. I didn't know what to make of Gillian's forthright willingness to confide in me. "Hmm," I said.

They packed the car with their tools: water bottles, lunchmeat sandwiches, fruit. I peered into the back and saw a few mysterious items: a black wooden box with a brass latch, and some pentagonal doodads made of string and sticks.

"Well," I said. "Good luck. What'll you do when you find it?"

Pierce cleared his throat. "Well, nothing at first. I'll need a little while to think about it."

I felt a rush of empathy for my brother and clapped my hand on his shoulder—too hard, maybe, but he stood steady. "Well, I'd like to be there when you open it."

"Yeah, yeah," he said. He made no effort to mask his alarm at the thought.

They climbed in and drove off. The little car, receding, looked like a giant groundhog, waddling down the driveway. An eroded sticker on the back bumper read MY OTHER CAR IS A BROOM.

I did my chores in the yard with something like ecstasy, barely recognizing it as such until I was almost done. I slowed, holding off the end until I had gotten my fill: the sweetness of rotting leaves and fish washed up on the shores of the river, not a hundred yards away; the sun-warmed air, just getting its baby teeth. I found myself reliving, with a kind of instant nostalgia, something that had happened the evening before at Ivy Homes: my mother, confused and narcoleptic as was now usual, had awoken from a sound sleep with an urgent need to be taken to the bathroom. I had been reading a magazine in the chair at the foot of her bed, in the shifting light of the muted TV. She couldn't seem to voice this desire and, like a cat staring mournfully at its empty bowl, only moved her eyes and head toward the toilet.

"The bathroom, Mom?" I said.

She blinked. "Yes."

I got up to find a nurse's aide, and though there were plenty of them purposefully navigating the halls, in the end I couldn't bring myself to ask their help with my own mother. I went back to the bed and helped her into her

wheelchair. If she could distinguish me from the usual help, she didn't indicate it, but all the same there were no complaints, no protests at my treatment,
and I was grateful. I wheeled her to the bathroom and lifted her out of the
chair: she was light as a child. I could say here that the entire process was like
helping a child, except that it wasn't, save for the absence of speech, the absence of embarrassment over the body. Otherwise she was still my mother, a
woman who had known ruin, had wrecked herself willfully and deliberately
escaping the onus of life with my father, whom she had ceased to love, and of
life without the man whom perhaps she did. I set her down on the toilet,
helped her raise her nightgown, cleaned her when she was through. And I
cried, not out of pity—though I did pity her imprisonment in this body—but
because there was dignity in her lack of shame for this sorry state, dignity even
in her helplessness. She met my eyes while I worked her gown back over her,
and if anything passed between us in that look, it was that she would let me
usher her into her death, would trust me to help her find whatever comfort I
could give her.

And to my surprise, I wasn't disgusted by this task, or even saddened. I
was moved by the revelation that this, like cartooning, like stepping out of bed
in the morning and opening the bedroom door, was work, and by definition
important, a discrete, fully contained act. It was an act of maintenance, and of
mercy, but it was good and useful and utterly proper. And when I had put my
mother back into her bed and she again fell to sleep, I felt a tacit acknowledg-
ment between us of the fact of her death, which waited for her like a gift from
a distant relative that had been shipped but had not yet arrived.

Out in the yard, shoving fallen branches into a metal garbage can, I let
happiness run its course through me, knowing that it wouldn't last, but also
knowing that it would always be somewhere waiting for me, if I made the effort to find it. This understanding seemed an almost criminally excessive piece
of good fortune, but for the time being I accepted it without question.

They came back at ten o'clock. Gillian aimed a knowing smile at me as she
crossed the threshold of the studio, but Pierce was in a fever, sweating, his hair
wild and damp, his hands talking to each other in the air.

"What?" I said. "What happened?"

"Oh, man," Pierce was saying. "Oh, man."

"What!"

Gillian threw an arm around Pierce, trying to contain him. "We found it," she said.

"Really? So the plan worked?"

"Oh, totally!" Pierce said, as much to himself as to me.

"Sort of," Gillian told me. "We skipped a bunch of them. Then we got to the twenty-fifth or -sixth or something, and I thought, this is it, and we asked the guy in the office if the key was his. And he said no, but that he knew the guy who had those kind of keys at his warehouses, and he gave us the address, and we went to this guy and he said it was to the Girard Avenue location, so we went there."

"And that was it?"

Pierce gaped at me. "It's fucking huge, Tim, it's totally huge! The door is like . . . you could fit a dump truck in there!"

"It's true," Gillian said. "It's a big door."

"We didn't go in. I couldn't. I can't."

"Sure you can," she told him, giving him a friendly shake.

"No way. Oh, man." He suddenly looked out the door at the house, as if he'd heard something there. "I gotta get a shower or a bath or something." He wriggled out of Gillian's grasp and dashed away.

She watched him go, then turned to me. "I know he seems a little riled, but he'll be okay."

"If you say so."

"So you're coming, right?"

"Whenever you're ready," I said.

She patted my shoulder. "You're a good brother," she told me, then went out after Pierce. I had been accused of a lot of things in my life, but never that.


The next morning I did a strange thing. While getting ready to visit my mother, I grabbed a sketchbook from the kitchen counter and a couple of number two pencils. I'd been inking in the sketchbook before breakfast, working on some cartoon versions of household items, but I couldn't remember what I had done with the pen. I felt a little pang of guilt over this—my father would no sooner have drawn in a sketchbook with a number two pencil than eat dinner with a garden trowel—but I let it pass. I don't know why I felt the need to bring the sketchbook at all. I just did it.

Gillian had spent the night, so the Caddy was available. I set the sketchbook and pencils on the passenger seat while I drove. The simple thought of them thrilled me. For a moment I considered turning around and going back to the studio, but I squelched the impulse and made it to Ivy Homes.

My mother was asleep. She woke up briefly when I got there, regarded me with an expression of plain surprise, then just as abruptly collapsed back onto the pillow and fell asleep again. The nursing home was quiet; most of the residents were at the nondenominational Sunday religious services the home provided and that my mother, even in her nonplussed half-consciousness, had the presence of mind to eschew.

I set the drawing supplies on the edge of the bed and watched her. It is often said of the dead or dying that they look peaceful in sleep, but my mother looked like she was deep in a drugged coma beneath the tent of an army field hospital. I don't think I'd ever seen someone so enervated, so utterly whipped. I glanced at her chart on the back of the door and read that already today she had woken up, sung several songs with the other residents, ate breakfast, went to the toilet and took her first of several handfuls of medications. It was no wonder she was tired. There was something vital missing from her face, as if life was only accessible to her during waking hours, rationed like wartime electricity.

So I tried to draw her, or at any rate to capture this absence on the page. How could you render nothing with a pencil? The first few tries were in vain; I was aiming for stark realism and got nothing but vaguely melancholy smudges. I tried to draw the cartoon Mom: first as a young woman, placidly dozing, then older, aging her in stages. What I came up with was not too bad. There was only an empty space, a cartoon void, between her cheekbone and nose, but in the first drawing the space implied a round, flushed cheek, and in the second a concavity, the sunken cheek of an old woman.

Still, the cartoon lacked anything of what I actually felt for my mother. It was the aged version of my father's creation, something that would never be useful in my career as the author of the Family Funnies. I started a fresh page and tried again, this time jettisoning the rigid toadstool-shaped coiffure and the angular calendar girl's nose and inserting my own interpretations, in a thick-lined cartoon shorthand, of her features. The nose, not a V but a gentle curve with a curious reverse loop at the nostril: my mother's were wide and expressive, like little mouths. Her eyes a set of parallel lines, as if desperately squeezed shut against an incomprehensible world. It took me several tries to get it right, but ten minutes later, there she was, both a cartoon and my mother.

"That's swell," said a voice at my ear, and I jerked so hard my chair barked against the floor like a car horn.

"Oh God! I'm sorry!" Bitty said in a piercing whisper. She was standing behind me, wearing a yellow sundress and a gigantic straw hat. My mother's face tumbled through a series of anxious quivers.

"Oh, Jesus," I said, my heart thundering. I gathered the pencils and pad from the floor. Bitty pulled Mom's wheelchair up beside me and sat down in it.

"I thought you knew I was here. I was right behind you!"

"I was kind of absorbed."

She pointed. "Can I see that again?"

I handed her the sketchbook unopened, and I watched as she leafed past my failed experiments. She lingered on the Family Funnies version, and then longer on the final version.

"This one back here looks like something Dad would have done," she said. It sounded like a curse, and I said so.

She bit her lip. "I don't like to think of him being here to see Mom like this. I mean, so far gone." Her eyes took on a faint gleam, and she blinked it away.

"No."

"So this drawing, the last one. It's good. It's the best of the bunch, you know."

"I was just thinking that."

"You ought to do something with it."

"Do something? Like what?"

She stared at it awhile. "I dunno. Maybe give it to me."

"Tear it out," I said. "It's yours."

"Really? Thanks." She tore cautiously, though it was a spiral notebook and there was no real need. She folded it in half, careful not to crease the actual drawing, which was small, and set it on her lap. "So," she said. "I guess she's coming home soon? I talked to Uncle Mal."

"A couple weeks," I said. Mal was buying a hospital bed, the kind with the sides that can be unlocked and pushed out of the way, and was finding her a good nurse, evidently a formidable task. We talked about these things as if they were established truths just waiting to be made manifest, but in fact it was not so simple, and I worried about all of them, from the nurse's fee to whether or not the bed would fit through the front door.

"We'll talk about my shifts?" Bitty said.

"When it's all set up, I guess."

Our mother stirred in her bed. She opened her eyes to the ceiling, then closed them again and fell, apparently, back to sleep.

"So things are a little dicey with Mike," she told me suddenly.

"Really? Why?"

"I'm knocked up, for one thing." She didn't give me time to react. Pregnant! I tried to picture Bitty swollen with child, and the image snapped into surprising focus almost instantly. "And also he's become kind of withdrawn." She said that Mike had set up a little mini-living room out in the garage, complete with an ottoman and tiny refrigerator, and sat there alone in the evenings watching television. "It's our only TV. I mean, I'd like to watch it now and then. But he said something about him being the breadwinner and it was his TV, and he could watch it alone if he damn well pleased." She made an exaggerated, horrified face. "I mean, really. Does he think I'm some sort of moron?"

"He just sounds like a guy to me. Does the knocked-up part have anything to do with it?"

"I think he finds me disgusting now that I'm a fully functioning female human being."

It occurred to me that this meant I'd have a new nephew. Or niece. "Hey, a baby. A baby will be good. It could play with Nancy and Bobby's baby someday."

She chortled. "Yeah, my baby will be a bad influence on their baby."

At that moment my mother sat up in bed, as rigidly and mechanically as if worked by hidden hydraulics. Her eyes were wide open. "Well, Carl," she said, "there we are."

"Mommy?" said Bitty, sounding small.

Mom's posture softened and she smiled, genuinely, sadly. "Just look at us!"

Bitty went to her, but she lay back down and went to sleep. That was all she said. When Bitty came back to the wheelchair she was crying. The crying turned into sobbing. I got up and touched her shoulder.

"Bitty," I said. "Hey, Bitty." But she cried and cried and would not stop.

## thirty-two

The last few weeks before my final submission to Burn Features, I felt much like Napoleon must have in the last days before invading Russia: suffused with visions of glory and power, with occasional distraction by a vague sensation of unease. My submission date had taken on the burnished gleam of legend, deep in the future history of my imagination, as the time when everything would become clear to me and my life would hoist its backpack onto its shoulders and set off, once and for all, onto its True Path.

Of course I recognized how stupid this was. Over those weeks I worked as hard and long as before, but now I had a heightened sense of this work as inherently absurd in its repetitiveness, the frenzied lever-yanking of a hormone-crazed lab rat. Rationally speaking, handing it in seemed to have no chance of solving anything, but my emotions had turned it into a talisman that I was foolishly convinced would protect me.

The work I filled my time with didn't always have anything to do with the strip. I kept drawing my mother in this new, slightly disturbing cartoon style, and the images I created stayed with me all through the day: her hunched, vulture's curve in her wheelchair, the rare stoop over her walker, the miserable wrinkle she made under a sheet. I hung out a lot at Ivy Homes. The nurses were getting to know me, and meanwhile Pierce and Mal were hard at work preparing the house for her presence, preparing her for it as well. That plan, anyway, seemed to be working.

Bitty and I often came to the home at the same time, and while I drew she read magazines and looked over my shoulder. She was mum about her pregnancy and about Mike, and I had no reason to press the issue; it did seem, however, that she felt more comfortable with me now that I knew, as if that confession was a piece of her I was carrying for safe keeping. And this was fine with me: it was so light that it felt like a piece of myself.

Wurster seemed to notice that I wasn't concentrating, but he didn't say anything about it. In the past months he had gotten to be less severe, more contemplative: a new Brad. I didn't much miss the old one. Once, during the last week of our classes—I was to have a few days off to do the final drafts of my submission cartoons—he told me, right in the middle of a lesson, to stop drawing.

"Why?" I said. "What's wrong?"

"Nothing," he said. He was looking at the paper in a funny way, as if something was crawling across it. "Just stop."

I sat back in the chair, and felt the muscles in my back loosening. "Okay."

"There," he said.

"There what?"

"How does that feel? Not drawing. Does it feel better than drawing?"

I shrugged. "I suppose."

He stood up, leaned past me and pulled open the window, which during my stint here had never been opened. Dust filled the room, and a gooey, filthy sort of light. He squinted into this light for a while, saying nothing. Then he turned to me. "Let's go outside."

"Why?"

"Let's just go out." He picked my jacket up from the floor and handed it to me.

It was really fall now. It had that smell. Leaves were getting the fragile jitteriness that meant they were thinking about taking the plunge. We sat in the scraggly grass, enjoying the yard's only patch of sunlight, and scootched around after it as it moved.

"Can I ask you something?" I said to Wurster.

"Shoot."

"What did my dad pay you for this?"

He sighed. "Nothing."

"Nothing?"

"I promised him I'd teach you. I didn't want to break the promise."

"You're doing this for free?"

He made a face. "It was a long time ago. I owed it to him. And besides," he said, his voice softening, "it was . . . instructive, working with you. I learned some things."

"No kidding?"

"No kidding," Wurster said.

And that was all he would say on the subject, and I never would find out what it was he owed my father for. In retrospect, I'm glad he didn't tell me. The older I get, the more reluctant I become to judge my father, or anybody else, so terribly harshly. But that's later.

The only other change in those last few weeks was in my relationship with Susan: I had fallen in love with her. At least I thought I had, anyway; I was reluctant to get close enough to find out for sure, the way you're reluctant, while enjoying a balmy and empty beach, to look too closely at the sign that might or might not say NO TRESPASSING. The possibility of love was thrilling to consider, but its implications were overwhelming. Susan and I ate together, slept together. She did her laundry at our house. But the emotions went unaddressed, and I was aware that she was waiting me out, and that her willingness to wait was finite. Our relationship was a beautifully wrapped gift that, when you listened closely enough, went tick, tick.

The day I went to the post office to mail away my two weeks of Family Funnies, Ken Dorn was waiting for me. He was leaning against the self-service counter, reading a paperback book. He looked up at me and smiled politely, much in the way you would smile at a man you've invited into your office to fire, and said, "Timmy Mix. What a surprise!" His goatee was fully in now, as neatly trimmed as a fairway.

"Fancy meeting you here."

"It's nearly eleven," he said. "I was certain you'd be here by ten-thirty." He pointed to my package, which had the words DO NOT BEND stamped on it in dark red block letters. "What have we got here?"

"Matzoh."

"Har, har. Just in time for Passover."

He followed me into the line, which was long. Everyone in it seemed to have the same cold, and kleenex fluttered before the regiment of noses like a dozen flags of surrender. "So, Tim, any chance of letting me check out the drawings?"

"They're all packed up," I said.

"Come on, for your old pal Ken? They can seal it up again at the counter."

I gave this some thought. "Stand a couple feet back," I said. "No touching."

"All right, all right. I wasn't going to spoil your little party." He backed off and crossed his arms smugly over his chest.

I pulled each drawing out slowly, held it up before Ken Dorn, and slid it back into the package before taking out another. Ken seemed to lose his snotty affect; the sneer disappeared from his face and he studied each drawing carefully, with a kind of scholarly detachment. I sealed them away and tucked the envelope under my arm.

"So," I said.

He nodded. "Those are good," he said with real sincerity. "I'm impressed."

I waited for pride to sweep me off my feet, but it never came. I was too far resigned to what fate would bring to care what Ken Dorn thought. The sentiment was touching, though, from such an insidious little man.

"Well, thank you," I said. "That's very kind."

"I mean it, they are very good." He shrugged. "Not that it'll make a difference."

I was less suspicious of the content than the delivery: the supercilious whimper had crept back into his voice. "What do you mean?" I said.

"I mean, it's a done deal. The Family Funnies is mine."

"I haven't even mailed these, Ken."

"No matter. I played nine holes with Burn yesterday. I'm as good as hired."

We moved forward in line. I was fuming. I said, "You came all the way to Riverbank to tell me that?"

"Mixville," he said. "And hey, Timmy, I thought you'd want to know. It's important news, isn't it?"

"If it were correct," I said, loudly enough so that several people turned their heads, "it would be news. As it is, it's just idle speculation. You're bluffing." I couldn't bear to look at him.

Dorn laughed. "Don't kid yourself, Mix. You know I have the inside track."

"Shove off."

I stole a glance. Across his face spread the priggish leer of a corrupt cop about to toss a ziploc bag of marijuana into my car. We stood glaring at one another for a few seconds before he turned, pointed at the counter, and said, "You're up, buddy."

I asked the clerk to next-day my package. She taped it back up and stuck a sticker on it. I scanned the place: Dorn was gone.

"That's fifteen bucks," said the clerk. I barely had the energy to take the money out of my wallet.


Two days later I had come down with the post office cold and was on my way to New York to meet Susan. I had a box of tissues wedged between the seat belt thingies and a lukewarm travel mug of mint tea in the pull-out drink holder. Pierce had put some foul powder into it that was supposed to ream out the sinuses, and though I winced with every sip, I breathed better than I had in eighteen hours. I made frequent and disgusting sounds into balled-up kleenexes, which coated the floor of the car to a depth of several inches. I was not one to pretend I wasn't sick.

Parking a Cadillac in New York was no small feat, so I gave up entirely and resorted to a garage. If things somehow managed to work out, I figured I could deduct the cost. I stuffed a wad of fresh tissues into my jacket pocket, and emerged into the cab-agitated air of New York. With my head in such a state, every gentle breeze felt like a sock in the jaw; I was convinced I could feel Brownian motion at work on every follicle of my hair.

I had expected to be on edge about Burn's impending decision, but for some reason—the inner dullness the cold had brought on, perhaps, or the fatalistic fog encounters with Dorn invariably put me in—I was completely relaxed. I rode the elevator to the syndicate with a kind of objective calm:

whatever happened, I told myself, it would have no more or less power over me than if I was watching it happen to someone else.

For this reason, I was more than a little surprised to find myself panicking at the sight of Susan sprinting past the receptionist's desk, holding a giant cardboard box. I leapt out of the elevator, head pounding, as she vanished into the stairwell. The receptionist sat very still, her eyes round as cherry tomatoes.

"Susan?" I said. The stair door sucked shut and I could hear her footsteps faintly echoing off the concrete walls.

I ran to the door and flung it open. "Susan! Is that you?"

The footsteps stopped. I could hear her breathing. I looked down the long shaft and saw a hand, two floors below, gripping the rail. "Who is that?"

"It's me, Tim!"

"*Tib?*"

"*Tim!*" I hollered. "I have a cold!" I hurried down the stairs, my throat feeling brittle and untethered, rattling loose in my neck. She had already begun walking again, slower now, by the time I reached her.

"Where are you going?" I said. Her face was tight and furious, like a welterweight's.

"Out."

I was having trouble keeping up. My nose had begun to run, and I fished a tissue from my pocket to wipe it. "What about Burn? I thought . . ."

"Don't bother," she said. "You didn't get it."

I stopped on a landing. She kept going. "I didn't?"

She reached the next landing, then turned, slumping against the wall. "No."

"Dorn got it."

"Dorn always had it."

"And you knew that?"

She put the box down. "No, I actually thought you had a chance. But you didn't. So."

"So?"

"So I quit."

I looked down into the box: tape dispenser, photos, plush armadillo toy. I started slowly down the steps, keeping my eyes on her face, which in its anger and humiliation had taken on a dozen harsh new folds. She looked like a pug dog. She was *mad*. My mind raced. "You quit?"

"Yes."

"You can't quit!" I blurted, and immediately I wanted to take it back, because the train of thought I had taken to get to it suddenly came chugging into view: if you quit, then who's going to support us when we move in together?

"Why not?"

"Because . . . Because . . ." I had almost reached her now. She bent over and picked up her box.

It was then that I had a kind of epiphany. I saw Susan, really *saw* her, in a new way. At first this perception wouldn't entirely reveal itself to me, the way a mysterious shape in a dark room takes a moment or two to resolve through light-drunk eyes. She was no longer the old thing but was not yet the new thing, with her blouse crooked around her neck and her bra strap cleaving the flesh of her shoulder. She was undergoing a kind of phase change.

And then, as she stood, I had it: I knew how I would draw her. I knew how I might do the liquid squiggle of her hair and the unlipsticked perpetual half-grin of her mouth, and the assemblage of concentric roundnesses that was her body. More significantly, I had at last come to a sense of the wholeness of her, of what she *meant*. Of her body's truck with her brain.

I also understood that this wasn't a revelation about her at all. It was about me.

"Do you think I like working for these people?" she was saying. "The boy king and his loyal subjects? I'm quitting because they insulted you, Tim."

"I . . . I love you," I said, apropos of nothing. Her jaw dropped.

"Bullshit!"

"No, really."

She put down the box a second time and moved a step closer. There was something unfamiliar in her eyes, something that looked like it might give. "You remember I said I'd kick your butt."

"I know. I . . . don't have anything. A job, money, anything. I'm living off my brother."

"But you love me."

"Yeah."

She took my hands and, stepping up to meet me, kissed me on the lips.
"Then it's safe."

"Safe?"

"For me to love you," she said.

I felt, however clumsily, that this was true, though I hadn't the where-
withal to figure out how. No matter. "Sure," I said. "It's safe."


We worked things out in the car. She would get out of her apartment, which,
having quit her job, she could no longer afford. She assured me that quitting
was a long time coming. "Don't go feeling all guilty about it," she told me.
"I've felt like scum since the day I set foot in that cathouse." And she would
stay with us for a few days until she could find a place somewhere—Mixville,
Titusville, anywhere—to live while she sorted things through.

It all sounded fine to me. We wouldn't move in together, not right away,
anyway, so that I could help get my mother settled. I told Susan I wanted to
live at home for a while to be with her. "And then, who knows?"

"Right."

We talked about our sudden freedom without regret, with something like
joy. I was beginning, on this ride home, to see my life as something I could fill
up, rather than something I was stuck in, and my family, for the first time, the
same way. For better or worse, my mother's decline would bring us together,
in the place we ought to have been truly together in the first place. I was full
of high hopes for everyone: for Bobby to relax, for Sam to sleep, for Bitty and
Mike to reconcile. I saw us rallying around our mother like destitute burghers
after a hurricane, eager to set things right, and secretly happy for the new op-
portunities, new beginnings.

Then we got home, the pair of happy failures, and walked into a house so
gummed up with gloom that we could barely push through the doorway. Mal
and Pierce sat across the kitchen counter from one another, their heads in
their hands, and Gillian stood behind my brother, gently running her hand up
and down his back. She looked up at Susan and me, and so did Mal, and I could
tell by the pitiful wrecks of their faces that my mother was dead.

## thirty-three

Three weeks later, the four of us—Pierce, Gilly, Susan and I—set off for Philadelphia in the Cadillac. Pierce had wanted Mal to come, but Mal had refused. Since our mother's death he had come frequently to the house for despondent little visits, and while this worried me—what was he putting himself through?—he seemed glad to be in our company, as if spending time with us was what he wanted all along. As well it might have been. Susan and Pierce and I began to lay a living claim on the house, emptying the place of ill-chosen items, painting, having the carpet cleaned. Possibilities of life in Mixville started turning up like found change where the bulky old furniture used to sit. I realized I had become attached to the studio and my regimen of drawing, so I cleared out all the Family Funnies junk and boxed it up in the garage, and continued sitting out there, drawing aimlessly, right on schedule.

And so I should have been happy. I had what I wanted, didn't I?—a life free from the pressure of dealing with my parents, with Amanda, with the barnacled anchor of the Family Funnies. But there is nothing like a lot of trouble to make a lazy man feel busy, and now that the trouble was gone I was back to square one: me. I was disappointed that Mom never came home, but the disappointment wasn't only for her lonely death at Ivy Homes: it was for my own superfluity. I was going to do something important! I was going to make up for all those years when I barely paid her a moment's notice! And now I had no project, no guiding principle but the rehabilitation of my soul, and nothing's less appealing than that.

"You have the key?" I said to Pierce as we pulled out of the driveway. He sat beside me in the passenger seat, Susan and Gilly in the back, and we were all in a pretty good mood, considering.

"Oh my God!" he said, and I slammed on the brakes. But he was holding the key up before me, grinning.

"Huh huh huh," I told him, and he sniggered like a scoundrel.

We drove along Route 29, past the giant outdoor flea market, empty today and cluttered with fallen leaves, past the dilapidated barn on the grassy hill, the Christmas tree farm, where I anticipated coming in a couple months for the U-Chop-It special, past the mottled box elders that canopied the road. I was feeling a little bit of nostalgia for the old days of driving up and down this road from West Philly, but not much. I relished the prospect of skipping my usual exit, of getting to enjoy a trip into the city that wasn't a cobbling-together of recreated past experiences.

I seemed to be the only one in the car with nothing to say. Gillian was telling Susan about witchhood, which by her description seemed to consist of equal parts Spiritualism, Celtic Gnosticism and Jungian psychology. They got onto a tangent about ghosts, and from there a talk about Weird Experiences, which everyone had had but me.

"I had a dog when I was a kid," Susan said. "One night he was out in the yard howling, and I went out to see what was going on. It was fall, a lot like this, and the ground was covered with leaves. By the time I got out there the howling had stopped, but Loofah—"

"Loofah?" said Pierce.

"I like it," Gillian told her.

"Well, thanks. Anyway, he came to me across the yard, and there was something weird about it, I didn't know what. So I patted his head and told him to go back to his little house, and like that, he turned around and did. But the weird thing was that his paws weren't making any sound on the leaves, and from where I was standing he looked like he was hovering about an inch off the ground."

A moment of silence while everyone took this in. "Creepy," Pierce finally said.

"I thought it was a dream or something, but the next morning he was dead."

Nobody seemed surprised. "Poor Loofah," said Gillian.

Pierce said suddenly, "I used to have a flea circus."

"No kidding?" Susan said.

"Yep. I was just a kid." And he began to tell them the flea circus story, the fleas he got through the mail, the books and pamphlets he read to learn how to train them. I knew the story, of course, but there were elements I hadn't heard, like the middle-aged gypsy woman who sent him letters, thinking he was older and might marry her, and the colony of fleas that simply disappeared in his room during the night without a trace. To my surprise, Pierce was a good storyteller. His timing was perfect. When he got to the tall man's visit, which I suppose was intended to be the weird part, I listened carefully. He said that he let the man in, showed him the fleas.

"And he totally put me down. I mean, he'd come hundreds of miles to wreck a kid's day. He told me I was just an amateur and that my fleas were no good, and that I ought to give them to him, because he could really teach them a thing or two."

"So did you give them away?" Susan asked.

"Nope. I torched 'em. I took them out in the yard and set them on fire. Tim remembers this."

"It's true," I said.

Pierce shook his head. "It was the cruelest thing I've ever done. I was a little Nazi. After that, I swore I'd never hurt another thing again. I still watch my feet to make sure I'm not stomping bugs."

Afterward, Gilly told a story about how she'd been in a car driven by a drunk kid, and it rolled over once in the middle of the road, landed on its wheels and kept on going, and nobody mentioned what had happened. But I wasn't listening too carefully. Instead I was thinking about Pierce and the mysterious man. Pierce had revealed, without provocation, one of the great secrets of his childhood, and it turned out to be utterly devoid of the intrigue we had all attached to it. The tall man was nobody, just some guy, probably very lonely and jealous and insulated from the world, who couldn't stand the paltry notoriety of a little boy, and came to steal that notoriety away. It occurred to me that maybe we had never actually asked Pierce what happened, that we had so built him up in our minds as a mythic, almost magical loner that we failed to recognize that he was just a sad, neglected kid in the early stages of a lifelong sickness. I wondered how many times we had let him stew like that in his own juices, how much we had contributed to his problems later. I was ashamed. I wanted to take my hands off the wheel, lean over and hug him, but of course I didn't.

We were all silent as the Caddy glided into the Philadelphia city limits. Gilly leaned over the back of Pierce's seat and held both his hands; in the rearview I saw Susan squinting through her glasses at the hazy skyline. For a moment our eyes met and we smiled twin nervous smiles.

The warehouse stood, dark and crumbling, on Girard Avenue, a wide two-way dissected by ancient trolley tracks. All the other cars looked like ours, but older and less kept up: hulking American tugboats from before the energy crunch. We parked easily, as the spaces were largely empty, or occupied by cars that hadn't been moved in months. It was chilly, and the air carried the subway smell I'd learned to identify and enjoy, an organic admixture of gear oil, urine and soft pretzels.

"That's it?" I asked Pierce and Gilly.

Gilly had a thin arm around him. She gave his shoulders a squeeze. "That's it," she said.

The building was surrounded by chain-link fence. We stopped at a gate, where a muscular man was listening to a transistor radio. Pierce showed him the key and he waved us through.

They were right: the door was the size of a dump truck. It was made of corrugated metal and fastened shut with a giant padlock and a swivel hook as big as my arm. Pierce stared at it, then at me.

"Will you do it?"

Now? I wanted to say. Shouldn't we bow our heads or something? Say a prayer? Susan and Gilly stood side by side, several feet behind Pierce, and

Susan put a tentative arm around Gilly, in a big-sisterly way. Gilly seemed to appreciate it. For the first time since I'd met her, she actually seemed uneasy, and I was glad that Pierce wasn't looking at her. "Sure," I told him, and held out my hand. He put the key into it.

The lock resisted for a second, then gave, and I threw all my weight into unlatching it. The hook groaned in its eye. Then it was open. I turned around: Pierce had stepped back and was holding hands with a newly composed Gilly. "I'm gonna do it," I said.

"Okay."

The handle was cool and rough with rust, and I adjusted the position of my fingers, less for a better grip than for the sheer physicality of it, the pleasure in the sensation. I can't describe how happy I was at that moment, so deeply involved in this adventure with these three people; I felt like I could spend every waking moment with them for the rest of my life, and be perfectly satisfied.

The door rumbled up without the least resistance, practically pulling itself after the first few feet. This was the first indication that my father had spent a lot of time in here, but while this was occurring to me I looked up and saw what was inside, illuminated by the scummy daylight.

"Wow," Susan said.

I couldn't help the first thought that came to me, which is that this thing he had made, this monstrous piece of what I instantly recognized as installation art, was *bad*. Of course my second thought was that the first thought was terribly unfair, but in that brief moment of cruel judgment I saw what a fool I'd been to take on the strip, and how obvious it was that my father knew this all along, and knew I would fall for it too. He must have known I wouldn't let him change my life, no matter how much changing it needed, unless he was dead, and far out of range for flinging I-told-you-so's.

Although this thing he'd made, this awful thing was telling me so. It was also apologizing, in ragged, gasping breaths. We walked in, our footsteps seeming to echo this sad fact: *Sorry,* they seemed to say, *sorry, sorry, I'm so sorry.*

What we saw first were the sloppy fifteen-foot-high Family Funnies figures painted on the walls: Mom, Bitty and me on one side; Bobby, Lindy and

Puddles on the other. And on the back wall, my father himself, with two new additions to the FF cast: Mal and Pierce.

Mal and Dad stood on opposite sides of Pierce, each with an arm around him: the son's two fathers. Mal was rendered with a doting, fatherly air, while my father had done himself with his usual world-weariness, bent, in a neat trick of perspective, out over the floor of the storeroom. Pierce, on the other hand, was a clumsy creation at best, with a cherubic, glowing face that he had never possessed and never would. He had the same ears as Mal, and was wearing a T-shirt Pierce used to have and that I had forgotten, which read, in bubbly black Jersey-Shore-iron-on letters, BLAME MY PARENTS.

There was more to it than just the walls, of course. We walked around the room like baffled souls thrown into purgatory, sifting through the rest, amazed that it could all have existed and been brought here, to become a part of this. At the foot of each painted character was a brand-new red metal wagon filled with junk: things my father had collected over the years that had been ours or had something to do with us. In my own wagon I found every report card I'd ever gotten, including the ones from college, which I couldn't remember ever sending home; all my medical records up to the age of eighteen; drawings I had made, presents I had gotten my parents for Christmas, clothes I had worn as a baby. And my penciled blueprint, blurred by the years and fuzzy at the folds, my drug-induced blueprint of our cartoon house, with all the superimposed rooms and imaginary spaces. I unfolded it gently, going easy on the creases, as if it were a map to buried treasure: the fading lines were palpable under my fingers, drawn with such vehemence they tore through in places. I could not recall the passionate anger that made them.

I went through Mal's wagon too. My father had filled it with things of my mother's—a tarnished silver barrette; a shot glass; a summer blouse, the fabric worn thin. There was a manila envelope containing black and white photographs of my mother and Mal, twenty, thirty years ago, walking through a park I couldn't identify, holding hands. The pictures were grainy and out-of-focus, and had the candid tawdriness of paid reconnaissance. There were other photos too, washed-out color snapshots my father had certainly taken, of my mother with Pierce: at the shore, holding him by his toddler hands above the roiling surf; in front of our high school, a mortarboard for him, a corsage for her. And dozens more, none that I had ever seen, none that had ever made it into the family albums. The spy pictures upset me, but these were truly shocking. How long had he hoarded them, intending someday to symbolically cede my mother to Mal? For all the misogynist presumption of the gesture, what truly amazed me was the endurance of his self-loathing: he had known for so long that he was no good, and never left the very people who reminded him of it.

It was Pierce's wagon that was strangest, though; he had the expected childhood relics, but his pile was comprised mostly of unfamiliar, unexplained objects. A corncob pipe, for instance, and a linen napkin stained with blood. The four of us gathered silently around him, picking through these things and spreading them out on the floor. A flashlight. A shoehorn. A deck of hand-made playing cards, drawn hastily in pencil and cut out of yellow lined paper. Ice tongs.

"I sort of remember these," Pierce said, picking up the tongs. It was the first thing any of us had said. "I found these in somebody's garbage. He took them away from me."

"What about the napkin?" Gilly asked him.

Pierce stared at it for a long time. Something was happening to his face, but he kept it in check. "I don't know about that," he said finally, and we didn't ask him about anything more.

Eventually, the three of us moved away and looked over the rest of it. There was a cartoon of our house executed in masking tape on the storeroom floor, and a lot of old bicycles—I recognized them from years before—hanging from the ceiling on ropes. The wall space between the characters was papered with fan mail to my father, adoring letters from children requesting drawings and signatures. I read a few, but mostly they were drearily similar, like kindergarten art projects. Pierce didn't get up, only worked his quiet way through his wagon, greeting each object with long, earnest concentration, like an anthropologist trying to decode the messages of the past. Which was what Pierce was doing, except the past was his own, of course, and not any of our business. We met up outside and waited for him, shivering a little in the cold, watching cars pass on Girard Avenue.

It seemed like hours. When he finally came out, he got into the back of the car without saying a thing, and Gilly got in next to him.

"Drive?" I said to Susan. She took the keys. All the silent way home, we held hands, listening to the sound the wheels made on the road and the even, exhausted breathing of Gilly and Pierce in the back.

# epilogue

My comic strip is called "The Family Facts." Susan, who despite her bad experiences with the Burn Syndicate remains my editor, is trying to get actual newspapers to run it. She is more optimistic about its prospects than I am. It's not that it's bad: it's just true, or at least true to my memory, which of course doesn't make it all that much truer than the Family Funnies itself. There *is* something funny about a family that falls apart, or almost does; I'm certain of it. But there is a family out there named Mix that doesn't fall apart, and Ken Dorn is its patriarch, and I wonder, Susan's enthusiasm notwithstanding, if people might prefer Ken's version of events.

The backyard studio is now a studio and office, home to Susan's upstart comics syndicate, which is called Cal-Mix Enterprises (her title; I think it sounds like a cat food). So far its cartoonists' stable echoes with the snorting of a single stud: Tyro proved easy to draw away from Fake Comix, and he is overhauling "The Emerald Forest" for its new run in an expanded number of urban free weeklies. Sometimes I visit galleries with him in New York, or he comes down to Mixville for dinner, which Pierce makes for everybody when he's in the right mood, which is not very often but more often than before.

We have not met Bobby and Nancy's new daughter, and it seems increasingly unlikely that Mike will be around for the birth of his son (I went to the doctor's with Bitty and saw him on the video monitor—pinioning his monochrome arms, his little heart winking like a firefly). Also Rose hasn't spoken to us since we told her about the warehouse, and I doubt she'll go down to see it. But that's to be expected. If there's anything I've learned from my new involvement with my family, it's that voluntary change in anyone is exceptional indeed, myself included. I am loath to imagine what I'd be doing now if none of this had happened to me; then again, I feel awful viewing my parents' demise as a great opportunity, even if that's what it turned out, in part, to be.

And I remembered a weird experience. I don't know why I didn't think of it on the trip to the warehouse, and in retrospect I can't understand why I ever forgot it at all, so singular is it in my life: it makes me wonder what else I've forgotten.

This happened during my sophomore year in college. The art supply section of the college bookstore was open late because it was finals time, and I was buying a bunch of pencils and newsprint for a drawing project I was working on. It was almost dark outside, and there was nobody else in the store save for the clerks. I was thinking about ringing up my purchases and leaving when I looked up at the counter, which stood about fifty feet from where I was standing, and saw somebody waiting in line who looked exactly like me.

Now, what was odd was that I knew everybody in the art department, and in fact had been keeping my eyes open for friends of mine, so if somebody had come in—especially somebody who was dressed in the same T-shirt and jeans I was, and from behind, anyway, had my precise haircut, posture, etc.—I figure I would have noticed. But I hadn't noticed anyone. And this guy seemed to have a newsprint pad and pencils, too, which he had to have gotten from the very section of the store I was shopping in.

As I watched, this person walked out the door, onto the sidewalk, and— I swear I saw this clearly through the bookstore window—climbed into my car and drove off.

I remember feeling agitated and more than a little embarrassed, because my car had been stolen before my eyes and I had done nothing to prevent it. At the same time, it didn't register as a terribly big deal to me: watching a doppelgänger steal my car was weirdly like lending it to my own brother. I walked to the counter and paid for my supplies. Outside, the car really was gone and I walked home.

The police found the car abandoned and, miraculously, unharmed on the shoulder of Route 90, and it was returned to me the following day. But the more I thought about them, the more the circumstances of the theft seemed incredible at best, and at worst invented. That, at least, was what the police appeared to think. I began to wonder if I had done this myself, in some sort of stress-induced daze, and if in fact I did similar things all the time, then obscured them in my mind. I wondered if I was beginning to get sick the way Pierce had. In the end I gave up thinking about it entirely, and my life went on as planned, which plan actually turned out to be no plan at all.

But now I wonder if that person really was me, and if he spent ten years wandering around, gathering the raw materials that a real life could be made from, in order to return them to the original me at some later date and make me whole. I wonder what that later date might be, or if perhaps it already passed without my notice, meaning that what I was for all those years was never very far from what I was supposed to be.

At any rate, I'm not going to hold my breath waiting for him to show up. Anna Praegel, who is recovered, divorced, and full of pithy advice, is fond of telling us what a great life she would have had if she hadn't sat around waiting for things to happen to her, because when they did they were invariably the wrong things. Nevertheless, it does make a good story, and I'm working on a way to fit it into the strip, which any day now should be reaching a college rag near you.

Not long ago I was cleaning out the cabinets under the sink when I came across a cardboard box addressed to my father. It was postmarked a few weeks after he died and had a Riverbank P.O. Box for a return address. It hadn't been opened.

I turned it over a few times and gave it a good shake. Something was loose in there, making a muffled, metallic sort of rattle. The box looked familiar, and I closed my eyes, remembering: it had sat on the kitchen counter, pushed back next to the broken radio, for several months, then was moved to the living room floor, just inside the sliding doors, when Pierce and Susan made pancakes together. A few weeks later it vanished, and now here it was again. I called out to Pierce, who was smoking cigarettes in his bedroom.

He walked out looking stricken, as if he'd been watching television for days on end. I held up the box to him and he frowned.

"Whassat?"

"You tell me."

He took the box and gave it a cursory look. "It came for Dad. I don't know what it is."

I opened a drawer and pulled out a dull paring knife with a green plastic handle. "Give it here," I said. He did, and I set it on the counter and sliced through the packing tape. Pierce came up beside me and watched. I folded back the flaps and picked up a piece of cream-colored linen paper with a letterhead printed on it. The letterhead read RIVERBANK FUNERAL SERVICES, INC.

"Uh-oh," said Pierce.

Dear Customer:

Enclosed are the remains of your loved one, and product #34195, Oriental Brass Urn, which you requested and paid for in full. You have our unconditional guarantee that this urn will meet with your complete satisfaction, or your money back.

The remains of your loved one are packed in a UV-protected plastic pouch which has been double-sealed and inspected to ensure that no remains are lost. To remove remains, shake to the bottom of the pouch, then remove the sealed end using a pair of scissors or sharp knife. Slowly pour remains into your urn and affix the lid. Store urn and remains in a dry place, to prevent sticking. Do not place urn on a surface where it may be jostled or knocked over. Keep away from pets.

We sincerely hope our services will help you to remember your loved one with pleasure and respect. Thank you for choosing Riverbank Funeral Services, Inc.

"Why was it addressed to *him?*" Pierce was saying.

"Got me," I said, and then, unnecessarily, "*That's* him in *there.*" We stared at the open package for a few minutes, lost in our private worlds of horror. Beside me, Pierce breathed his labored cigarettey breaths.

"So what do we do with it?" I said.

"We can't keep it in the house. We have to scatter it or something." The remains of our father had become "it," which made things easier.

"But then we have to take it out of the bag."

We could easily have stood there all day. I took the urn out of the box. It was ornate and artificially aged, with foreign writing and pictograms all over it, and a small curved handle. The lid had a rubber lining, to ensure a tight fit. The bag of ashes was inside the urn, so I stuck my hand in there and worked it through the opening. The ashes were barely visible through the ultraviolet-proof coating, coarse and multicolored, with large black hunks of what pretty much had to be bone.

"Oh my God," said Pierce.

I dropped the knife back into the drawer and clattered around until I found a scissors, then followed the instructions in the letter. A fine gray dust rose as our father cascaded into the urn.

"Oh, yuck, yuck!" Pierce was saying. We backed away, terrified of inhaling him. From across the kitchen we watched the dust settle. After a safe interval, I clamped the lid on, threw the box into the trash and wiped up the counter with a rag.

"How about the river?" I said to Pierce in the car. He drove while I kept the urn on the floor, clamped between my ankles.

"What if it floats? It'll float, and then it'll just get tangled up in some old branches and mud on the bank."

"We could go down the shore."

"No way," he said. We were tooling around on some narrow county road. "We'll throw it in and it'll come crashing right back on us. And then it'll be all over our clothes." He bit his lip. "I was thinking of renting a plane or a helicopter or something and dropping it out."

"What if it blows back in?"

"Ew, ew," he said.

"We could just bring the urn to the Salvation Army in some little town. Somebody would buy it and put it on the mantel."

"We could leave it by the side of the road."

"We could leave it on a golf course."

"We could dump it in the Pine Barrens."

We didn't talk for a long time. Somewhere, Pierce pulled over at a gas station. We sat silent and still while the attendant pumped. Super Unleaded, our father's grade. While Pierce was paying I got out and put the urn in the trunk, wedged between a plastic milk crate full of motor oil and a busted starter motor in a greasy cardboard box. That's where it is today.

While writing this I consulted excellent books on cartooning by Morts Walker and Gerberg. Judy Moffett, thank goodness, made me attend a science fiction conference. For crossing t's and dotting i's, thanks to Rhian, Ed, Jill, Andy G and Julie; for their ongoing dirty work thanks to Lisa and Jeff. Thank you Ruben Bolling for your fine photography, and boosters Ruden, Prose, Bukiet, Spencer and the Art Museum of Missoula. I am grateful to all River-headbangers and to dispersed West Phunnydelphians Lee Ann, Andy C, Host, Kevin, Shauna, Luggage, Biscuit, Kristen, R.C. Thanks to every card, clown, ham, wag and cutup I've ever known, who ought to have the good humor to forgive me for not naming them. And finally I must thank my family, who provided me with God's gift to comedy, New Jersey.

**J. Robert Lennon** is the author of *The Light of Falling Stars*. He lives with his wife and son in Ithaca, New York.

**a note on the type**

The text of this book is set in Fournier. The display typeface used is Journal Bold. The images for the ornaments appear courtesy of Archie McPhee & Company.